The Tie That Binds

CATHARINA MAURA

Contents

For my husband, who has always supported me with every single thing I've ever done. Thank you for being my number one fan and for believing in me when I fail to do so myself.

Daniel & Alyssa's Playlist

You can find Daniel & Alyssa Playlist on my Spotify account

Daniel's song for Alyssa, in particular, is *Speechless* by *Dan + Shay*

One

I stare at the priest who morosely preaches about loss, death and heaven. He tells us all how good of a person my father was, and that we should rest assured because he's without a doubt in a better place now. Though I'm certain that's true, I fail to understand how the priest would know that, considering my father hasn't set foot in a church in at least a decade. He was, after all, a devout atheist. My father's belief in God died the day my mother did.

He would have hated this funeral. It isn't him at all. Not even remotely. He would've wanted a simple ceremony with no more than a handful of mourners. Instead, I'm standing in a graveyard that's filled to the brim with people I barely even recognise.

I look around me, my eyes settling on my grandmother. In the days following my father's sudden passing, I'd been so grateful to have her with me. She patted my back and told me not to worry about a thing. And indeed, she'd taken care of everything while I foolishly nodded along. I should've known better. There's a reason my father cut her off, after all. A woman who would embezzle from the company my father put his blood, sweat and tears into, isn't someone I should've trusted to honour his final wishes. I regret placing my trust in her. I wish I'd been more on top of things. I convinced myself that involving her in the funeral would be the right thing to do. That it would give her the closure she'd need to say a final farewell to her only son. I was wrong. Based on the amount of politicians and businessmen present, it's obvious she didn't know my father at all, and I'm starting to be grateful for it.

"Alyssa."

I blink and look to my right. Dominic, my best friend, has clearly been trying to get my attention for some time. He smiles at me, his eyes as red as mine. He clutches my hand and gently places a rose in it, closing my fingers around the stem.

I look down at it numbly. I know they're expecting me to drop the rose on top of my father's casket to signal the start of the burial, but I can't do it.

"It's time, Lyss," he whispers. Dominic's mother, Mary, nods at me with tears in her eyes. The only thing getting me through this day is the Devereauxs. Without them, I'd truly be alone. I guess from today onwards, I really will be.

I stare at the rectangular hole in the ground, my mind blank. I shake my head, panic slowly building in my body. I can't do this. I can't say goodbye to the man that has raised me single-handedly. Who is going to hold my hand when life gets tough and make me the perfect cup of tea when I'm feeling down? My dad will never see me take his position as CEO and he will never walk me down the aisle. I'm not ready to say goodbye. There are too many things we still should've experienced together.

A heavy arm drops around my shoulder, and I look to my left. Daniel. Dominic's older brother and my father's co-CEO. If anyone is hurting as much as I am today, it's him. Daniel tightens his hold on me and gently takes the hand I'm holding the rose with. He looks at me and I nod. A single tear falls down my cheek as he raises my arm and the rose falls onto my father's casket. Daniel keeps hold of my hand and clenches it tightly, as though he's hanging onto me in an attempt to keep it together.

The sound of sobbing fills the graveyard. People I've never

seen before are holding back sobs and, oddly, it infuriates me. Where were these people when my father was alive? When they still had a chance to spend time with him.

The priest drops a small amount of soil onto the casket and suddenly it feels so final. I feel an insane urge to demand that everything stops. To claim that my father cannot be gone. I feel panic creeping its way through my body, starting low in my belly until it constricts my throat. My breath is laboured and I can almost feel the hysteria bubble up in my throat. I remember being devastated and sobbing when my mother passed away, but that was different. When the cancer took her, we'd known it was coming. We weren't any more prepared for the day to come, but it was different nonetheless. This time, my dad is just gone. There were no goodbyes and no long talks at night to make sure we told each other everything we needed to. The heart attack ended his life with no warnings. Part of me can't even fathom that it's my father lying in that casket. I haven't even cried since he died. Not the way I did when my mother took her last breath. I haven't sobbed like the people around me. My eyes have filled with tears countless times today, but I've refused to let them spill. Crying would only make it so much more real. You only mourn those that are truly gone. I wonder how long I'll be able to hold on to this numbness. How long will I be able to hold the panic at bay?

Dominic's arm wraps around my waist as he starts to lead me back to the parking lot. I let him drag me along, grateful to move away from my father's grave. The further we get, the easier it becomes to breathe.

To my surprise, Dominic walks me to his brother's car instead of his own. I stare at it, my heart clenching painfully. An Aston Martin Vulcan in matte black. The only reason I know the name of the car is because my dad and Daniel picked it out together. They scrutinised and researched every single detail. At one point, they even made a cost-benefit analysis for the different customisation options. Why they did that is beyond me, since the car set Daniel back millions. I didn't think a couple of grand extra would've mattered, but according to my dad and Daniel, it did. The two of them shared a bond I've always been jealous of. At times I was certain Daniel was the child my dad wished he had instead of me.

Dominic and Daniel's father died a few years after my mother did, and ever since my dad has embraced the two of them as his own. Daniel more so than Dominic. I guess he thought that Dominic at least had me, while Daniel had no one. I don't think there's been more than a handful of days in the last couple of years that my dad and Daniel didn't see each other. My dad trained Daniel until he was ready to take on his father's vacant seat as his co-CEO. They worked together every day, but outside of work they were more like father and son. I always aspired to have a similar relationship with my dad, but it's too late for that now.

"Will you take her?" Dominic asks. Daniel hesitates, and truthfully, I don't want Dominic to leave me. I need him with me, now more than ever. I stare at him pleadingly, but his eyes are on his girlfriend, Lucy. She's standing next to his mum with a sweet smile on her face.

I can't help but feel slightly bitter and hurt about it. I feel foolish for expecting him to stand by me today. Things between us haven't been what they used to be. Not since my drunken confession a few months ago. Dominic has slowly but surely been distancing himself from me, and I only have myself to blame.

"Pathetic," Daniel murmurs as we watch Dominic rush towards Lucy. He didn't even wait for Daniel to agree to drive me home. Nor did he ask me if I'd be okay.

"Must be some magic pussy for him to abandon his best friend on a day like this."

A tiny smile pulls the edges of my lips up and Daniel grins as he opens his car door for me. I feel relieved to see him smiling. Though he hasn't shed a tear in my presence, his red-rimmed eyes and the bags underneath them tell me this has been just as hard on him as it has been on me. I've never seen Daniel cry or be overly

THE TIE THAT BINDS

emotional at all. The most emotion he ever shows is his perpetual boredom. His stoic expression has gotten him in to trouble more than once. I even vaguely recall one of his ex-girlfriends breaking up with him over it.

"When are we going to discuss everything?" I ask, my voice barely above a whisper. Daniel's hands tighten on the steering wheel. He doesn't have to ask me what I'm talking about. As my father's sole heir, I'll be inheriting his 26 percent shareholding in DM Consultancy; the parent company that stands at the top of our conglomerate empire. The Devereaux's own 25 percent while the rest of the shares are distributed amongst other family members and early investors. So long as the Devereaux and Moriani families stay united, we'll remain in absolute control.

However, with my dad being gone so suddenly, the company is in turmoil. The share price has already plummeted in the few days since his death. On top of that, Vincent, the company lawyer, told us that my dad's will is unconventional and that we need to see him as soon as possible for fear that the company may be in peril. He refused to discuss the details over the phone. To make things worse, the press has been writing scathing articles about the future of the company now that its visionary is gone. Many have expressed doubts about Daniel's ability to run the company without my father, adding to the emotional turmoil he's already feeling.

Truthfully, I fear not only for my own empty and bleak future, but that of the company too. I have full faith in Daniel, but I'm not sure how long it'll take him to become comfortable in his new role. I know better than anyone how much he relied on my father.

"Not today," Daniel says, sounding exhausted. "Today is for mourning and honouring the man we all loved. To say our good-byes and make peace with a devastating loss. The company isn't going anywhere."

I nod. I'm grateful Daniel hasn't set the meeting with Vincent for today. I have no idea how I'm going to deal with that when it comes. I'm sure my father has some sort of unpleasant surprise for me, and I'm not ready to face my own inadequacy yet. DM Consultancy was my father's first love and more often than not I wondered if he loved it more than he loved me.

"We're here," Daniel says, sighing as he parks the car in my driveway. Neither one of us moves. Instead, we sit there in silence as we stare at the countless cars lined up in front of my house.

"Are you ready?" he asks.

I shake my head. "No," I answer, my voice breaking. I clear my throat and look out the window. "But let's do this anyway."

Two

All conversation stops when Daniel and I enter my house. I'm not surprised to find my grandmother in the middle of all of it. She seems to bask in the attention she's getting when she should be mourning.

Everyone looks at me; their eyes filled with pity. I've been pretending to be deaf to the rumours, but I'm well aware of what everyone has been saying and what they're truly worried about. Most people here are investors or stakeholders of some sort. They aren't here to offer me their condolences or to pay their respects to my father. They're here because it's a rare chance to speak to Daniel in person. They're here to find out what the company's future holds.

I recognise many of the people in the living room, but I don't actually know many of them. It makes me feel like a stranger in my own house. The last thing I want to do right now is entertain people my father didn't even like. The whole concept is weird to me. Why would you hold a literal pity party at someone's house after a funeral? My father would've hated this, and he would've hated my grandmother for allowing these vultures easy access to Daniel.

My grandmother walks up to me and grabs my arm with more

force than necessary. I wince and try to pull away, but she won't let me.

"Dear, where did you go after the funeral? You just disappeared. There are so many people we must greet. We mustn't let your father's hard work go to waste. It's up to us to reassure everyone that everything is fine. We must maintain the connections your father established. I saw the Mayor here. He brought his son and he mentioned that you're acquainted. We best go say hello."

I'm overcome with disgust. The last thing I want to do is socialise, but it seems to be all that's on her mind. She seems positively giddy at the prospect of conversing with the Mayor and it sickens me. I regret inviting her to the funeral at all.

I gently pull my arm out of her clutches, at a total loss for words. Before I can come up with an appropriate response, Daniel intervenes.

"Thank you kindly for the help you have provided in the days leading up to the funeral, Mrs. Moriani. Though you haven't been in touch with Alyssa since she was a toddler, she has really appreciated your presence here in the past week. Please have a seat and help yourself to the refreshments we have provided. As always, the catering is provided by Deluga Catering, so I'm certain you'll enjoy it. I wouldn't want anyone to think we don't treat our guests well, so please help yourself."

Daniel's voice is loud and as always, when he speaks, people pay attention. Those who'd been falling over themselves to gain her favour hear the warning loud and clear. My grandmother isn't associated with DM Consultancy, and she and I aren't close.

Daniel takes my hand and leads me away before she can retort. The whispers around us increase as we make our way through the room. Daniel leads me to the kitchen where Dominic is already waiting with a cup of tea in his hands. Making a cup of tea was what my dad always did when I was sad or upset. The thought that he'll never do it again breaks my heart.

Dominic hands me my favourite mug. It's the one that says

Boss Lady on it, and my heart breaks a little more. My dad gave it to me for my 22nd birthday a few weeks ago, telling me he was going to step up my training so I'd be ready to take over his role within a few years. He had so much faith in me, and now he won't ever see me accomplish the goals we set together.

My eyes fill with tears and Dominic opens his arms. I walk into his embrace and hug him tightly, barely keeping my tears in. A stab of pain twists my heart at the knowledge that I won't ever see my father at the office again. I won't be able to drop by the office he shared with Daniel for a quick cup of tea and a chat. I can't ask for his advice anymore when I don't know how to handle a situation.

Dominic puts his index finger underneath my chin and gently lifts my face up to meet his. "Hey, I'm here. I promise I'm not going anywhere. We'll get through this together. I promise you won't be alone," he whispers.

I stare into his grey eyes, willing myself to believe him. I've felt alone ever since he started dating Lucy. No one has ever been able to get between us, and both of us have had to end relationships because our partners couldn't accept our friendship. But Lucy is different. She's been vocal about her dislike of me, and Dominic has been giving in to her. He's been distancing himself from me lately. I can't even remember the last time he and I were alone. Lucy and he are a package deal now. If I want to see him, I have to see her too. I can't even blame Lucy for her distrust of me, or Dominic for giving in to her. Just as Lucy suspects, I do have feelings for Dominic. I'd never act on them or jeopardise his relationship, though. I wish he could see that.

Lucy walks up to us with outstretched arms and tears streaming down her face.

"Alyssa, there you are! I'm so, so sorry for your loss. What can Nic and I do for you? Please, let me know how we can help," she says, her voice loud and shrill. I cringe a little and step away from Dominic. I've tried my best to like Lucy, but I can't do it. I cannot understand what Dominic sees in her. She's loud whereas he's quiet, and she's adorably silly whereas he is intelligent beyond compare. They don't suit each other. Lucy is the type of person that neither of us has ever liked.

"Do you know more about the will yet?" she all but shouts, her face crunched up in what I assume is worry. My eyes automatically find Dominic's. I can't believe he told her that. When I told him what Vincent said to Daniel and me, I told him it was confidential. Her shouting what she did could easily cause more unrest amongst our biggest shareholders, many of whom are present today.

Some of the women in the kitchen pause and tune in to our conversation. I sigh uneasily, surprised at her lack of sensitivity... and, well, her common sense. Sometimes I wonder if my dad was right about her when he called her a dimwit.

Daniel glares at Lucy and puts his hand on my shoulder, reassuring me without words. He exchanges a look with Dominic that tells him what he thinks of her behaviour, and Dominic lowers his eyes in shame.

Lucy trembles and starts crying as she throws herself into Dominic's arms. I'm not even sure whether she's crying because of the funeral or because Daniel just glared at her. Somehow Dominic ends up consoling her instead of the other way around. Dominic lost a father figure today, yet he's wiping away her tears instead of shedding his own.

I take a step back and look at the two of them together. I could never compare to Lucy with her supermodel figure and her long blonde hair. In comparison, I look like an Oompa Loompa, with my overly full unfashionable curves and my petite stature. It's no wonder Nic never fell for me the way I fell for him.

He pats Lucy's back as she cries on his shoulder, but his attention doesn't seem to be on her. He's looking at me, his eyes filled with worry and sorrow.

I turn away to find Daniel leaning against the kitchen counter. He's looking at me with a pained expression, and I can't help but wonder whether he knows how I feel about his little brother.

Whether he understands how much it hurts to need Dominic so badly, yet having to watch him hold someone else instead.

Daniel holds his hand out, and I bridge the few steps that separate us. He takes my mug and wraps his arm around my shoulder, offering me a bit of consolation. He stares at Lucy and Dominic disapprovingly as he takes a sip of my tea. Daniel usually ignores me, but I'm happy he's showing me some solidarity today.

"I don't think we should wait till tomorrow," I murmur. Daniel looks at me with a knowing look in his eyes. I don't need to explain what I'm talking about. He knows. Thanks to the rumours Lucy has just helped spread, we'll need to take action as soon as possible. The uncertainty we currently face might be harmful. He knows as well as I do that my dad always had something up his sleeve. It'll be the same now. We'll both rest easier if we know what it is, especially if it pertains to the company.

Daniel nods. "I'll call Vincent."

Three

Another two hours of fake tears and gossipy whispering pass at an excruciatingly slow pace. When the last guests leave, only Daniel, Vincent, my grandmother and I remain. I asked Dominic to stay and be there with me when the will is read, but he told me he needed to drive Lucy home. I didn't have the energy to beg for a bit of consideration. He's made it clear where I stand in his life now. I can't keep clinging to him the way I have been. The small amount of pride I still have won't let me.

Daniel leads us to my father's home office as though it's his own, navigating my house with ease. It should be weird that he's been in there more often than I have, even though I live here, but it's not. It's what Daniel and my dad were like.

He walks to the little bar in my dad's office and pours us both a shot of whiskey. He hands me the glass and we both empty them in one go. My throat burns as the liquor goes down, and my discomfort must have been obvious because Daniel chuckles. It's the first time I've heard him laugh in weeks.

I roll my eyes at him and walk towards the plush sofa in the corner. I plop down unceremoniously and wait for Daniel to sit down next to me.

"All right. Let's get this over with," Vincent says, sounding tired. I know this isn't easy for him. My dad has always been a close friend of his. Dad was one of Vincent's very first clients before he made him our legal counsel. Vincent runs a hand over his face and then inhales deeply before speaking.

"Mr. Moriani is leaving the cottage in France to his mother. Everything else goes to his only daughter, Alyssa Moriani."

He clutches the will in his hands, indicating that things aren't as simple as that. He's about to elaborate when my grandmother jumps up, her eyes flashing with anger.

"That can't be all he left me. That little cottage? What about money? Who is going to pay me my monthly stipend? I assume he expects Alyssa to be responsible for that now?"

My heart sinks with disappointment. I'd been trying to convince myself that she was here to mourn her son and to be with me. I'd been hoping I was wrong about her, even though every sign told me she was just after my father's connections and money. She disgusts me. I'm trembling with anger and can't wait for her to leave. She should count herself lucky my dad left her anything at all.

Vincent stares at the will for a few seconds before responding. "The only thing he left you is the cottage. There is no request for Alyssa to pay for your maintenance."

She stares at me with a calculative look in her eyes and I can guess what's on her mind. She'll try to milk me for all I've got. I'll be lucky if she returns to France at all.

She smiles to herself and nods. "Very well," she says. She glances at me one more time and then walks out of the room, slamming the door behind her. She's undoubtedly hatching some sort of plan.

Vincent sighs and shoots me a wary look. I tense, bracing myself for the worst. "There's a clause in the will, Alyssa. It's about your father's shares in the company." Vincent speaks carefully, and it only worries me even more. I freeze, mentally preparing myself for whatever bad news he's about to spring on me.

"The clause states your shares are to be given to your grandmother unless you marry the man of your father's choosing within a month from now."

Daniel inhales sharply and closes his eyes in resignation. He leans forward and holds his head in his hands. This news is as bad for him as it is for me, worse perhaps. If she gets her hands on those shares, she'll run my father's company to the ground. Everything Daniel and my dad have worked for will be for nothing.

I shake my head. "That can't be," I whisper. "I'm only twenty-two. I just graduated from university. I can't get married. My dad always discouraged getting married too young. There's no way he'd ask it of me now. No way he'd put his company on the line to make it happen."

I stare at Vincent, half expecting him to smile and tell me that this is his weak attempt at a joke, but I've never seen him look so grim. He hesitates and looks at Daniel before continuing.

"Your father's wish is for you to marry Daniel. There isn't anyone he trusts more with his company and his daughter."

I sit there in shocked silence and slowly turn to Daniel. He looks distraught and furious, but he doesn't look surprised.

"Did you know about this?" I ask, my voice dangerously soft.

He shakes his head. "Lately your father had been making some strange remarks. He kept pushing me to take you out for dinner and continuously insinuated that he thought we'd make a good couple. I never expected this though."

"I can't believe this," I murmur. "You're ten years older than me. And he knows. He knows I..."

He knows how I feel about Dominic, so how could he ever expect me to marry his older brother? How could he do this to me?

I start pacing the room, a million thoughts running through my mind. I feel the rage course through me and embrace it. I latch onto it and let it drive away the pain I'm feeling.

"Show me that," I snap, ripping my father's will out of Vincent's hands. He looks at me apologetically, even though it isn't his fault, and I instantly feel bad about snapping at him. I pause as I read through the will, my heart sinking. Daniel reads through it over my shoulder and curses. The will clearly states that my father's last wish is for me to marry Daniel and to continue my training to take over my dad's role as CEO as soon as the board and Daniel deem me ready.

I want to be angry at my dad. I want to shout at him and ask him whether he's lost his mind. I want to ask him what day and age he thinks we're living in and why he doesn't trust me enough. Why he feels the need to entrust me to Daniel, rather than trusting I can stand on my own two feet. But I can't ask him any of those questions, because he's gone. I'll never get the answers I'm seeking.

Daniel runs a hand through his hair and closes his eyes. "What was that old man thinking," he whispers to himself. He walks back to my father's bar and pours himself a tall drink and empties his glass in one go. He turns and leans back against the drinks cabinet, his eyes on me. He looks at me with a pained expression as his eyes trail down my body before he looks away. He clenches his teeth and inhales deeply.

I'm suddenly overcome with an intense sense of rejection. It's clear the mere idea of being with me disturbs him, and whether I like it or not, I'm instantly reminded of Dominic. Does he feel the same way when he looks at me? What will he say when he finds out about the will? I wish he'd been here with me. He would've known what to say and do.

"We can't lose those shares. If they fall into her hands, the company will never recover. It'll never be the same."

I stare at my feet, knowing that he's right. How could my father do this to me? To us. Did he have no faith in me at all? Did he do this because he didn't trust me with his company? How could he possibly have trusted my grandmother more than me?

"He always wanted you as his son. I guess he's getting his wish granted in death," I say bitterly. I feel hurt, and part of me blames Daniel for what's happening. He glances at me and starts pacing like I had been.

"We can do a paper marriage, Alyssa. We can both keep our lives. Nothing needs to change. You won't have anything to worry about. We'll have an iron-clad prenup, so you'll be protected. Whatever you own, you'll keep, including your shares. I won't take advantage of you in any way. We'll divorce in a year and you'll have your estate and anything you might have earned during our marriage."

Daniel sounds unwilling and detached, as though he's discussing a minor business deal that's a waste of his time. His attitude annoys me even further.

Vincent clears his throat and looks at us with a cautious expression. "There's more," he says. I look at him, wariness clouding my vision. Of course there's more. This is my father we're talking about, after all. If he wants us together, he won't make it easy for us to escape his wishes. When my father wants something to happen, he'll get it done.

"The two of you will have to live together and stay married until Alyssa either becomes CEO or turns twenty-five. If you two separate or divorce before then, the shares are still to be given away. We could potentially contest the will, but I'll tell you now that I won't be the one to take that case on. I won't disrespect your father's last wishes like that."

I always thought my father loved his company more than he loved me, and this seems to prove it. What was he after when he wrote his will? He raised me to be independent, yet his last wish is for me to get married to a man I didn't choose. A thousand questions flash through my mind, each making me feel worse than the last.

Daniel and I both sit in my dad's office for what feels like hours. Neither one of us knows what to say or what to do. I didn't even notice Vincent leaving.

"I can't believe he'd do this to us," I whisper for the third time. Daniel runs a hand through his hair. I look up and stare at him for a couple of seconds. He looks so tired and sad.

"I know you're stuck between a rock and a hard place, Alyssa. You either marry me and lose a part of your personal life and a chance to make that unrequited love of yours work. Or you lose the company that's rightfully yours. It's a tough situation, but it's no walk in the park for me either. The last thing I need is to be saddled with a teenybopper for the next few years. However, I will marry you if you're willing. Even if it's just to honour your father's last wish. He's never asked anything of me before today and I won't let him down now."

I cross my arms and glare at him. "Teenybopper, really? Okay, boomer. Don't forget that you're getting something out of this too. If you don't marry me, the company is doomed and so is most of your fortune."

I ignore what he said about pursuing my unrequited love. I didn't know that he knew about that. If he knows, who else does? I thought I kept it hidden really well. Have I been making a fool of myself the entire time?

Daniel looks at me with an amused expression. "Yes. I won't deny that there are benefits for me too. The last thing I want is to lose the absolute control your father and I had over the company. We had a vision that I intend to realise, but I can't do it without major interference. And yes, if your grandmother were to interfere with the way the company is run, the share price would likely drop, which would indeed affect me financially."

My dad always told me how important it is to him that I never sell his shares, so why is he now choosing to give them away to the one person he ruthlessly cut out of our lives? Did he regret cutting her off in the end?

Daniel and I are at an impasse, and neither one of us seems to know how to move forward.

"I guess we'll have to get married," I say. Daniel looks away and nods. He stares out the window and sighs, a wistful expression on his face.

"I guess there's only one thing left to do."

He walks to me and drops down on one knee. I'm so startled that I freeze in disbelief. He grabs my hand and looks into my eyes with an intensity I've never seen before.

"Alyssa Moriani, will you do me the honour of becoming my wife?" he asks, his voice soft but clear.

I inhale deeply and nod, praying to god that I'm doing the right thing.

Four

I stare at my reflection in the mirror. I'm wearing a white knee-length dress with my favourite old nude stilettos that make my legs look endlessly long. I'm wearing blue underwear and borrowed Mary's earrings. I'm not sure why I even bothered with the old tradition, but it just seemed wrong not to.

The dress I'm wearing is gorgeous and figure hugging, but it isn't a wedding gown. It's something I could easily wear to the office without feeling overdressed. It certainly isn't what I imagined I'd be wearing on my wedding day.

I feel numb. It doesn't feel like I'm getting married, and I definitely don't look like a bride. I can't believe I'm doing this. I'm about to get married to the wrong Devereaux. In every marriage fantasy I've ever had, it's always been me getting married to Dominic. Becoming Mrs. Devereaux in my mind always meant becoming Dominic's wife.

Who would've thought I'd end up marrying Daniel instead? Daniel, who has always barely tolerated me. Daniel, who is ten years older than me and who is rumoured to have bedded half of London. I know this isn't a real marriage, but my nerves are feeling pretty real.

I turn when someone knocks on the door. Dominic walks in, his eyes widening when he catches sight of me.

"Wow. You look stunning," he says. The way he's looking at me right now is how I've always wanted him to look at me. Granted, I rarely wear clothes that are this fitted, but still. I look away and try to smile but fail. It hurts to see him today. It hurts to know that today marks the end of any feelings I've ever had for him. Once I marry his brother, Dominic will never see me as a woman again. He'll be out of my reach entirely. I feel like I'm losing everything in life today. I lost my father and now I'm losing my first love. Why couldn't it have been Dominic? Why couldn't my father have asked me to marry the man he knew I loved? If it's a way to unite the Devereaux and Moriani families, then asking me to marry Dominic would've sufficed. I don't understand what my father was thinking at all.

Dominic walks up to me. His eyes are filled with the same heartache I'm feeling, and for a second I wonder if he ever saw me the way I see him. Did he ever wonder what we could have been? Did he ever consider stepping over the boundary we drew between us as kids?

He cups my cheek gently. I see the love and regret that I'm feeling reflected in his eyes as he rests his forehead against mine.

"I can't believe you're marrying Daniel," he whispers. I close my eyes and inhale deeply.

"I can't believe it either," I reply. Dominic pulls back and hesitates before he speaks.

"Couldn't it have been me? If all you had to do was marry a Devereaux, then why not me?" he asks, his voice breaking. I swallow hard as tears start to gather in my eyes.

Dominic buries his hands in my hair, messing up my hairstyle. His eyes are filled with an anguished expression I've never seen before. He's so close yet so much further away than he's ever been.

"It's not just any Devereaux, Nic. The will specifically states I had to marry Daniel. Besides, you've got Lucy. I'd never ask something like this of you. I wouldn't dare."

Dominic inhales deeply. "She's not you, Alyssa. She'll never be you."

I don't know what to make of his words, and I don't dare to hope anymore. Not now. Not when it's already too late.

Dominic leans into me, his lips only an inch from mine. The energy between us sizzles with love, desire and heartache. He moves closer to me, millimetre by millimetre. My eyes fall closed as I wait for the moment his lips finally touch mine, the moment I've waited for pretty much all my life.

I feel his breath tingling against my lips and lean in eagerly. His lips brush against mine and when I'm certain he's finally about to kiss me, the sound of knocking on the door interrupts us.

We jump away from each other as Mary walks in. She looks from me to Dominic with a displeased expression, and I know she realises what we'd been up to.

"Are you ready to escort your future sister-in-law down the aisle?" she asks, her tone sharp. Dominic clears his throat and nods, his eyes filled with regret.

Mary walks up to me and rearranges my hair carefully. I don't dare to look into her eyes, scared she'll know what almost happened.

Just as I'd been avoiding her gaze, Dominic avoids mine as he walks me down the aisle. I've got my hand through his arm and he's clutching my hand tightly. We walk slowly, as though both of us know things will never be the same when we reach Daniel. For the minute or so that it takes to walk down the aisle of our local church, I imagine Dominic will stop me. That he'll tell me not to make the biggest mistake in my life and that he didn't know what he was missing until I almost became someone else's.

But he doesn't. He can't. If I don't marry Daniel today, I'll lose everything my father has worked so hard to build, and

Dominic knows that. He hesitates for a second before putting my hand in Daniel's and then stares at our joint hands with clenched teeth. My eyes follow him as he turns and walks right out of the church instead of sitting in one of the pews. Daniel's hand tightens on mine and I turn to look at him. His expression is carefully blank, but there's a mocking smile on his lips. I close my eyes and inhale deeply, reminding myself of what I'm doing this for.

Daniel leans in, his lips brushing my ear. The touch sends an unexpected thrill through my body.

"I guess that love wasn't as unrequited as I thought," he whispers.

I pull my hand out of his and glare at him, directing all my helplessness and pain at him. He looks unfazed, and much to my regret, stupidly handsome in his tux. I glance at the empty church. Our only guests are Vincent and Mary, who serve as our witnesses. If it had been up to me, Daniel and I would've signed our papers at city hall and called it a day, but Mary wouldn't have it. Since Daniel is her first child to get married, she insisted on having a church wedding. It seems like a big insulting joke to me to get married in the house of God against your will. I guess my father was right. If God truly existed, I wouldn't have found myself standing here with the wrong Devereaux.

Despite the beautiful church, the ceremony feels empty. I can't help but feel oddly disappointed, which is quite the accomplishment considering my low expectations.

I turn back to Daniel, who is studying me intently, his expression unreadable. He's basically a more rugged and taller version of Dominic. Where Dominic is still boyish in many ways, Daniel is all man. He fills his suit out nicely with muscles I know Dominic works for but has yet to achieve. Daniel's attractiveness pisses me off more.

The ceremony is over before I even realise it. I know at some point Daniel and I both said 'I do', but that's about it. We sign our marriage certificate in silence, the pen shaking in my hand as I put down my signature. To me it feels like signing my own death sentence and I have to breathe in deeply before I can make myself do it. I stare at it in shock as both our witnesses sign as well. It's done. I've officially become Mrs. Devereaux, just not how I imagined it.

Five

Daniel drives me to my house in silence. The last few days have been such a blur. We haven't even had a chance to discuss the details of our marriage. If the two of us have to live together, where will we be living?

I follow behind Daniel quietly. He lets himself into my house with ease. My dad put Daniel's biometric details into our security system years ago, allowing Daniel access to our house at all times. I've gotten so used to Daniel being here that it never struck me as weird until now. He's far too comfortable here, but then I'm pretty comfortable at the Devereaux mansion too.

As soon as the door closes behind us we hear the sounds of laughter. He looks at me in surprise and I shake my head, indicating that I have no idea who it might be. We follow the chatter to the sitting room, where we find my grandmother surrounded by some of the most influential women in London. Daniel's eyes darken and he grabs his phone immediately, sending several texts.

"Grandma," I say, nodding at her before greeting the other ladies present. She's invited the Mayor's wife as well as the wives of several high ranking DM Consultancy employees and some politicians. They're all having tea and she waves me over with a smile.

I've got to admire her guts. She's invited people she barely knows to a house that isn't hers. I don't think I'd ever dare to do something like this. The ladies present all light up when they see Daniel and it makes me chuckle. It's like seeing teenagers eyeing a cute boy. Their elegance just melts away in front of Daniel.

"You two look stunning. Did you attend some event today?" My grandmother asks, looking peeved. Neither Daniel nor I informed her about our wedding, so she probably thinks we attended some corporate event she would've loved to be at.

Daniel places his hand on my shoulder and smiles at her, though I'm not sure you can call that a smile. Even I shudder at the way he looks at her.

"Mrs. Moriani, you're still here," he says. "I've booked you a room at the Shangri-La and a flight back to France in two days. My driver is waiting for you outside and will help you with your luggage."

She looks at him with wide eyes and then laughs. "Oh there's no need. I'll be staying here for the foreseeable future. After all, Alyssa shouldn't be alone now. She'll need me."

The ladies surrounding her nod in agreement, and so does Daniel. "Indeed. That's why she's coming home with me. As you're well aware, my younger brother is her best friend and my mother is as much of a mother figure to her as your son was a father figure to me. She indeed needs to be surrounded by people who know and love her. People she's used to."

She stands up, her cheeks reddening in anger. Daniel speaks before she can attempt to talk her way into staying in my house.

"As such, Alyssa won't be able to host you. Of course, if you wish, you could extend your stay in London by finding a place to live or by extending your stay at the Shangri-La. I've already pre-paid your two nights there, but I'm sure you'll be able to extend that if you wished."

He then turns to the ladies that are present and bows slightly.

"All of you lovely ladies, please accept my sincerest apologies for cutting your teatime short. Please allow me to make it up to you. If you give my secretary your contact details, I'll be sure to set up an afternoon tea appointment for next week, should your schedules permit it."

The ladies all smile, none of them even remotely angry. If anything, they look excited to be having tea with Daniel himself. One by one the ladies leave, until only my grandmother is left. Daniel leans back against the wall and stares her down. It looks like she wants to argue with me, but then her gaze falls back to Daniel and she rises instead.

The two of us stand in silence as she packs her things and leaves in a huff. I didn't think I'd get rid of her so easily.

"Thank you, but I could've handled that myself, you know."

Daniel smiles at me and ruffles my hair like I'm a child. I pull away from him in annoyance. "Yes, but you don't have to," he says.

Daniel calls my security team and instructs them to deny my grandmother access to any of my properties while I walk through the house in search for anything she might have left behind. I'm not surprised when I find more than a handful of her belongings and pack them all neatly. I have no doubt she intended to worm her way back into the house under the guise of collecting the things she forgot. I'd rather not deal with that all.

I call my head of security and ask him to drop off my grandmother's things at her hotel as Daniel takes a seat on the sofa. He pulls his bowtie off and leaves it around his neck. I hate how handsome he looks.

"Come and sit for a minute," he says.

I nod and sit down opposite him so enough distance remains between us.

"I know I just told your grandmother you'd be staying with us, but that was just to get her out of your house. If you'd like to stay here then I can move in here."

He places a stack of documents on the table. At a glance I can tell what it is. It's a copy of the various clauses relating to our marriage.

I look around the house and bite down on my lip. This house is filled with memories of my dad and I'm not sure I'll be okay here.

"Would it be okay if we stay somewhere else for a little while?"

Daniel nods, the same lost expression on his face. He's got just as many memories in this house as I do, and I'm sure it isn't easy for him.

"Would you like us to stay with my mother or in my apartment?"

I hesitate. What I crave is time in isolation which Daniel's apartment would give me, but I know it's not what I need. Even though things are awkward between Nic and I, I do still need both him and Mary.

"I'd like to stay with your mother."

Something flashes in Daniel's eyes but it's gone before I can identify it.

"Very well."

He stares at me for a couple of seconds before clearing his throat.

"We need to discuss the specifics of our marriage," he says.

I nod uncomfortably.

"I'm happy to do this verbally, on a trust basis, but we can draw up a contract if you feel more comfortable with that."

I shake my head. "I doubt that'll be necessary. We have an iron-clad prenup that protects both our assets, what more could we need?"

Daniel nods in agreement.

I speak up before he does. "I want our marriage to remain between us. I don't want it publicly announced and I don't want anyone to find out about it."

Daniel looks startled for a second before his expression becomes guarded. He nods slowly.

"Very well. Nonetheless, there are some things I expect of you, and some things we must abide by per your father's requirements."

I nod for him to continue.

"I'm happy to keep our marriage a secret, but this doesn't mean I'll condone cheating. As long as we're legally tied to each other I expect you to be faithful to me, as I will be to you."

I frown. "What? That's ridiculous. Do you seriously think you'll be able to keep it in your pants for three years? You're photographed with a different model every weekend."

Daniel's eyes darken and the way he looks at me sends a delicious thrill through my body. I subconsciously clench my thighs. Daniel blinks and whatever was there is gone, his usual stoic expression back in place.

"Hmm. Nonetheless, I won't condone cheating, Alyssa." His voice is low and dangerous but I decide to push my luck regardless.

"How about we both just do our own thing discreetly? After all, you need this marriage just as much as I do."

Daniel's eyes darken and he pins me down with a stare. He chuckles humorously.

"That's where you're wrong, sweetheart. I'm a Devereaux. I never worked for DM Consultancy because I needed the money or the shares. That's not why I married you, either. I did it because I loved your father like he was my own. We Devereauxs have more than enough money to fund the next couple of generations comfortably."

I gulp. He's right, of course. My dad was rich, but not like the Devereauxs are. They're old money rich with ties to every industry and every significant politician. Daniel doesn't actually even need to work at all. He crosses his arms and stares me down.

"Rule number one," he says. "We'll be faithful to each other. Defy that rule and I'll divorce you, shares be damned."

I nod reluctantly and indicate for him to continue.

"Rule number two. You'll keep an appropriate distance from Dominic. I don't want to hear any rumours about you two, or about any other men for that matter."

I laugh. "You're crazy if you think you can keep me away from my own best friend. I know you're ancient but this isn't the Middle Ages. These days you don't get a say in your wife's life."

Daniel smiles. "Try me."

"You're an asshole, Daniel," I whisper.

He grins and looks away. "I said *an appropriate distance,* Alyssa. Be as close to him as you want to be, so long as you keep things appropriate."

I can't even disagree with him because what he's asking for isn't unreasonable.

"Very well. Rule number three is that we keep our marriage a secret. I don't want anyone to know beyond the people closest to us. If anyone needs to be told I'd prefer that we discuss it before-hand. In three years we'll divorce, and I don't want to be known as your ex-wife for the rest of my life."

Daniel nods, agreeing. "The rest of the rules... we can make up as we go," he says.

Six

Daniel carries my luggage into the guest room I've always used at the Devereaux mansion. It's right next to Dominic's bedroom and opposite Daniel's. I'm fairly certain it didn't used to be a guest room until I started to stay over regularly. He looks around the room as though he's never seen it before, and he might not have. I don't remember him ever coming in here in the last couple of years. He sits down on my bed and watches me unpack with a frown.

"Are you sure you want to stay here and not in the downtown apartment?"

I nod. "At least here I'll have your mum and Dominic. I know what your working hours are like. If we lived in the apartment, I'd always be alone."

He doesn't say anything as I slowly unpack. I've always felt at home in this room, but this time I feel off. I feel out of place. Daniel nods and leaves to unpack his own things. I get the feeling I'm not the only one who feels a little out of place here.

Before I know it, it's time for dinner. One of the maids knocks on my door, startling me. I've never felt comfortable with so many staff members around, but I guess I'll have to get used to it. The Devereauxs employ at least twenty people at their residence, ranging from cleaners, cooks and drivers to security personnel. My dad and I had a housekeeper who came over every day, but that can't be compared to this. The Devereauxs have an entire quarter just for their staff to live in.

I follow the girl to the dining room where the rest are already waiting. Much to my annoyance, Lucy is in the seat I usually sit in. I smile politely as I take the seat opposite Daniel instead. Dominic looks at me apologetically and then smiles at Lucy, his entire face lighting up. It looks like I was the only one who thought we might've had a moment before I got married. It's better this way, anyway. I eat my dinner quietly as Lucy and Dominic chat and laugh. Daniel glances at his phone as he eats, reading the news as usual.

"Have you unpacked, my dear?" Mary asks.

I nod and smile at her. "Yes, thank you for having me."

She shakes her head. "Don't be ridiculous. This is your home as much as it is the boys'. It always has been, but even more so now."

Lucy sits up and looks at me, anger flashing through her eyes. "You're staying here? How long?"

I nod, unfazed. "A couple of weeks at least. I don't really want to be alone right now."

I don't bother to tell her about my marriage to Daniel. We've already informed everyone we'd like to keep it a secret, so I doubt Dominic will tell her. He'd never let his older brother down like that. He might be okay breaking my trust, but he'd never break Daniel's.

I'm surprised to see a flash of insecurity in her eyes. She starts to cling to Dominic and feeds him bites of her food. Just looking at them makes me feel uncomfortable, and it's clear Mary feels the same way. Daniel glances at them, looking amused, and resumes eating in silence.

I excuse myself as quickly as possible and walk back to my room feeling dejected. I hate seeing Lucy and Dominic together and I hate knowing it'll never be me with him.

I sit down on my bed and grab the photo of my dad from the nightstand. There's a letter next to it that wasn't there when I left the room. I frown when I realise that my dad's wax seal is on it. I pick it up with shaking hands.

I can't help but wonder what he was thinking, asking me to marry Daniel. The age difference between us is too large and my heart has always belonged to Dominic. My dad knew that.

I wish I could ask him what was on his mind, what game he's playing. I wish I could argue with him, but more than that, I wish I could just see him one more time.

I carefully open the letter, tears falling from my eyes as I recognise my father's handwriting.

My beloved Alyssa,

If you're reading this letter, then unfortunately, that means I'm no longer here and I've had to leave you behind. It also means you've chosen to honour my wishes and married Daniel. I wish I could've been the one to walk you down the aisle. I have no doubt you looked beautiful, and I wish I'd been there for this important occasion.

I know you're angry, princess. I know you'd like to argue with me, and I know you can't understand my reasoning. But please trust me when I say I'm doing this because I love you.

Please know that it's not because I don't believe you can run the company in my stead. I know you can, and one day you will. I might not be there to see it happen, but rest assured that I left this world knowing you'd get there one day.

I know I've already asked a lot of you, but please allow me to ask you one more thing. Give your marriage with Daniel an honest chance. Don't keep him at a distance and don't avoid him. Let him in, Alyssa. He's not just an excellent business partner. I truly believe he'd be an excellent husband to you as well. You might not see it now, but one day you'll understand.

My greatest accomplishment in this life is and always has been you. I know you'll continue to make me proud and I'll be watching over you as you conquer the world.

I love you, baby girl
Daddy

Tears stream down my face as I clutch the letter to my chest. I lie back on my bed as a sob escapes my lips, my heart shattering. For the first time since my dad passed away, I fall apart. I cry until I've got no tears left and stare up at the ceiling. Eventually, I drag myself out of bed and into my bathroom. I'm still wearing the dress I got married in and my mascara runs in ugly lines down my face. I look like a mess and I feel even worse.

The shower helps me feel better, but not by much. Not even my favourite silk nightgown helps to lift my spirits. I settle into bed, praying I'll be able to fall asleep without memories of my dad assailing me.

God must have heard me and decided to punish me for my lack of faith, because as my head hits my pillow the sound of a girl moaning fills my ears. I freeze in disbelief, whatever was left of my heart shattering beyond repair. Dominic is in his room with Lucy. His bed and mine share a wall, and though the walls are thick, they aren't soundproof. He knows I'm in this room. He knows I'll hear them if they're too loud. How could he do this to me?

More tears run down my face and I sniff, trying my best to keep them at bay. I'm heartbroken. It feels like I've lost everything within a couple of weeks.

My bedroom door opens suddenly, and I sit up in surprise. Daniel is leaning against the door wearing nothing but long sleeping bottoms. His eyes find mine and he sighs.

"I knew you'd be crying," he says, his voice soft.

He walks up to me and gets into my bed. I'm surprised, but

welcome the comfort he's offering me. He takes me in his arms and shifts so my head is resting on his chest. I sniff and he carefully wipes away the tears that won't stop falling.

"I'm sorry," he whispers.

"It's not your fault."

He sighs and tenses. "I was the one who put the letter there. Vincent asked me to give it to you after the wedding, but maybe I should've... I don't know. Maybe I should've told him to do it himself, maybe I should've given it to you personally. Maybe I should've just thrown that girl out so you wouldn't have to listen to this shit."

I snuggle into him and shake my head. "It's not your fault, Daniel," I repeat. I listen to his heartbeat and my tears slowly abate. When is the last time Daniel hugged me? It must've been years ago. He spoiled me rotten when I was a child, but things changed when I got older. He started to treat me differently and slowly but surely, we grew apart.

"Thank you," I whisper.

Daniel kisses the top of my head like he used to when I was a child. "Anytime, sweetheart."

Seven

Daniel is gone when I wake up, but I'm sure he spent all night with me. I don't remember the last time I slept so peacefully.

I brush my teeth and wash my face before slipping on my silk robe. It matches my nightgown perfectly, and it's always made me feel like a queen. I tie the sash around my waist and follow my nose to the kitchen.

To my surprise, Daniel is standing behind the stove, frying bacon in one pan and eggs in another. I lean back against the doorframe, silently admiring the view. He's still only wearing his pyjama bottoms. I hate to admit that he looks sexy as hell.

It takes me a few minutes to realise that I'm not the only one ogling Daniel. Lucy is leaning against one of the kitchen counters, looking at Daniel appreciatively. She's barely wearing anything. I'm fond of skimpy nightgowns, but hers cannot be called a nightgown at all. Not even remotely.

"I didn't know you could cook, Daniel. You're a man of many talents, huh?" she says. I bite back a smile when he ignores her. I walk into the pantry and grab one of the aprons, purposely picking the hot pink one that Mary loves, to mess with him. I walk up to him and place my palm on his lower back. He shifts out of my reach with an angry scowl on his face, startling me. I freeze and almost drop the apron I'm holding. I ignore the brief jab of pain in my chest and the sudden feeling of rejection. It makes no sense for me to feel this way.

"Oh, Alyssa. Sorry," he says. He brushes my hair out of my face gently and smiles. "I didn't realise it was you. Hungry?"

I nod and hand him the apron. "Wear this. The oil might splash on you." My eyes subconsciously move towards Lucy and Daniel follows my gaze.

"Hmm," he says, taking the apron from me with a smile. My heart skips a beat when I take in his chest and abs. His lower abs taper into a V and I struggle to drag my eyes away from his body. He's stupidly hot. I knew he was muscular underneath his suits, but I never realised quite how much. I wish I'd taken the time to appreciate how his body felt against mine last night. I breathe a sigh of relief when he finally puts on the apron, covering most of his body. To my knowledge, Daniel hasn't spent many nights here since he moved into his downtown apartment. He was certainly never here when I was. I'm pretty sure I'd remember him wandering around the house half-naked.

I feel strangely possessive. I don't want Lucy staring at him the way she was, even though our marriage isn't real. Daniel finishes cooking breakfast with a bright smile on his face and I start to set the table.

"How come you're cooking today?" I ask.

"Sundays are family days, remember? Most of the staff have the day off. Usually my mum would've cooked, but I was up earlier so I thought I might as well."

I nod and help him place the food on the table as Mary and Dominic come strolling in. Just like Daniel, Dominic is wearing only pyjama bottoms, but it's different somehow. Dominic is far leaner than Daniel is and I guess I just got used to seeing Dominic like this.

Yeah, that must be what it is. The reason my heart fluttered was because I'm not used to seeing Daniel half-naked.

THE TIE THAT BINDS

Daniel takes off his apron and takes his seat opposite me. We all dig in to our food and though I'm trying my best not to, I keep catching myself staring at him. The way his muscles move when he reaches for something and his messy bed hair... I've never noticed him the way I do now. I guess it's because I've not seen him in such an informal setting in years. He's always in work mode, regardless of whether I see him at the office or at my house with my dad. This is the first time in years that I've seen him looking so... relaxed, and so casually dressed. He'd usually spend his weekends at his apartment. I haven't seen him here in a really long time.

Dominic clears his throat and both Lucy and I look at him, startled. "I said have you settled in okay?" he snaps.

My eyes widen, and I nod. What's he so pissed off about? "Yes, thanks for asking."

"You might want to change rooms, though," Daniel says. "There are plenty of other guest rooms, so just pick whichever one you want."

I nod at him, my mood plummeting. The last thing I want is to hear Lucy and Dominic again. If her staying over is going to be a regular occurrence, then choosing a new room isn't a bad idea.

"What? Why would you pick a new room? The room you're in has been yours since we were kids."

Daniel levels him with a pointed stare. "You and your girl-friend kept us up most of the night with your little show."

Dominic blanches and looks at me with wide eyes. "You heard us?" he asks. I look away and take a sip of my tea, unsure how to reply.

He looks at his brother, confused. "But how did you... did you two... were you together?"

Daniel crosses his arms and stares his brother down. "Alyssa lost her father and just moved into a new place. Her best friend, the one person she should've been able to count on, was too busy screwing his girlfriend to realise she shouldn't be left alone. Of course I was there to console her. The question is, why weren't you?"

I look up in surprise. He went as far as making it a rule for me to keep my distance from Dominic, yet now he's berating him for doing just that?

"Did you know she read a letter last night that her father left her? You're so preoccupied with yourself that you haven't even taken the time to ask her if she's okay."

Dominic looks down in shame. "I'm sorry, Alyssa. He's right. I've been a terrible friend. Let me make it up to you."

I shake my head. "It's fine, Nic. You had other things on your mind. I understand."

And I do understand. I'm not a priority in his life. Not anymore. I can't keep pitying myself or keep vying for his attention. Enough is enough. Friendship isn't something I should ever have to beg for.

"Moving rooms isn't a bad idea, Daniel. I'll have a look at the other rooms. Thank you for suggesting it."

I smile at him, and he nods at me. When the awkward silence becomes too much to bear, I get up and take my dishes to the kitchen. I rinse them and load them into the dishwasher while Dominic hovers around me. I ignore him and walk back to my room, but he's hot on my heels. I'm angry and want to slam my door in his face, but he's too quick.

I groan and sit down on my bed as he stares at me pleadingly. "I'm sorry, okay."

I nod. "I said it was fine, didn't I?"

Dominic chuckles. "Fine? Fine? We both know it isn't fine when you say it's 'fine'."

I sigh. "What do you expect me to say, Dominic? Daniel's right. You weren't there. You haven't been there for me in months. When is the last time you and I even had a private conversation? You didn't even drive me to my house from my father's funeral. You didn't accompany me to the reading of the will even though I asked you to and you didn't check up on me last night. You've made it quite clear that you don't give a damn about my wellbeing. What exactly do you expect me to say, huh?"

The fight leaves him and he sits down on the floor in front of me. He grabs my hands and entwines them with his.

"I've been a terrible friend. Lucy has just been so insecure about you and reassuring her has meant continuously letting you down. The bond between us has always been strong, so I knew we'd be fine. Both of us keep being dumped because of our friendship... I didn't want that to happen this time, but I also didn't mean to hurt you the way I did. I'm so sorry, Alyssa. It's hard for me to find the right balance between you and her. It's hard for me to keep you both happy."

I don't know what to say to that.

"Nic, I'm not asking you to choose me over her. I've never asked that of you, nor have I ever expected it. All I wanted was for you to look out for me a little, but you haven't. You haven't been there. It's like you don't even care. I was there for you when your dad died, but now that I'm in the same situation, you're not there for me."

"You're right. I know you are. Please, Alyssa. Please give me a chance to make it up to you? Let's go get some ice cream tonight, just you and me. Just like the good old days?"

I nod reluctantly, hoping he won't let me down yet again.

Eight

I stare at my reflection and turn around in a circle. I'm wearing another form-fitting dress and I'm starting to like them on me. I've gotten so used to not dressing up and wearing comfy baggy clothes that I forgot how good it makes me feel to dress up. I should make a habit out of it.

I grab my clutch and slip on a pair of heels. I know it's just ice cream, but Dominic and I haven't been out together in so long. I haven't been out in forever, full stop.

I pull a hand through my long brown hair, loving the feel of it. Straightening my hair always makes me feel good. I touch up my lipstick one more time and nod to myself, satisfied.

I walk out of my door at the same time Daniel does. He pauses and looks at me, surprised.

"Where are you going?" he asks, his eyes roaming over me slowly. I instantly feel guilty, even though I know I'm not doing anything to feel guilty about.

"Oh, Dominic and I are going out for ice cream."

Daniel walks up to me and I automatically take a step away, my back hitting my closed bedroom door. He puts his forearm against the door and leans into me, almost caging me in with his body.

"You're going for ice cream dressed like that?"

His voice is soft and dangerous. He's standing so close that taking one step closer would have him pressing his body against mine.

"Dressed like what?"

He chuckles and pushes my hair behind my ear with his free hand, truly caging me in now. "Are you sure this is appropriate?"

I bite down on my lip, my heart racing. "Of course."

He scowls at me and stares me down as though he thinks I'll cave and admit I'm doing something wrong.

"Daniel? Alyssa?"

I jump and Daniel pulls away from me, both of us turning to Lucy who's staring at us in shock. Her gaze keeps jumping between us as though she can't believe what she's seeing. It's like she caught us making out or something.

"Are you also joining us for ice cream, Daniel?" she asks.

My heart sinks. Dominic told me it'd just be the two of us. I thought we'd finally be able to catch up again, and that this would be his way of making up for his absence. My heart aches and I inhale deeply. I drop my head back against the door and close my eyes. Another night of watching Lucy and Dominic falling over each other.

"No, I'm not. Change of plans. I'm taking Alyssa out for dinner. Please let Dominic know she won't be joining you."

Lucy smiles and nods. "Oh, dinner sounds great! We'll come with you. We can always do dessert afterwards."

Daniel chuckles. "Yeah, no."

I bite back a smile and look at my shoes instead.

"What?" she says, a confused look on her face. It's clear that she isn't used to people refusing her anything, and her baffled expression is amusing as hell.

Daniel ignores her and grabs my hand, pulling me past her. We walk past Dominic who is waiting in the hallway and Daniel waves at him. "Enjoy your date," he says.

Before Dominic can reply, Daniel has pulled me out the door, slamming it closed behind him. He walks me to his car and opens the door for me. I sit down quietly. He seems angry and I have no idea why.

He's quiet as he drives us to one of the most expensive places in town. It's a five-star hotel with a beautiful rooftop restaurant, but it's always fully booked.

I follow behind him quietly as he walks to the lift that goes straight to the top. It's clear that he's been here before.

"Are you okay?" I ask once the doors close behind us. He hasn't spoken once since we got into the car. He looks at me and smiles absentmindedly.

"Yeah, fine. Just lost in thought, sorry."

I nod, unsure of what to say. Should I warn him we probably won't get into this restaurant?

The hostess smiles at us politely. "Welcome. Do you have a reservation?"

I shake my head and her smile falls. Daniel takes out his wallet and for a second I'm scared he's trying to bribe her into giving us a table, but then he takes out a black card and hands it to her. Her eyes widen as she swipes it. She nods at us politely as she hands it back to him, her hands trembling slightly.

"I didn't recognise you, Mr. Devereaux. Please forgive me," she says. She leads us to a small secluded table in the corner of the terrace. It's hidden behind a wall and I wouldn't have noticed it if she hadn't led us straight to it.

Rather than putting the card back into his pocket, Daniel gives it to me. I stare at it curiously. It's a black metallic card similar to a credit card, but instead of numbers on the front, it's got the golden Devereaux family crest on it. The same one as Devereaux Inc's company logo. Sometimes it's easy to forget that DM Consultancy isn't Daniel's only job. The main reason my dad didn't make Daniel the full-time CEO is because Daniel doesn't have time for it. Besides doing this he's also on the board for Devereaux Inc.

"What is this?" I ask as I sit down.

"Put it away and keep it on you. It'll give you access to any facility owned by the Devereaux family. We always have at least one table for VVIPS at every one of our restaurants and at least one room in our hotels. It'll also give you discount at all the shopping malls and other stores owned by us. Every Devereaux has one of these cards. This one is currently registered to me, but I'll transfer it to you tonight."

I stare at it with wide eyes. "I had no idea something like this even existed. Dominic never told me about it. I've never seen him use it either."

Daniel nods. "Hmm, yeah. I developed it a few months ago. He doesn't have one because I don't trust him with it. Probably didn't tell you because he's bitter as fuck about it. Last thing I need is that little asshole racking up bills everywhere and demanding superior treatment. He can have one when he finally grows the fuck up."

I sit back in surprise. I know Daniel and Dominic aren't as close as they used to be, but I didn't realise Daniel's impression of him was this bad. I want to stand up for him, but realistically I know Daniel is right. Dominic does have a bit of a penchant for showing off. Putting a card like this in his hands would only make his behaviour worse.

I stare out the window and lean on my elbow, admiring the view. When I look back at him, Daniel is leaning back, looking much more relaxed.

"Thank you. You didn't have to take me for dinner, you know."

He looks at me with such a sweet smile my heart skips a beat.

"And let you sit through a night of Lucy and Dominic's PDA? I wouldn't wish that on anyone."

I laugh as Daniel fills my glass with champagne before filling his own. He raises his glass to mine and looks into my eyes as they clink together. "Here's to us."

43

I nod and take a sip, my heart racing. The waitress takes our order but struggles to keep her eyes off Daniel. I can't help but feel offended, even though this isn't actually a date.

"How long has it been?" he asks when she finally leaves.

"How long has what been?"

He looks out the window and sighs. "How long have you been in love with Dominic?"

I freeze and stare at him. He's called me out on my unrequited love before, but I didn't think he'd ask me so directly.

"I — why do you ask?"

He shrugs. "Just curious."

"I don't even know, to be honest. I think I've always loved him. It was a very gradual thing."

Daniel smiles bitterly.

"What about you?" I ask. "Is there anyone you love?"

He pauses and takes a big sip of his champagne before nodding. "Yeah, there's a girl. I'm not sure I'm in love with her, per se. But there's someone that I can't seem to get off my mind."

My stomach tightens in what I've come to realise is jealousy. I brush it off and smile at him.

"How? I've seen the tabloids and the photos that get stuck on your office door. You make it in there almost every week, photographed with one model or the other, and that's been ongoing for as long as I can remember."

Daniel laughs. "It's complicated. That girl wasn't available. I couldn't pursue her."

He's after a married woman? Or at least someone in a serious relationship. My mind automatically replays his words, my anxiety rising. "Wasn't?"

He nods and smiles at me. "Yeah. I think I might have a shot now, but like I said, it's complicated."

I tense and unintentionally glare at him. "Yes. And you're married."

He grins and looks away as the waitress brings over our meal.

She sets it down in front of us, but my appetite seems to have waned. I wait until she leaves before probing further.

"How long has that been a thing?"

He takes a bite of his fish and chews slowly, like he expects to get out of the question that way.

"You're curious tonight, aren't you," he murmurs.

I swirl my champagne in my glass and take another big sip before smiling at him.

"Hmm, well, I answered your questions, so it's only fair."

I try my best to pretend the answer doesn't matter to me, as it shouldn't. Just as he did, I take a bite of my food and chew slowly. The food looks delicious, but my nerves render it tasteless.

"A couple of years. Since around the time I did my MBA, I guess."

My heart tightens and I try my best not to show how crestfallen I suddenly feel.

"That was four years ago. Quite some time to hold a torch for someone."

I feel jealous and bitter, even though I don't have the right to be.

"Who is she?"

It's likely someone from our social network unless he knows her from work or from his MBA. Daniel shakes his head and smiles. I'm annoyed by his refusal to answer. Part of me wants to insist that he tells me since he knows all about Dominic, but doing so would be beyond childish.

Since she was unavailable until recently, she must've just gotten out of a relationship or she just got divorced. Considering Daniel's type of tall skinny models, it won't be that hard to figure it out. Who got out of a long-term relationship recently?

"Well, if you want to pursue her, I won't stand in your way. If you've waited four years for her, I won't make you wait another three years until we divorce."

He looks at me thoughtfully, as though he's actually considering it. "Is that so?" he asks.

I panic. Considering how strongly he seemed to feel about that rule, I thought for sure he'd shoot me down straight away. I didn't even realise I was bluffing until now.

"I, well, yeah. If that's what you want, it's fine by me."

I grab my glass and empty it. I'm angry and I don't even know why.

"Hmm. There's no need. If she's the one for me, then she'll still be there in three years."

I laugh. "You believe in fate?" I ask, shocked. Daniel is the most level-headed person I know. While he's very chivalrous, I can't imagine him being romantic or believing in fate.

He shrugs and smiles at me as if to say so what.

I shake my head. "You're crazy. Life waits for no one.".

He leans forward in his seat and looks at me, his eyes twinkling.

"I'll make you a bet. If I propose within the next four years and she says yes, then you'll owe me a new Aston Martin. It'll have to be whichever model has just come out. If you win, I'll buy you an apartment the equivalent of the Aston."

I laugh and shake his hand. "That's a deal, Daniel. I'll start looking at apartments."

He shakes his head at me as though he's certain that he'll win, and if I'm honest, it hurts a little to know he wants someone so badly that he sees himself marrying her. Daniel is the ultimate bachelor. Girls come and go in his life, and no one has ever lasted for more than a few months.

"You should come back to work soon, Lyss."

I look down and nod. He's right, of course. I've not been in the office since my father died. I can't stay on leave forever.

"There's someone joining our executive training programme soon. I'm hoping you can take him under your wing. I owed his father a favour, so he's starting halfway through the programme. I tried to warn him that the competition will be even fierce because his peers will know it's blatant nepotism, but he said he didn't care so he's on his own with that one."

I nod. I'm pretty sure this dude will quit within a couple of weeks anyway. DM Consultancy is an extremely competitive place. Not many who come in through nepotism are able to last.

"Yep. No problem, boss."

Nine

I step through the doors of DM Consultancy with a wide smile on my face. This place is like home to me and I've been away for too long. I hum all the way up to the top floor, giddy with excitement. It feels like my first day all over again. I forgot how much I love being here.

"You're back!" Linda says, hugging me tightly.

Luke nods at me, silent as ever. The guy is brilliant with numbers, but not so much with words. The three of us are the only ones in the executive office. Others come and go, but the three of us have lasted. Throughout the last couple of years, we've become good friends and allies. We quickly learned to put up a united front to survive Daniel's rigorous training.

Daniel walks out of his office with his secretary on his heels. I hate how handsome he looks today. The suit he's wearing looks sexy as hell on him, and my eyes linger on his body far longer than appropriate. Much to my dismay, a guy I know all too well follows behind Kate, Daniel's secretary.

I stare at my ex in surprise. What the hell is he doing here? My eyes slowly drop to the name tag around his neck. "You've gotta be kidding me," I murmur.

Daniel smiles when he sees me. "Alyssa," he says. "Meet Jake, your new colleague."

I stiffen. I was hoping I was mistaken. Out of all the people that could've joined, it had to be Jake. He turns to Jake and hands him a stack of documents. "Alyssa will be your senior and mentor from now on. She'll help you get started and she'll be the one you can reach out to if you have any questions."

Jake and I stare at each other. Our breakup was messy, to say the least. Jake was the guy I thought things might actually work out with. I attended university using my mother's surname. I never told Jake about my family and never gave him any indication that we were even remotely wealthy. It's what my father wanted. He wanted me to learn what it's like to grow up as a regular kid as much as possible. It's the reason he told me to use Alyssa Carter at work too. Our top executives know who I am, but beyond that most of my colleagues are blissfully unaware, as was Jake.

Right when our relationship got serious, he told me we'd never have a future because I'd never be good enough for him and would never fit into his life. He said that his family was rich and they wouldn't ever accept a Cinderella into the family. He told me that the two of us could have fun until we graduated, but it'd never be more than that. I'm glad he showed me his true colours a few months into our relationship, rather than stringing me along even longer. I was furious nonetheless. I dumped a cocktail on his head and threatened to castrate him if he ever dared show his conceited face again.

"Alyssa," he murmurs, surprised. "I didn't know you worked here. The executive programme, as well. You've done surprisingly well for yourself."

I barely manage to keep from rolling my eyes. This asshole. Surprisingly well? DM's executive programme is one of the toughest in the country, and my dad would've kicked me off without remorse if I wasn't good enough. He warned me beforehand that he'd fire me and make me work for someone else if I couldn't cut it at DM. I worked harder than anyone else here to make sure that never happened.

Daniel looks at me. "You two know each other?"

I sigh and nod, part of me too embarrassed to admit I dated this douchebag. Daniel looks at me with raised brows but Jake answers him before I can.

"Yes, we attended the same university. We dated for a while."

Daniel looks at me coldly and I almost want to take a step back.

"Hmm, really now?" he says, his voice low.

I nod. "We broke up because he said I'd never be good enough for his rich family," I tell Daniel, a mischievous grin on my face.

Daniel stares at me in disbelief and then starts laughing. "Must not have been that serious then."

I nod in agreement. It was never serious enough for him to even find out my real name. It's not like I go out of my way to hide who I am. I do have social media profiles and all that, it's just that I keep them relatively private and usually pretend I don't do social media.

"Join me in my office for a minute, Alyssa."

I nod and follow him, pausing at the threshold. My father's desk is still there, untouched. Daniel closes the door behind us and I blink away the tears that have gathered in my eyes before he notices.

He walks to his desk and shakes his head. "That guy?" he says. "Really?"

I roll my eyes. "Don't judge. I've seen some of the girls you've been with."

He leans back in his chair and shakes his head. "No, Lyss. You've seen some of the girls I've been photographed with."

I blink in surprise. Surely he isn't insinuating that not everything I've seen is real. I know the media likes to twist things to get a juicy story out, but there's often a grain of truth to it. Daniel pushes a folder my way before I can overthink it.

"Luxe. One of our oldest clients. Out of everyone, they are the one client I thought would stick with us, no matter what. But now they're threatening to terminate our contract after we deliver the new packaging designs and our proposed marketing strategy, unless we give them twenty-five percent discount. They're saying they don't have faith in us without your father here."

I shake my head. "Impossible. We need them to let us implement the marketing strategy. We can't afford to give them more discount because we're barely making any money on them as it is. If we give them more discount. that'll set a precedent I'm not comfortable with."

Daniel nods at me. "Exactly. Can you handle this?"

"I'll try, but if they're intent on leaving us, then they'll do so."

Daniel sighs and pulls a hand through his hair, messing it up. "Are you doing okay?" I ask. I walk around his desk and lean against it, looking down at him. I haven't actually stopped to wonder whether he's doing all right. He's doing my father's job now on top of his own, and he's constantly confronted with his loss in this office.

"We can remove the desk, you know. You shouldn't leave this all here. I can pack it all up. Looking at it all day will just be hard for both of us."

Daniel stares at the desk opposite him, looking so lost that my heart breaks. "Hmm... I'll get someone to do it this weekend. I don't think it's something you or I are ready to do so soon, but it needs to be done."

I stare at him, unable to determine whether he's really okay or whether he's putting up a good front. It's been over a month since my father died. Has he been staring at my dad's desk all this time? We've been married for two weeks and he never once showed me how much pain he's in, but the agony I'm seeing in his eyes as he stares at my dad's desk tells me everything I need to know.

"Okay, all right," I murmur. I comb through his hair with my fingers, carefully straightening out the mess he made. I smile when I'm done and pull back to find Daniel staring at me with wide eyes. I realise what I did and cradle my hand.

51

"Oh, I'm so sorry, Daniel. I didn't mean to..."

I feel mortified. In the last couple of days, the lines between Daniel and I have begun to blur. I've gotten so used to him throwing his arm around my shoulder or playing with my hair that I didn't think much of it. I forgot that we're at work and that my behaviour isn't appropriate.

He shakes his head and smiles. "It's fine. I don't mind. Thanks for fixing my hair." The way he smiles at me is sweet and almost shy. It makes my heart skip a beat and I step away from him, feeling flustered.

I all but run out of his office, praying my cheeks aren't flaming. Jake is standing at my cubicle when I walk back and I sigh. I really can't be bothered with this guy.

"You can sit there," I say, pointing at the empty cubicle next to Luke's. He nods, but rather than going to his cubicle, he hesitates and lingers at mine.

"Lyss, we're good, right?" he asks.

I groan. "Yeah, we're fine. Get me all the data on Luxe. They're one of our oldest clients. I need summaries of the information we have. I need details of our past contracts with them, employees who have worked with them most frequently, details on our key contacts there and a copy of our latest proposal, including a full breakdown of costs."

Jake looks startled. "I won't repeat myself, Jake. You'd better have gotten all that. I need it on my desk within the hour. If one of the interns hasn't shown you how to use our systems yet, then I recommend you learn quickly."

He looks angry and I can't wait to see what kind of bullshit is going to come out of his mouth now. "I'm not your little bitch, Alyssa. I get that you're still bitter about our breakup, but you can't take it out on me at work. That's unprofessional. I'll let it slide this time, but I'll be reporting you to HR if you pull this shit again."

I roll my eyes. "Are you an idiot? Did you get into uni the same way you got into DM? Didn't you hear the way the CEO introduced you to me? I'm your senior, so yes, you are my little bitch. Now get to work or get the fuck out."

Linda whistles while Jake's face keeps getting redder and redder. He looks at Daniel's office as though he wants to storm in and demand retribution, but he probably knows Daniel is just as likely to throw him out. His father might have gotten him in here, but he won't be able to keep him here. After stewing for a couple of minutes, he finally stalks off and gets to work.

"Fifty-three minutes," I yell. He clenches his jaw and starts typing furiously.

Luke chuckles. "Don't worry," he says. "She's been here longer than any of us. She's everyone's senior, not just yours. And yes, she's just as tough on us. Don't take it personally."

Sadly for me, but fortunately for Jake, he actually gets the information to me in time, robbing me of an excuse to get rid of him. I mull over it and draw up a plan, but I'm not a hundred percent confident.

I knock on Daniel's door with the outline of my plan. He's on the phone when I walk in, so I stand and wait in front of his floor to ceiling window. The skyline looks stunning as the sun slowly sets.

Daniel joins me when his call is done. He stands next to me, his arm brushing against mine.

"I think they're bluffing," I tell him. "I've gone over the data and calculations over and over again. None of our competitors can afford to give them the rates we do. I'm eighty percent sure they're bluffing."

Daniel turns to face me and nods. "I agree."

I look away and try to gather the courage to tell Daniel my plan.

"Would it be okay if I request a meeting with them?" I ask, my voice soft. Daniel looks at me and tilts his head in question.

"I want to talk to them in person. Remind them of the relationship they had with my dad and how much of a betrayal it is for them to do this to us right now. I'm a Moriani, after all."

Dan smiles at me and nods. "That might just do the trick. Have your ex sign an NDA and bring him with you."

I hesitate. "Are you sure?"

Daniel nods. I sigh as I walk back to my cubicle to print the non-disclosure agreement and set the appointment with Luxe. I don't want to bring him, but since Daniel suggested it, I have no choice. I slap the NDA on Jake's desk. "Sign this. The boss told me to bring you to tomorrow's meeting with Luxe."

He frowns. "I already signed an NDA when I signed my contract."

I shake my head. "This NDA is specific to me. Read through the terms. It states that nothing you hear during meetings you attend with me can be revealed. Not even intra-company. The NDA you signed only covers sharing information with those outside of DM."

Linda jumps up, dismayed. "Seriously? I had to wait three months to attend a meeting with you and he gets to go in his first week? What kind of bullshit is that, Alyssa?"

I run a hand through my hair and shake my head. "It's not me, Linda, I promise. I don't want to take him either. It's the boss's orders. Go take it up with Daniel."

She grits her teeth and sits back down, and I sigh. She's going to sulk all day without a doubt and nothing I can say is going to convince her that I'm not playing favourites.

"We're meeting Liam Evans on Friday," I say, pushing a post-it his way. "This is the address, you'd better not be late."

Jake grins like he's got the upper hand. "I know Liam. I've met him a couple of times. We'll be fine. He's a great guy."

I roll my eyes. Everyone knows everyone in the same social and business circles. That doesn't mean shit, but whatever. Let him find out the hard way.

Ten

I'm absentminded on the way to the restaurant. This entire week back at work has been tough. It's odd not seeing my dad walk out of his office to chat with me or to offer us all a cup of tea. Even this client meeting is tough. This is the first time I'll have to do one by myself, without Daniel or my dad present.

Much to my annoyance, Jake is already there even though I'm fifteen minutes early. He hasn't messed up once this week, no matter what I threw at him. He follows me silently as the waitress leads us to the table. If he's surprised that the meeting location changed, he hasn't shown it.

I sit down and go through the points I want to make in my head. Liam is tricky, and if he so much as suspects that I'm bluffing, he'll call me on it and I'll be done for. A couple of minutes after we've sat down, Liam walks up to us. Jake jumps up and shakes his hand before I even stand up.

"Hey, Liam. How are you? It's good to see you again," he says, excitedly.

Liam smiles at him but clearly has no idea who he is. "Yeah, good to see you too," he says, before turning to me.

"Well, I'll be damned," he murmurs. "Alyssa Moriani in the

flesh. Isn't it sad that the only time I get to have dinner with you is when it's for work?"

I chuckle as he kisses the back of my hand. I pull it from his grip, wiping it on my skirt.

"Ever so heartless," he says, shaking his head.

"What?" Jake says. "Moriani? No, her name is Alyssa Carter," he tells Liam carefully, clearly trying to be as polite as possible about it.

Jake looks at me reproachfully. "You're still going around using your mother's surname?"

I shrug and sit down. Liam looks at Jake sympathetically. "It's fine," he tells him. "She does this to all the newbies. Her father has always been a bit odd like that, insisting that she remains low-key amongst the staff even though all of us in the upper social circles know her. Somehow it actually works out for her. Don't be too shocked."

Jake looks at me and lowers his eyes in shame, but I don't actually care about his past behaviour. What's in the past can stay there. If Daniel hadn't asked me to bring him, he wouldn't have found out at all. I would've preferred it that way. The last thing I need is for him to suddenly think things can work out between us.

"God, you look amazing," Liam says.

I blush and look away, unable to hide my smile. "You don't look so bad yourself," I tell him truthfully. Age has only made him more handsome. He's grown out his sandy brown hair and his eyes are the colour of the sky on a gorgeous clear day. Liam has always been handsome, and he's always known it.

"I would've been happy to come to your office for the meeting, you know."

Liam smiles. "I know. But this is the only way I can get you to agree to have dinner with me. God knows how many times I've asked."

I smile and look away, feeling a little embarrassed.

"You know this is just a business meeting, right?"

"For now," he murmurs.

I shake my head and burst out laughing.

"You're unbelievable," I tell him.

I order us a jug of sangria and tapas to share. "I love your choice of restaurant," I say.

Liam smiles from ear to ear. "I was hoping you'd like it. The last time we met you said you really wanted to try sangria, and this place has great sangria."

I look at him in genuine surprise and think back to the last time I saw him. It must've been over a year ago. If I'm not mistaken, it was a couple of weeks before my twenty-first birthday and we'd gone to a tapas place similar to this one, but my dad wouldn't let me try the sangria. It seems like such a long time ago.

"Wow. I can't believe you remember that," I say softly. Liam's cheeks redden and he shrugs.

I take a careful sip of my sangria and grin. "Oh my god, this is delicious!"

Liam grins, a cute twinkle in his eyes.

"So, you know why I'm here, right?"

Liam nods, still smiling. "Yes. My company is bullshitting yours and you're here to charm me into making them get their shit together."

I raise my eyebrow in surprise and chuckle. "Well, that's one way to put it."

Liam's smile widens. "I've missed you, you know. I was really sorry to hear about your dad. I'm sorry I couldn't make it to the funeral."

"I missed you, too," I say, my voice soft. I pretty much kept to myself ever since I started university. My focus was entirely on succeeding my father... and on Dominic. "I miss your scandalous stories about all the terrible things you got up to at uni."

Liam laughs and looks away. "That's all behind me, Lyss. I'm a changed man now." I nod. "Yeah, right."

"No, really," he says, his gaze turning serious. I take a sip of my sangria and I look at him, not sure what to make of him. I

CATHARINA MAURA

decide to go into my sales pitch instead, in case things become awkward between us.

"I looked into the figures and I'll be honest with you, Liam. We're already giving you a far better rate than you'll find elsewhere. I know you're well aware of that. I can't give you a twenty-five percent discount," I say simply. "What I can do for you is give you a smaller team comprised of more experienced people that are already familiar with Luxe. The campaign will take longer to complete, but it should cost you slightly less. I can cut off about eight percent of the costs that way."

Liam looks at me, surprise flickering through his eyes. He nods slowly.

"I don't want to lose Luxe as a client, Liam, but I can't give away our services for free either. If I give you more than eight percent discount, I won't make a profit on this contract at all. I'd rather put my resources to work for a client that gives me a high profit margin, rather than taking the opportunity cost I'm absorbing by sticking with Luxe."

I smile at him, but my heart is pounding. I'm scared he'll call me on my bullshit. Even with an eight percent discount, we'll be making a large profit on this contract. If Liam decides to walk away now, we'll likely lose Luxe as a client forever.

Liam nods slowly, a wicked grin on his face. "So what's stopping me from moving to one of your competitors, Alyssa? I'll be honest with you too. Your father was behind all the genius campaigns for our firm, whether it was marketing or restructuring. He was great at all of it. Now that I'm not sure who the mind will be behind our campaigns, I can't have the same blind trust I used to have in DM."

I nod. I understand what he means and it's true. Daniel and I have both been missing my dad's great ideas and solutions, but I have faith in us. The only thing I can do is hope others will too.

"I'll be one of the minds behind your new campaign, Liam. And while I might not have my father's years of experience and expertise, I can assure you that he's trained me personally. The

THE TIE THAT BINDS

other main contributor to your campaign will be Daniel Devereaux himself."

Liam raises his eyebrows in surprise. "Daniel will be working on the campaign himself?"

I nod. "Of course, Liam. Luxe is one of our most important and oldest clients. We will continue to deliver the quality you're used to. I can assure you of that. Needless to say, you're always welcome to speak to Daniel or me at any time," I say, pushing Daniel's business card towards him. "His private business number is on here and you can reach him directly." I purposely didn't ask him to call Daniel's secretary for an appointment. I need Liam to feel special and cherished as a client. I need to keep this as personal as possible. That's the best way to approach our current predicament.

Liam leans back and nods. "All right, Alyssa. I'll sign the implementation contract. Have your office send the contract over to mine and I'll get it back to you within the week. We'll pay full price, but I need you to update the timeline. I need this done quicker than outlined in your proposal. I'll email you the updated timeline so you can draft a new contract."

I exhale in relief and lean back, sipping my sangria to hide my victorious smile. I did it. I nod at Jake. "Perfect. Jake here will hand deliver the new contract to you once we've redrafted it."

Jake stares at me with newfound respect. I don't think he actually expected me to be good at my job, and for a couple of seconds I allow myself to be proud of what I've accomplished today. He hasn't interrupted me once during the meeting and has been taking notes diligently. If he keeps this up, he might actually make it at DM.

"I'll take you up on that offer to meet with Daniel. I've heard a lot of good things about him, but I'll rest easier once I've met him myself," Liam says.

I nod. "That won't be a problem. Just tell me when and where and I'll arrange it."

Liam hesitates as we get up. "What would you say if I asked

you out to dinner? Not a business meeting this time. Just you and I and a candlelit dinner somewhere, maybe a bottle of wine."

I freeze. My heart hammers in my chest and my thoughts automatically turn to Daniel and the rules we agreed on.

"I can't, Liam." I'm not sure how to explain myself. Should I tell him I'm seeing someone? I won't be able to tell him who it is thanks to the rule I came up with myself, and if Liam asks me again in a few months when I'm clearly not in an official public relationship, he'll think I've been lying to him all along. I don't want to do anything that'll damage our working relationship or our friendship.

"I'd say that now isn't the right time. Not now that you've got a contract hanging over my head."

Liam lowers his eyes in shame and nods briefly. "But that isn't a definite no, is it?" he says softly.

I shake my head, unable to answer any other way. "No, I suppose it isn't."

Eleven

I'm exhausted by the time I get home and slightly tipsy from the sangria. Much to my surprise, Daniel is hanging out with Dominic and Lucy in the sitting room. Hell must've frozen over. He's changed out of his suit, so he must've been home for some time at least. It's unfair that he looks even hotter in jeans and a tee than he does in a suit.

Dominic sees me and his eyes linger on my body for a couple of seconds. He rarely sees me in work clothes, and he's obviously startled. Startled in a good way, I guess, since he blushes when I catch him staring.

"Alyssa, you're home," he says, waving me over. Usually the first thing I do is go to my room and change into comfy clothes, but today I walk over and plop down on the sofa right next to Daniel.

"How was work?" Daniel asks. I lean into him subconsciously and he raises his arm to wrap it around me, side-hugging me. The two of us have gotten more comfortable with each other over the last couple of weeks. He'll usually throw his arm around me if we're sitting next to each other and he's taken to brushing my hair out of my face randomly too. It's not much, but it's a big change from the distance we used to keep from each other. We aren't as formal and polite anymore. I guess that's only natural since we see each other in our private time too now.

"It was fine. They'll pay full price, but we need to move the timeline up and deliver sooner. Liam said they'll sign the implementation contract this week."

Daniel looks at me in disbelief. "You're kidding me," he says, and I shake my head.

"Nope." I smile at him, unable to hide the pride I feel. Even I wasn't sure I'd get this done so quickly. I thought it'd involve a lot more negotiation.

"Liam Evans?" Dominic asks, sitting up. He pulls away from Lucy and looks at me through narrowed eyes. I nod and Dominic rolls his eyes. "That guy has had a hard-on for you for years. If you told him you wanted to raise the price, he probably would've agreed. Let me guess. He asked you on a date in return?"

Daniel tenses, his grip on my shoulder tightening. "Did he ask you out?" Daniel asks. I freeze. I was going to tell him, but I didn't expect to be telling him like this.

"Yeah. We should probably discuss that later," I whisper. I glance at Lucy, who's staring at us with interest.

"Holy shit," she whispers. "Liam Evans is wicked hot. I hope you said yes to that." Dominic glares at her and she looks at him sheepishly. I feel awkward and stand up and excuse myself, telling them I need to get changed. Truthfully, I just want to escape.

"Wear a cute dress," Lucy tells me. I stare at her blankly. "Tonight is the annual bonfire, remember?"

I sigh, finally remembering. I've had such a busy week at work I totally forgot I agreed to go with them. No wonder Daniel is hanging out with them.

I change quickly, not wanting to keep them waiting even longer. I reapply my lipstick and change into a cute spaghetti strap dress paired with my comfy slippers and rush back to the sitting room. I'm usually excited to attend the bonfire. I can't believe I actually forgot about it.

"We'll get the driver to drop us off in mum's soccer van. We'll probably all be drinking anyway," Dominic says. I nod and follow them quietly.

Daniel glanced at me once and has been ignoring me since then. I can't quite put my finger on it, but he seems a bit off. Usually he'd smile or make some small talk, but it's like I'm not even there. He remains quiet throughout the journey, typing away on his phone. Every time he smiles at his screen, I wonder who he's talking to. It's late, so it's probably not a client.

He jumps out of the car and walks to the beach without waiting for any of us. I've gotten so used to him offering me his hand when we get out of a car that I sit there for a couple of seconds, startled.

I'm not the only one who notices his odd behaviour. Dominic laughs as he looks at Daniel's disappearing form. "Does he have a hot date or something?" he asks.

I frown. Surely not. Is it that girl, maybe? The one he said he can't get off his mind. This bonfire is attended by almost everyone we know. The location is kept secret and only those with an invite are told where it'll take place. If the girl he's after is of a similar social status as us, she'll be here tonight.

The three of us follow Daniel at a leisurely pace. Lucy and Dominic are already in their own little world, but oddly enough it doesn't make me feel as awkward as it used to. I guess I've gotten used to their PDA now.

I watch Daniel disappear in the crowd and run after him, scared to lose him. With the amount of people present, it'll take me forever to find him again. I push through the crowd and when I finally catch up to him I find him embracing someone.

"Kate?"

She turns and smiles at me. "Hey, Alyssa! I didn't know you'd be here too."

She comes over and hugs me. "Did the boss invite you too?" she asks. Why is she even here? Why would Daniel invite her?

I shake my head. "No, I've attended for years. I was invited," I tell her.

She nods and looks around, her eyes twinkling. I've never seen her in anything other than work suits. Her figure looks great in her shorts and crop top, but it definitely doesn't leave much to the imagination. She looks as wide eyed as I was when I first attended. The annual bonfire isn't actually just a bonfire. It started as one, but it slowly turned into an event with live music, food stalls and plenty of games to play.

"It's even better than I imagined. I haven't been out in forever. Now that my divorce has finally come through, I'm so ready to just celebrate and let loose," she says.

I glance at Daniel, whose eyes are firmly pasted on Kate. He's smiling at her and it irks me.

"Divorce? I didn't know. Congrats, I guess?"

She laughs. "Congrats indeed, thank you."

She grabs Daniel's arm and hooks her arm through it. "They have cotton candy, should we get some?"

I freeze, my eyes zeroing in on where she's holding Daniel. My heart feels funny and I'm filled with irrational anger that turns into fury when he smiles at her instead of brushing her off. He lets her drag him away and I'm left to follow them, feeling like a third wheel.

I get even more angry when he buys cotton candy to share with her without even asking me if I want any. He's the one that insisted on the no dating rule, so what is happening here?

"God, this reminds me of that time we went to the carnival in San Fran. Except they had that pretty blue and pink cotton candy, remember?"

Daniel nods at her indulgently.

"When did you go to San Francisco together?" I ask, my voice harsher than I intended. Daniel glances at me, his expression blank. It's almost like he forgot I'm even here, or like he's surprised I'm still here. If it wasn't clear that I'm intruding, then it is now.

"Ah, we did our MBA together at Stanford. That's how we met. Didn't you know? Daniel offered me a job as his executive assistant when we finished. We keep things professional at work but we usually manage to hang out every couple of weeks at least."

My heart twists uncomfortably and I take a step back from them. Recently divorced and they did their MBA together? It doesn't take a genius to figure it out. I inspect Kate and laugh to myself. Tall, skinny and long hair. What a surprise. My stomach clenches with jealousy and my heart aches. My marriage to Daniel isn't real and I shouldn't be feeling the way I do, but that doesn't mean I'll stand here and watch my husband flirt with someone else.

"Guess I'll be buying you that Aston Martin, after all," I snap, failing to hide the anger I'm feeling. Daniel's eyes widen slightly, like he's surprised I figured it out. I glance at their joint arms and turn around, in need of a drink.

Twelve

"What's going on?" Linda whispers to Luke as she eyes me. Luke shakes his head with wide eyes, silently telling her to shut up. I've been in a bad mood today and I'd like to say that I'm better than taking it out on my colleagues, but I'm not. I feel terrible for snapping at them, but I can't help it. Every time Kate giggles or Daniel smiles at her, my mood worsens. They're more chatty today than they previously were, so it looks like they had a great time at the bonfire. They must have, since Daniel didn't come home until well into the night and then disappeared for the rest of the weekend, coming home only to go straight to bed.

Daniel walks out of his office with a stormy expression on his face. "Alyssa, I asked you for the info on Takuya. Why is not on my desk yet?"

I lift my head and twist my desk chair towards him. "You asked for it fifteen minutes ago, Daniel. Do I look like a robot to you?"

He glares at me. "I didn't ask for sass. I asked you to do your damn job. I should've had it on my desk five minutes ago."

He storms back into his office and I try my best not to throw my apple at his head. Such an asshole.

THE TIE THAT BINDS

The entire office is silent, and I sit up, staring them down. "What the hell are you all looking at? Help me get this shit done, damn it."

They all turn back to their screens and start typing as furiously as I am. I'm enraged. Every little thing that comes out of his mouth makes me even more angry.

Twenty-five minutes later, I have the report in my hands. It required four people to get it done, so how he expected me to do it by myself in ten minutes is beyond me.

Jake hesitates and then looks at me. "I can go give him the report if you want."

"Yeah, that would be great." I smile at him gratefully, relieved I won't have to face Daniel again. I'm not sure I'll be able to get through a meeting with him without resorting to violence at this point.

I focus on the rest of my work as Jake walks into Daniel's office. Within three minutes I hear Daniel shouting. Jake walks back out, his face scarlet. He looks like he might burst into tears any second. I inhale deeply and massage my temples. I should've expected that Jake wouldn't know how to answer Daniel's questions.

"Alyssa!" he shouts.

I pull a hand through my hair to compose myself before I walk into Daniel's office, shutting the door behind me.

"You called for me?" I say. He's standing by the window and turns to face me. I don't think I've ever seen him look this angry. He never used to show any emotions at all, making it impossible to guess what he's thinking. He's got no problem showing his emotions today though. He's snapping at me one minute and smiling at Kate the next.

"Explain to me why Takuya is threatening not to sign with us after all the effort we went through."

So he asked for a five-page report and didn't even bother to read the first couple of sentences? Fucking fantastic.

"Their R&D is through the roof and they have nothing to

show for it. Their profitability has been decreasing every quarter since Mr. Takuya's son took over. Looks like they'll run into liquidity issues soon. They need us to save their company. They definitely won't be able to do it themselves. We just need to convince them they need us. I suggest going in person. The issue will be more that Mr. Takuya's son won't want to admit to his failings, and he probably knows hiring us will result in that."

I walk up to his desk and grab the report to show him my calculations and forecasts. I turn around as Daniel walks up to me. I take a step back until my hips hit his desk. He leans in and cages me in with his arms.

My heart starts racing at his proximity and I try my best not to show it. "What are you doing?" I whisper.

"Tell me why you've been so mean to me all morning," he replies.

I place my hands against his chest to push him away but end up sliding my palms up to his shoulders.

"I'm not being mean."

I didn't realise it wasn't just my colleagues I've been snapping at. I've been trying my best to keep things professional between Daniel and I, but I've been irrationally angry and jealous. Pretending to hide it has just resulted in me being irritable.

"You are. What's got you so worked up?"

I shake my head and grab his tie, straightening it out. He's so close. What would he do if I leaned in and kissed him? My eyes drop to his lips and I subconsciously lick mine.

I drag my eyes away and shake my head. "It's nothing. I'm sorry. I didn't realise I wasn't behaving professionally, but then neither are you."

He raises his brows and looks at me.

"You keep smiling at Kate and she keeps giggling at you. Do you think flirting at the office is appropriate?"

His eyes widen and I worry that I just gave myself away. "I've been treating her the same way I always have," he says. He takes a step closer to me, closing the remaining distance between us. My body is pressed up against his and I love the way he feels against me so much that I struggle to hold on to my anger.

"So you've always been flirting with her and I only just noticed? No wonder you said you didn't need to amend our rules to win the bet."

Daniel buries a hand in my hair and shakes his head. "I'm not flirting with her, Alyssa. It's just friendly banter."

I laugh humorously and try to pull my hair out of his grip, but he won't let me.

"Speaking of our rules. Sounds like you had a great time with Liam Evans."

I glare at him. "It was for work. It wasn't even just the two of us. Jake was there too."

Daniel smiles. "Yeah, but you agreed to go out with him again, didn't you? How are you going to accomplish that while still abiding by our rules?"

I push him away and walk to the window. "The same way you seem to be getting away with it. Asking Kate to the bonfire. Letting her put her arm around yours and sharing cotton candy? All the while making it obvious that your own wife is the third wheel. If you can do that, then why can't I? Seems like your definition of not cheating is just not having sex with someone else. I'm pretty sure I can manage that."

Daniel joins me by the window, an amused twinkle in his eyes that pisses me off more.

"Come to think of it. Where the hell have you been all weekend?" I snap.

He bites down on his lip and it looks an awful lot like he's trying to hide a smile. He slips his hand in his pocket and takes out his wallet.

"I've been at home, sweetheart. In my own home, my apartment. Being at my mum's is overwhelming at times. I needed a bit of rest and some time to clear my mind. I came back to sleep at my mum's so we don't breach the terms of the will. We can only stay away from each other a total of fifteen nights a year, so it's best if we keep those for emergencies."

He hands me a keycard with his apartment building's logo on it. "You can keep this. It's the access card for the building. The entrance to the apartment itself is through biometrics. Security is the same firm as your house and the Devereaux mansion, so I asked them to transfer your existing biometrics to my apartment as well."

I waver, suddenly second guessing myself. He's just been at home all weekend?

"Were you alone?"

Daniel nods and brushes a strand of my hair behind my ear before cupping my face. "Yep. You can check the guest log if you don't believe me. There are cameras by the entrance as well. I registered your name to my residence so you're formally a co-habitant of my apartment. You have access to all the same security feeds that I have access to."

I shake my head. Like I'd ever go as far as checking camera recordings. I exhale in relief. At least he didn't spend all weekend with Kate.

I lean into his hand and Daniel moves closer to me, his hand sliding over my skin until he's holding the back of my neck.

"I didn't realise living at your mother's house would be tough on you. I guess it makes sense. You haven't called it home in so long. Maybe we should stay at your apartment during weekdays at least? It's closer to the office, anyway. We could stay at your mum's on the weekends."

Daniel looks at me gratefully and nods. "I'd really appreciate that, Alyssa. Let's give that a try, and if you're not comfortable there, we'll move back."

I nod and clear my throat, hesitating before I speak. "I think we should add some more details to the rules. Cheating from now on includes anything ranging from flirting to sleeping with someone else."

70

Daniel grins and looks away. He looks shy and cute, and I hate how much I love his expression.

"Very well. If you say so, Wifey. Those rules apply to you too, though."

My heart skips a beat at the endearment he uses and I blush. "I evaded Liam's request by saying he couldn't ask me out while he's got a contract over my head, but it's been signed now and he asked me to go celebrate with him. I thought of saying I'm seeing someone... but if in a few months I'm clearly not dating, then he'll just think I was lying all along."

Daniel takes a step closer and presses his body flush against mine. He looks down at me with an intense gaze that has my heart beating wildly. "So just date me, wife."

I bite down on my lip and look away. "I — I guess we can think about our options when the time comes," I stammer.

"Hmm, yeah. Think about that, Alyssa," Daniel says.

Thirteen

I follow Daniel into his building. The security is definitely over the top. Daniel swipes his access card and the doors swing open automatically. There are two security guards standing by the doors who both smile at him.

"Welcome home, Mr. Devereaux."

He nods at them and pauses, placing a hand on my lower back as they take our luggage from us. "This is my wife, Alyssa. She'll be moving in with me. Please treat her the same way you treat me."

My heart skips a beat. This is the first time he's ever introduced me as his wife, and I'm surprised by how much I like it. It gives me an odd sense of security and makes me feel all giddy.

The security guards nod at me politely. If they're curious about me, they don't show it. Daniel walks into the lift and grabs my hand, startling me.

"Biometric scanner," he says. He pushes my finger against the scanner and the lift starts to move up automatically. I look around but can't find any buttons except for an emergency call button. He answers my question before I even voice it.

"Guests need to sign in at the reception desk downstairs and are then escorted up. My mother is the only other person besides us that has access."

The doors open right into the apartment, revealing a large entrance hall. I follow Daniel inside, barely able to contain my curiosity. I've never been here before and for some reason I always imagined it as a small cute apartment. It's nothing like that at all. It's far bigger than I could've imagined and decorated tastefully. It's nothing like the bachelor pad I was expecting to find. It does indeed look like a home.

"I love it. No wonder you've missed this place so much."

He shows me to the living room and I sigh in delight. His sofa is large and comfy looking. There's so much natural light coming in that the space looks even bigger than it is. One entire corner of the room is made of glass, overlooking a magnificent skyline. His open plan kitchen is a dream come true, with every single appliance I could imagine. He's even got a waffle maker. I can't wait to rummage through the cupboards and find out what else he might have. Each room Daniel shows me is more stunning than the last.

"There is one guest room that my mother usually uses, but you can have that one now. Unless you prefer the master bedroom?"

I peek into the room he points out and can clearly see Mary's touch all over it. The wooden bed frame and the daisies on the bedsheets don't suit the modern apartment at all, but it's so her. Daniel has already moved past the guest room and walks into another room. I follow him in curiously.

"This is my bedroom. I think you might be more comfortable in here, so you're welcome to have it."

He walks into the room and sits down on his bed as I take it all in. The master bedroom is huge. He's decorated it in dark colours while maintaining a modern, state of the art feel. Even the lamps on his bedside table look as though they were carefully selected. Similar to the living room, one of the walls is made entirely of glass.

He's silent as I explore his bedroom, unable to suppress my

curiosity. His walk-in wardrobe is much bigger than mine at home. He's even got a little dresser in there with aftershave and other cosmetics, every single thing in its own place. Much to my surprise, he's got two photos on the dresser, right behind his little collection of perfume bottles. One is of Daniel, Dominic, Mary and me last Christmas. I remember my dad taking this photo, but I didn't realise he even sent it to Daniel. The other photo is of my dad, me and Daniel on the last birthday we got to celebrate with my dad. It was his 58th birthday. I barely remember taking the photo. I think we went out for dinner to celebrate and afterwards we got some dessert. All I remember is that my dad and Daniel spoke about buying Daniel's new car most of the night.

I touch the photo with my fingertips and walk through the other door in his bedroom. His bathroom consists almost entirely of marble. It looks luxurious and inviting. There's a large jacuzzi in one corner that I'm dying to try out. Just Daniel's bedroom, wardrobe and bathroom must take up at least a quarter of the total size of this apartment, if not more.

"God, I can see why you'd miss this place. It's wonderful. I wouldn't dare take your room though. I'm happy with the guest room, but I may have to sneak into your jacuzzi one night."

Daniel's eyes darken, and I realise what I said. "I — I mean... when you're not there, I mean."

Daniel smiles and shakes his head, thankfully disregarding my awkwardness. "You're welcome to use anything here, my bathroom included. We're married, Alyssa. This place is yours as much as it is mine."

I bite down on my lip and nod. It's been easy to forget that we got married, especially because we've been living with Mary. While there, we didn't spend that much time together, so it never felt like we were married. I guess it's what we both wanted, though. It's a marriage of convenience after all.

I jump when I hear footsteps nearby and Daniel stands up. "Suitcases," he tells me.

"How many of the staff have access?"

Daniel shakes his head. "Not many. Two designated security officers, one housekeeper and a cook. The housekeeper comes once a day, and the cook comes whenever I ask her to. It's up to you when you want them to come. Would you prefer for us to do our own cooking?"

I nod. My dad and I always cooked for each other a few times a week. It was kind of our thing; our way of showing appreciation for each other. We'd sit down and have dinner together. My dad never missed it, even if it meant he had to work overtime in his home office. Our little tradition meant that Daniel often ended up eating with us and spending the evening in my dad's office. My heart aches at the memory. Knowing I'll never taste my dad's food again breaks my heart.

"Maybe we can just cook ourselves a few times a week? If you don't want to, then I can do the cooking?"

Daniel's expression softens, as though he knows what I'm thinking. He walks up to me and cups my cheek gently. "Of course. I'd be happy to do that. Though you'll have to promise you'll make it home for dinner every day like you did with your dad. I'll do the same. If we have to work overtime, then I have a big enough home office to facilitate us both. I'll get you a desk chair so we can share my desk."

My heart melts. How does Daniel always know the right thing to say? "Yes, of course. I promise."

He smiles at me, and my heartbeat accelerates. His entire face transforms when he smiles like that. It's oddly intimate, especially because he rarely smiles.

I drag my eyes away from him and take a step back, hoping he doesn't notice that I'm blushing. "I — I'll go unpack," I tell him, rushing away to my new bedroom. I hear him chuckle as I close his bedroom door behind me and rub my chest to try to calm my raging heart.

Since when has Daniel impacted me so much? I guess it's been easy to ignore how hot he is since he always used to keep a certain boundary between us. My dad was always with us too. I don't think I've really spent any alone time with Daniel in the last couple of years.

The room I'm in doesn't feel like my own at all. It's clearly Mary's room. There are even some spare clothes of hers in the cupboards. It almost feels like an intrusion to be in here. Even after unpacking I still feel uncomfortable.

When I'm sure I'll be able to keep my erratic heart in check, I head to the living room. Daniel is sitting on the sofa, legs outstretched. He's changed into pyjama bottoms and a tight t-shirt. He's got black framed glasses resting on the tip of his nose as he goes through a stack of documents, and my heart does it again. It freaking skips a beat.

The way his t-shirt stretches over his muscles barely leaves anything to the imagination. I wonder which is worse, the tight t-shirt or nothing at all. Both are torture, that's for sure. Daniel looks up and catches me staring at him like a total pervert. I look away and pray my cheeks aren't flaming as I walk towards the sofa.

"You changed," he says. I look down at my outfit and clutch my fluffy robe. I showered and put on some of my favourite jammies, but I wasn't sure if it would be inappropriate for me to walk around the house half-naked, so I threw on my trusty old bathrobe.

"Ah yeah, so did you," I say, my eyes lingering on his muscular arms. It's a shame he covers them up with suits every day.

I sit down next to him somewhat awkwardly. The sofa is huge and I'm not entirely sure where I'm supposed to sit. Sitting too far away from him would be awkward and potentially rude, but so is sitting too close.

"I — I like the glasses," I stammer. Daniel blinks as though he forgot he was wearing them and pushes them up. He looks at me and smiles, and my heart skips another beat. How can a man be adorable and hot at the same time?

I clear my throat to distract myself from my own thoughts and peek at what he's working on. He shuffles closer to me and throws his arm around my shoulder, pulling me to his side. I glance at him in surprise, but he keeps his eyes on his documents. I lean into him and get comfortable, putting my feet up next to his.

"What's this?" I ask, not recognising the documents.

He turns to look at me, his face far closer to mine than either of us expected. He pauses, his eyes dropping to my lips for a second before he turns back to the papers in his hand.

"It's for Devereaux Inc. My mother can hold her own as CEO, but every once in a while I actually have to put some work in as the CFO. This year I want to focus on tightening our internal controls, but it isn't easy. I'm thinking of hiring a team from DM Consultancy to implement the strategy I have in mind."

I look at him in awe. I remember he used to come in around noon when my father was still his co-CEO. I guess he spent his mornings working for Devereaux Inc. while he spent his afternoons at DM. Since my father passed away, he's been handling DM all by himself. He's usually the first to get in and the last to leave, so how has he been getting everything done for both of his jobs?

"How can I help?" I ask, suddenly feeling guilty. Daniel hooks his arm around my neck and pulls me closer to kiss the top of my head.

"You can help me by training as hard as you can. Within one or two years you'll be able to take over as my co-CEO. Who knows, you might even want to be the sole CEO."

I frown. Me becoming Daniel's co-CEO means our marriage would come to an end. If the idea of that happening is already unappealing now, then how will I feel in two years?

Fourteen

I stand next to Daniel as he cooks dinner. The two of us have been in our own little bubble for the last couple of weeks, and I've loved every second. I've never lived with a man other than my dad, and I didn't realise it'd be so... exciting. Catching Daniel in half-dressed states has become my new hobby. My favourite is when he comes back from the gym, his body slick with sweat. Daniel making breakfast in the morning half-naked is a close second though.

I stare at him suspiciously as he chops up vegetables, but it looks like he actually knows what he's doing. "You know, I've never eaten dinner you've made. Yet, you've had dinner made by me so many times, both at my house and here."

Daniel grins at me. "Guess I've got some making up to do, huh?"

"I think you should tackle dinner this week and I'll do break-fast. Deal?"

Daniel pretends to think it over and nods. He's so different in his own home. So much more relaxed. I didn't even realise he was uncomfortable at his mother's, but the difference is obvious now.

"Are you going to hover over me or are you actually going to be helpful?"

I giggle and shrug. "Hover."

Daniel shakes his head and throws the peppers in the pan. I never thought watching a man slice vegetables could be hot. Turns out it is if Daniel does it.

"I liked the pink apron better on you."

He's wearing a neat black one that only makes him look more handsome. It isn't fair. He shouldn't be allowed to be a good cook and handsome as well.

"Buy me one and I'll wear it, but you'd better get yourself a matching one too."

I laugh. "Joke's on you. I like pink."

Daniel laughs too and shakes his head. "No, you don't. You hate pink, thoroughly dislike purple, and you love maroon."

I stare at him in surprise. How does he know that? He looks away and tosses the vegetables in the pan like a total pro. I'm beyond impressed. I thought I was a good cook, but I definitely don't have the same skills he does.

"Is it weird that I kinda hope the food won't taste good? It's just unfair if you're an amazing cook too."

He frowns. "What do you mean?"

I shake my head. "Never mind. Doesn't matter."

He looks at me funny and shakes his head. "Come here," he tells me. I move closer and Daniel hooks his arm around my waist to pull me to him.

"Stir this for me while I crack the eggs," he says. I melt into him and nod. He smiles down at me and it looks like neither one of us wants to let go of the other. I've loved these small touches. At Mary's, Daniel would throw his arm around me if we watched TV together, but that's about it. Here in our own space he's far more comfortable. He's been touching me without even realising it. Last night, he spooned me on the sofa after falling asleep while we watched a movie. I find myself wanting more of his little touches.

I take the spoon from him and purse my lips in disappointment when he lets go of me to grab the eggs.

He walks back and stands behind me. I'm startled when he reaches around me to break the eggs. He's essentially hugging me from the back and I'm tempted to lean back so my head rests on his chest.

When he's done cracking the eggs, he takes a step closer so his body is flush against mine. My heart is racing and I'm blushing fiercely, but thankfully he can't tell. He puts his hand on top of mine and stirs the vegetables. My heart is beating loudly and I'm hyperaware of his movements. How would he respond if I turn around now and press my lips against his? Would he kiss me back?

I turn around and place my hands on his chest. His entire body feels strong and I can't help but wonder what his naked body would feel like on top of me. I bite down on my lip and look up at him. His expression is heated. Is he feeling what I'm feeling?

Daniel tears his eyes away from mine and takes a step back. He smiles at me without a single trace of lust, and I force myself to swallow down my disappointment.

"Dinner's done," he says. I nod and escape the kitchen under the guise of setting the table. By the time he's joined me at the dining table, I've got my raging heart under control. I haven't felt this type of crazy attraction since I was a teenager. Surely he must feel it too?

"I wonder if it'll be as good as it looks. Where did you even learn your mad knife skills? Food Channel?"

Daniel bursts out laughing and shakes his head. "No, I took some cooking classes when I moved out of my mother's house. It was that or eat macaroni cheese every day."

I take a cautious bite of the stir-fry he cooked us and moan. "Holy shit. This is amazing!"

Daniel looks down shyly and I can't help but giggle.

"Really, it's awesome."

"Hmm," he says, his eyes twinkling. "You know, I could probably get away with not working tonight. We could watch a movie, and I promise I won't fall asleep this time."

I smile at him, already knowing he's going to break that promise. "Okay but I get to pick the movie," I say.

Daniel shakes his head, and I know it's because I always get to pick the movies.

"How about Star Wars?" he asks.

I frown. "That's a trick question. Which episode? Original trilogy or the prequel? Or any of the newer ones?"

Daniel grins at me. "How about The Empire Strikes Back?"

I stare at him in surprise. I didn't think he could get any more perfect, but it looks like he can. Did he know that one's my favourite?

"Hmm, well, I guess we can," I murmur, trying to hide my immense excitement. I know every single line of the movie and I'm definitely going to struggle to not talk along.

I'm almost jumping with joy when Daniel puts the movie on after dinner. He sits down in his usual seat, and I literally shriek when the iconic intro starts. I jump onto the sofa like an excited child and Daniel chuckles. He hooks his arm around my neck and pulls me into him. He shifts so that he's spooning me the way he did when he fell asleep on the sofa last night.

It's a good thing he suggested a movie I've seen a million times, because there's no way I could focus on it while his arm is wrapped around me, his fingers only an inch away from the underside of my breasts. I'm tempted to squirm so I can push my body flush against his and move his fingers to where I want them, but I'm scared he'll pull away. It drives me crazy that I can feel his body right behind me, so close but not touching me.

I try my best to focus on Yoda as he messes with Luke, right before he decides to train him, but I can feel Daniel's breath on my neck. He lowers his cold nose to my neck and my eyes fall closed. He gently traces a line from behind my ear to the middle of my neck. I almost stop breathing when he presses his lips to my neck, kissing me so gently I might not even have noticed if I wasn't so hyperaware of him.

I'm breathing erratically and I'm eager for more. I'm about to turn around so I end up in his arms when he brushes his lips against my ear, eliciting a shiver from me.

"Baby, your phone has been ringing non-stop. Maybe you should check who it is," he whispers. It takes me a couple of seconds to realise what he said. My brain is still stuck on him calling me baby in such a husky voice. I sit up and grab my phone in annoyance, which makes way for surprise when I realise Dominic has called me nine times. Daniel looks over my shoulders and tenses when he sees who's ringing me.

He sits up and crosses his arms as I pick up the call. "Hey, what's up?" I ask, somewhat annoyed that he's interrupting us, even though all we were doing is watching a movie.

"Why didn't you pick up? God, I've called you like twenty times. Where are you?"

I lean back and drop my head on Daniel's shoulder. He's still tense and doesn't put his arm around my shoulder.

"I'm home. Where else would I be on a Sunday night?"

Dominic sighs. "You're not home. I dropped by your house and the security guard said you haven't been there in weeks. I dropped by the coffee shop you go to as well, couldn't find you."

I glance at Daniel, but he's staring at the TV screen and ignores me. "Yeah, I'm at the downtown apartment, I mean. Not my dad's place."

Dominic scoffs. "You mean you're at Daniel's? Since when is your dad's place not your home? When did Daniel's apartment become your home? You've only been there for what, three weeks?"

I grit my teeth, annoyed. "Anyway, what's up?" I ask, eager to end this conversation already. I'm not sure what's rubbing me the wrong way, but I'm annoyed.

"Lucy and I had a huge argument. I'm at the hotel bar we always go to. Will you come have a drink with me?"

I look at Daniel who's pretending to watch the movie when he's clearly focused on my conversation and I just want to stay home with him. I want to go back to three minutes ago when he

THE TIE THAT BINDS

had his lips against my skin. What would've happened if Dominic hadn't called?

"Please, Lyss. I need you," Dominic says. I haven't heard him sound so distressed in a long time.

I sigh and close my eyes. "Yeah, of course. I'll be there in twenty minutes or so, okay?"

Daniel clenches his jaw but doesn't say a thing. He seems tense as I hang up the phone, and it makes me hesitate.

"I — Dominic called..."

He cuts me off before I even get my explanation out and shakes his head, a humourless chuckle escaping his lips.

"Let me guess. My little brother called and you're going running?"

I frown at him. "It isn't like that. He seems distressed. I'm just going to check up on him."

Daniel nods at me and turns back to the TV. I run a hand through my hair and make my way to my bedroom to change. I feel like I'm stuck between a rock and a hard place. I'll let someone down whether I go or not.

Fifteen

The doorman stops me before I enter the bar and looks at
me apologetically. "I'm sorry miss, we don't allow anyone
in with trainers on. Our dress code is smart casual."

I look down at my outfit. I threw on jeans with a black tee and
my trusty old converse. I probably look like a teenager trying to
sneak in.

I stare at the intricate logo of the hotel and rummage through
my bag to find my wallet. I fish out the black card Daniel gave me
and show it to him.

"Does this help?" I ask him. He stares at it and speaks into his
headphone quietly. Within a minute someone comes running up
with a tablet that has an inbuilt card reader. He swipes the card
and stares at the screen in disbelief for a couple of seconds before
he hands it back to me. I'm oddly nervous. What if it shows
Daniel's name and they think I stole the card?

The man hands me my card back with two hands, as though
it's precious. "I apologise, Mrs. Devereaux," he says, bowing his
head. I blink in surprise. Mrs. Devereaux? I bite back my smile.
The sound of that gives me butterflies. I guess the system shows
that I'm Daniel's wife.

"Please show the card to the bartender as well. He'll put all your drinks and anything else you wish to consume on your tab. Our kitchen is also at your disposal should you wish to have a late dinner."

I glance at my watch and frown. It's almost 10pm. Surely their kitchen is closed now? I thank the doorman and enter. I walk to the end of the room and find Dominic sitting in our usual spot. I smile at the bartender and order myself a cup of tea and Dominic some water. He looks at me with raised brows but nods nonetheless.

"You're here," Dominic says. He smiles and his eyes light up. I'm surprised when the sight that used to make me feel all giddy doesn't even stir my heart.

"You look like shit, Nic." His eyes are red and tired. Looks like he hasn't been sleeping much.

Dominic looks at me and laughs. "I missed you," he murmurs.

"You saw me a few days ago."

He shakes his head. "No, I mean, I've missed you these last few months. We've barely spoken and I know it's my fault."

I sit in silence. I don't know how to respond to that. I don't want to agree with him, because I don't want to make him feel even worse, but it's true. He hasn't been there, even when he was physically present.

"So what happened?" I ask.

Dominic sips the water I gave him and looks away. "She's really insecure and keeps accusing me of cheating when I've been nothing but loyal. But then she'll ogle Daniel all the time. She's been to our house every day that he was there, always hanging around him and trying to talk to him. I've seen the way she looks at him. The way you both look at him. I mean yeah, he's so much more muscular than me, but then she's my girlfriend, you know? She hasn't come over the last few weekends, and it just so happens to coincide with me telling her Daniel moved out. I thought maybe she was just insecure about you being there, but I didn't actually tell her you moved out too."

I'm at a loss for words. I also thought she was far too interested in Daniel and I didn't like the way she looked at him, but I thought maybe I was being possessive, that it might've been in my head.

"Do you think things might get better once she feels more secure in your relationship?"

Dominic looks down, dejected. "I don't know. This is the first time I've given a relationship all I could, and it just doesn't seem like it's enough. Seems like I'm not enough. I just have this weird feeling. I'm hoping it's just jealousy. Maybe I'm jealous that she seemed to find Daniel attractive."

I nod. I usually have great advice for him, but today I truly don't know what to say.

"Good communication is key, Nic. You should tell her how you feel and explain to her how her behaviour makes you feel. It sounds like you're already doing all the right things, but maybe you should talk to her more too."

Dominic looks at me in wonder. "Yeah, you're probably right."

It's almost like he didn't expect me to give him any advice at all. Surely he doesn't think I'd drive a wedge between them when he's already down in the dumps?

"Sometimes I wonder, you know. What if your confession last year hadn't scared me? What if I hadn't been so scared to lose you? What if I'd had the courage to love you the way you deserve to be loved?"

I look away. These are words I longed to hear a mere few months ago, but things are different now. The way he treated me after my father died changed the way I feel about him. It made me realise how young and selfish Dominic still is. I doubt I was even in love with him. I guess it was more infatuation than anything else.

"There's no point in wondering, Nic. I was drunk. I wasn't

even being serious. Besides, I'm married to your brother now. If anything was going to happen between us, it would've happened long before I married Daniel. You made the right call. If you and I hooked up, we would've both regretted it."

Dominic looks at me in disbelief. "Surely you don't actually believe that? Your marriage with Daniel isn't even real. Three years will be over before you know it. Anything is possible."

I smile sardonically. Why do I keep being reminded that my marriage with Daniel is only temporary? And why do I hate hearing it so much?

"Even so, I'm married. Daniel and I promised we'd stay faithful during our marriage. I have no intention of breaking my word."

Dominic looks startled. "Whose idea was that?" he asks, his voice rough.

"Does it matter?"

Dominic crosses his arms and stares me down. "Hell yeah, it matters. My brother can't keep it in his pants for more than a couple of weeks. Haven't you seen the countless women he's always with? All those models and actresses? How long do you think that fidelity bullshit will last? If it was him that suggested it, then that only means one thing. He's expecting to bed you."

Dominic looks angry and I'm not sure whether I should be flattered or upset.

"So what?"

He looks at me in disbelief. "What do you mean, so what?"

I shrug. "He's my husband. So what if he wants to fuck me?"

Dominic's incredulity makes way for concern. "Lyss, please don't tell me you and my brother... that you two are... you know."

I laugh at his awkwardness. He's never had a problem telling me the ins and outs of his sex life, yet now he can't get his words out?

"No, we aren't sleeping together. But yeah, we're married. We'll be stuck together for three years. At some point, who knows?"

Dominic shakes his head. "Don't, Alyssa. Seriously. I love him to bits, but I love you more. He's been moving from one woman to the other for as long as I can remember. His last long-term relationship was like five or six years ago. He doesn't do commitment. If you end up sleeping with him, he'll end up breaking your heart when he moves on to the next girl."

I bite down on my lip as I consider his words. The romantic in me wants to believe that he'd just been moving from one woman to the other because the one he truly wants wasn't available. I'm not one to think that I could change a man. I truly believe change comes from within and no external factors can influence it as much as willpower. But still, part of me believes Daniel isn't the womaniser the world seems to think he is.

"Anyway, we aren't here to talk about me. We're here to talk about you."

Dominic crosses his arms and looks away. I know that look. He's annoyed with me and he's going to make sure I know it.

"Come on." I sigh. "Let's just get you home."

Sixteen

I wake up to the smell of coffee and follow my nose, only half
awake. I pause in front of the kitchen, my eyes widening at
the sight I'm being presented with. Daniel is standing in
front of the coffeemaker in his pyjama bottoms but without the
shirt he usually wears with it. I don't think I'll ever get used to
this. He's hot. Daniel turns and I sigh at the view. Muscular chest,
a six-pack complete with V muscles and a thin trail of hair on his
lower abdomen that disappears into his pants. I should probably
try harder to hide the lust I'm feeling, but I'm weak this morning.
I blame the lack of coffee.

I look up and almost miss Daniel's dark eyes. His gaze trails
over my body, lingering on my chest. I've gotten comfortable
enough to ditch the robe, and if I'm honest, I've been enjoying
the way he looks at me when I'm wearing nothing more than a
skimpy nightgown. Daniel blinks a couple of times and then his
stoic expression is back on his face, all traces of lust gone. The
attraction I could've sworn I saw was gone so quickly that I'm
second guessing myself.

He smiles at me and hands me a cup of coffee. I accept it
gratefully and take a big sip before lifting myself onto the counter.
I swing my dangling feet as Daniel moves around.

"Pancakes?" I ask, as I watch him stir what looks like some type of batter. He nods as he works quietly. I lean back and admire the way his body moves. I've been making breakfast all week, so I guess he feels like it's his turn today. If this is the view I'm presented with whenever he makes breakfast, then I'm certainly not complaining. I might even sacrifice his delicious dinners for it.

"Can you show me how this coffee machine works later?" I ask, staring at the huge monstrosity that really should be in a coffee shop instead of a home. He's made coffee every morning while I was making breakfast, but at some point I'll need to figure it out.

Daniel chuckles at my expression and nods. "It's quite simple once you get the hang of it."

I shake my head. "Making coffee isn't something that should come with a learning curve."

Daniel laughs again and the butterflies in my tummy go wild. "You know, you never laugh at work. You rarely even smile. It's a good thing, too. The girls would be all over you even more."

I speak without thinking, and it isn't until Daniel looks at me with a smug expression that I realise what I said.

"Hmm, maybe I should start smiling more."

I bite down on my lip. What does that mean? Does he want the girls at work to be all over him? The idea doesn't sit well with me.

"Well, come to think of it, you have no problem smiling at Kate. It's just the rest of us you can't be bothered with."

Daniel turns off the stove and walks up to me. I grip the counter tightly and contemplate jumping off so I can create more distance between us. He looks intense and somehow I feel like I'm in trouble.

He puts his hands on my thighs and spreads my legs as he pulls me flush against him. I squirm as his abs push against my inner thighs. His skin against mine feels amazing. I place my palms behind me and lean back on the counter, inadvertently pushing my barely covered breasts out. Daniel grabs me. His large hands cover my tiny waist almost entirely. His eyes fall to my breasts and he bites down on his lip. His gaze slowly trails up until he's looking into my eyes.

"This again, Alyssa?" he murmurs. I'm breathing hard and I'm struggling to remember what we were even talking about. "I told you I'm treating her the same way I always have, but if you think the way I treat her is inappropriate, then I'll be sure to address that. You're my wife, Lyss. You're the only woman in my life. Why is it you insist there's something between me and her when there isn't?"

I narrow my eyes at him. "Nothing there? How would you feel if I ignore your existence and invite someone else to an event we'll both be at? If I let him hold my hand in your presence? Besides, she's the woman you met during your MBA, isn't she? The one that was unavailable. She's divorced now, so I'm not surprised you started flirting with her. Sharing cotton candy with her was quite cute, I gotta admit."

Daniel pulls me closer and drops his forehead to my shoulder. "Lyss, I'm sorry. You're right. It was a shit thing to do, but isn't it the same thing you've always done to me when Dominic's around?"

I look away because it's true. Even after we got married, I've probably prioritised Dominic, even when he didn't do the same for me.

"Dressing up to go for dessert with him when you've never once dressed up for me. Laughing with him and making inside jokes that you know I won't get. Making me feel like an outsider even though I'm your husband. It doesn't feel nice, does it? How would you feel if I go running as soon as some other woman calls me, even though you cleared your busy schedule to spend some time with me?"

I stare at him, realisation suddenly dawning. He cleared his schedule to watch a movie with me last night? Come to think of it, he's been working on the sofa every night while I watched movies beside him. Did he work longer hours so he'd be free last night? I'm racked with guilt.

"I didn't know, Dan. I'm sorry. I don't know what you expect me to do. He's still my friend. He seemed so upset last night on the phone..."

I'm making excuses and I know it, but there's nothing I can say that will make this better. I didn't realise Daniel felt like he's been second best. I didn't really think he cared about anything I do at all.

Daniel pulls away from me and walks out of the kitchen, the half-baked pancakes still on the stove. I sit there in a daze as the last couple of weeks flash through my mind.

He's right. Every single day I've made him feel like an outsider, but then isn't that what we were going for? Didn't we get married under the assumption that nothing between us would change?

I jump when Daniel's bedroom door slams closed. Seconds later, I hear the ding of the lift. I hop off the counter and walk to the living room only to see the doors close again, only a sliver of Daniel visible before the doors shut.

I groan and make my way to the bathroom to get ready. I'm running late because I spent all morning overthinking things.

I stare at my outfits and decide to go for something sexier than usual. Something that might distract Daniel from his anger.

Seventeen

"You're late," Linda says. She looks worried. "The boss is in a terrible mood today. You'd better get to work quickly before he realises. He's already threatened to fire Jake twice."

"Oh damn. What happened?"

Linda shakes her head. "Nothing interesting, to be honest. Liam Evans called to book in an appointment with him to discuss phase two of Luxe's implementation plan. The boss snapped at Kate when the call came in. Other than that, not much has happened. He was pissed off because Jake left a small typo in one of the memos. That one's Jake's fault, though. He should've waited for you to look it over, but he stupidly thought he'd get more credit if he went to give it to Daniel himself."

I bury my hands in my hair and inhale deeply. Liam. Is that what set him off, or was it our argument this morning? Can you even call it that?

"Did he come in annoyed or was it Liam's call that annoyed him?"

Linda blinks and tries to think back. "He came in annoyed for sure. He usually has a blank expression on his face, but this morning he was scowling. He didn't even say good morning and slammed his office door closed. Even Kate was staring at his door for a couple of minutes before she dared to brief him on today's schedule."

I stare at his door and contemplate talking to him. I'm feeling uneasy about our argument this morning. The way he held me so intimately, followed by the things he said. He was opening up to me and I'm not sure what to do with what he told me. He seemed serious when he said there was nothing going on between him and Kate, and he seemed genuinely hurt when he mentioned Dominic. I want to make him feel better, but I don't know what to do or say.

I bite down on my lip and get to work on my proposal for the Takuya project. At some point he'll call me in. Hopefully, he'll have cooled down then and I'll be able to apologise.

I wait all morning for him to ask me about one of our projects or one of the documents that the rest of my team brings in for him, but he doesn't ask for me at all. Instead, he keeps shouting for Linda. In the first hour she did fine, but her nerves are clearly getting the better of her, because she's shaking as he shouts her name yet again.

"Give it to me," I tell her. She looks at me, equally relieved and doubtful. "It's fine. I'll go."

She exhales and nods, handing me the documents with both hands, almost reverently. She looks at me as though I'm her hero, and I can barely keep the smile off my face.

Kate sends me a tense warning look as I knock on Daniel's door. I enter before he gives me permission like I always have, my heels clicking on the floor. Daniel doesn't look up from his screen.

"Did I tell you to come in?" he snaps.

"No." I'm tempted to ask him if I should walk back out, knock, and then enter again, but I'm sure he'd actually take me up on it today, so I rein the sass in.

"Why are you here? I asked for Linda."

He looks annoyed to see me and looks back at his screen in dismay. My heart twists. I'm not sure what I was expecting, but annoyance and dismay wasn't it. Did I misread the signs this morning? I hesitate before answering him, and he looks up again to glare at me.

"I asked you why you're here," he repeats.

I jump into action and walk to his desk. I hesitate and then decide to walk around his desk. Before we got married, I always maintained an appropriate amount of distance. Walking around his desk to stand right next to him isn't something I used to do, but recently it's always felt right. Today it feels like I'm over-stepping.

Daniel frowns at me when he finally notices the dress I'm wearing. Somehow I expected at least a bit of appreciation, but all I'm seeing is dissatisfaction. I freeze, suddenly feeling vulnerable and insecure. When did his opinion start to matter to me so much?

He glances at the modest amount of cleavage I'm displaying and grits his teeth. He looks annoyed and my self-esteem takes a hit. I suddenly wish I could cover up. I feel like a fool for dressing up today.

"The document you requested."

I place it on his desk and wait for him to respond or to ask me anything about it, but he remains silent. When he realises I'm not going to leave, he leans back in his chair and stares at me.

"Noted. Dismissed," he snaps.

I sigh and lean back against his desk. "Can we talk?" I ask, my voice soft.

Daniel looks away and focuses on his screen, dismissing me without words. Part of me is ready to walk out and bury the feelings that have started to develop. I feel oddly humiliated, even though he hasn't actually done anything wrong. All he's done is treat me like the rest of my colleagues, but I guess that's just it. Throughout the last few weeks I've started to think that he sees me differently and now I'm wondering whether I was seeing things.

I bite down on my lip hard and make up my mind. I lift

myself onto his desk the way I did on the kitchen counter this morning, my feet dangling off. Daniel turns to me, looking so outraged that I'm certain he'll push me off himself.

"What the hell do you think you're doing, Ms. Moriani? Get the fuck off my desk or I'll be making a call to HR."

I'm taken aback but try my best not to show it. He hasn't called me Ms. Moriani since before we got married, and even then he'd only do it when I was purposely annoying him. I look down at my thighs, second guessing myself already.

I breathe in deeply and gather my courage. "Enough," I say, my voice barely above a whisper. I hook my foot through his armrest and pull his chair closer until he's sitting right in front of me. He moves to get up so I place my red bottomed shoe against his chest and push him back down. He sits back, looking completely stupefied. Before he can respond, I spread my legs so they cage him in, my heels brushing his outer thighs. His eyes drop between my legs in shock. I'm giving him a clear view of my red lace panties, but at this point I don't even care.

I grab his tie and pull on it. He looks bewildered and flustered when he looks up at me, his anger temporarily gone. I glance at his desk phone and pick it up, handing it to him.

"Go ahead. Call HR. I'd love to see how that goes. Go ahead and tell them Mrs. Devereaux, your wife, is harassing you."

His eyes drop back to my thighs and the red lace that I know contrasts against my skin provocatively. He licks his lips and blinks.

"Hmm? Not calling?"

He looks back up at me and shakes his head. I place the phone back in its holder and tighten my hold on his tie.

"Come here," I tell him.

Daniel stands up between my thighs and I hook my legs around his hips, pulling him in closer. He puts his hands on the desk, either side of my hips, preventing me from pulling him flush against me.

"Now tell me what's going on, Daniel. What happened? One

second we were having breakfast together and the next you stormed out. We had a great weekend together, so I don't get where this is coming from. If you don't talk to me, then how am I supposed to know what's on your mind? If you don't tell me where I went wrong, how can I learn from my mistakes?"

Daniel stares somewhere over my shoulder instead of looking at me. "I'm sorry, Daniel. I'm sorry I haven't been putting you first. That'll change now, if you'll give me a chance."

He shakes his head, his expression hardening. "No. Why would it? Why would you do that? When we got married, we said things would stay the same between us. Our marriage is nothing but a piece of paper. We have no obligations to each other. I've been too narrow-minded. My view of marriage has always been traditional, but this isn't a real marriage. Fidelity and loyalty... they aren't things I expect of you. Hell, they aren't even things I want from you."

My heart is shattering. Over the last month or so, I've started to see Daniel differently. I've started to see him as a man, but also just as my person. I didn't realise it until he said it, but I do want fidelity and loyalty from him. Was Dominic right? Is he incapable of it? Is he already tired of the couple of months of celibacy?

"I'd really prefer it if you and I could remain the way we were before we got married. Let's forget about the rules too. I'd like us to start seeing other people."

I stare at him in shock. "You... you want to start seeing other people?" I repeat numbly. Daniel clenches his jaws and nods.

I shake my head. "No," I say, panicking internally.

Daniel chuckles darkly. "You don't have a say in this, Alyssa. Divorce me, for all I care. I love DM, but it's just a company. It isn't the same without your father here anyway. I have plenty on my plate with Devereaux Inc."

I stare at him and barely even recognise him. Daniel is known for his ruthlessness, but he's never shown me this side of him. I don't even understand why it hurts so much.

I let go of him and cross my legs, deeply ashamed of my

behaviour. Somewhere along the line I thought Daniel and I felt the same way. That the attraction was there, and that it wasn't just me. Now it looks like I was wrong. He was just being nice to me and trying his best to behave the way he thought he should as a married man.

"What, you just can't wait to get back to fucking a different model every weekend? Not having sex for a few months was too much for you?"

He looks as though he's going to object to what I'm saying, but then he looks away, as though he knows I'm right and can't be bothered to come up with an excuse.

My heart feels as though someone twisted a knife in it. The idea of him with someone else makes me feel sick.

I stare down at my fingers and nod. He's right. He's got Devereaux Inc. I'm the one that stands to lose everything if we were to get divorced. He'd be fine.

"Very well, Daniel. If that's what you wish... if that's what'll make you happy, then that's what we'll do. It's not like I can keep you from doing what you want."

Daniel looks at me, his expression unwavering. "Yes," he says. "That's what I want."

Eighteen

"So what exactly is going on between you and my brother?" Dominic asks.

I balance my phone between my ear and shoulder as I swipe my access card in the lift. Only executive staff have access to the top floor and while I understand the security measure, having to swipe my card every time I get in the lift is pretty annoying.

"Nothing. What do you mean?" I ask. Thankfully, I'm alone in the lift. "Connection might drop. I'm at work now."

"What, you two don't go to work together? Why did you move out and move in together if nothing is going on?"

I roll my eyes. "The apartment is just closer to work, that's all. Things are still the same between me and Daniel. I told you that."

"Good. Then you won't be hurt when you see today's tabloids."

I freeze. Daniel has been coming home late most of the week since our argument and wasn't home much at all during the weekend, but I assumed he was just at the office. When he was home, he was quiet and distant. No matter how cheerful I tried to be or how much I tried to make him smile, all I was met with was cold politeness. The politeness hurt more than an argument would have. I'd rather have him shout at me than have him treat me with indifference. He hasn't even been coming back to have dinner with me. I thought we might have a chance to get closer again last weekend, but he stayed away and only came back to sleep.

I walk into the office to find Luke and Jake grinning down at this week's tabloids. I grimace at the thought of our old office tradition. For the last couple of years, we've always stuck a tabloid photo that was taken the weekend before on Daniel's office door; the more scandalous the better. We'd usually keep it up for up to a few weeks until another girl inevitably replaced the old one. There hasn't been a photo on the door for months now, but like Dominic said, he didn't last long.

I watch as Jake and Luke stick the photo on Daniel's door. I walk up to it and stare at the photo. He's with a beautiful woman. Another skinny model, no doubt. She looks familiar, so she must be quite famous. She's got his suit coat over her shoulders and looks up at him adoringly as he smiles at her. She's holding on to his arm as he walks her the final few steps to his Aston Martin. Looks like they walked out of a well-known romantic restaurant. It's also got a waiting list of three months, and I've never even been there. I guess that's how he was spending some of the evenings that he didn't eat at home.

I wonder if he fucked her. If she's had what I've never had. Did he come home to me after sleeping with someone else? Did he fall asleep in the room across from mine with another woman's scent still all over him?

"Are you okay?" Kate asks. I blink in surprise and look at her. I struggle to smile and nod at her politely. "Yes, of course. Why wouldn't I be?"

She glances at the photo and then back at me. "It's probably some sort of publicity stunt, you know. I bet he was working on some ad with her for Devereaux Inc."

I laugh. Does she realise how stupid she sounds? Do they look like they're working on some sort of advert?

"Why would I care what our boss does in his free time?" I snap. I turn and make my way to the bathrooms. I swipe my card to access the executive bathroom. It's large and has a shower in it as well as a regular toilet and sink, but most importantly, there are no other stalls in here. I lower the toilet lid and sit down on it as the first tear escapes my eyes. I bury my hands in my hair and allow myself a couple of moments of heartache. A couple of moments of my hopes dying.

I was stupid to think that Daniel was different. He's always shown me exactly who he is. Those photos have always been up. The tradition started when I was still an intern years ago. It continued all the way through when I worked part time during uni and only stopped when my dad passed away. I've seen the photo of every single woman he's been with, so why am I still surprised? I can't compete with those women, and it seems I couldn't capture his attention for more than a few weeks, anyway. I'd rather find out now than later.

I pull myself together and fish my eyedrops from my handbag. I've spent years wanting to quit and crying in the bathroom because clients were difficult or because my dad was tougher on me than anyone else. I never thought I'd sit here and cry over a man, though. I shake my head at my own foolishness.

By the time I make it back to the office, everyone is dead silent and the photo is gone. Daniel probably came in and ripped it up, though why he tries is beyond me. One of the boys will have a new one printed and stuck on there within the hour.

I sit down and get to work. Daniel made it clear last week that he wanted things between us to go back to what they used to be. I just didn't listen. I held out hope where there was none. I don't even understand why I'm so hurt. We were never together. We never even kissed.

I was never this hurt over anything Dominic ever did, so why are things so different with Daniel? Is it because he's my husband? Is it because I feel possessive?

I print out the timeline and agenda for the meeting with Takuya. Daniel will have to travel to Singapore for it. I wonder if he'll find someone to warm his bed there too. I don't doubt he knows a couple of actresses or models down there. If not, Mr. Takuya will be happy to introduce him to some.

I knock on his door and wait for his permission to enter. He looks stressed and distraught when I walk in. He looks at me cautiously, as though he's wondering whether I've seen the picture and how I might react.

I stand in front of his desk and slide the itinerary his way. "This is the proposed timeline. I contacted the Singapore office and they agreed to assist with the presentation. The itinerary has been approved by Sasuki, Mr. Takuya's son."

Daniel stares at me. I wonder if he heard a thing I just said. "Daniel?"

He blinks and nods at me. I smile politely and repeat what I said. Daniel nods along but he's absentminded. He's probably still thinking about last weekend's girl. I wonder how long she'll last. They rarely make it beyond three weeks.

"You — are you all right?" he asks, his voice soft. He sounds concerned, and I wonder if my eyes are red despite the eyedrops.

"Why wouldn't I be?"

Daniel shakes his head and looks over the itinerary. "Come with me to Singapore. You know this project better than anyone else. You can take the lead."

I nod. "That's a wonderful opportunity, boss. I won't let you down."

Daniel stands up and leans forward, his palms on his desk. "Boss? You haven't called me boss in months. What's going on?"

I shake my head. "Nothing. Would you prefer it if I call you Daniel at all times?"

He looks at me warily and then looks down. "You saw the photo."

I inhale deeply and nod. "Yes, of course. Me and everyone else at the office, and probably a couple hundred thousand other people. She's pretty."

He looks at me in disbelief. "She's pretty?" he repeats.

I purse my lips and look away. "If that's all, Daniel, I'll get back to work."

I turn to walk out of his office, but he grabs my wrist before I reach the door. I turn back to look at him and raise my brows.

"That's all you've got to say?" he snaps.

I look away. "She's just your type, isn't she? Tall, blonde and with no curves to speak off. No wonder you wanted to start seeing other people. All the girls you've been with are the opposite of me. Like I said, she's pretty. What else am I supposed to say? Well done?"

I'm average height with dark brown hair, green eyes and more curves than he can fit in his hands. I'm not even remotely fat, but I'm certainly not catwalk thin either. I've always been told that I'm pretty, but I'm not drop dead gorgeous like the women Daniel dates.

"You asked for things to go back to how they were before we got married, and I guess you made it happen. I hear you now. I get it. I'm sorry I kept clinging to you all week last week. I kept pestering you to watch movies with me and to eat with me. I won't do it again. I apologise. You were quite clear when you told me you wanted to see other people... that you wanted us to be the way we were before we got married. I'll work to make that happen. I won't overstep again."

Daniel tightens his grip on my wrist and pulls me closer. I stumble in my heels and only just manage to balance myself.

"Alyssa, no. That's not..." He inhales deeply and looks away. "Look, nothing happened between me and her. It was just a business meeting. That's all."

I laugh. "I don't remember ever attending a meeting and holding a business partner's arm while his jacket is wrapped around my shoulder. But sure."

I yank my wrist out of his grip and walk to the door.

"I didn't cheat on you, Alyssa. I swear. She's just an old friend that had a proposal for me. That's all."

I turn back and smile at him. So at first it was a business

meeting and now she's an old friend? "You don't need to make excuses, Daniel. Our marriage isn't the type where that is required. Like you said... You'll do what you want and there's nothing I can do about it if I want to inherit my father's shares. Point taken. You needn't worry. You've made it clear that I don't have any rights to you. I'll stop now. I'll stop seeing things that clearly aren't there."

I walk out and pray some of my heart will remain when our marriage inevitably comes to an end.

Nineteen

When I walk into the apartment I'm met by acoustic music, dimmed lights and the smell of something delicious. I walk into the dining room curiously and find Daniel setting the table. He hasn't been home early in a week and a half, so what is he doing here today?

My heart sinks at the thought that he might be expecting someone. This is his home, after all. This is probably where he'd take the girls that he used to date.

"Hey, you're home," he says. He smiles at me sheepishly. He looks good. He's still in his suit, but he's ditched the jacket and tie, and rolled up his sleeves to expose his forearms. I nod and glance at the table. Candlelight, lasagne, salad and some delicious-looking dessert. He went all out.

"Do you have plans?" I ask. "If so, I can just leave."

He freezes and looks at me in disbelief. "No. Of course not. I just thought we could have dinner together."

This is all for me? I guess he's feeling bad about so blatantly seeing someone else a few days after informing me he would.

"I'm not really hungry. Thanks, though."

I turn to walk back to my room, but Daniel runs up to me and holds my shoulders from behind.

"But it's tradition, isn't it? Weren't we going to have dinner together a couple of times a week? How about we do twice a week? You'll cook once and I'll cook once."

I pull away from him and turn around. "I didn't think that was still a thing considering you didn't show up for dinner once last week. It's not a tradition if you only keep to it when it suits you. Besides, it isn't something we used to do before we got married. You wanted things to be like what they were before we got married, right? You don't need to humour me with this," I wave my hand towards the table. I actually waited up for him every single night last week, but he never bothered to come for dinner. He never informed me he'd be late either.

I move to walk away, but Daniel stops me yet again. He grabs my hand and entwines it with his before pressing them to his chest.

"I take it back. I take it all back, Alyssa. I don't even know why I said that. I don't want things to go back to how they were before we got married. I wasn't thinking clearly. I didn't mean it at all. I just didn't want you to... I didn't want either of us to feel forced in this relationship. I didn't want you to feel like you're just with me because you have no other choice. I wanted us to be able to do whatever we want, yet hopefully still choose to spend time together."

I look at him, confused. What exactly is he trying to say? I pull my hand out of his grip and smile wryly. "So I can cheat on you tomorrow and then tell you I want to take it back? That I wasn't thinking clearly when I clearly told you I wanted to see someone else? Also, how fickle are you? Didn't you tell me you had someone you wanted to pursue? Didn't you bet you'd marry her? So who is this girl you're seeing now?"

Daniel runs a hand through his hair and groans. "Fuck, Alyssa. I'm telling you. I didn't cheat on you. Do you want to ask Giselle? I can call her right now."

I blink. "Giselle? The girl you were with last Saturday is your ex? The one that miraculously lasted more than three months?"

His eyes widen and he purses his lips, as though he's finally decided to shut up. I shake my head. The tabloids had a field day with Giselle and Daniel. She's the one the whole world thought would last. I haven't actually read any of the articles published about them, but I'm sure the media is excited about seeing them together again.

"Just have dinner with me, Alyssa. Please. I understand that you're angry, but I swear it's not what you think at all. If you can't give me anything else, then at least give me a chance to have dinner with you twice a week. Let's be friends? We'll live together for at least the next couple of years. Won't it be so much more comfortable if we're friends?"

I hesitate and eventually nod. Daniel pulls out a chair for me and I sit down reluctantly. He seems anxious as he serves me dinner, and if I didn't feel so numb I'd find it cute.

"So how about we spend some extra days in Singapore to do some sightseeing?" he asks.

I bite down on my lip. I don't want to spend time with him, but I've always wanted to go to Singapore, and he probably knows it.

"We can stay in the Sands for a couple of days?" he adds.

I glance at him in surprise. "The hotel with the infinity pool?" I ask, my curiosity piqued. He nods and grins at me as though he knows he's got me now.

"Sure, but you're paying for it."

He shrugs. "You got it, babe."

I stare at my plate while he continues to carry the conversation by himself. "We can also go see the Gardens by the Bay and one of my friends recommended a beach club in Sentosa. I think you'll really like that."

I look up at him and nod. "Sounds good."

Daniel grins at me. "It'll be great."

I get up as soon as I'm done eating. Daniel looks startled and rises with me. "Thanks for dinner," I tell him. "Let me know when you're done, and I'll come tidy it all up."

Daniel shakes his head. "No, that's fine. I'll do it. But I was thinking of watching the rest of The Empire Strikes Back. We didn't get to finish it last time, remember?"

I'm tempted, but I shake my head. What I need is a long shower to clear my head. "I think I'll head to bed," I tell him.

He looks dejected but nods and bids me goodnight. I walk away before he tempts me into staying.

After spending at least forty minutes in the shower, I sit on my bed and go through my social media feed for lack of anything better to do. There's one headline that captures my attention.

Daniel Devereaux sues tabloids and denies rumours about him and Giselle

I click on it, my curiosity getting the best of me.

Daniel Devereaux was spotted coming out of Regale with former beau Giselle on Saturday night. The two were caught smiling at each other intimately as they made their way to Daniel Devereaux's two-million pound sports car. In our photos, it's obvious that Giselle is wearing Daniel Devereaux's jacket and the affection in her eyes is unmistakable. Nonetheless, Mr. Devereaux's spokesperson denied involvement of the two, while Giselle has refused to comment. To our knowledge, Mr. Devereaux has never taken legal action against the countless rumours floating around about him. One can't help but wonder whether there might be a reason, or a lady, behind the former Casanova's sudden surprising actions. After all, he hasn't been spotted with anyone in months now.

I stare at my phone blankly. He sued them? I'm not sure how to feel about that or what to even think of it. I stare at my bedroom door as the sounds of the movie Daniel's watching fill the apartment and bite back a smile. Daniel hates it when the volume is too loud, but he's obviously turned it up so I can hear the movie from my bedroom. I hesitate for a second before I make my way to the living room. He's lying on the sofa wearing shorts and nothing else, his elbow behind his head. His hair is still wet, so it looks like he just walked out of the shower.

"Oh, hey," he murmurs lazily. "Come watch with me."

He turns back to the TV and pats the seat beside him. I walk up to him slowly and sit down slightly further away than I usually would, keeping some distance between us. There's plenty of space for both of us on the part of the sofa that has the ottoman, but tonight I need some distance. Usually the first thing Daniel would do is hook his arm around my waist and pull me closer, but today he looks at me curiously and smiles to himself. It's a big change from last week, when we both avoided each other entirely.

I lean back and try my best not to murmur along to the lines. I'm so invested in the movie that I didn't even notice Daniel had moved closer to me. He puts his arm on the back of the sofa above my head and lies down, extending his legs. I glance at him when I'm sure he isn't looking. He looks way too hot like this. The shorts I thought he was wearing are clearly just boxer shorts. Why did he ditch the pyjama bottoms? I can clearly see the outline of his... package... and if that's what he looks like when he isn't hard, then how big is he?

I glance over his abs and pecs. I'm dying to touch him. To trace every muscle with my fingers and then with my tongue. I want him badly. I wonder what he'd think if he knew that. I try to look away but can't. Daniel shifts and rests his hand across his lap, obscuring my view a little. I remember the way he stood between my legs when I sat on the kitchen counter. The way he couldn't tear his eyes off my breasts. He might not fully realise it, but he's attracted to me too. I don't know what to make of the way he's lying here half-naked. Does he think it won't tempt me?

Daniel grabs the throw we keep on the sofa and covers most

of his lower body with it, much to my chagrin. He smiles at me and tilts his head. "Wanna join?" he asks. Do I want to press my body against a half-naked Daniel? Hell yes.

I nod and scoot closer to him. Why can't I stay mad at him? It's not uncommon for Dominic and I to spend months not speaking to each other over issues neither one of us can even recall. Yet now, when I should be keeping Daniel at a distance, I can't get myself to do it.

He extends his arm and I cuddle into him the way I've gotten used to, with my back against his side and my head resting on his arm. He places a hand on my waist and turns back to the movie. It isn't long before his breathing deepens. No matter how hard he tries, he always falls asleep while we watch a movie.

I turn in his arms so I'm facing him and gently place my hand on his chest, careful not to wake him. His muscles are hard and tempting. I trace a finger down his chest and over his abs until my hand disappears underneath the blanket. I gently trace my fingers over his abs, right over the trail of hair on his lower stomach. I place my palm on the edge of his boxer shorts, not daring to go down further than that.

I pull my hand away and turn off the TV. I glance at Daniel one more time as I tiptoe to my bedroom.

Twenty

I'm on my third cup of coffee and it's only ten in the morning. There's so much prep to do for our trip to Singapore on top of my regular workload. Recently Daniel has been giving me more responsibility and while it's been exciting, it's also been nerve-racking. The learning curve has been steeper than I expected, and I'm constantly exhausted.

I look up when I hear the clicking of high heels and freeze. The entire office falls dead silent. While Daniel has been with many women, none of them have ever shown up at the office. I stare at her in surprise, my eyes falling to the paper bag in her hand. She's clearly bringing Daniel food. It's from Regale, on top of that. So much for nothing happening between them. My heart aches and my stomach twists.

Part of me is hoping that she'll be denied entry, but I know that's wishful thinking on my part. Kate glances at me and looks annoyed before she lets Giselle into Daniel's office. I'm tempted to follow her in. I'm curious about what she's doing here. It's almost like I want to catch Daniel cheating. Like seeing it will finally make it real.

Kate leaves Daniel's office door wide open and she huffs as she walks back to her seat. Looks like she isn't a fan of Giselle either. I can't focus on work at all as her laughter rings through the office. The sound of it grates on me.

Daniel walks out of his office with a wide smile on his face and looks at me. "Lyss, can you come to my office?"

I look up at him and back at my screen.

"No. I'm busy."

Jake looks at me with wide eyes. "Have you lost your mind?" he whisper-shouts.

I shrug. What's Daniel gonna do? Fire me?

Linda looks at me and tilts her head towards his office, silently urging me to get up and go already. I'm sure my refusal is increasing her anxiety, even though she isn't the one that's being asked to go in.

"Please, Lyss," Daniel says, still smiling. I glare at him and get up, walking painfully slow. He places his hand on my shoulder as soon as I'm within reach and closes the door behind us.

"What is it?" I snap, not bothering to hide my annoyance. Daniel grins and walks up to Giselle.

"Come have some food with us, Lyss. Giselle brought some Tapioca pudding. That's your favourite, isn't it?"

I look at him like he's crazy. "Have you lost your mind? That's what you called me in for? Stop wasting my damn time, Daniel.".

Giselle smiles at me and looks as though she's curious about me, even more so after my outburst. "Liz? Is that short for Elizabeth? It's nice to meet you. I'm Giselle," she says.

I nod at her politely. "It's short for Alyssa, actually."

I turn to walk back out, but Daniel grabs my hand and holds on tightly. I glance at him, dismayed, while Giselle jumps up.

"Oh my god, Daniel. This is Alyssa? Your Alyssa?"

She smiles from ear to ear and I look at him, beyond confused. He nods at her and smiles just as wide. He pulls me closer and throws his arm around my shoulder.

"Yep. This is my wife, Alyssa."

Giselle shakes my hand, and there's not a trace of jealousy or displeasure on her face. She seems genuinely excited to meet me.

"Oh, my god. I've been hearing about you for years. To think Daniel and you finally ended up together. I'm so happy for you," she gushes.

I glance at Daniel, whose smile falls just a touch and frown. What is she talking about? I guess she might've heard about us having grown up together. I smile at her but can't help but feel awkward.

She looks at her watch and grabs her bag. "I need to go now, but thank you so much for hiring my cousin as Regale's sous-chef. I promise she won't let you down. She made these dishes for you as a thank you, and I told her you'd fire her if she makes the smallest mistake. She reassured me she's got this, though."

She walks to the door and turns back. "Oh yeah, before I forget. I already instructed my PR team to deny all allegations about me and you, Daniel. I apologise, Alyssa."

I nod at her, dazed. She smiles at us and then walks out, closing the door behind her. Daniel picks up the tub of pudding and takes a bite before offering me a spoonful. I reluctantly open my mouth and let him feed me.

It's pretty damn good, but I'm in no mood to admit it. Daniel sits down on the settee in his office and pulls me over. I stumble and end up on his lap. Rather than let me go, he throws his arms around my waist and shuffles my weight to balance me onto his knee.

He pushes my hair away and rests his chin on my shoulder. "Told you I didn't cheat on you, Lyss. It really was just a business meeting. Her cousin was there too, but she stayed back to talk with the chef. When I said I wanted to take back everything I said to you, I meant it. I take it back. Let's reinstate the no cheating rule."

I'm silent as I think things through. What is he thinking?

"I don't know, Dan. It might be better if we do see other

people. Considering your track record, it'd be a surprise if you can actually last three whole years without getting laid."

Daniel chuckles and tightens his hold on me. He brushes his lips against my ear, eliciting a shiver from me.

"Who says I'm planning on going without sex for three years?" he whispers. He presses a soft kiss against the back of my neck and my eyes fall closed, desire pooling between my legs. Is he saying what I think he's saying?

"Surely you don't think I'd actually sleep with you," I say, my voice far huskier than I intended it to be. Daniel chuckles and another wave of desire crashes through me.

"Do you want to bet on whether or not I can make you beg for it?"

I clench my thighs and shift in his lap. How does he get me wet so quick? I'd be mortified if he found out.

I move to get off his lap, but Daniel wraps his arms around me and holds me captive. "Tell me you'll be faithful to me, Alyssa. I'm not asking you to sleep with me. I'm just asking you not to sleep with anyone else."

He presses another kiss to my neck and my lips fall open, barely suppressing the moan longing to escape.

"Tell me you'll be mine for as long as we're married, Alyssa. Promise me you'll be mine like I am yours."

I lean back against him with my eyes still closed. "Are you mine, Daniel?" I ask, my heart racing.

He grazes my neck with his teeth before biting down softly. The way he nibbles on the most sensitive parts of my neck sends delicious tremors down my back.

"Yes, sweetheart. I'm yours," he says. "I promise."

I involuntarily arch my back, grinding my hips up against his leg. I'm overcome with desire. I want him to touch me. I want his hands on me and his lips on mine.

Daniel's hands wander up slightly until he's holding me right below my chest. He draws circles with his thumb on the underside of my breasts and I whimper.

"Daniel…" I whisper.

I turn to face him just as his office door opens. I jump up and straighten out my clothing as Kate walks in. She glances at me and then nods at Daniel, a small smile tugging at the edge of her lips.

"Your eleven am meeting is commencing soon. I escorted Mr. Davis to conference room A," she tells him.

Daniel pulls a hand through his hair and sighs before nodding at her. I look down in embarrassment. We almost got caught behaving inappropriately. I'm certain my face is scarlet and I can't walk out of Daniel's office looking like this. But then again, my team will probably just think I got scolded for something.

Kate smiles and then walks out of the office, leaving us standing alone. Daniel looks at me and brushes my hair behind my ear.

"I need you to promise me, Alyssa."

I cross my arms over my chest to hide my hard nipples and look away. "And what if I won't? I'm not the one who decided to create or abolish the rule in the first place. You do whatever the hell you want and expect me to agree. What if tomorrow you change your mind again?"

Daniel closes the distance between us and buries his hand in my hair to tip my head up. "I won't change my mind. We can get it down on paper. I'm happy to sign a contract. I'll give you my DM shares if I ever cheat on you."

I look at him wide-eyed. "You're really serious about this, huh? Why did you say you wanted to start seeing other people only to change your mind again two weeks later?"

He drops his forehead to mine. "It's complicated, Lyss. Just know that I didn't and won't ever cheat on you. Can you say the same?"

I look into his eyes and nod. I can't imagine wanting someone else, and that's before we've even slept with each other.

"Yes. Okay. I promise you fidelity, Daniel. But this time we're signing a contract."

He grins at me and kisses my forehead gently.

"I'll get Vincent to draft it," he says. His eyes linger on me before he walks out, leaving me standing there with my heart racing.

Twenty-One

I've been antsy all day. It's been four days since Daniel made me promise him fidelity, and true to his word, we did sign a contract this time. We defined cheating as sexual intimacy with someone else; the fine being our respective shares in DM Consultancy.

I expected us to get a little closer, but neither one of us has had time to spend together. Daniel is working late at Devereaux Inc. most days while I'm at DM. By the time we get home we both collapse. I'm hoping it might be different since at least we'll be together all weekend now. I'm not even sure what exactly I'm hoping for, but I miss him.

I exhale in relief when I walk into our house to find Daniel sitting on the sofa with his glasses on and documents littering the place. I walk up to him and throw my arms around him. He freezes for a second and then pulls me onto his lap and hugs me back.

"I missed you," I whisper without thinking.

Daniel tightens his hold on me. "I missed you too, baby," he murmurs.

My heart flutters at the endearment he uses and I blush. I hide my face in his neck and relax in his hold. We stay that way for a couple of minutes, neither one of us saying anything.

"Tired?" he asks.

I nod and inhale deeply. "You must be pretty tired too. I've barely seen you."

Daniel nods, his stubble brushing against my hair. "Exhausted," he whispers.

I pull back and sit down next to him. "Are you going to work all weekend again?" I ask, pouting. Daniel chuckles and pets my hair, earning him a glare. He always used to pet my hair when I was a kid and I used to love it then, but I hate it now. It makes me feel like he still sees me as a child.

"I won't. I'll keep Sunday free, okay?"

I nod and get up to cook. Daniel grabs my hand as I walk past him. "Let's just get some takeout. Why don't we open a bottle of wine?"

I nod and walk to the wine fridge. "How about red?" I ask. Daniel nods at me from the sofa and leans back to watch me as I fill two glasses.

I hand one to Daniel while I put the bottle on the coffee table. I sit down on the small patch next to him that isn't cluttered and hold my glass up to his. He clinks his against mine and takes a big gulp. I chuckle and take a sip of my wine.

"Pretty damn good," I mutter.

Daniel winks at me. "We only have the best in our house, babe."

My heart flutters. Does he even realise what he's calling me? Does he realise he's referring to his apartment as ours?

"Go on. Go take a shower and get into comfy clothes. I'll order some Italian. It'll be here by the time you get out."

I nod gratefully and walk to my room, eager to get out of my work clothes. As promised, the food's here by the time I walk back into the living room. Daniel's eyes roam over my clothes and I tighten my robe. I'm wearing a short navy silk and lace nightgown that's far sexier than anything I've ever worn before, hidden behind a thick and fluffy robe. He has changed into his pyjama bottoms with nothing else on.

The way Daniel looks at me makes me think he's wondering what I'm wearing underneath the robe. How would he respond if I take it off?

He pats the sofa and hands me a plate. I can't remember the last time I felt so comfortable with someone. So at home.

"Delicious," I murmur as I take another bite of my pasta. Daniel chuckles and wipes his thumb across my lips. He brings his thumb to his tongue and licks it, rendering me speechless. I grab my wine glass and take another big sip, which does nothing to calm my raging heart.

"Should we watch a movie later?" I ask. "We can put something on while you work, maybe."

Daniel nods and hands me the remote. I scroll through the list of movies we saved on Netflix before settling on a chick flick, while Daniel continues to read through documents. I feel content sitting here with him, doing essentially nothing.

Daniel puts the plates away when we're done with dinner and then joins me on the sofa, a stack of papers in his hands. He pushes his glasses up and my heart skips a beat. He's far too alluring with those glasses on and his muscles on display. I sneakily grab my phone and take a photo of him. He raises his head and looks at me suspiciously. I'm in such a rush to hide my phone that I nearly drop it. Daniel takes it from me, but thankfully I managed to lock it in time. I'm blushing and it only increases his suspicion.

"What are you doing?" he asks.

I shake my head and smile innocently. "Nothing," I say far too quickly.

Daniel points the phone towards me and unlocks it using facial recognition. As it unlocks, the first thing on the screen is the photo I took of him. I look at him in outrage and lunge for my phone. Daniel grins and turns me over so I'm underneath him, his documents wrinkling and flying off the sofa.

"Taking unauthorised photos of me, Wifey?"

He holds himself up on his forearms and pushes my legs apart with his knee, settling between them.

"I... no, I would never. Why would I?"

His face hovers above mine. Just a smidge lower and our lips would touching.

I place my trembling hands on his chest and slowly slide my palms up to his shoulders and then around him. Daniel's eyes drop to my lips and my heart rate increases.

I can feel him hardening against my inner thigh, but just when I think he's going to kiss me, he pulls away. He pushes himself away from me, my arms slipping away. He sits up and runs a hand through his hair as he grabs some random documents and tries to sort them. I sit up, confused. Why didn't he kiss me? I'm sure he wanted to. I could feel his desire.

"Daniel," I whisper. I rise to my knees and look at him, suddenly feeling both insecure yet certain of what I want.

"Hmm?" he murmurs, not looking at me. I undo the tie on my robe and let it fall open as I gather my courage and scoot closer to him. I cup his cheek gently and turn his face towards me. He looks at me, his expression unreadable.

I'm terrified of overstepping, but I'm even more scared of going to bed filled with regrets and what ifs all over again.

My eyes drop to his lips and I lick my own in anticipation. I'm breathing hard and my heart is beating wildly. I slowly lower my face to his, giving him enough time to pull away. I kiss the edge of his mouth and then press my lips against his, once, twice, before gently sucking on his lower lip. Daniel is tense and doesn't kiss me back. Instead, he sits there, frozen. I pull away, filled with regret.

He stares at me and I look away, mortified. I was so sure he wanted me too.

"I — I'm sorry," I stammer. Daniel doesn't respond, which only adds to my humiliation. I stand up and walk away, intent on hiding away in my room. Forever, if need be. I've only taken three steps before he's behind me. He grabs my arm and pulls me back against him. I stumble and place my hands on his chest to stabilise myself. He tangles one of his hands in my hair and puts the other around my waist. He tips my head up and his lips crash against mine hungrily. He moans against my lips as he kisses me. I rise to my tiptoes to deepen the kiss, and Daniel tangles his tongue with mine. His hands roam over my body eagerly. He tugs on my robe and lets it fall off my shoulders. It pools at my feet and I step out of it. Daniel lifts me up and I wrap my legs around his waist as he pushes me against the wall. He drops his forehead against mine, both of us panting.

"Alyssa," he murmurs. The way he says my name turns me on even more. I tilt my head and capture his lips again, desperate for more. He kisses me roughly and pushes his hips against mine. He's rock hard and I grind against him, trying to create more friction. I need him desperately.

"Daniel," I moan. He pulls back a little to look at me. His eyes drift down to the nightgown I'm wearing. It barely covers me.

"Fuck, Alyssa." He presses another lingering kiss against my lips. "You have no idea how long I've wanted to do this," he whispers.

I smile at him and nip at his lips. "You have no idea how long I've been waiting for you to kiss me," I tell him.

He looks into my eyes and the butterflies in my tummy go wild. He makes me feel like I'm all he can see. Like I'm cherished.

"I — I thought... I didn't know—"

I cut him off by kissing him again. Now that I've finally got a taste of him, I can't get enough. He smiles against my lips and kisses me back, deeply and gently this time. My heart feels so full that I'm feeling emotional. Is it possible for a single kiss to make you feel deeply loved?

I run my hands over his shoulders and down his arms. I've been dying to touch him so freely, and his muscles feel amazing underneath my palms.

The sound of an alarm goes off and Daniel pulls away from

me, startled. He carefully lowers me to the floor and walks towards the lift.

"What is that?" I ask, following him.

"Means security has tried to contact us on our phones and they couldn't get through. They checked whether we're home, so they've now sounded the alarm to let us know one of them is coming up to speak to us. They usually only do this if it's urgent, though."

Daniel groans as he stares at the camera feed on the intercom and closes his eyes.

"Go grab your robe, babe."

I nod, confused, and walk back to pick it up. I've barely got it tied around my waist when the lift doors open to reveal Bennet, our security guard, holding up a clearly drunk Dominic.

"Good evening, Mr. Devereaux. Your brother showed up here thirty minutes ago and refuses to leave. He isn't on your approved list, so we couldn't grant him access, and we were unable to reach you or Mrs. Devereaux."

Daniel sighs. "It's fine, Bennet. You did the right thing."

Bennet lets go of Dominic, who glares at him. He straightens out his clothes and walks into the apartment. He walks straight past Daniel and throws his arms around me.

"I broke up with her, Lyss."

Twenty-Two

Dominic hugs me tightly and buries his face in my hair. I sigh and hug him back, gently patting his back.

I look at Daniel over Dominic's shoulder. He looks stricken for a second before his eyes fill with resignation. He looks away, dismayed, and turns to walk to his bedroom.

I grab his wrist as he walks past us and he pauses, his eyes dropping to where I'm holding him. His stoic expression is back on his face, making it impossible for me to read him.

"Why don't you make Nic a cup of tea?" I murmur. He hesitates and then nods at me. I lead Dominic to the sofa and he clings to me the entire way. He sinks down into the pillows and pulls me down with him, his head resting on my shoulder.

Daniel looks at the two of us, and I see it clearly now. He's jealous and insecure, but I don't know how to make it better without letting Dominic down.

"What happened?" I ask, my voice soft.

Dominic looks up at me with heartbreak in his eyes. "She just wasn't the one for me. I tried so hard to make it work. I had to... I had to try."

Daniel puts down two teacups with more force than required. He's tense and I can tell he wants to walk away again, but I tilt my head and indicate for him to sit down next to me. He hesitates before he sits down. I grab one of the teacups and hand it to Dominic.

"Have some. You'll feel better."

He takes it from me and glares at Daniel in between sips. "Why the fuck are you walking around half-naked anyway? You did it at our house too, when Lucy and Alyssa were around. Don't you think it's inappropriate?"

Daniel inhales deeply and ignores Dominic.

"I'm asking you a question, asshole." Dominic sits up, his tea sloshing over the edge. I take the cup and scowl at him. "Watch it," I snap. "I'll kick you if you spill any on my sofa."

Dominic looks at me in surprise. "Your sofa?"

I didn't even realise what I said until he repeated it after me. "Fine. Daniel's sofa. The sofa."

Dominic kicks off his shoes and folds his feet underneath him. "We broke up because of you, Alyssa. She's convinced I'm in love with you."

I stare at him in disbelief. "That's bullshit. I know she's insecure, but that's taking it too far."

Daniel tenses beside me, and Dominic looks at me with an expression I know all too well. It's guilt.

"Is it, though, Lyss? I started dating her shortly after you told me you're in love with me. I was terrified of what being in a relationship would mean for us and what might happen to our friendship if we dated and ended up breaking up. I felt like the only way to get over wanting you was by dating someone else. I guess she could always tell I wasn't a hundred percent committed to her."

I'm speechless. I would've loved to hear this before I married Daniel, but it wouldn't have mattered. I still would've had to marry him, and in hindsight I'm glad I did. Dominic was right to worry about our friendship. A relationship between him and I never would've lasted, and it would've destroyed our friendship.

Daniel gets up and walks to his bedroom, not looking back

at. I want to chase after him and reassure him that this changes nothing. I can see his insecurity and I want to rush and take it away. I think back to when he asked me how long I'd been in love with Dominic, back when he took me out for dinner. I told him I'd always loved Dominic. But now I know better. What I felt for him wasn't romantic love. It doesn't even come close to what I'm feeling for Daniel, and I already know I have yet to fall further. I'm worried Daniel will distance himself from me now. That he'll think Dominic and I are mutually in love and he's the one standing between us. Nothing could be further from the truth.

"I don't get it," I say to Dominic. "You said you broke up with her? Why did you do that? Were her insecurities becoming too much?"

Dominic shakes his head and walks up to Daniel's liquor cabinet.

I frown. "Don't you think you've had enough? You'll be hanging like crazy tomorrow."

Dominic takes a shot of whiskey and returns with the bottle. He puts it on the coffee table and grabs my hand as he sits down.

"I broke up with her because I realised it wasn't fair on her. It wasn't fair of me to use her to get over the feelings I have for you. I know it's months too late, but I haven't been able to think of anything but you. I don't want to put our friendship at risk, but I had to tell you. I need you to know I feel the same way."

I take my hand out of his and run it through my hair. "You're not in love with me, Nic. Just like I wasn't in love with you. We're just used to each other. We're comfortable with each other, and out of that comfort came infatuation. It's not love, and it'll pass."

Dominic shakes his head. "You can't truly believe that. I know you feel the way I do, Alyssa. I'm sorry I didn't realise it straight away. I'm sorry I made you wait for so long."

I shake my head and get up. "Where is all this coming from so suddenly? What's gotten into you?"

Dominic jumps up and grabs my hands, a pleading look in his

eyes. "It's not sudden. I've known all along, I just didn't know what do."

I shake my head. "What makes you think now is a good time? I'm married, Dominic — to your brother."

"It isn't a real marriage anyway, Lyss. Do you really think he'll care if we date?"

I close my eyes and try to think of the best way to handle this. What do I even say to that? How can I make him see reason?

"Nic, I'm sorry your relationship with Lucy didn't work out. But I hardly think jumping into another one, only hours later, is a good idea. Besides, I won't cheat on Daniel for as long as I'm married to him."

Dominic looks at me in disbelief. "That's bullshit. You might be faithful to him but he'll never be faithful to you. Why waste those three years? Didn't you see him in the tabloids with Giselle?"

I sigh, unwilling to get into this with Dominic. I'm not willing to listen to him tearing down my relationship with Daniel. I don't even get the animosity between them. Dominic always looked up to Daniel. When did that change?

"I'm sorry you broke up with Lucy, Nic. But I'm proud of you for not stringing her along when you realised it wasn't going to work out."

He nods and looks away. I can tell he's not ready to drop the topic, but I know we're going to end up arguing if I don't end it now.

"Come on, let me help you to bed. You'll feel like hell tomorrow if you don't get some rest."

He purses his lips and then lets me drag him to my bedroom. I avert my eyes as he undresses and then tuck him into the sheets.

"Sleep with me tonight, Lyss. No funny business at all. Just like when we were kids."

I sigh and lie down on top of the blankets while he's underneath them. He stares at me until his eyes flutter closed and his breathing evens out.

Twenty-Three

I place a glass of water and two painkillers on my nightstand and tiptoe out of the room. I glance at the clock and sigh. It's almost midnight already. I carefully open Daniel's bedroom door, relieved to find it unlocked.

His room is bathed in moonlight and much to my surprise, he's sitting up in bed, staring at the skyline outside his window. He seems lost in thought and doesn't even notice me walking in. I close the door behind me and lean back against it. His sheets have bunched up around his waist and his side profile looks enticing. How can a man be so beautiful? I open my robe and let it fall to the floor. The sound catches Daniel's attention and his head whips towards me. He looks surprised to find me standing there.

I walk up to him slowly until I'm standing right beside him. I'm feeling insecure and I'm scared he might push me away.

"I put Dominic in my bed," I tell him quietly.

He stares up at me as though he can't quite figure me out. "Hmm," he answers.

I want to push his blankets away and climb on top of him to kiss away any misunderstandings that might have occurred, but I don't dare. Instead, I fidget with the hem of my nightgown and walk around the bed. I hesitate before slipping underneath the covers on the empty side of the bed. Daniel follows my movements with his eyes but doesn't say a thing until I'm in his bed. I sit up against the headboard, mirroring him.

"What are you doing?" he asks, crossing his arms.

I look down at my hands. "I told you. I put Dominic in my bed."

Daniel studies me with a carefully blank face. "That doesn't explain why you're in my bed, Alyssa."

I freeze, suddenly second guessing myself. Does he already regret our kiss earlier? I don't understand why he's suddenly being so distant.

"I... well, I mean... if it's okay with you, could I sleep here tonight? If you're uncomfortable, I'll move to the sofa, it's not an issue. Actually, maybe that might be better." I'm rambling, but I can't help it. He's making me nervous.

I lift the sheets to get up, but Daniel places his hand over mine and shakes his head. "It's fine. You can stay."

I nod and turn to him, expecting him to say something more. Anything. But instead he lies down and turns his back to me, seemingly going to sleep. I'm surprised, but follow his lead. I lie down and stare up at Daniel's ceiling. I expected him to want to talk. To question me about Dominic's drunk confession. But there's nothing.

I'm nervous just being in the same bed as him, but he seems unaffected. I turn to my side like he has and scoot closer to him, little by little, until there's barely any distance left between us. I gently place my trembling hand on his shoulder and let it glide down his arm until I'm covering his hand with mine. I close the remaining distance between us and press my body against his, my breasts crushing against his back and my hips against his strong, muscular ass.

Daniel doesn't respond. He doesn't even grab my hand. I rest my forehead against his back and slip my hand underneath his arm to caress his abs. His muscles tense where I touch him; he's definitely not asleep. He's ignoring me. I slide my fingers down his abs until I reach the waistband of his pyjama bottoms. I hesitate before slipping my fingers underneath. Daniel grabs my wrist and keeps my hand in place.

"You're playing with fire, Alyssa," he murmurs.

I press a kiss to his back and wiggle my fingers, trying to reach deeper. "I thought I was playing with my husband. I mean, you're hot... but likening yourself to fire is a bit over the top, isn't it?"

Daniel's grip on my wrist weakens, but he doesn't let go. I expected him to reply, but he's gone back to ignoring me. I sigh and press soft kisses to the back and side of his neck. When I hit the right spot, he shivers and tightens his hold on my wrist.

"Go to bed, Alyssa," he whispers, sounding pained.

I smile to myself and graze his neck with my teeth before sucking on it softly, leaving red marks on his skin. It won't bruise and turn into a kiss mark, but seeing the red spots gives me an intense feeling of satisfaction.

Daniel groans and suddenly turns around so he's on top of me. He grabs my wrists and pushes them above my head, pinning me down with his weight. He settles his erection right where I want him and glares at me, his eyes flashing with anger and impatience.

"Stop," he snaps. "Go to sleep. Don't try me Alyssa, or so help me God, I will throw you out."

I freeze, my playfulness vanishing. He's rock hard and was clearly responding to my touch. So what is happening?

I nod slowly and look away, unable to look into his eyes. "I'm sorry, Daniel," I whisper. "I... I'm sorry. I shouldn't have touched you without your consent. I wasn't thinking."

I can feel tears gathering in my eyes and I'm burning with shame. I turn my head away. I'm unable to escape while he's keeping me locked in place, but the sofa is starting to look like a good option. I regret walking into his bedroom.

Daniel sighs and lets go of my arms. Instead, he holds himself up above me on his forearms, his lower body still locked with mine. I wrap my arms around my chest protectively. I feel vulnerable and exposed, and all I want to do is hide.

"Hey, look at me," he whispers, adopting a gentle tone. I look out the window and ignore him.

Daniel lowers himself a little and holds himself up on one arm so he can cup my cheek with his hand. He turns my head towards him as a tear escapes my eye. I look up at him, all my insecurities on display.

Daniel looks hurt, even though I'm the one crying. He kisses away the tear that's rolled down my cheek, his lips lingering on my skin.

"It's not you who should be sorry, baby. I'm sorry for snapping at you. You always have my consent to touch me. Whenever, wherever. I told you I'm yours, right?"

I sniff and shake my head. "You say that, but then you'll change your mind and go eat your stupid cotton candy with Kate, or you'll tell me you want to see other people and ignore me for a week straight. You say one thing and do another. I'm tired of guessing, Daniel. I'm tired of wondering whether you want me too. I'm done."

I push against his chest in a feeble attempt to throw him off, but he lowers his upper body against mine and presses a sweet kiss to my forehead. He pulls back a little to look into my eyes.

"Alyssa... you do the exact same thing. You agree to go on a date with Liam Evans, then you go running when my brother calls, and even now you disregard me as soon as he's here. I bet you're happy he returns your feelings after all. You've loved him for as long as you can remember, right? Must be nice to have him love you back. You don't need to come in here and pretend it changes nothing when it changes everything. I bet you really regret signing that fidelity contract now, huh? How long do you think you'll last before it's his bedroom you'll be sneaking into?"

He looks distraught and... jealous. I smile to myself, which only increases his anger. He's behaving this way because he's jealous?

"Hmm. Well, I see your point," I tell him, my own annoyance mounting. "By that reasoning, and since you're threatening to throw me out of your bed if I so much as touch you... I guess I'll just return to my own bed. To the person you say actually loves me back."

A burst of panic flashes through his eyes before he manages to control his expression. "Very well," he says, pulling away from me. He lies back on his own side of the bed and throws his arm over his face.

"I'll have the share transfer agreement ready for you tomorrow morning," he says, sounding angry but resigned.

I rise to my knees and stare at him, a wide grin slowly transforming the scowl I had on my face. So Daniel behaving this way is him lashing out in jealousy? Interesting. He doesn't snap or behave in any obvious ways, he just pulls away from me.

I pull the sheets out of the way and straddle him. He's no longer hard, but I make myself comfortable. He pulls his arm away from his face and looks at me, dazed and confused.

"What are you doing?" he asks, tensing.

"You did just say that you're mine, right? That I always have your consent? That I can always touch you? Didn't you say something along the lines of whenever and wherever?"

Daniel stares at me, his confusion mounting. "Alyssa, I'm not in the mood to play games with you," he says. I see it clearly now. He's feeling as insecure and vulnerable as I do.

I lean forward and kiss his chest. I make my way down his abs, kissing each one gently. Daniel's muscles tighten where I touch him, and he pushes himself up on his elbows to look down at me. I don't stop until I reach the waistband of his pyjama bottoms. He's breathing hard and his eyes are glazed over with desire.

"I promise I'm not playing with your feelings, Daniel. But I can't promise I won't play with your body."

I kiss his erection through the fabric and he twitches. He's staring at me intensely, like he's scared to find out what I'll do next.

I grab the edge of his pyjama bottoms and slowly pull them down, exposing more of his delicious V line. Daniel swallows hard as he grabs my hand. I look up at him, disappointed. He shakes his head and sits up to grab me by my waist. In one fluid motion, I'm flat on my back with him above me.

He kisses my cheek before he hovers his lips above mine. How could he possibly still be hesitating? I thread my fingers through his hair and pull his lips down on mine. He relaxes on top of me when our lips finally meet, his insecurities resolved. He kisses me gently at first, but within seconds the kiss turns scorching hot. It doesn't take long for me to be moaning against him. I wrap my legs around his and roll my hips underneath him, eager for more.

Daniel kisses my neck, nipping at me the way I did to him. He moves down slowly and pauses at the top of my breasts. He looks up at me for permission and I nod. He hesitates before his lips brush over my nipples through the fabric. I'm eager for more. I want his lips on my skin already.

"Daniel... more," I plead.

He grins and drags my nightgown down with his teeth. He inhales sharply when my breasts come into view and grabs one while he lowers his lips to the other.

"So fucking perfect," he whispers. The way he flicks my nipple with his tongue sends ripples of pleasure straight to my core. I never knew I was so sensitive.

I whimper in disappointment when he lifts his head and moves back up. He grins and shuts me up with another long kiss.

When he pulls away, we're both panting. "We need to get some rest, my love," he whispers. I look at him in disbelief. Rest? Now?

He kisses me again, gently this time. Then he turns onto his back and pulls me into him, hugging me. He closes his eyes and I stare at him, confused.

How could making out be enough for him? I huff and close my eyes, knowing it'll take me forever to fall asleep feeling this hot and bothered.

Twenty-Four

By the time Dominic wakes up, Daniel and I have already had breakfast. He didn't even twitch when I walked in to get myself a change of clothes this morning.

I chuckle as he walks into the living room looking like a mess. He groans and sits down next to me, dropping his head on my shoulder. I laugh and pet him gently.

"That's what you get for drinking so much."

Daniel glances up from his laptop for a second before refocusing his attention. It's clear he isn't pleased with Dominic's behaviour, but at least he isn't scolding him.

"Feed me, Lyss," Dominic pleads. He repositions himself so he's lying down with his head in my lap. "I'm dying."

I chuckle. "It's your own fault, you know. I told you to stop drinking, but you weren't listening. You barely even drank the water I gave you either. Daniel made some pancakes earlier. I think we might have some left. Do you want some?"

Dominic shakes his head. "I want your scrambled eggs," he says, sounding cute and whiney. I sigh and gently slide out from underneath him.

"You're the best! Love you," he shouts as I walk to the kitchen.

"Yeah, yeah. Love you too," I reply automatically. It's so common for us to say this to each other that I never stopped to think that it might make Daniel uncomfortable, the way it made Lucy feel insecure.

"You want some coffee too?"

Dominic shakes his head from the sofa. He looks like that one small movement is taking its toll on him and I bite back a smile. Serves him right for drinking so much.

I put his plate and a glass of orange juice on the coffee table and help him sit up before putting the plate in his lap. "You're so useless," I tell him.

He smiles at me sheepishly and kisses my cheek. "Thanks for breakfast, Lyss."

I shake my head and grab the remote. I glance at Daniel. "How do you feel about a rom com?" I ask him. He looks up at me blankly and nods before looking back down at his screen.

"Ugh, no, can't we watch something interesting?" Dominic says.

I roll my eyes. "Adding random explosions doesn't make a movie more interesting."

Dominic looks at me in disbelief. "You jump every time a planet explodes and stare at the screen open-mouthed when the Death Star explodes, even though you've seen it happen a million times."

I pout and look away. He's got a point, but I'm not admitting it. Instead, I scroll through the movies on Netflix and put on Two Weeks Notice.

Dominic groans. "We've seen this like a hundred times. We both know you just want to watch Hugh Grant."

I shrug and don't bother to deny it.

"I don't even see the appeal. He isn't that hot."

I ignore him and settle in to watch the movie. Usually I'd be sitting cuddled up to Daniel, but today it feels inappropriate. Thanks to Dominic's confession and Daniel's distant behaviour, I'm stuck sitting between them with plenty of space either side.

It's like Dominic can read my mind because he looks at me and smiles. "I might have been drunk, but I meant every word, you know."

Daniel tenses and glances at me. I give him a reassuring smile before turning to Dominic. "How're you feeling this morning, anyway? Feel sick?" I ask, ignoring what he just said.

Dominic pulls a hand through his hair and looks at me, exasperated. "Is this payback for ignoring your confession last year?" he asks.

I shake my head. "Nothing like that. I just don't think right now is a good time to discuss this."

Dominic looks away and glares at the TV while I awkwardly try to focus on the movie. Not even Sandra Bullock can save me from the tension in this room.

"When you moved out you said you'd be back on the weekends, but you haven't been back at all in a month now."

I nod. Daniel and I did intend to go back, but neither one of us mentioned it. Weekends are the only time we get to spend whole days together without other people around. And though neither one of us has said it, I know it's something we both enjoy.

"Mum misses you, you know? You should come back tonight. She's been making your and Daniel's favourite dishes every weekend because she keeps expecting you to turn up, but you never do."

I bite down on my lip, suddenly flooded with guilt. Mary has always been like a mother to me. She's never once treated me differently from the boys. If anything, she's always treated me better. She'd always side with me in arguments and spend time going shopping with me or taking me to beauty salons when I was old enough. She's the one who bought me my first bra and helped me through my first period.

"I didn't know," I whisper. I glance at Daniel, who clearly feels as bad as I do. "Dan? Maybe we should go back soon." I murmur.

Dominic nods. "Let's all go back together today," he says

excitedly. I glance at Daniel, who nods at me before looking away. He looks uneasy and I'm not sure why. Over the last couple of years Daniel and Dominic have grown apart, but it's never been clear to me why. I'm worried I might become another thing that stands between them, and I'm not sure what to do about it.

Daniel clears his throat. "Why don't you go shower, Nic. We can go home together once you're done. I'll take my work with me."

Dominic yawns and nods. "Borrow some of your clothes?"

"I'll put some in Alyssa's room for you."

Dominic looks at me in surprise. "That reminds me. Did you sleep okay? You weren't there when I woke up. I hope I didn't thrash in my sleep."

I smile and try my best to keep a blank expression on my face. "I slept fine, but you did seem out like a log."

Dominic chuckles as he walks to the bathroom, while Daniel's expression darkens. He puts his laptop away when the bathroom door closes and turns to face me.

"He thinks you slept with him last night?"

I fidget with the hem of my skirt. "Seems that way."

Daniel crosses his arms, drawing my attention to his biceps. He looks far too good in a simple tee.

"Why would he think that?" he snaps.

I swallow and stare at him with wide eyes. I've done nothing to feel guilty about, but I somehow still feel on edge.

"Did you get into bed with him before you sneaked into my room?"

"I — why do you have to say it like that? It wasn't like that at all. I just put him to bed and waited till he fell asleep. That's all."

Daniel searches my eyes for something and purses his lips in disapproval.

"Did you get into bed with him or did you just put him to bed?"

I hesitate. How am I supposed to answer this without him overthinking?

"It's a simple question, Alyssa."

"I — I... It's not like that. I did lie down next to him for a bit, but that's all."

I see the devastation in Daniel's eyes before he manages to hide it.

"God," I whisper. "What is going through your mind? He's my friend, Daniel. We grew up together. You tucked us into the same bed countless times. Don't you remember?"

Daniel laughs humorously. "Don't pretend it's the same as when you two were five. You got into bed with him after he told you he loved you."

I don't know what to say to that, and I don't know how to make it right. Last night it seemed like the right thing to do.

"Just because he uttered a drunk confession doesn't mean he suddenly ceased to be my best friend."

Daniel pulls a hand through his hair, messing it up. "You can't act like it doesn't change anything, because it does. Besides, he told you he meant every word. He's not drunk now, is he?"

I close my eyes and inhale deeply. Nothing I say will make this better. Daniel shakes his head and starts packing his briefcase. He's done speaking to me and I know I'm in for some silent treatment.

Twenty-Five

"How have you been, my dear? Has Daniel been good to you? Are you comfortable at his apartment?"

Mary started fussing over me instantly, making me feel even worse for staying away so long.

"Of course. He's always good to me, you know that. The apartment is amazing. The views are stunning and I'm so in love with the kitchen."

She grins as she takes her famous apple pie out of the oven. "Yeah, me too. Back when Daniel first bought that apartment, I'd go over all the time just to play around with all the fancy equipment he put in there. Such a dream kitchen."

I laugh and help her cut the pie. "I did wonder how he accumulated so many utensils that he never seems to use."

She smiles at me fondly. "So you two have been eating well? Have you been having dinner together?"

I nod at her. "Most days we manage it. Work has been busy and Dan is so busy with Devereaux Inc too. Even at home he's always working."

She nods thoughtfully. "The boy works too hard. He needs to hire more staff and delegate more. He can't keep overworking himself."

I nod in agreement, but we both know Daniel won't do that. There are too many things he has a hand in directly. Too many projects that are close to his heart.

Dominic walks up to me and hugs me from behind, startling me. He presses a kiss to my hair and reaches around me to grab a piece of apple pie.

"Delicious," he murmurs, his eyes on me. Mary clears her throat and looks displeased but doesn't say anything. She looks torn, which is exactly how I feel. Dominic and I have always been close and him hugging me isn't anything special, but it feels different these days. It feels like he's flirting with me. I'll need to talk to him soon enough, but I'm avoiding having that conversation. I don't want to hurt him, and I don't want to strain our friendship.

I didn't notice Daniel leaning against the kitchen doorway until he turns and walks back out. How long had he been standing there? I close my eyes and sigh. Why does this have to be so difficult?

"What's wrong?" Dominic asks. He moves to brush my hair out of my face and I dodge him instinctively. I've gotten so used to Daniel doing it that having anyone else touch my hair feels wrong now. "Headache?" he asks. I nod absentmindedly, not wanting to explain myself. He grabs my hand and pulls me along. "Come on, let's get you some painkillers. I'll massage your head for you."

We walk past Daniel's bedroom. The door is open and he's sitting on his bed staring at his phone. His eyes drop to our joined hands and he stares at us expressionlessly as we enter Dominic's bedroom.

"Nic, what are you doing?"

He sits down on his bed and looks up at me. "You and I have always been in my room together for hours on end. No one has ever thought it was weird. Seriously, what's gotten into you lately? It's like my brother's moodiness has rubbed off on you."

I pull a hand through my hair and frown at his words.

"I just wanted to talk to you in private. I told you I meant every word."

I sit down next to him. "I know you said that, but I doubt you actually mean it. We're best friends. We'd never work out as a couple. Plus, I'm married to Daniel. I can never undo that. Do you really want to be the guy who hits on his sister-in-law?"

He grimaces. "Your marriage to him is only on paper, and no one knows about it. No one will ever know, so why does it matter?"

I shake my head. "You and I will never be together, Dominic. You need to get the idea of us out of your head. If we were meant to get together, it would've happened long before now. Not now that I'm out of reach."

Dominic chuckles. "What? You think I suddenly want you because you're married to my brother? You're crazy. You're the best person I know. My favourite person. The only reason I didn't pursue you before now is because I didn't want to ruin our friendship."

I shake my head. "Even so. Even if you're serious about this, I don't feel the same way. I might've had a crush on you because we were so close and so familiar with each other, but that's it. It's in the past. You're right to say it's not worth putting our friendship at risk over."

I sigh. Truthfully, I don't see Dominic the way I used to. I always used to think the world of him, but that illusion shattered when my father died and he left me to deal with it myself. His behaviour showed me what both Daniel and Mary have seen all along. That Dominic has a long way to go in terms of growing up. I don't want to be the one he learns his lessons through. Dominic has an amazing heart, but both his mother and brother have spoiled him rotten. So have I, for that matter. I've always given in to him, and I've always done everything he ever asked of me.

"You're only saying that because I've been such an asshole recently. I'll be better, Alyssa. For you, I'll be better."

I shake my head. "No. I don't want or need you to be better. I need you to be my friend. That's all."

Dominic chuckles. "What? A year ago you were crying your eyes out because I said I just wanted to be friends. And now you're the one telling me you just want to be friends? Why? Did something happen between you and Daniel?"

I cross my arms over my chest. "What happens between me and my husband is none of your concern, Dominic."

He looks at me with raised brows. "You and your husband? What, did you fuck him, Alyssa? Did you fucking sleep with my brother?"

I haven't, but I don't want to admit that. I don't want him to think there's any hope left that we might work out.

"Yes."

Dominic's shoulders relax, and he smiles. "You're lying," he breathes out. I blink at him and shake my head.

"Yes, you are. You could never lie to me, Alyssa. If you haven't slept with him yet, then it won't happen at all. I've heard the rumours about Daniel. I know my brother better than anyone. He's impatient and ruthless in bed. If he wanted you, he would've already pursued you. Since that hasn't happened, the only way he'll sleep with you is if at some point it's convenient. If he's got an itch to scratch. It won't be out of desire or blinding lust, like his weekend girls."

I pale at his words, because he's voicing out my inner demons. I'd have to be deaf to not have heard the rumours about Daniel. To never be in contact with the countless women in our social circle that he's slept with. I've heard the giggling and the whispering amongst the women that he's been with. The inevitable drunk comparison notes in club bathrooms and their eagerness to have him again. Even I know he fucks hard and fast and leaves women wanting more. He's relentless in his pursuit, but he's never once shown me the type of passion he seems to have shown other women.

"Even so, I'm married to Daniel and it'll remain that way for the foreseeable future. Regardless of what happens between Daniel and I... you and I will never be together, Nic. I don't want to lose you as a friend, but I need you to drop this now."

He looks down. The agony in his eyes makes my heart ache, but there's no other way to handle this. I need him to understand we can never be together.

Twenty-Six

I twist and turn in bed, unable to fall asleep. Daniel has been keeping his distance from me, the way he always used to at his mum's house. It's unsettling. It feels like we've taken twenty steps back. He didn't even question me about what Dominic and I spoke about, and he didn't voice the slightest bit of displeasure when Dominic pulled me into his bedroom.

I guess this is why I dreaded coming back here. Because Daniel is an entirely different person here. He feels so distant. So out of reach.

I hesitate and then slip out of my bed. He wasn't that mad when I sneaked into his bedroom last night. Tonight I don't have an excuse, but I'm hoping he won't question me. I'm hoping he's missing me too.

I glance around the silent hallway and then tiptoe into his bedroom. The room is pitch black and my eyes are struggling to adjust. I blink a couple of times and carefully walk to Daniel's bed, taking tiny steps to make sure I don't bump into anything. I sigh in relief when my knees hit his mattress.

I tug on his blanket and slip into his bed, my body hitting his. He wakes up suddenly and grabs my arms. He turns me over and pins me down with such force that I whimper. He looks enraged. The anger in his eyes dissipates when he realises it's me.

"Alyssa, it's you," he whispers, obviously relieved. He lets go of me and turns onto his back, inhaling deeply.

"Who else would it be?" I ask, suddenly suspicious. I have a sinking feeling that I'm not the only girl that's ever tried to sneak into his bed while sleeping over at Mary's.

"No one," he replies. "I was just surprised. I was fast asleep."

I nod uneasily.

"What brings you here?" he asks, sounding far too formal. Far too distant.

"I — I couldn't sleep."

Daniel chuckles. "So you thought you'd get into my bed? You could've just shaken me awake, you know."

I blush. How clueless is he? "Ah, yeah," I murmur.

Daniel turns onto his side and looks at me tenderly. I scoot closer to him and to my surprise he shuffles back, maintaining distance between us.

Dominic's words ring through my mind, an unwelcome reminder. The only way he'll sleep with you is if at some point it's convenient. If he's got an itch to scratch. It won't be out of desire or blinding lust, like his weekend girls.

Just lying next to him makes it nearly impossible for me to keep from touching him. A single kiss has me soaking wet, yet he actually moves away from me when I try to get close?

"You must be enjoying this visit back home. Would you like to come back every weekend?" he asks.

Fuck no. I love Mary, but I don't want to be here if he'll turn into a stranger every time we set foot in this house. I sit up, distraught.

"Why do you move away from me? Am I that repulsive to you? You seemed fine kissing me yesterday, so what happened? Do you regret it?"

Daniel sits up and stares at me with wide eyes. "Repulsive? What kind of bullshit is that? No, of course not. It's just... being here is weird. Besides, I saw you walk into Dominic's bedroom earlier. You spent hours in there with him."

I shove against his chest but barely manage to move him. I shove him again with all my strength and he captures my hands in his, keeping them against his chest.

"What's going on?" he asks, more confused than annoyed.

"You... you just infuriate me," I snap.

He looks at me with raised brows. "I infuriate you?" He huffs, a sliver of emotion finally escaping his armour. "You're the one that spent hours with my brother while ignoring me, but I infuriate you?"

I exhale in relief. My worst fear is him not caring at all. I can deal with jealousy and anger, but I can't deal with indifference.

I smile at him and throw myself on him. He falls onto his back and I lower my lips to his. He freezes when I kiss him, but I don't let that deter me. He's already pushing me away. What else do I have to lose?

I tangle my legs with his and scrape my nails across his scalp. I melt against him when he finally kisses me back. He buries his hands in my hair and pulls tightly as he kisses me without abandon. I let my hands roam over his body and slip my fingers down his boxers before he has a chance to stop me. I gasp against his lips when my fingers curl around his erection. He's fucking huge and thick. He'll never fit inside me. Daniel moans into my mouth and trembles as I move my hand up and down, but he doesn't stop me.

"Baby, you drive me insane," he whispers. He starts to tug on my nightgown and I let go of him to let him take it off.

"You too," I whisper. Daniel pauses and stares at me as though he's trying to make sure I know what I'm asking for, and then he tugs off his pyjama bottoms. "These too," I snap, pushing down his boxers. He chuckles and presses a quick kiss to my lips before shrugging out of them. He lies back on top of me naked and I moan in delight. His lips find mine and he kisses me deeply, grinding his hips against mine. We're only separated by the panties

I'm wearing, and I long to push them aside. Every time he slides up against me, he pushes into me the tiniest bit, as much as the fabric allows him to. It drives me insane.

I'm panting and bucking against him. All I want is to feel him slide into me. I groan in frustration when he moves down to tease my nipples with his tongue. I lift my hips in a silent bid for more, but he merely chuckles against my skin. He swirls his tongue around my nipple and I arch my back, pushing more of my breast into his face.

"Please, Dan," I whisper. I pull on his hair and he finally moves back to my lips.

The way he kisses me has me panting and ready to burst. He slowly moves his hand down my body, his lips never leaving mine.

I moan loudly when he trails a finger over my soaking wet panties. "Fucking hell, baby. Your pussy is soaking wet," he groans. He pushes my panties to the side and slides a finger deep into me.

"Oh fuck, yes... Daniel."

I bury my face into his neck and place my lips against his ear as he pulls his finger back out and over my clit. My entire body tenses as he teases me. He lifts himself up on one arm and looks down at me as he touches me.

"So fucking wet for me, Alyssa. I could slip right into you, baby."

My eyes close under the intensity he looks at me with, a blush slowly extending across my cheeks.

"I'm always wet for you, Daniel."

He groans and kisses me roughly while my own hands find his throbbing hardness. He twitches in my hand as I move up and down, my grip tight.

"Baby, you've got me ready to come for you like a horny teenager. You gotta ease off with those hands of yours," he pleads. I grin up at him and shake my head. He looks at me through narrowed eyes and pushes two fingers into me while stroking his thumb over my clit. My lips fall open and I moan loudly as he pushes me towards an orgasm.

"Daniel, no. Oh God. I can't take it, please. Dan... Fuck."

I let go of him and instead wrap my arms around his neck, holding on for dear life. I don't know where he's touching inside me, but it's incredibly sensitive. Combined with the way he's stroking my clit, it's almost too much. I've never felt such intensity before, and I'm panting and moaning.

"Please, Dan. Please, baby. Please," I whimper, not even sure what I'm asking for. Daniel increases his pace until it's all too much and I erupt. My entire body shakes and he smothers my moans with his lips. He doesn't pull his fingers away until the last ripple passes through my body. I collapse against the mattress and look at him in equal parts bliss and shock. "Wow," I whisper.

He kisses me gently. "Wow indeed," he says, smiling smugly. I blush and pull him down, loving his weight on me. He gets comfortable as I wrap my arms around him, hugging him tightly. I brush my lips against his ear. "My turn," I whisper. Daniel chuckles and shakes his head, not budging.

"No. Now we sleep, beautiful."

Twenty-Seven

I wake up when the door to Daniel's bedroom opens and freeze. Thankfully, Daniel is on his side with me tucked against his back. He gasps as he's startled awake and I scoot down a little, hiding myself. Daniel pulls the blankets tight and clamps it underneath his arm so he creates a little tent around me.

"You're still asleep, darling?" Mary asks. I don't dare to move. I'm wearing nothing but my panties and Daniel is naked. I'm pressed up against him, my face against his back. I desperately try to remember where we threw our clothes. Daniel's clothes must still be tangled somewhere in the sheets while mine are on the floor on my side of the bed. So long as she doesn't walk around the bed, she won't see me or my nightgown.

"How come you're sleeping in? Usually you'd be up by now in the kitchen. I was looking forward to your breakfast, you know. It was so nice to have you back in the house for a couple of weeks. No one takes care of me like you do."

I relax against Daniel, my heart melting. "Uh... Mum... I'm just tired. I thought I might sleep in longer. Why don't we have a chat later?" he says, sounding genuinely sleepy. I hear Mary shuffle into the room and if I'm not mistaken, she's just sat on the lounge chair by the door. It doesn't seem like she has any intention of leaving, but at least she won't be able to spot me from where she's seated. I exhale in relief and place my hand on Daniel's waist, making myself a little more comfortable.

"I guess Alyssa and Dominic are still asleep. I thought for sure things would've changed between you and Alyssa with you two being by yourselves in that apartment of yours, especially since you two haven't been coming back here much... But she and Dominic seem closer than ever. The way he hugged her yesterday and then dragged her off to his room surprised me. You weren't there and I didn't know what to say either."

Daniel's entire body tenses and I shake my head gently, trying to reassure him wordlessly. I slip my arm over his chest and squeeze myself against him tightly, crushing my breasts against his back.

"I used to think they were just friends, but now I'm wondering if I was just blind to what was happening between them... Daniel, if I'd known I'd never have let you get married to Alyssa. I would've made that nasty grandma of hers an offer she couldn't refuse and buy back the shares."

I press a silent kiss against Daniel's spine and push my forehead against his skin. I was foolish to think there'd be nothing wrong with following Dominic, when I knew full well that my friendship with him makes Daniel uncomfortable. I guess it's not actually the friendship he dislikes, but the feelings he thinks I have for Dominic. How do I now convince him otherwise when a couple of months ago I admitted to being in love with Dominic?

"You should start seeing someone, Dan. I've let you be and let you sow your wild oats, but you aren't getting any younger."

I freeze, my entire body tensing against Daniel. Why would she say that to him when she knows we're married?

"Mum, I'm only thirty-two. Chill," he murmurs, relaxed. I'm tempted to poke him and ask him what the hell he means by that. He should be reminding her he's married and not planning on seeing anyone else.

Mary huffs. "Yeah, but it'd probably take you a year to find a good girl, then another year or two of dating before you finally get engaged. Then another year while we plan the wedding. By the time I'm finally holding my grandchild, five or six years will have passed."

Daniel chuckles. "There we go. So that's your real objective. You just want a grandchild. Why don't you just go adopt one?"

"I want a grandchild that looks like you. You'll have to make me one, and I'm running out of patience. You and Alyssa won't work out. You've been married for months and you're still sleeping in separate bedrooms. You didn't even speak to each other all day yesterday, and I checked. She was with Dominic all day while you hid in your room. You two don't even seem to be friends. I would've loved to have her as my daughter-in-law, but your marriage is clearly just a paper marriage. It shouldn't stop you from seeing someone. I'm sure if you find the right person, she'll understand the situation. Or otherwise you just buy out Alyssa's grandma and divorce her. Lord knows we can afford it."

I squeeze my eyes closed and tighten my hold on Daniel. I don't want that. I don't want him to see anyone else, and I don't want to divorce him. Thank god we've got the fidelity contract. Though technically that won't stop him from seeing anyone, so long as he doesn't have sex with them. The thought of Daniel on dates with someone else doesn't sit well with me.

"Mum, I don't know. I'm still married. It would feel too much like cheating to me. I'd rather not," he says carefully, but even to me his response sounds lacklustre, like he doesn't actually care but can't be bothered dating.

"Hmm," Mary says. "Well, you have no choice. I invited Olivia and her mother over for lunch today. They should be here in an hour or so. Do you remember her? She's always been crazy about you. Besides, she's a university professor and she's really pretty. Very sweet and polite too. I think you'll like her."

I remember Olivia very well. I never liked her. She always used to tag along whenever her mother came over for lunch or dinner at the Devereaux mansion. She'd spend the entire time staring at

Daniel as though she wanted to drag him to the nearest room and have her wicked way with him. She's indeed always been polite, but something about her rubs me the wrong way. It always has.

"Seriously, mum? With Alyssa here? What are you thinking?" he snaps, his anger rising.

His mother tuts. "She won't care. I doubt she'll even notice that I'm trying to matchmake you. It's just lunch, isn't it? Not like we've never done that before. It'll also relieve your brother's guilt. Maybe Alyssa's too."

"So, what? You're trying to push me towards someone else so Dominic can covet my wife without feeling guilty about it?" he asks, his tone harsh.

Mary sighs. "Nothing like that, and you know it. Those two aren't right for each other. Maybe they need to get it out of their systems or something. It doesn't matter. It's not like you and Alyssa are actually together. She's only your wife on paper, Daniel. Besides, I'm sure you'll really like Olivia. Just give it a chance, sweetheart. Please. Just do it for me. I'm tired of worrying about you."

Daniel scoffs but nods at her. "Yeah, okay mum. Anything to make you happy," he says, sighing. Pure liquid fury runs through my body. He fucking agreed? I pinch his waist and he yelps.

"Are you okay?" Mary asks, confused.

"Uh, yeah. Just cramp," he stammers.

I hear shuffling in the room before the door opens. "Wear something nice, okay? Maybe a nice button-up? What do girls these days like? Maybe a t-shirt, actually. Just don't come out wearing your pyjamas like you have been doing."

She closes the door behind her and I push the covers off me, my eyes blazing. Daniel looks at me, his expression unreadable. I glare at him, gritting my teeth in anger. I sit up, not caring that I'm half-naked. Daniel's eyes fall to my breasts and a flicker of desire shatters his unreadable mask, transforming his face. I get out of bed and storm into his walk-in wardrobe, giving him one hell of a view of my barely covered ass.

I grab two of his ties and walk back into the bedroom, making my way to the door to lock it. He follows me with his eyes but doesn't say a thing. He doesn't even try to make excuses for agreeing to let his mum arrange a date for him.

The small sliver of daylight that still manages to find its way in through the curtains makes the room look dusky, allowing me to see him clearly as I pull the blankets off him entirely. I pause, startled. He felt big last night, but to see him like this. That's definitely more than I can take.

I glance at his face. He's lying back with his arms behind his head, his eyes on me. He doesn't even try to hide his body. There's not a trace of embarrassment on his face.

I climb back on the bed and straddle him, his eyes widening as I do so. I lean over him and grab his wrists, tying one of his ties around each before linking them together. He doesn't fight me. He just looks at me with heated eyes, as though he's waiting to see what I'll do next.

I raise his arms and tie his knotted wrists to his bed frame. He tries to tug his hands loose but fails, and I smile in satisfaction.

"What are you doing?" he murmurs, his voice husky. I glare at him, still infuriated. His eyes drop to my breasts and he tries to tug his tied wrist loose again. He fails and licks his lips, watching me hungrily.

"Punishing you," I snap. I lie down on top of him and bury my hands in his hair, pulling on it hard enough to make him tilt his head. I lean in and place my lips against his neck, right below his ear, and bite down before sucking on his skin harshly.

Daniel moans and turns his head to the side to give me better access. "Fuck, Alyssa," he whispers, sounding turned on beyond reason. He bucks his hips, squirming until he's sliding against me. My underwear prevents him from entering, but it doesn't stop him from driving me crazy. It was meant to be me torturing him, but before long I'm panting and close to coming.

I tighten my grip on his hair and turn his head to settle my lips against the other side. I bite down bang in the middle of his neck and suck harshly, leaving a clearly visible kiss mark. Daniel moans loudly and I cover his mouth with my hand. He presses a soft kiss against my palm and thrusts against me more frantically. I love seeing him so out of control. So desperate for me.

I lower my lips to his collarbone and he groans. "No," he whispers. Moving down meant he's no longer pressing his erection into me and he tugs on his restraints before hooking a leg around me to try and move me up. I chuckle and take my time giving him kiss marks on his collarbone, and then his chest before moving on to his abs. He's breathing hard and watching me with heated eyes as I press my lips against his adonis belt, marking that too.

I grin up at him as I follow the trail of hair on his lower abs down and down with my lips, pressing small kisses against his skin. Daniel is lying still, his body tense. He watches me with ardent eyes as I grab his throbbing erection, wrapping my fingers around the base.

"Baby, you'd better let go of my dick now.".

I smile at him. "Or what?" I ask, lowering my lips to kiss the tip. He moans and bites down on his lips.

"What if I don't want to let go of your... dick?" I whisper, almost stumbling over the word. Daniel gulps and stares at me with wide eyes as I slowly take the tip of him into my mouth. His eyes close and he moans loudly when I swirl my tongue.

"Alyssa, baby. Please," he moans. "Oh fuck, Lyss."

I bob my head up and down, taking him in deeper each time. With each of his moans, I get wetter myself. I never thought this would turn me on as much as it does. I clench my thighs together as Daniel roughly pulls on his ties.

"Baby, you gotta stop. I'm gonna come. Lyss, I — I can't..."

He tries to pull his hips away from me, but I take him in deeper, trying my best not to gag. Daniel's moans get louder and his pleas get more desperate.

"Please, my love. Alyssa... I can't hold it..."

He bucks his hips and pushes deeper into me, coming deep in

my throat. I struggle to swallow it all down and pull away, coughing. I wipe my lips and look at him, pleased with what I'm seeing. He looks spent and intensely satisfied. Daniel looks at me through lowered lashes and grins lazily. The mere sight of him has my heart skipping a beat.

"Baby..." he says. "I don't think you quite understand the definition of punishment."

I burst out laughing and shake my head. "Don't you provoke me. I'm tempted to leave you tied here so you'll miss that damn date you should never have agreed to in the first place. If this wasn't your mother's house and if I didn't love her so much I would've really done it."

I lean over him and loosen the tie enough for him to be able to get out of it while giving myself time to escape his room. I glance at him one more time, satisfied with the countless bites on his skin that mark him as mine.

Twenty-Eight

I walk to the outdoor dining table, fuming. Daniel is sitting in the corner wearing a button-up that covers most of his kiss marks. The one right below his ear that's still exposed, he covered by putting a plaster on. He smiles at me and winks when I glare at him. I sit opposite him in the seat that's marked for Mary. I grab the name cards and switch mine with hers before nodding politely at Olivia and her mother, Dana.

It doesn't escape my attention that Olivia is in the seat next to him, right in the middle of the table, while I would've been next to her, at the other end of the table. In that seat, it wouldn't be easy for me to speak to Daniel without leaning over Olivia. Mary placed Dana opposite Olivia while Dominic would've been sat opposite me. It's clear what she's doing and I don't like it at all. With this setup, Daniel and I would have been at opposite ends, unable to even see each other. I try my best not to glare at Olivia. She's pulled her seat so close to Daniel's she might as well be in his lap.

We all rise when Mary walks up to us. She pauses and looks at me curiously and then at the one empty seat that's left before greeting our guests with a smile.

"Gosh, Olivia. You look prettier every time I see you. Isn't she pretty, Daniel?" she says.

I glance up at him to find him staring down at her with a sweet smile. My heart clenches painfully when he nods at his mother. Perhaps sitting where I can't see him would've been easier. I look away so I'm not caught glaring at him.

We all sit down as the staff take our drink orders. I order a double gin and tonic. There's no way I'm making it through this completely sober.

"It's so lovely to see you again, Alyssa. I was so sorry to hear about your father," Olivia says, smiling at me.

I nod at her politely and try my best to smile back. "Thank you, Olivia. It's lovely to see you too."

One of the serving girls places my drink in front of me and Olivia frowns. "Oh, Alyssa. You shouldn't! You're still underage, aren't you?" she says, sounding genuinely concerned. I sigh, already tired of this lunch, and the first course hasn't even been served yet.

"I'm twenty-two."

Olivia chuckles. "Wow, you've grown up," she says. She glances at Daniel and smiles. "Do you remember being twenty-two, Daniel? Fresh out of university. God, those were the good old days."

Daniel merely smiles at her noncommittally and she turns back towards me. "So you'll be starting your career soon, huh? That must be exciting."

"Yeah, I'm working for DM Consultancy," I tell her, a tinge of pride ringing through my voice.

She frowns at me. "Oh, Alyssa. Don't you think it'll be better to get a real job rather than relying on nepotism? Your father's company will always be there, but it's so important to work for an actual boss first. Someone who doesn't care about your surname. I worked for my dad's company for a while, and it was so easy compared to working for the university. Take it from me, sweetie.

It'll really build character to work elsewhere. I have plenty of connections if you struggle to find a job."

She turns to Daniel and smiles at him. "Or Daniel can help you find something. I'm sure you'd help your little's brother's friend, right?"

She places her hand on his arm and grins at me. "He's always been so supportive. He's actually the one who introduced me to the professor I currently work for. I still had to go through the whole interview process, but it was nice to have someone to talk to beforehand."

I glance at her hand on his arm and then at him before looking away. Just seeing her touch him so intimately annoys the hell out of me. "I'll keep that in mind, thank you, Olivia," I say.

No matter how hard I work, people will always think I don't deserve my successes. This is the main reason my dad instructed me to use Carter as my surname at work, but it doesn't make it any easier. We have plenty of staff who've been with us from the start of their careers and who have climbed their way up to executive positions, the way I'm doing. But just because my surname is Moriani, people will always assume I was handed everything on a silver platter.

"Actually, Alyssa has a real job," Daniel says, an edge to his tone. "She works harder than any of my other staff members and has been with DM since she was eighteen, often working sixteen-hour days to get all her work done in addition to attending university. In four years she's worked her way up to becoming a managing consultant. Are you insinuating that my company is guilty of nepotism when all we're doing is nurturing talent? That we hire and promote unfairly?"

Olivia blanches and my heart feels more at ease to hear him standing up for me. Mary clears her throat and sends Daniel a warning look. "Of course not. That's not what you meant, right Olivia? She's just looking out for Alyssa. She doesn't know much about DM, after all. Maybe you should show her around."

Olivia nods. "Yes, I'm sorry if that came out wrong, Alyssa. I meant well. I would love to see DM. Maybe I can bring you some lunch sometime, Daniel?"

Mary nods happily. "Oh, that'd be wonderful. How about sometime next week? I'll give you the phone number for Daniel's secretary so you can set up a lunch date."

My heart sinks. He hasn't rejected her advances once. I take a large sip of my G&T, drowning out the conversation as I pick at my food. Olivia smiles at everything he says and in return he nods and listens intently as she tells him about her job. I can see why Mary selected her. She's taller and thinner than me. She's only half a head shorter than Daniel while I barely reach his chin, and she's got a supermodel's body that she undoubtedly works hard for. Mary seems to know her son well.

I look away and finish my second glass of gin and tonic while Olivia and Daniel reminisce about the events they've both attended. From the sounds of it, they share more memories than I realised.

Olivia giggles and I look up. "We got so drunk, do you remember?" she says.

Daniel smiles at her fondly and my heart wrenches. Does he ever look at me like that? "We didn't get drunk. You got drunk. I had to carry you home," he says, laughing.

I thought they were merely acquaintances, but it sounds like they're pretty good friends at least. It makes sense. Their mothers are good friends and they're close in age. Olivia is only three years younger than Daniel.

"It's been so long since we've had a chance to catch up. I'm so happy to see you today. We should really do dinner sometime soon. How about that new Italian place?" she says.

Daniel smiles at her and glances at me. I look away, pretending to be bored, and finish my third G&T. My heart is aching and I feel oddly betrayed, even though Daniel hasn't exactly done anything wrong yet. All he's done is be polite and kind to her while honouring his mother's arrangements. Mary was right. If I

THE TIE THAT BINDS

hadn't known better, I wouldn't have thought anything of this lunch.

"So, Alyssa," Dana says, when Daniel ignores Olivia's question. "You've grown up to be a beautiful, hardworking young woman. Are you dating anyone?"

I smile at her tightly. She takes my non-responsiveness as denial and nods happily.

"You might remember my son, Oliver. He's only a couple of years older than you are. He's twenty-five. Perhaps you and he could go for drinks sometime? He's only just moved back to London. It'd be nice for him to date a little. He's become such a hermit these days."

I smile, remembering Oliver. He was always really sweet.

"Actually, Dana... I'm sorry, but I'm seeing some right now," I say.

She looks surprised and disappointed. "That's too bad," she murmurs. "I've heard such great things about you from Mary and Christopher."

I look up at her with raised brows. "Christopher from Accounting at DM?"

She nods and smiles. "I think he's the Head of the Finance now, but yes, him. He's a family friend and speaks very highly of you."

I nod in understanding. "When I started he wasn't the head of the department yet, so in my mind he's always Christopher from Accounting. That's still how he signs any emails he sends to me," I say, chuckling.

I sip my fourth G&T as dessert comes around, feeling pleasantly buzzed. I can't wait for this to be over. I just want to go back to my bedroom and hide out in bed. I'm feeling hurt and insecure and I hate it. I felt so empowered this morning in Daniel's bedroom, but here, now, it seems like it never even happened. He's pleasantly chatting with Olivia and even though I'm sitting opposite him, he's barely spoken three words to me all afternoon. Is it that easy for him to separate intimacy and public appearances? This must be what all the women before me have felt like. It's excruciating to feel so special in bed, only to be made to feel like I'm insignificant outside of it. I'm ready to call it a day when Mary smiles at Olivia brightly.

"You did bring your swimsuit, didn't you?" she says. Then she turns to Daniel and grins at him. "I told her you'd take her for a swim since the weather is so lovely out. We can all sit by the pool and sip some cocktails. Wouldn't that be wonderful?"

I groan. I'd rather burn in Hell.

160

Twenty-Nine

" I 'm not feeling all that well. I think I'll sit this one out and go take a nap," I murmur, smiling politely. I can't watch Daniel with Olivia any longer. My heart aches and I'm tired. I just want to get into bed and fall asleep with the hope that tomorrow might be better. At least I get to go back to work tomorrow.

Dominic shakes his head and grabs my hand. "Nope, you're coming," he says. He pulls me away from the rest of the group. The two of us fall behind them and he throws his arm over my shoulder.

"You got it bad, huh?" he murmurs. I frown at him, confused. "You know he's just messing with you, right? His eyes were on you every time you looked away. He's just trying to make you jealous."

I pause and glare at him. "What are you talking about?"

He sighs, and a brief expression of hurt flashes through his eyes before he smiles at me. He gently pats my hair and strokes my cheek.

"All I've ever wanted was for you to be happy, Alyssa. I know I'm selfish. I know I've been a terrible friend to you. But I do truly love you. You're my heart, Alyssa. I want the world for you."

He hesitates and inhales deeply. "I also know you better than anyone else, and I know you've never once looked at me the way you were looking at Daniel today. You usually hide it so well that I didn't realise..."

He shakes his head. "It's nothing. Go put on your red bikini. You know the one, right? You look wicked hot in it. Go put that on, and trust me just one more time. Can you do that for me?" I look away, unwilling. Dominic cups my cheek gently. "Trust me, Lyss. I would never do anything to hurt you. Do this for me now, and I swear you won't regret it."

I shake my head. "I don't feel like it. I don't want to swim. I just want to leave."

Dominic pulls me against him and hugs me tightly. "I know, Lyss. I know. But if you do that, if you run away now... then you and Daniel will keep going around in circles. My brother is hard to read, but I know exactly what he's thinking. If you want to be with him, then you'll need to chase him aggressively, until he finally gets it through his thick skull that it's him you want. Until he finally believes it. So come to the pool with me and trust me. Let me make at least some of my behaviour up to you."

I hesitate, but he pushes me into the direction of the house before following me, as though he doesn't trust that I'll actually come back out. He looks pleased when I walk back out wearing the bikini he told me to wear and offers me his arm. He changed in record time and has a spare pair of swim shorts in his hands. "For Daniel," he says, winking at me.

When we reach the pool, Daniel's eyes immediately find mine. He stares at Dominic's hand around my shoulder and grits his teeth. Dominic chuckles and leans into me. "He's stupid for thinking he wouldn't pay for making my best friend suffer through that bullshit lunch."

A small smile tugs at my lips, and I shake my head at him. "Don't provoke him," I tell him. "I don't want to do that to him."

Dominic smiles at me with a twinge of longing and presses a

long kiss to my cheek. "I wish, Alyssa. I fucking wish," he whispers.

"Where were you two?" Daniel shouts.

He walks up to us, looking furious. "Went to change, bro," Dominic says. "Do you like the bikini I picked for Alyssa?"

I look at him through narrowed eyes. This bastard. He winks at me and holds my hand, twirling me around. Daniel's eyes drop to my breasts and he grits his teeth. The bikini I'm wearing showcases my body perfectly. The tiny bottoms are shaped so that my waist looks small while my ass looks nice and round, and the top has enough support to push my already full boobs up. Even I think it's sexy as hell.

Dominic hands Daniel the spare swim shorts he brought and Mary walks up to us, excited. "Oh, fantastic. See, problem solved, Daniel." She glances between us curiously, an amused look in her eyes.

Daniel shakes his head. "I really don't think that'll be a good idea, mum," he says, looking at her sternly. I laugh mockingly. So he doesn't want Olivia to see his kiss marks. I brush past him, regretting coming here at all.

Daniel grabs my wrist and pulls me back. I stumble and brace myself against his chest. He looks at me intensely like he wants to say something, but then he shakes his head and lets go of me, his eyes lingering on my body.

He leans in and whispers into my ear. "You asked for this, Alyssa. I have no problems showing your lover boy all the marks you so happily left on my body. Let's see if he's still so keen on picking you out bathing suits when he sees what you did to me this morning."

I chuckle humourlessly and stand on my tiptoes. I grab his shirt and yank him closer to me. "Don't pretend to be the good guy here, Daniel. You just don't want Olivia to see the kiss marks. You went as far as putting plaster on to make sure she didn't see them. Don't want to ruin your chances, do you? I wonder if she'll still go for dinner with you when she finds out my lips have been all over your body..."

I let go of his shirt and push past him and an astonished Mary. "What did she say to you?" she inquires as I lie down on one of the empty lounge chairs. Daniel shakes his head and storms past her into the boathouse while Dominic sits down by my feet. He's smiling at me, but his smile is bittersweet.

"Wow, you really grew up, huh?" Olivia says, glancing at my body. She's wearing a black bikini and her abs are enviable, but she's flatter and thinner than I thought she'd be. If that's the body type Daniel likes, then he'll never be satisfied with me. I smile at her politely as Daniel comes storming back in. He's changed into his swim shorts, but he's still wearing his shirt. He drops his trousers on the seat next to mine and glares at Dominic before he slowly unbuttons his shirt. I ogle him through my sunglasses as it falls opens. He might piss me off, but he's still hot as fuck. He grins smugly as he shrugs his shirt off, letting it drop to the floor. Everyone stares at him with wide eyes. Olivia pales while Dominic looks away, hurt flashing through his eyes. I look down, feeling terrible about hurting him and embarrassed at the sight of the damage I did. Daniel has over a dozen kiss marks on his body, all the way from his neck to the waistband of his swim shorts. I didn't think I'd left so many. I obviously wasn't thinking clearly when I did it. It's evident that he was passionately manhandled recently.

Mary clears her throat and looks shocked. Her eyes automatically shift to me and back to Daniel. She looks contrite for a moment before she purses her lips to try and hide a smile, her eyes lighting up with amusement.

"Cramp, my ass," she mutters. I inconspicuously cover my face with my hair to hide my crimson cheeks. What was I thinking...

Daniel walks towards the pool and smiles at Olivia. "You wanted to swim, right, Liv?"

She stares at him and blinks a couple of times before nodding uncomfortably. "I — you... uh, your chest, Dan..."

He looks down at the kiss marks I left on his skin and smiles to himself. "Oh, that... yeah. To be honest, I didn't expect to walk around half-naked today or I would've told my girlfriend to behave. She wasn't pleased with a decision I made recently. We had a disagreement and worked through it... vigorously."

Daniel smiles and shrugs, looking far too pleased with himself. This nut job. Did he seriously insinuate we had an argument and makeup sex? His not-so-subtle vulgarity is embarrassing as hell. Also, did he just call me his girlfriend?

Dominic glances at me and shakes his head. There's a flicker of jealousy in his eyes, but he does his best to suppress it. "Fucking hell, Lyss," he whispers. I look away and run a hand through my hair awkwardly. Thank god Olivia and Dana don't realise it was me. I don't dare to look up at Mary, though. I'm not sure I can ever face her again.

"I didn't know you had a girlfriend, Daniel," Dana says, sounding just as disappointed as Olivia. He grins at her and then glances at Dominic.

"I do," he says.

Thirty

aniel was quiet the entire way home. We didn't get a chance to speak to each other privately between entertaining guests, packing up to go back home and finishing some last-minute things for work tomorrow.

He looks pissed off as we enter the lift, and he's yet to say a word to me. I don't understand what's making him so angry. He's the one that exposed his kiss marks, and he's the one that declared he had a girlfriend, only to avoid me afterwards.

He drops our luggage to the floor as soon as we walk in and scoops me up. I yelp as he lifts me into his arms, one hand underneath my knees and one wrapped around me. He carries me to his bedroom and kicks the door open before placing me on his bed.

I'm surprised when he helps remove my flip-flops and kicks his own off before lying down next to me. He rolls on top of me, glaring.

"What's wrong?" I ask, my voice quivering.

"Nice bathing suit you had on today. Dominic picked it out for you?"

My eyes widen. "Oh, that," I murmur nervously.

"Hmm, that," he repeats. He glances at the red strap that's

peeking out from underneath my sundress, his eyes darkening. If I'd known it would upset him this much, I would've taken it off at the mansion. I kept it on because it dried nicely while I sunbathed, and I figured I'd want to shower before bed, anyway.

He grabs the hem of my dress and lifts it up. "Off," he orders.

I raise my arms obediently and let him take it off. He throws my dress on the floor and stares down at my body hungrily.

"I've gotta say, it does cup your perfect tits beautifully," he says. He grabs a handful of my breast and squeezes. He glares at my bikini top and puts his hands on the cups before pulling it apart in one fell swoop. The fabric tears like it's nothing, and I gasp as my breasts spring free. He throws the remains of my bikini top on the floor with force, as though it personally offended him. He leans down and takes my nipple into his mouth. I moan and arch my back, making him chuckle. He roams up my body and places his lips against my neck, sucking harshly. My eyes fall closed as a thousand different sensations crash through my body. Daniel pulls back and looks at the mark he made with satisfaction before doing the same thing on my collarbone, my chest and my stomach.

He pauses when he reaches my bikini bottoms and stares at it in anger. He looks up at me. "I saw you. I saw the way you hugged him. I saw the way he stroked your hair and held your hand. The way he pulled you away and towards the house. Did you let him into your bedroom? Did he go through your outfits to pick out the one he liked best?"

He trails his nose against my inner thigh before sucking down and leaving another mark. I tremble underneath him. I'm beyond turned on. He's never been this rough with me before, and I'm almost embarrassed to admit that it drives me crazy.

Daniel glances up at me and grins before tearing off my bikini bottoms. He kisses my lower stomach and moves down until I'm trembling with need. He looks up at me and then drags his tongue down my slit He moans at the same time as me. "I knew you'd be fucking delicious," he whispers. He swirls his tongue around my clit and has me ready to come within seconds. I bite down on my lip and try my best to hold on as he tortures me with both his tongue and his fingers. The combination of the two is almost too much for me, but every time I'm about to come, he pulls away.

"I don't want him even thinking about you," he snaps. "You're mine, Alyssa, and I'm done playing games. I'm done stepping aside and trying to do the right thing. You're mine."

He pushes a finger against my g-spot while he swirls his tongue around my clit and I almost lose it. "Ohh, fuck. Dan. Please..."

"Say it, Alyssa," he whispers.

"I — what?" I can barely think straight.

He finally pushes me over the edge and I shatter on his lips, coming harder than I ever have before. I'm still trying to catch my breath when Daniel gently lifts me into the bed and pulls the covers over both of us. He rolls on top of me, his clothes cold against my skin.

He brushes my hair out of my face and kisses me so sweetly that my heart feels like it might burst.

"Tell me you're mine, Alyssa. Officially from now on. No more games. No more blurred lines. No more flirting with other people and making each other jealous. No more guessing and no more miscommunication. I want you, heart and soul. Tell me you want that too."

He looks so vulnerable as he stares down at me. I pull him to me and kiss him as gently as he kissed me. Is he actually asking me what I think he's asking? My heart is racing and hope blooms within me.

"Only if you promise me, there'll be no more pulling back and hiding your thoughts and emotions, no more unwarranted jealousy and definitely no more separate bedrooms," I whisper.

Daniel exhales in relief and drops his forehead to mine. "I promise, Alyssa. I promise." He glances at his walk-in wardrobe and grins. "I better make some space for you, huh?"

I giggle and throw my arms around him. He nuzzles my neck and pulls back to kiss me. I moan against his lips, already wanting more.

A thought crosses my mind and I suddenly feel vulnerable. I pull away and glance at him.

"What is it, baby?" he whispers.

"I... do you... it kind of seems like, I don't know. Do you not want to sleep with me?" I say, my words coming out rushed. I'm blushing and feeling embarrassed that I have to ask at all.

Daniel looks at me with wide eyes. "What?" he says. "What the fuck?"

He grabs my hand and shoves it down his shorts, making me feel how hard he is. "Alyssa, you could merely glance at me and I'll want you. Hug me, and I'll be hard. I always want you, baby. What could possibly make you think I don't?"

I hesitate.

"Communication, right baby?" he reminds me.

I nod. "It's just that you never seem to want to go all the way with me. You'll kiss me and then just go to bed... or you know... you'll touch me and then you won't let me touch you in return and just go to sleep. It makes me think you might not really want me."

Daniel groans. "Alyssa, I've been trying to treat you respect-fully. I didn't want to rush into anything with you. You're not some one-night-stand or a girl I know I'll dump in a few weeks. You're my wife. I wanted to do right by you."

He pulls a hand through his hair and shakes his head. "God, Alyssa. I'm dying to sink my cock deep inside you. Fuck, you were so wet just now, all I could think about was how you're going to feel wrapped around my dick. I'm throbbing at the mere thought of it. I need you so desperately, baby... But you're not just a quick fuck. I wanted it all with you. I wanted to make out with you and play with you without any expectations. Just pleasuring you brings me enough satisfaction."

I bite down on my lip and throw my arms around him,

169

hugging him tightly. "Okay," I whisper. "You've done it. You've done right by me. Don't make me wait much longer, Daniel. A few more days and I'll jump you myself."

He smiles and kisses me tenderly. It's been a long time since everything has felt so right in the world, but tonight it truly does.

Thirty-One

"You got laid, didn't you?" Linda says, grinning.

I frown at her. "What are you talking about?"

"You keep smiling at your screen and zoning out. That's never happened to you before. You're always hyper focused on work, so it can only mean one thing. A man is involved. Besides, that's obviously a hickey on your neck."

Jake and Luke stare at me with wide eyes, both of them obviously curious. Jake looks at me wistfully, as though part of him is hoping it isn't true. He hasn't tried to pursue me since he started working with me, and I'm so relieved. It'd just get messy, especially if Daniel caught wind of it.

I glare at Linda. "Fine," I admit. "I'm dating someone. We've been seeing each other for a little while and finally made it official. I'm just kind of giddy, I guess."

Linda squeals and claps. "Oh, my god! You're actually dating someone!" I roll my eyes. She seems more excited about it than me. "Wow, you've never dated in all the time I've worked with you. Not that I know of, anyway. I've never seen you this happy before. It's kind of weird to see you looking your age."

Linda is five years older than me and started at DM just before I did, though I did get promoted faster than her. I've always appreciated that she takes me seriously despite my age, but I guess part of it might be that I've always been really serious. Her smile drops when Daniel walks into the office. She nudges me and looks down. "Don't tell the boss," she whispers.

"Why not?" I ask, confused.

She shakes her head and turns back to her screen. "Just don't," she murmurs.

Daniel pauses at my desk with a wide smile on his face, causing the butterflies in my tummy to go wild. He places a coffee cup on my desk before holding a couple of other cups up for the rest of the team.

We woke up together this morning and got ready for work together. It was incredibly sweet and exciting. I loved it. I wish we could've gone to work together, but Daniel had a meeting at Devereaux Inc. I discreetly ogle him as he hands out the rest of the cups. He's wearing the tie I picked out for him this morning. We barely managed to get dressed between the kisses. I take a sip of my coffee and look down at it with a wide smile. He got me a mocha? It's my ultimate guilty pleasure, but I rarely let myself have one. How did he know? Daniel winks at me and walks towards Kate to give her a cup of coffee before he disappears into his office.

I'm antsy and eager to get some time alone with him. I need his lips on mine. I try to focus on work as best as I can. We'll be going to Singapore together next week and I'm so excited about it. It'll be our first trip together, and I want it to be perfect.

"Alyssa," Daniel shouts. I jump up, immediately back into work mode. I think back to my schedule and whether anything could've gone wrong but come up empty. I walk into his office and close the door behind me.

I walk around his desk. "What's wrong?" I ask. He grins at me and lifts me onto his desk. He parts my legs and stands between them, cupping my head gently. He lowers his lips to mine and kisses me.

"God, I missed you," he whispers. His hand trails down my

leg as he kisses me until he reaches the lace fabric of my panties. He pushes it aside and moans against my lips. "So wet for me already, baby."

He pulls away and sits down on his chair. I try to close my legs, but he shakes his head, his hands keeping them open.

"Do you remember that time you sat down on my desk and caged me in with your legs? We were arguing and I was being cold to you."

My smile vanishes. "Yeah. You told me you wanted to see other people," I snap. I try to jump off his desk, but he holds me in place.

He rises and presses a kiss to my lips. "Easy, baby. Let me finish. I thought you were the most beautiful thing I'd ever seen. And when you sat down on my desk, your stunning legs on either side of my thighs and those damn red lace panties right in front of me... All I wanted was to bury my face between your legs."

He grins at me and leans in to kiss my inner thigh. "So let me overwrite that bad memory, my love," he murmurs, before pushing my underwear aside and finding my clit with his tongue. He laps me up and then inserts a finger, playing with my body expertly. He makes me come hard right there on his desk, his name on my lips. I cover my mouth with my hand and try my best to keep my moans quiet as I shatter.

Daniel pulls back and puts his finger in his mouth with a wicked grin. "Fuck. So good," he moans. "I'll never get enough of watching you come for me, Alyssa."

I blush fiercely and jump off his desk, unsteady. Daniel grabs my waist and helps me balance until my legs finally decide to work again. I'm trembling and panting, my head still spinning from how hard I just came.

"You — you..." I snap.

Daniel stares at me, his brows raised.

"Did you actually need something?" I say eventually. He shakes his head and grins up at me so cutely I can't even be mad.

"No playing around at work," I warn him, before storming

out. I must've looked angry with my red cheeks and my mild annoyance because my team immediately falls silent and work diligently.

I've only been working for about ten minutes when the intranet messaging system pops up. I click on it, expecting it to be someone from one of the other departments. Instead, it's Daniel.

Daniel Devereaux: *but I like playing with you, Wifey. There are so many things I've been fantasising about doing to you. Surely you won't begrudge a man such a small request?*

Alyssa Carter: *Have you lost your mind? This is the work intranet! It's on my screen! What if someone walks past me?*

Daniel Devereaux: *I'll fire them. Do you know how long I've wanted to bend you over my desk and fuck you? Baby, I want you kneeling down between my legs underneath my desk. I want you sitting on top of your desk with your legs spread wide... You can't just kill my dreams, my love.*

I clench my thighs together. I just came and I'm already ridiculously turned on again. How does he do this to me?

Alyssa Carter: *You can't just fire someone, Dan. There are these things called labour laws. You'd better get to work. Stop making me wet and desperate for you.*

Daniel Devereaux: *Wet and desperate, huh? How do you expect me to work now? All I can think about is your tight, hot pussy. I'm taking you tonight, Alyssa. I can't wait any longer.*

My eyes widen, and I gasp. Linda glances at me and I immediately click away my chat with Daniel.

"You okay?" she asks.

"Yes, it's nothing. Just forgot to plan a meeting. The boss will kill me if I don't do it ASAP," I blurt out randomly. She nods in understanding and gets back to work.

All I do for the rest of the day is count down the minutes until Daniel and I are finally alone in the privacy of our home.

Thirty-Two

I jump up from the sofa self-consciously when the lift doors open and wrap my arms around myself. I'm wearing a revealing silk negligee that made me feel sexy when I put it on, but now it just makes me feel shy and nervous.

Daniel walks in looking exhausted and freezes when he sees me. "Wow," he whispers as he drops his briefcase to the floor. He stares at me with such intensity that I blush. He grins and walks up to me. As soon as he's close enough, he pulls me to him and lowers his lips to mine. He kisses me eagerly and buries his hands in my hair. I moan and tug on his tie, loosening it before I pull it off. Daniel takes it from me and throws it on the floor.

"You can't be trusted with ties," he whispers, and I look away shyly. I must've lost my mind when I tied him up the way I did.

Daniel kisses me like he can't get enough of me and runs his hands over my body. "This... is this for me?" he asks, his eyes wide.

I glance down at my outfit and grin. "Who else could it be for?" I whisper. I tug on his jacket and he shrugs out of it, his lips back on mine. He groans when I pull away and push him against the wall. He looks down at me with heated eyes as I slowly unbutton his shirt.

"I need you," I tell him. "Those messages you sent me today... did you mean it?"

He tugs a strand of my hair behind my ear and cups my cheek. "About wanting you? Yes, I meant every word."

"Good." I push his shirt off his shoulders. Daniel shrugs out of it and lifts me into his arms. I wrap my legs around him as he kisses me and starts walking towards his bedroom. The way he kisses me is so passionate that my entire body feels sensitive. I'm aching with need.

I almost sigh in relief when he finally places me on the bed. I rise to my knees and undo his belt and zipper. He grins down at me and helps me get it off. Before long he's standing in front of me wearing only his boxer shorts.

Before I have a chance to pull them down, he gets into bed and rolls on top of me, kissing me gently. He cups my face and runs his thumb over my lips.

"Alyssa, I can't believe you're really lying here with me," he whispers. "You're so fucking beautiful."

He leans in and kisses me so gently, so tenderly, that my heart aches. My eyes shutter closed and I wrap my arms around his neck, wanting him closer. He pulls away a little and kisses my forehead, and then my cheeks, my nose and finally my lips. I moan as his tongue brushes against my lips.

I tug on his boxer shorts and he smiles before finally giving in and taking them off. He plays with the hem of my negligee and pushes it up. "You're breathtaking in this, but I want you naked." I nod and lift my hips to help him take it off. It falls to the floor as Daniel's fingers close around my panties. He pulls them off and drops them on top of my discarded negligee.

"I've waited far longer to have you than you can imagine," he whispers. He tangles his hands into my hair and rolls on top of me, his lips hovering over mine as though he's hesitating. I cup his head and pull him closer, pressing my lips against his. He sighs and kisses me tenderly, like I'm breakable. I spread my legs and shift underneath him so he presses up against me.

Daniel tangles his tongue with mine and slowly moves his hips up and down, sliding against my wet heat. He angles himself so he's aligned with my entrance but doesn't push in. Instead, he keeps teasing me, sliding against my clit every time he moves.

"You're so wet," he whispers. He pulls back a little and lifts himself onto his forearms so he can look down at me. "So beautiful, Alyssa. I can't get enough of you."

He kisses me again, gently and slowly, taking his time. When he pulls back, his eyes are filled with emotions I don't recognise. He's never looked at me like this before, and my heart goes into overdrive. I wrap my arms around his neck.

"I want you, Alyssa."

I nod and push my hips up so he slides into me slightly. His lips fall open and he moans. His entire body tenses and he drops his forehead against mine.

"Fucking hell, Alyssa," he whispers, pulling back out of me.

"No," I whimper. "I need you, Daniel. Please. I can't wait anymore."

He kisses me and then tangles one hand in my hair while he cups my cheek with the other. "Are you sure you want this, baby?" he asks.

I roll my hips up and his eyes fall closed, a soft whimper escaping his lips. "Yes, Daniel. I want you," I whisper.

He fumbles around for a condom and I grab his hand. "When's the last time you got tested?" I ask, my voice quivering.

He freezes and looks at me, bewildered. "I've never fucked anyone without a condom, Lyss. Not even once. I had my annual check-up a couple of weeks before we got married. I'm clean. I... I didn't know you were worried about it. I'm sorry, I should've told you."

I blush and shake my head. "I wasn't worried, Dan. It's just... I'm on the pill. I've been on it for years to regulate my periods."

Daniel looks at me with wide eyes. "I — you... are you saying you want me bare?" he asks, his eyes darkening with desire.

I bite down on my lip. "Yeah," I whisper. I'm embarrassed and turn my head away, suddenly feeling shy.

Daniel grins and leans in for a kiss. "Look at me, baby," he whispers. I tilt my head, staring into his eyes. He's looking at me so lovingly that my heart feels ready to burst. It's like I'm all he can see, all he'll ever want or need.

He pushes into me slightly and my lips fall open. He's thick, and stretching me out more than I've ever been. I push down a sliver of panic. Should I have told him?

"You're so tight, baby. Damn. Is this okay?" he whispers. I nod and scrape my nails over his back. He pushes in deeper, slowly. "Fuck. So tight," he groans. He pulls back out and then pushes into me all the way, fast and hard. I cry out in pain while Daniel cries out in pleasure.

"Shit, are you okay, Lyss?" he asks, panicked. I nod as a tear escapes my eyes. "Fuck, baby. What's wrong?"

I pull him closer to me and kiss him. "It's nothing. It just hurt more than I expected," I whisper. Daniel looks concerned, and I shake my head. "It's nothing, Dan. Just kiss me for a little while, just a few minutes. Let me get used to your size."

My muscles involuntarily contract around him and he moans, his forehead dropping against mine. "I could come just like this," he whispers. I giggle and wrap my arms around him. He leans on one elbow and cups my face with his free hand.

"I... did I hurt you? You're definitely wet enough, I don't understand. Should I pull out?"

I shake my head and caress his face, trailing a path from his forehead down his nose and lips with the tip of my finger.

"Dan, it's okay. The first time is meant to hurt. It'll be okay soon enough," I whisper. His concern makes way for shock and then panic. He moves to pull out of me, but I tangle my legs with his.

"Please," I whisper, my eyes filling with tears. "I promise I'll be okay soon, please don't stop." I sniff as a tear runs down my cheek. "Next time will be better, I promise. I'm sorry."

Daniel looks at me, heartbroken. He wipes my tears away with his thumb and kisses me so tenderly that even more tears end up falling down my cheeks.

"Alyssa, my love, don't cry. Please... You're breaking my heart, baby."

He kisses every tear away and cups my face gently. I look up at him, distressed. "I just... I just wanted it to be perfect. I've wanted this for so long, and I — now I... I ruined it."

Daniel leans in and kisses me, over and over until I relax again and my tears subside. He pulls away and smiles at me. "I'm still rock hard. I'm still inside you. How is anything ruined, beautiful? We haven't even started yet, and this is already the best sex I've ever had. You feel amazing, Lyss. So wet for me, so tight. This is absolutely perfect, my gorgeous wife. So much better than I ever could've dreamed."

He pulls back slightly and pushes back in, moving little by little. It doesn't hurt anymore, but it also doesn't feel as good as I thought it would. It's tight and uncomfortable.

He kisses me as he moves in and out. His lips caress mine so gently that I'm filled with tenderness. "Daniel," I whisper. He leans back a little to look at me. He looks tense and turned on, and it's the hottest thing I've ever seen. "You don't need to hold back," I whisper, worried that it doesn't feel good for him. He closes his eyes and bites down on his lip.

"Baby, I've been ready to burst from the moment I sank into you. I'm not holding back, I'm just trying my best to make sure your first time lasts more than a couple of thrusts, but fuck. I've wanted you for so long and so badly..."

I laugh and rake my nails over his scalp. I pull him towards me and kiss him deeply. He moans against my lips and picks up the pace. He leans back a little to look into my eyes and then thrusts hard. "Alyssa, my love... I can't... I'm gonna come, baby." I nod and tilt my hips up to meet his frantic thrusts. "Yes... Fuck yes, Alyssa," he moans. His entire body tenses and he closes his eyes as he collapses on top of me.

Well, damn. That's gotta be the hottest thing I've ever seen.

"Sorry, I must be heavy," he whispers. I shake my head and hug him tighter. He slowly softens inside me, the sensation novel to me. After a couple of minutes, he slips out and presses a quick kiss to my lips.

"Stay here, babe."

He comes back a minute later with a wet wipe in his hands and lifts the sheets. I gasp in horror when I look down and clutch the blankets, trying my best to cover myself with them again. My thighs are stained with what looks like a mixture of sperm and blood. I'm sure there's not actually that much blood, but it looks horrific.

Daniel kneels down in front of me and brushes my hair behind my ear. "Let me, my love. It would mean the world to me if you'd let me take care of you now."

I bite down on my lip and nod, releasing my death grip on the covers. Daniel tugs it away gently and spreads my knees. He looks at me so intently that I can't help but look away. "Daniel, it's embarrassing," I whisper.

He shakes his head and wipes my thighs, cleaning me up delicately. "It's not, Lyss. It's fucking beautiful," he says, genuinely sounding like he's in awe. I glance at him and he's looking at me so adoringly that I blush, a smile tugging at my lips.

"Come on, baby." He grabs me and lifts me into his arms. "I'm running you a bath. That'll make you feel better for sure."

Thirty-Three

"Ugh, I knew you'd be unbearable once you started dating. I'd rather have the ice queen back instead of this giddy, giggly mess," Luke mutters, his disapproving eyes roaming over me. Usually I would've glared at him, but today I grin and blow him a kiss. He shudders and looks away, much to my amusement.

After spending ten minutes coming up with an excuse, I finally walk into Daniel's office with a document he needs to sign. He looks up and smiles at me as I approach. He hugs me and I relax in his arms. He's been at Devereaux Inc. every morning, and the office just isn't the same without him. I rise to my tiptoes and press a kiss to his lips.

"How're you feeling?" he whispers.

My cheeks burn. "Fine, just a bit sore."

Daniel drops his forehead to mine and sighs. "I'm sorry, Lyss. I didn't know. I wish you'd told me you were a virgin. I would've gone easier on you. Maybe stretching you out first would've helped."

My embarrassment increases and I shake my head. "It was fine," I murmur. And it was. It hurt at first and it felt uncomfortable for a while, but towards the end it was all right. I struggled to get used to his size, but I'm sure it'll be fine over time.

Daniel pulls away from me and shakes his head. "Maybe we shouldn't have," he whispers, and my heart drops. "Why did you wait to lose your virginity? Were you saving it?"

I panic. The truth is that I thought I was in love with Dominic, and throughout the years no one managed to convince me otherwise. Even when I dated, my heart wasn't really in it, so none of my relationships went any further than second base.

"I wasn't saving it, per se. I just... it just never happened."

Daniel stares at me thoughtfully, a hint of agony flashing through his eyes. "Hmm, I see," he says. He takes a step away from me and I miss him instantly. "You'll be sore for a while." He looks torn and regretful, and I don't know what to make of his reaction.

"It's fine. I'll be fine. I'm okay. I'm sure it'll be better next time."

He nods at me but looks uncomfortable, which in turn only makes me feel more awkward. I take a step closer and wrap my arms around him. I push my breasts against his chest and drag his head down towards me. I kiss him and relax against him when he kisses me back, passionately this time. A small moan escapes my lips and I feel him harden against my stomach. I slide my hand down his chest until I'm cupping his hardness, but he jumps back. I freeze while Daniel looks at me with wide eyes.

What just happened? "Ah, we're at the office, Lyss," he murmurs. I glance at the desk behind him. The same one he lifted me onto before he buried his face between my thighs. The same one he said he wanted to bend me over.

"Uh, yeah," I whisper. I clear my throat and hand him the document I wanted him to sign, both of us suddenly stiff and awkward. I can't help but feel like something is wrong as I walk back to my cubicle, but I can't figure out what.

Thirty-Four

By the time I walk into the apartment, Daniel is already sprawled on the sofa surrounded by documents, his glasses on the tip of his nose. He got home before I did for a change.

I rush into our bedroom to take a quick shower and change. I bought a new nightgown, and I can't wait to see his reaction. Daniel has been distant and awkward all day, but I'm hoping that was just because he doesn't know how to behave around me at work now.

He looks up when I walk in and his eyes roam over my body appreciatively. My new nightgown is mostly sheer with some lace covering my privates, and it's obvious he can't get enough of it.

"Hey, Lyss," he murmurs, his eyes shifting back and forth between my face and my breasts. He clears the space next to him and hands me a takeout box awkwardly. "Got some Chinese on the way home," he says. He tries to focus on his paperwork but keeps glancing at me with heated eyes.

I grin to myself and take a bite of the stir-fry as I start scrolling through our list of favourited movies. Eventually I settle on The Lord of the Rings and Daniel grins at me when I click play. I belatedly realise it's his favourite movie. He always teases me for being a nerd for loving Star Wars, but he's even worse with his Lord of the Rings obsession. He leans in and presses a soft kiss on my cheek as the movie starts, putting my heart at ease. Thank god he isn't being awkward at home. I'm not sure what I would've done.

I settle against him comfortably and eat as he works; the two of us content with our regular routine. It's not until halfway through the movie that I'm starting to feel needy. I glance at him and gently tug his documents out of his hands before climbing onto his lap. He hardens against my butt instantly, and I bite down on my lip to hide my smile.

Daniel throws his arms around me and kisses the top of my head. "Hey, I was working," he whispers, trying his best to sound annoyed and failing miserably. The cute smile that tugs at his lips gives him away.

"Hmm, I know. But I feel neglected. Give me ten minutes of your time and I'll let you get back to work."

Daniel laughs and stretches out his legs, shifting us both into a more comfortable position. He spoons me and I sigh in delight when he starts to kiss my neck, trailing a path from my ear to my shoulder and back. I turn around and bury my hand in his hair to pull his lips against mine. He kisses me back eagerly and before long I'm panting, already wanting more. I hook my leg around his to get him where I want him and he moans against my lips. He rolls on top of me and grinds against me.

"Daniel," I moan.

He pushes himself up to look at me, and I blush. I'm sure I'm a dishevelled mess. "This thing you're wearing... it's torture," he whispers. He leans in and sucks on my nipple through the lace that covers it. I arch my back and moan. My entire body feels sensitive.

Daniel smiles and moves his lips to my other nipple, sucking on it eagerly. I buck my hips against his and scrape my nails over his back before sliding my palm down his abs. He freezes when my fingers grasp at his erection and pulls away, out of reach.

"Your ten minutes are up," he says, sitting up.

I stare at him in disbelief. "You're kidding, right?"

He shakes his head and stands up to move away. I grab his hand and try to pull him back to me, but he won't have it. "Dan... you can't leave me like this," I whisper, my voice husky. He glances at me and shakes his head.

"Lyss, I'm sorry. I've got a video call with Liam Evans in a couple of minutes."

He makes his way to his home office and I sigh in relief. At least he's got a genuine excuse. For a second I thought he just didn't want to take things further.

I hesitate for a couple of minutes before I follow him into his office. He looks up in surprise when the door opens and I grin evilly.

"Everything okay, bud?" Liam asks.

Daniel looks back at his screen and nods. "Ah, yes. My girlfriend just walked in. I apologise," he answers.

"I didn't even know you had a girlfriend. Can't believe someone finally managed to lock you down. Who's the lucky girl?"

I walk up to his desk and sink to my knees so I can crawl underneath it. I place my hands on his thighs. Daniel looks down at me and back at his screen, panicked.

"Uh, we're keeping it quiet for now. We haven't been official for long."

I unbutton his suit pants and tug on his boxers to reveal his rapidly hardening dick. I lick my lips and look up at him. He shakes his head with wide eyes and grabs my hands to stop me, but I lower my lips to him and take his dick into my mouth. Daniel moans and tries to cover it up with a cough.

"No wonder you haven't been seen with anyone in months. I'm surprised the press hasn't caught you with your girlfriend yet," Liam muses. "Can't wait to meet her. The girl who tamed Daniel Devereaux."

I take him deeper into my mouth and bop my head up and

down as quietly as I can. Daniel tries his best to answer Liam's questions about Luxe. He buries his hand in my hair and gyrates his hips, urging me to go faster and harder.

"You okay, Daniel? You don't look so well," Liam says.

I look up to find that Daniel has buried his face in his hands. "Yep, fine. Just uh... just a headache," he says, sounding breathless.

Liam is silent for a while before he starts laughing. "Fucking hell, your girlfriend is still there, isn't she? What a girl. You fucking lucky asshole."

Daniel shakes his head frantically, making himself look even more suspicious. "No! She's uh... she's in the living room," he says, the words tumbling out of his mouth in a rush.

"How do you know?" Liam asks, laughing heartily. "She just walked into your office and then allegedly back out, so how do you know where she went?"

Daniel gulps and Liam laughs even harder. "Anyway, I'm happy with the answers you've provided. Let's do lunch sometime next week? I want to meet this girlfriend of yours."

Daniel nods, clearly just wanting to get him off the call. "Uh, yeah, sure. Thanks for your time."

As soon as he ends the call, he moans loudly and pulls his hips away, jerking as he covers my neck and chest.

"Fucking hell, Alyssa. You're going to fucking kill me, baby."

He pushes his chair away and then pulls me onto his lap, still breathing hard. He grabs a couple of tissues from his desk and cleans me up before hugging me tightly. "Fuck," he whispers, making me giggle.

He picks me up and carries me to our bedroom. I laugh at his tortured expression. I'm giddy with excitement and eager for more.

If I'd known Daniel had no interest in continuing what I started, would I still have done it? If I'd known he'd carry me back to our room only to tell me to go to bed while he finishes his work, would I still have seduced him?

Thirty-Five

I'm nervous as we walk into Mary's house. Though Daniel and I have shared a bed every single night since we officially decided to be together, he hasn't done more than kiss me ever since we had sex a week ago.

He pulled away from me further after I crawled underneath his desk. He treats me with warmth and respect, but not with intimacy. He'll kiss me back if I initiate a kiss, but he won't let it go further than that. He won't respond if I walk through the bedroom half-naked and he'll block my hands as soon as they start to wander. He hasn't even touched me from the waist down, and he's not letting me touch him either. I'm scared the sex was so bad that he doesn't want to do it again, and being here with Mary and Dominic is definitely not going to help.

I'm startled and oddly hurt when he carries my luggage into the bedroom I'm always in, instead of his own. I freeze in the doorway and bite down on my lip. I can't help but wonder if he wants some distance, and if that's the case, then I don't want to push myself on him.

He seems awkward and avoids looking at me as he walks out of my room and into his own. I don't know what to make of his behaviour. I've been insecure all week. Every time I try to initiate more than a kiss, he'll pull away, and he's gone back to being mostly professional at work. I'm not sure how much longer I can take the rejection.

I'm absentminded when I walk into the living room, my thoughts still on Daniel who has disappeared into his room.

"Hey, what's up?" Dominic asks. He side hugs me and drags me onto the sofa.

I lean into him and sigh. "Nothing."

Mary smiles at me as she puts my favourite apple pie on the table. "Looks like you had a long day, sweetie," she says. "Where's Daniel?"

I sigh again. "He's in his bedroom."

Dominic laughs. "God, why are you sulking?"

I pout and grab the remote control to log into Netflix. Dominic keeps poking me and annoying me as I decide on the chick flick I want to watch. I throw him my dirtiest glare, but it merely amuses him. Daniel walks in as the movie starts and glances at us before sitting down in his usual seat on the sofa.

"Dude, what did you do to her? She's been sulking ever since she walked in," Dominic says. I glare at him and poke him, which only amuses him further. I stand up with a huff and go sit down next to Daniel, taking the remote control with me.

Mary laughs and sits down next to Dominic, occupying the seat I just vacated. "The Notebook? Good choice," she says.

I scoot closer to Daniel until our sides are touching. Usually he'd already have thrown his arm around me, but today he leans away from me a little. I'm frustrated and annoyed. He's the one who said he wanted to make things official between us, and he's the one who sent me all those messages saying he fantasised about fucking me. So why is he now the one to pull away? I guess I didn't live up to his fantasies. Maybe he lost interest now that he's had me.

I wrap my arms around myself and try my best not to over-think things. I want to focus on the movie, but my mind keeps wandering. Eventually I get up and make my way to my bedroom.

When I'm feeling this shit, the one thing that might help is a nice long soak in the tub.

I stare at myself in the mirror as I undress, unable to figure out what it is about me. Is it my figure? Is it because he doesn't like inexperienced women? I understand that sleeping with me probably isn't as exciting as sleeping with someone who knows what they're doing, but there's nothing I can do about my lack of experience.

I lie down in the tub and close my eyes, half expecting Daniel to at least come check on me, but he doesn't. Even when I get into bed hours later, he still hasn't so much as peeked into my room. My heart sinks when I eventually hear his door close opposite mine and I close my eyes, feeling dejected.

I've been chasing him all along. I've sneaked into his bedroom twice and I was the one who kissed him first. It was also me who pretty much begged him to finally fuck me. Daniel on the other hand has always kept a cautious distance between us. When I got possessive and marked his skin with countless kiss marks, he hid them and even put a plaster on the one he failed to hide with clothes alone. He didn't tell his mother that there's no way he'd be seeing anyone else, even though we signed a fidelity contract. And he didn't reject Olivia's advances. Instead, it was me he ignored. I can't keep chasing after a man that only wants me when I've worn him down. What man would deny a woman that's literally begging him to fuck her?

I curl into a ball and hug my pillow. I refuse to pity myself. I went after what I wanted, and I can't regret that, but I do need to maintain a sliver of dignity.

My heart soars when I hear my door click open and I sit up in excitement, only to be disappointed when Dominic walks in. I sigh and fall back onto my pillows, turning my back to him.

"Jeez, thanks for the warm welcome," he mutters. "First time a woman has been so disappointed to see me walk into her bedroom. Just bulldoze my ego, why don't you."

I roll my eyes and pull my blankets over my head, intent on

ignoring him. All I want right now is Daniel. I'm in no mood to entertain Dominic. I've learned the hard way that these days he only comes to me when he needs me. He sits down at the edge of my bed and pulls my blankets down to expose my face.

"Why are you in here while Daniel is in there?" he asks, tipping his head towards my door. I sit up and hug my knees. Dominic sighs and pulls me closer. He throws his arms around me and rests his chin on top of my head.

"What happened?" he asks, his voice gentle. I shake my head. What do I even say? I'm too embarrassed to admit the things I've done and the way Daniel has been avoiding and rejecting me. Dominic sighs and hugs me tighter as a tear rolls down my cheek.

"It's nothing," I whisper, my voice breaking. "I'm just... I guess I'm just insecure, that's all."

Dominic shakes his head. "Did you guys argue or something?"

I shake my head and wipe away my tears. "Okay," Dominic whispers. "What do you want to do? You wanna watch another movie? We both know you aren't going to fall asleep when you're upset."

I nod and Dominic smiles at me, his eyes sparkling with affection. He turns his back to me. "Okay, go on," he murmurs. A small smile tugs at my lips and I throw my arms around him as he lifts me onto his back like he's done since we were kids.

He carries me back into the living room and gently puts me on the sofa. I smile at him as he drapes the blankets over me and presses a kiss on top of my head.

"I'm gonna make you a cup of tea. Pick a movie in the meantime, okay?"

I nod and settle in. I'm tempted to pick a movie that'll make me cry, so I can let go of the heartache that's been gripping me, but I know Dominic will see straight through me. Eventually I settle on Die Hard, knowing that it'll keep him occupied enough not to question me too much.

Dominic hands me my cup of tea and then wraps his arms

around me, the two of us getting comfy on the sofa. He gently pats my arm while I rest my head on his shoulder, and I'm grateful to have him here with me. I wish he'd been there for me like this throughout the last few months. If he had, would things be different now? Maybe I wouldn't have embarrassed myself with Daniel as much as I have.

Thirty-Six

I'm startled awake by a loud sound and open my eyes, groaning.

"Ugh," Dominic mutters as he stretches; both of us disoriented and sleepy. Dominic squeezes his eyes closed and buries his face in my hair. The two of us are tangled together on the sofa. We spent most of last night watching one Die Hard movie after the other until we inevitably fell asleep. I sit up, still feeling drowsy, and yawn.

My eyes fall to Daniel's as I stretch, and I freeze. He's standing in front of the sofa, his arms crossed over each other and his expression carefully guarded. I glance back at Dominic and pinch him hard enough to wake him up. He yelps and sits up with an angry scowl, only to freeze like I did when he finds Daniel standing over us.

The two of us straighten and send each other an alarmed look before we both look down. I straighten my clothes, trying my best to ignore the way Daniel's gaze is burning on my skin. Like usual, I'm wearing a silk nightgown that's perhaps a bit too revealing to watch a movie in. Dominic and I definitely look as if we were up to no good.

Daniel doesn't question us. He just stares with a blank expression. He doesn't look jealous, and he doesn't look angry to find us on the sofa together. I must be crazy for wanting him to lose it. I expected him to demand an explanation, but he doesn't.

"Breakfast is ready," he says, and my heart sinks. He finds me lying on the sofa intimately entwined with Dominic and that's all he says?

I nod at him, and he walks away, presumably back to the kitchen. I fall back onto the sofa and throw my arm over my face. That's all? If it were me, I'd already be losing my shit. How much longer will I deceive myself? How much longer will I trick myself into believing that he feels the same way I do?

Daniel is reading the paper when Dominic and I finally make it to the dining room, both of us dragging our feet. Though neither one of us would admit to it, we both hoped he'd be done with breakfast and back in his bedroom by the time we made it to the dining room. But no such luck. He's sat in his usual seat in his usual pyjama bottoms, his torso bare and a newspaper in his hands. He glances up briefly as we walk in and then looks back down. Dominic looks at me questioningly, but I ignore his gaze.

Dominic and I eat in silence, neither one of us able to get much down. Daniel doesn't say a thing. He just sits there and stares at his newspaper. Eventually, I clear my throat to catch his attention.

"Uh, about just now... Dominic and I were just watching movies last night and fell asleep on the sofa," I murmur, feeling oddly guilty. Daniel glances at me and nods before turning back to his newspaper.

"It's fine. I don't care," he says.

I freeze. "You don't care?" I repeat slowly.

He sighs and puts his newspaper down. "What is it, Alyssa?" His tone and the way he looks at me makes me feel like I'm a petulant teenager.

Dominic stands up in an attempt to interrupt our impending argument. "Uh, Lyss. I thought maybe we could go swimming today? Let's lounge by the pool. What do you think?"

he says. He seems nervous and I sigh. I don't want to drag him into any issues I might have with Daniel, especially because he isn't to blame. Things between Daniel and I have been weird all week.

"Hmm, yeah, sure," I murmur. Daniel picks his newspaper back up as though he's relieved our conversation has ended. He doesn't even glance at us as Dominic drags me out of the dining room.

"Jeez. What the hell is going on with you guys?" he asks. I shake my head. I don't even know what's going on, so how am I supposed to answer?

I walk into my bedroom and my mind flashes back to the way Daniel ripped off my red bikini. He told me he didn't even want Dominic thinking about me, so why is he so unfazed to find me asleep on the sofa with him?

I grab a coral-coloured bikini I've had for years. I've kept it at the Devereaux mansion ever since I was sixteen, and I definitely don't fit into it as well anymore. It's far tighter and revealing than it was years ago, but it should work for what I have in mind.

I smile to myself as I make my way back to the dining room, wearing nothing but my bikini. I purposely left my robe in my bedroom. I'm relieved to find Daniel still sitting in the same seat I left him in. He glances up when I walk in and does a double take.

"You wanna come swimming with us?" I ask, walking right up to him. His eyes darken and he reaches for me without thinking. His hand wraps around my waist and he bites down on his lips as his eyes drop to my chest.

"The weather is great, and we don't have a pool in our apartment. Might as well make use of the one here. Who knows how long we'll be able to enjoy this weather."

Daniel blinks and then looks up at me, his expression unreadable. "Hmm, I think I will," he says. I grin and walk away, giving him a spectacular view of my ass, most of which is on display thanks to this itty bitty suit.

Dominic is already doing laps when I make it to the pool. He stops and swims towards me as I lower myself on the ladder. He takes one look at my bikini and bursts out laughing.

"Let me guess. You walked past my brother looking like that?"

I bite down on my lip and look away, a blush slowly spreading on my cheeks. "Not a bad call," Dominic says. His eyes drop back to my body and there's a flicker of appreciation in them before he looks away, but I don't miss the regret he tries to hide.

He grabs my hand and pulls me towards the unicorn float the staff have put in the water for us. "Your love for floats is so child-ish," he tells me, grinning.

I punch his arm, and he laughs. I try my best to lift myself onto the unicorn, but it keeps slipping away and I fall back into the water. Dominic laughs and lifts me into his arms. I throw my arms around his neck and I glare at him.

"Keep looking at me that way and I'll throw you back in the water instead of helping you up the horse."

I roll my eyes. "It's a unicorn, dumbass."

He bends his knees suddenly, making me feel like he's drop-ping me, and I squeal as I tighten my arms around his neck. He laughs as I throw him another dirty look. "Asshole," I mutter.

Dominic grins at me mischievously and I shake my head. "Don't you dare!" I shout, as he drops me into the water. I stand up, coughing, and kick his shin. I nearly slip in the process, but it's worth it.

Movement behind Dominic catches my attention and my eyes land on Daniel. He's changed into swim shorts and he's staring at Dominic and me with his arms crossed. His expression is blank, and I can't tell whether he's even remotely angry or jealous.

Dominic and I both turn to him as he makes his way into the pool. He swims towards us leisurely and stands up in front of me. The water glides down his skin and I'm a goner. He looks sexy as hell as he pulls a hand through his wet hair.

"Struggling to get onto the float, Lyss?" he asks as he tips his head towards my unicorn. I nod and he smiles as he takes a step closer to me. He bends down and lifts me into his arms before

196

placing me on top of the unicorn. I'm disappointed when his hands don't linger on my skin.

Instead, he turns away and starts swimming laps. Dominic grins at me before he follows his brother. I lie back on my float and close my eyes, soaking up the sun until Dominic and Daniel eventually swim back towards me.

As soon as he's within reach, Dominic grabs my arm and yanks me off the float. I cough out water as I stand up to find him already on my float.

"You asshole," I shout. I push at him, intent on shoving him off, but he holds on for dear life.

Daniel throws his arms around my waist and pulls me back and away from Dominic. I struggle against him and kick the float in one last attempt to dislodge Dominic before Daniel pulls me out of reach.

He laughs and pulls me flush against him, my back to his chest. "It's fine, Lyss. Just let him have it for a while. Why don't we go soak in the jacuzzi for a bit?" I glare at Dominic and follow Daniel to the jacuzzi next to the pool. I sigh in delight as I sink into the heat. One of the staff members hands me a glass of mango juice and I close my eyes as I lean back in my seat, my back pressed up against one of the jets.

"You look like you're enjoying that," Daniel says. I glance at him, surprised that he's speaking to me at all. I'd already mentally prepared myself for him giving me the silent treatment. I'm not sure how to feel about his behaviour now. Usually when he's jealous or hurt, he'll pull away from me. Does that mean he doesn't care about finding me with Dominic this morning?

"I am," I tell him. "The jets are amazing. It's like getting a tiny massage."

He holds his hand out to me, and I grab it instinctively. He suddenly pulls me out of my seat and onto his lap. I yelp, which only makes him laugh. Within seconds he's got his arms wrapped around me, my butt nestled onto his lap.

"You — what are you doing?"

Daniel nuzzles my neck. "I'm sorry," he whispers. "I didn't stop to think about how my behaviour would affect you, and I broke one of the promises I made you. I didn't communicate well at all. It took my brother snapping at me before I realised what I did to you. I'm sorry, baby."

I stiffen in his arms, unsure of how to respond. "I was worried. I was scared I'd hurt you again. I know having sex wasn't even remotely enjoyable for you, and I didn't want to put you through that again. I stopped you every time because I didn't want you to do anything out of obligation."

He stands up and turns me around before pulling me back to him as he sits back down. I fall onto his chest and find myself straddling him, my legs wide open. He pulls me close and leans back in his seat.

"I always want you, Alyssa. Always. But I never want to put you in a position where you're doing something just because you think I might want or expect it."

He cups my cheek gently and pulls my face close to his. I subconsciously freeze and wait to see what he'll do. When his lips find mine, I relax against him and kiss him back. His hands roam over my body before eventually settling on my ass, and he leans forward a little more to shift me right on top of his erection. He moans into my mouth and grips me tighter.

Part of me is still in disbelief. Part of me still believes he'll pull away soon. That he won't do more than kiss me. But then one of his fingers slips underneath my bikini bottoms and right into me. I moan and pull away from him, gasping for air and overcome with desire. Daniel grins as he plays with me, the two of us mostly obscured by the jacuzzi's bubbles. We're so wrapped up in each other that we forget we aren't alone.

Dominic pulls us back into the present by throwing a bucket of water over our heads. I jump away from Daniel and glare at Dominic, but he merely sticks out his tongue and runs away.

"Hmm, well, I guess we had that one coming," Daniel says.

Thirty-Seven

I'm still cursing Dominic as I walk into the shower. That's the closest Daniel has gotten to me all week, only for it to end like that.

"Ugh!" I shout, unaware that I'm no longer alone. Daniel steps into the shower with a wide smile on his face.

"What's got you so frustrated, baby?" he asks.

I look at him with wide eyes, my eyes roaming over his body. It feels like forever ago since I last saw him naked. He walks up to me and I take a step back until my back hits the wall. Daniel grins and lowers his lips to mine. "Now where were we?" he whispers, right before he kisses me.

His body slams against mine and he moans when I snap out of my stupor and kiss him back. He lifts me into his arms and pushes me against the wall as I wrap my legs around him. "Fuck. I missed your body. You have no idea how hard it was for me to stay away from you. I'm fucking craving you so badly," he groans.

Daniel buries a hand in my hair and tugs on it to expose my neck. A delicious shiver runs down my body as he bites and kisses me in places I didn't even know were sensitive. I subconsciously tilt my hips, bucking against him in an attempt to make him slide in. He shifts out of reach and it's like getting cold water thrown on me all over again. Daniel feels the change in me and pulls away a little to look at me.

"Babe," he whispers.

I shake my head, grateful that the shower disguises the tears that have started to fall down my cheeks. "Just put me down," I snap.

Daniel shakes his head. "No," he murmurs. He turns the shower off and walks out with me in his arms, both of us dripping wet. He sits me down on my bed and wraps me in a towel as he sinks to his knees in front of me. I didn't even notice him grab a towel. He's incredibly gentle as he carefully dries me off, ignoring all my protests.

"I can do it myself," I mutter and try to grab the towel from him. He shakes his head and scowls at me when I yank the towel out of his hands.

"Looks like you're going to be difficult. Very well," he says as he stands up and walks to my wardrobe butt naked.

He walks back holding one of the scarves Mary gave me and grins. He's hard, naked and gorgeous. I hate that I feel a tingle of desire at the mere sight of him.

Daniel lifts me into his arms and repositions me on my bed so I'm lying flat on my back. He grabs my wrists and ties them up so quickly that I don't have time to fight him.

"Daniel, release me," I say, sounding tired.

He shakes his head and ties my wrists to my bed frame. "I seem to recall you doing the same thing to me with one of my ties. Payback's a bitch, huh, Lyss?"

I stare at him, speechless. Daniel merely smiles at me and yanks my towel away, letting it fall to the floor. He looks at me hungrily and leans in to kiss me. I move my head away and for a second Daniel's expression falls. But then he smiles to himself and kisses my neck instead, slowly and softly. It's not like in the shower, when his movements were frantic. Instead, it's gentle and loving. He keeps kissing me until I'm out of breath and needy. When he moves back to my lips, I kiss him eagerly. He chuckles against my lips and deepens the kiss, torturing me until I'm panting and moaning.

He keeps his lips on mine while his hand slides down my body. His finger slips into me easily and he freezes. "Fuck," he groans. "So fucking wet."

He slips another finger into me and I arch my back to try and get him in deeper. I'm surprised when he pulls away from me. He reaches underneath my pillow and grabs something that definitely wasn't there before.

"Dan, what's that?"

He smiles at me sheepishly as he fidgets with the bottle, unwrapping the plastic around it. "It's... uh... it's lube."

I stare at him in disbelief, totally confused. "Dan, I don't think we need that," I tell him quietly.

He shakes his head and gulps. "I googled it. I think it hurt so much because maybe you weren't wet enough..."

I bite back a smile and tug on my restraints. "Baby, could you please undo this?" I ask.

Daniel hesitates and then nods. I wrap my arms around his neck and pull him in for a kiss as soon as my hands are free.

"What exactly did you google?"

He clears his throat and hides his rapidly reddening face in my neck, his weight nice and comforting on top of me.

"I just googled why sex might hurt, and what we could potentially do to make it better for you. Maybe you just weren't turned on enough, or maybe you weren't wet enough. For some people it hurts the first handful of times, but it seems like lube might help."

I close my eyes and try my best not to laugh at how incredibly cute he's being. "I see," I whisper. "Dan... it didn't hurt that much last time. Only at the start, and then it got better. I was just uncomfortable because of your size. I wasn't in pain. I just kind of felt overly stretched out. Honey, the lube isn't going to make a difference. There's no way I could possibly get wetter or more turned on."

He pushes himself up to look at me and my heart flutters.

He's so cute. He looks so distraught and caring. I cup his cheeks and bring his lips to mine. He kisses me gently and my heart overflows with tenderness. It's not until I rake my nails over his scalp that he deepens the kiss. His hands start to wander and he plays with my nipples as his tongue tangles with mine. Every touch sends a burst of liquid fire through my body, making me wetter and wetter. I can feel my arousal moisten the inside of my thighs and smile to myself. How could he possibly think I wasn't turned on enough?

Daniel's fingers finally find their way back between my legs, and he slips two fingers in with ease. My entire body jerks when he slides against my g-spot and he grins against my lips. He kisses me harder as he slides another finger inside me, stretching me out as he keeps stimulating me. I moan and pull my lips away.

"Baby, I want you," I tell him. Daniel pauses with his fingers still inside me and looks at me. He looks so overcome with desire, so passionate and so desperate to have me. Yet he still shakes his head.

"No," he says, sounding agonised. "Let me make you come first."

I smile at him and press a lingering kiss to his lips. "Hmm, Google tell you to do that?"

He blushes and pushes against my g-spot harder, almost making me come right there and then. I moan loudly and shift my body out of his grasp. Instead of letting him touch me, I grab his dick and line it up to me. His entire body tenses and he groans.

"I need you now, Daniel. Won't you fuck me? Won't you slide into your soaking wet wife?"

His lips fall open and he stares at me in shock before he grins and pushes into me ever so slightly. He pauses when the tip is in and glances at his bottle of lube. He looks worried and pained.

I chuckle and pull him on top of me, kissing him with all I've got. I tilt my hips up and take him in as far as I can. Daniel moans and thrusts the remaining bit into me, unrestrained and out of control. He pauses immediately after and looks at me panicked.

"Shit, Lyss. I'm sorry. I did it again. Fuck. Did it hurt? Are you okay?"

I shut him up by kissing him, and he relaxes on top of me. "I'm fine," I whisper.

Daniel looks at me and frowns. "Fine?" he repeats, almost fearfully. I chuckle and lean back.

"I'm perfect, baby. Please, Daniel. Will you give it to me or not?"

He exhales in relief and pulls back out almost all the way and then pushes back into me fully. I moan loudly and bite down on my lips to try and silence myself.

"Fuck," I groan. Daniel smiles and fucks me slowly as his lips find mine. He kisses me as the two of us lose ourselves in each other.

"Dan, it's so fucking good. Don't stop," I whisper. He chuckles and bites down on my lower lip. He pulls away from me and grabs my legs, pushing them over his shoulder and I moan in delight.

"Hmm, seems like those yoga classes of yours were worth it after all," he says. He pulls back and thrusts again, but this time he stimulates my g-spot with every thrust.

"Is this okay, Lyss? Does it hurt? Is it too deep?"

I shake my head, almost incapable of forming a response. Daniel grins and fucks me harder. The louder my moans get, the closer he seems to get.

"Daniel... I — I can't hold it," I groan. He increases his pace and comes seconds after I do, my name on his lips.

He grins at me and hugs me tightly, both of us satisfied. "You stayed away because you were scared of hurting me?"

His grip on me tightens and he nods tersely. I sigh and cuddle into him. "Baby, why didn't you just talk to me? If you'd told me, then I wouldn't have started to overthink everything. I thought the sex was so bad that you didn't want to sleep with me again."

Daniel pulls away to look at me, disbelief written all over his face. "What the fuck, Alyssa. How could you possibly think that?

Fuck. Do you know how bad I felt knowing that the worst sex you've ever had, is the best sex I've ever had?"

I pull him back to me and kiss him. "Hmm, well, I didn't know sex could be this good. You know, we're spending a couple of days in Singapore next week. How about you show me what I've been missing out on?"

Daniel's eyes darken with desire and I already know our trip is going to be one to remember.

Thirty-Eight

I'm oddly nervous as we board the plane. Daniel and I have cabins next to each other while Kate's is further down. I'm worried she'll catch on to us. Paying attention to minor details is literally her job. It won't take her long to figure us out. She'll only be with us for a few days, though. Right until the contracts are signed.

I'm quiet as the flight attendant converts our seats into a double bed. Daniel lies down and pulls me over. "What's going on, Lyss? You haven't spoken a word in hours. Are you tired?"

He massages my shoulders and my eyes fall closed. I sigh in delight. "No, not tired. Just kind of worried. What if Kate finds out about us? And what about our accommodation? She probably booked us two different rooms." Just the idea of being away from him for a single night annoys me. Daniel smiles at me and tugs a loose strand of my hair behind my ear.

"That's what you're worried about? You don't want her to find out?"

I look up at him, startled. "I mean... yeah, we're keeping our relationship a secret, right?"

Daniel looks dismayed, and suddenly I wonder whether he might actually be okay with her knowing. "I guess so," he murmurs. He turns away from me and lies down as he scrolls through the list of movies absentmindedly.

I sit up on my knees and tug on his clothes. "Hey, do you wanna join the mile high club?" I ask. I bite down on my lip and blush furiously. Daniel stops sulking and grins. He jumps on top of me and tackles me down to the bed. I laugh at his response, but my smile melts off my face as a sudden thought occurs to me.

"Hey, you haven't, right? You — have you ever..."

Daniel kisses me and shakes his head. "Nope. Never. You'll be my first and only, Lyss." I giggle and throw my arms around him. Both of us are impatient as we frantically undress each other. I'm hyperaware of every single movement on the plane and try my very best to stay quiet.

"Thank god I'll have at least one of your firsts," I murmur. Daniel sinks inside me and covers my lips with his hands.

"Shh, baby," he whispers, smothering my moans. I giggle against his lips and he kisses me to keep me quiet. Neither one of us lasts long. Within minutes, Daniel is the one that's struggling to keep quiet. He looks at me and bites down on his lip the way he does when he's trying his best to hold on.

"Come for me, Dan," I whisper. His body stiffens and his lips fall open as he fills me up. He pulls out of me immediately and finds my clit with his fingers, sending me over the edge within seconds.

The two of us collapse against each other and he kisses my forehead, his arms wrapped around me. He turns so he's on his back and I'm half on top of him, my leg over his.

"You've had so many of my firsts," he whispers. "You're the first girl I ever bought flowers and chocolates for, other than my mum. The first girl to sit in my car after I got my license. The first and only girl I've ever picked up drunk at a nightclub." He chuckles at the last one and presses a lingering kiss to my lips. "You're the only girl I've ever taken to the ballet and the only one I've ever sat and watched movies with on my sofa. You're also the only girl I've ever cooked for and the only one to have entered my apartment. It's a sacred space to me, and I've only ever shared it with you, your dad, and my family. You might not have had my every first, but you'll have all my lasts. You'll be the last girl I'll ever sleep with. The last one I'll ever take on dates and the last one I'll ever kiss."

My heart soars at his words. If only that were all true. We both know our marriage won't last. It came with an expiration date straight from the start, and by the time it's over he'll be relieved to get out. I know Daniel well enough to know that he doesn't like commitment and that his relationships don't last long.

He seems to sense my insecurity and kisses me, hugging me tightly as we both drift to sleep.

Thirty-Nine

Daniel is tense as we check into our hotel. He seems annoyed and keeps glancing at me as though he's waiting to see what I'll do. My stomach flutters at the idea that it might be because he doesn't want to hide our relationship. Daniel has never publicly admitted to having a partner, even though he's often been photographed with women. As far as I remember, he hasn't called a single one of them his girlfriend in the last couple of years. I automatically assumed he'd treat me the same way, but what if that isn't the case?

Kate looks at us awkwardly. It's obvious that something is wrong and I feel bad for saddling her with an atmosphere she had no hand in creating.

"Um, this is yours, Alyssa," she says, handing me a room card. She then hands another one to Daniel while she holds onto the last one. I glare at the card in my hands.

"Is everything okay?" she asks, frowning. I blink and nod at her.

"Yes. Of course."

Daniel stares down at the floor the entire time. He seems dejected but doesn't say anything all the way up to our rooms.

Daniel and I are on the same floor, but at other ends. I hesitate before I finally walk to my own room.

I sit down on my bed in the lavishly decorated room and stare at my suitcase. It only takes me a couple of minutes to realise I'm being an idiot. I smile to myself and drag my suitcase back out of my room. I press the bell by Daniel's door and wait. Minutes pass by and I worry he won't open the door. What if he's mad at me?

I sigh in relief when the door opens, and a flustered Daniel appears. He's wearing a bathrobe and his hair is still wet. He glances at me and then at my suitcase, a wide smile transforming his face. He doesn't say anything. Instead, he opens the door and drags my suitcase in for me, putting it next to his own. I walk into his arms and press my face against his chest. He hugs me back tightly.

"I'm sorry," I murmur. "I was being stupid. I wasn't thinking at all. I lasted about three seconds before I realised I can't spend a whole night without you."

Daniel leans in and kisses me. His eyes are dark and passionate when he pulls away. "Thank god, because I was about ten minutes away from cancelling my room and joining you in yours."

I look around his room and laugh. "You're crazy. You should've just thrown me over your shoulder and shown me this suite. Not a chance I'd want to stay in my room then."

Daniel laughs. "Hmm. I was going to tell you something's wrong with my room and they're fully booked, so I have to stay with you."

I grin. "You really thought that one through, huh?"

He looks so cute as he blushes and looks away. I push away from him and move to unpack my suitcase in the bedroom. I slept through my allocated shower time on the plane and didn't end up showering. I feel icky and tired.

By the time I walk out of the shower, Kate's voice and the smell of delicious food fills the suite. I change quickly and join them on the balcony. She looks surprised to find me here, probably because the doorbell didn't ring and she didn't let me in.

"Hey, come sit," Daniel says, patting the seat next to his. I nod and smile at him as he pushes a plate towards me. "I got the wagyu and the sea bass. Couldn't choose between them, so I thought we'd share.". I nod and take a bite of the fish as he pours me a glass of wine.

"Feel better now?" he asks. I nod and smile at him. It's a knowing and intimate smile. Over the years I've come to learn some of Daniel's character traits, and this is one I know well. It's one he used on my dad a lot. He's not going to bother hiding our relationship from Kate, but he doesn't know how to tell me he wants it out in the open either. He's had to learn the hard way that the only effective way to deal with Moriani obtuseness is by ignoring our silliness altogether. Both my dad and I can be stubborn even when we know we're wrong.

"Hmm, good," I murmur, nodding at him. I glance at Kate and smile at her. "Was the flight okay for you?" I ask. She nods but glances at me, looking confused. I've always treated Daniel politely, even in private, so it's probably confusing for her to find us smiling at each other in such a relaxed manner.

Daniel places his hand on my thigh, and I bite down on my lip. He's definitely going to make it hard for me to keep this from her. Very well. I steal a bite of food from his plate and Kate's eyes widen. She clears her throat. "Is your room to your liking, Alyssa?" she asks. She keeps glancing between me and Daniel, her brows furrowed.

"Well, to be honest, I like this one more." I turn to Daniel and smile at him. "Why don't you let me have this room," I ask, a dazzling smile on my face.

He blinks at me, his expression softening. "Hmm, it's yours."

Kate looks at me in disbelief. She glances at Daniel and genuinely looks worried about him. I just about keep myself from laughing. Looking at her, you'd think I'm taking advantage of him somehow.

Daniel lifts his fork to his lips and I grab his wrist, closing my lips around his fork and stealing his food. He chuckles and brushes a strand of my hair out of my face.

"You want it?" he asks, pushing his plate towards me. I shake my head. "Just wanted a bite."

He leans back and puts his arm around the back of my seat. "By the way, if you wanted to book any tours for our holiday afterwards, just let Kate know," he says, a wicked grin on his face.

I shake my head and smile at him. "Hmm, you're going to make it impossible, aren't you? Are you gonna be like this throughout the entire trip?" I ask. Daniel grins and bites down on his lip, looking ridiculously cute and unapologetic.

Kate looks at us blankly. "Oh, yes! I'm looking forward to spending some free time here. That was a really good idea, Daniel. You're the absolute best," she gushes. "What should we do?" she asks, looking excited.

My smile drops, and I look up at him. She's staying with us? I thought she'd leave straight after our work here was done. I cross my arms over my chest, suddenly annoyed. I was looking forward to spending some time together, just the two of us. Daniel chuckles at my irritation and throws his arm around me. He leans in and presses a quick kiss to my cheek, startling both me and Kate.

He turns to her and smiles apologetically. "I'm sorry, Kate. I promised my girl some alone time," he says, glancing at me. "Cancel Alyssa's room while you're at it. She'll be staying with me."

Kate looks at us in disbelief, and then she smiles, surprising me. "You two finally got together, huh? Good for you," she says, her eyes twinkling.

I look away, embarrassed. Part of me still thought something had been going on between her and Daniel, but it looks like I was definitely wrong. Daniel visibly relaxes now that she knows, and my heart flutters. I'd been so certain he'd want to keep us a secret, and I'm pleasantly surprised to find I was wrong.

Forty

"You're truly as beautiful as my father claimed you were," Sasuke says, smiling at me. Daniel's fingers tighten around his glass. He's been putting up with Sasuke's blatant flirting all evening, and I'm worried he'll snap soon.

Mr. Takuya smiles at his son and nods. "Alyssa is very clever and very beautiful. You should date a girl like her. All you do is work, work, work. You should give me a grandchild to play with now that I'm retired."

Daniel grits his teeth and smiles. "Hmm, there aren't many women like my Alyssa," he says, wrapping his arm around me in a clear warning. The father and son look at him, startled. Daniel has kept his calm all evening and has been ignoring all of Sasuke's flirting, but I've noticed him grow more and more agitated.

Mr. Takuya looks at me and then back at Daniel. He then proceeds to pour Daniel a glass of sake and pushes it towards him. "You've done well, son," he says, laughing. Mr. Takuya being here means we probably won't get anything signed and done. He prefers to socialise and drink first and do business after. I was hoping it'd be different with his son. Daniel is already well on his way to being drunk, and I'm definitely tipsy.

Mr. Takuya surprises me when he eventually nods at me with

a serious look in his eyes. "I read your proposal, Alyssa. I was very impressed. You inherited your father's mind. If you work on the project personally, then Sasuke and I will sign the contract."

I smile at him gratefully and try my best to hide my surprise. "I'm honoured you think so highly of me, Mr. Takuya. My father would be proud to hear your words. I'll be sure to work on your campaign myself. I'll make sure to live up to your expectations."

He nods, and it's done. I know he'll sign the contract if he's given his word. Sasuke doesn't look annoyed at all when his father makes a decision that should be his. Instead, he looks somewhat contrite, as though he knows it's the right call and he's glad he didn't have to make it himself. His father claps him on the back and all of us share another shot of sake to seal the deal.

By the time we stumble back into our hotel room, Daniel seems frustrated, even though we accomplished what we came here to do in far less time than expected. He grabs me as soon as the door closes behind us and pushes me against it. He kisses me harshly before pulling away.

"I need to put a ring on you, Wifey," he says. "A tiny little collar for your finger. I'm sick and tired of men hanging around you, coveting what is mine."

His lips trail over my neck before they return to my lips. "A wedding ring?" I ask, my heart hammering. Could it be? I doubt Daniel would ever consider such an obvious display of commitment.

"Yeah," he answers, seemingly excited about the idea.

He buries his hands in my hair. "We still have some time. It's only 10pm. Is there anything you'd still like to do?" he asks.

We have three more days here, and neither one of us wants to waste a single second of it. I mentally go through my list of to do's in my head. "The thing I wanted to do most was to see the light show at the Gardens by the Bay, but I think we're too late now. We might've already missed it."

Daniel chuckles and grabs his phone as he strokes my cheek.

"Baby, if there's something you want, then I'll make it happen. Let me make a call. You go get changed."

True to his word, an hour later we're standing in the middle of a closed park, no one else around us. We sit back and watch the light show that they've put on just for us. How he's made it happen is beyond me. Daniel isn't known for misusing his status or his wealth, and usually I love that about him, but tonight I'm flattered and honoured he did this for me.

He wraps his arm around me, pulling me close. "So, is it everything you thought it would be?"

I shake my head and kiss his cheek. "Better. It's even better."

Forty-One

Daniel proudly holds my hand as we roam through the streets. Holding hands in public is something we don't really do back home, and it wasn't until we started doing it here that I realised how much I enjoy it. Daniel intertwines his fingers with mine and pulls me along as we explore Haji Lane.

We sit down at one of the outdoor tables and Daniel pulls out his phone, taking what's gotta be the hundredth photo of us together. We're like two tourists that are travelling outside of their own country for the first time. I pose with the laksa I just ordered and Daniel laughs as he takes a photo. He snaps another few of me taking a bite of the noodles and I have to snatch his phone from him to get him to stop.

"I love this place. We should just move here," I murmur.

Daniel smiles at me wistfully. "Hmm, I wish. What would happen to Devereaux Inc. and DM if we just moved?"

I sigh and nod at him. "Hmm, I know. I was just kidding. I'm just having such a great time here. I definitely want to come back."

Daniel nods. "We can look into buying some property here if you want?"

I nod thoughtfully. "Might actually be a good idea."

The mere idea of buying a house with Daniel excites me. The apartment we currently live in is his. It's a place he picked and decorated himself. While I've been able to add personal touches, it still isn't really mine as much as it is his.

Daniel holds my hand as we continue to scroll down the countless alleys until we end up on a big road again. He glances at a large jewellery store and drags me towards it.

"Let's go have a look," he murmurs. The security guard lets us in, and Daniel immediately moves towards the counter with the rings. "I know we never did rings, but if our marriage was different... If you'd been proposed to with a ring, what would you have liked?"

The question makes my heart ache. Even though I'm beyond happy with Daniel, it does sometimes feel like I missed out on a lot. We didn't really date and then discuss marriage. I've never fantasised about how he might propose, or what ring he might choose. I didn't get to pick bridesmaids or go on a bachelorette party, and I didn't walk down the aisle with a heart full of love. "This," I say, pointing at the three carat cushion cut diamond with the pave band. I've always known what kind of ring I might want one day, but I doubt a true proposal is something I'll ever get to experience.

Daniel nods and asks the clerk to take it out for him. "Oh, no. I don't want to try it," I say, my mood souring instantly.

"Hmm, we're here anyway. We might as well," Daniel says. I shake my head and turn to walk out of the store, suddenly annoyed. I don't want to be reminded of how we started our marriage. I don't want to be reminded that it might end.

"Hey, what's wrong, babe?"

Daniel runs after me and throws his arm around my shoulder. I shake my head and rise on my tiptoes to press a kiss on his cheek. "It's nothing, honey. Come on. Let's go to the hotel. I can't wait to spend the afternoon in the pool. It's been on my bucket list forever."

Daniel fusses over me as we make our way back to our hotel. I'm giddy with excitement. It's almost like we're newlyweds on our honeymoon and I love the feeling. The two of us take dozens of photos together and of each other. The staff indulges us and takes one photo after the other without complaint.

Daniel has champagne delivered to the pool and we toast. "To us," he says, reminding me of the dinner date he took me on early in our marriage. It's crazy how quickly time has flown by.

"To us," I say, clinking my glass to his. Daniel and I spend the afternoon in the pool, drinking champagne and cocktails. Afterwards we hole up in our room, entangled in our bedsheets. We got out of bed once, and that was just to order room service.

Forty-Two

"Alyssa, could you look this over and sign here please," Jake says. I sigh and look up at him, annoyed that he's interrupting my daydreams about Singapore. I'm not pleased to be back at work. Daniel and I were in our own little cocoon over there, and it felt great. It was just us. No work. No distractions. Just the two of us and endless great weather.

I scan through his report and initial it before handing it back to him. Jake has a million questions for me today, and so does the rest of my team. I expected them to function better than they did without me.

"I'm sorry," Linda says. "I promise we all tried our best, but usually if the boss isn't here, then you're here to help us. This time you both weren't here."

I nod and take the stack of papers she gives me, my annoyance slowly but surely climbing. Just going through the mountain of issues that occurred last week takes me half the morning. Then there's my email inbox that's overflowing.

I groan when the messaging system pings and rest my forehead on my desk. As if it's not enough that my own department keeps harassing me. I click on the message and smile when I realise it's Daniel.

. . .

Daniel Devereaux: I can't stop thinking about you. It's only been a few hours since we've been apart and I miss you already.

I smile to myself and try my best to keep from blushing. He's developed a penchant for saying the cheesiest things to me lately.

Alyssa Carter: *Aren't you in a client meeting?*

Daniel Devereaux: *I am in the meeting, but I can't focus on it at all. I need you... alone... in my office.*

Alyssa Carter: *I fucking wish. I miss you too, baby. Too much work to do, though. I have a literal pile of documents on my desk and 300 emails to get to. I'm not even exaggerating.*

The mere idea of getting Daniel alone makes me smile. While in Singapore, I finally found out what the rumours about him are based on. The man is insatiable. But then again, I'm just as bad. Thinking about being alone with him has me clenching my thighs.

By the time he walks back into the office, he looks grumpy, and I'm sure my own expression mirrors his. "Lyss, a word please," he says, his tone biting.

I frown and follow him into his office. Daniel slams the door closed behind him and then slams my body against it, his lips crashing down on mine. He kisses me with impatience and desperation, and I kiss him back just as eagerly. Daniel pulls away from me only long enough to carry me to his desk. He shoves a bunch of things on the floor without looking and puts me down. I open his zipper as he shoves my underwear out of the way and slides a finger inside me.

"Now," I pant. "Need you now."

Daniel groans and sinks inside me deeply. I close my eyes and lean back, but Daniel isn't having it. He grabs my hand and pushes it between us, urging me to touch myself as he fucks me. I moan and kiss him, the two of us moving together frantically.

"Alyssa, fuck. I fucking adore every single piece of you."

He thrusts into me hard and fast, and I can barely think straight. It doesn't take us long to lose control and shatter. I giggle against his lips as we both try to catch our breath. Daniel does his best to straighten out my hair and I help him zip up while he helps me fix my clothes. The two of us are giddy with excitement and deeply satiated.

"I thought you needed a word," I murmur.

Daniel laughs and kisses me deeply. "Hmm, I did. The word was now. Please would've worked too."

I glare at him and shake my head. "I have to get back to work. No more of this. We're at work, you know."

Daniel sighs. "Does it matter? Who cares if people know about us. I mean, yeah, we probably shouldn't get caught having sex in my office... But you know."

I frown contemplatively. "I'm not sure. I don't even tell people at work my actual name. I can't really imagine sharing my relationship with colleagues. I think work and private life should be kept separate as much as possible."

Daniel looks annoyed but nods at me as he starts to tidy his desk. I sigh and walk out, feeling oddly unsettled.

The hours fly by and it seems like Daniel is doing his best to stay away from me. He tries his best to keep things professional between us, but we've gotten so used to each other that it's hard. We've gotten even closer while we were in Singapore. He hardly let go of my hand while we were there, and he'd sneak kisses and small touches in the entire time. It's hard for me to stay away from him too.

"Hmm, this," he says, pointing at something on my screen. He's standing behind me and leans over the back of my chair, his face close to mine. "Those numbers don't add up," he murmurs. I turn and my lips graze his cheek. Daniel smiles at me, his eyes twinkling. I blush and move away from him a little, flustered.

"Boss, maybe I can help you instead. Alyssa is quite busy," Jake says. He looks tense as his gaze shifts between me and Daniel.

Daniel stiffens and pulls away from me. He looks troubled, and I instantly feel guilty. It's not surprising that our proximity makes Jake uncomfortable, and in any other circumstance I would've thanked him for intervening. Right now, though, I'm anything but grateful. Daniel grits his teeth and straightens.

"It's quite all right. I'll do it myself, Jake." I turn to Daniel, who looks irked and refuses to look at me. I understand his frustration. As my boyfriend, he's not doing anything wrong, but as my boss he is. Daniel sulks for the rest of the day, and nothing I do or say cheers him up.

"Hey, will you be okay?" Jake says as he grabs his bag.

I glance at my watch and nod. "Yeah, of course."

He glances at Daniel's office and it takes me a while to realise what he's worried about. He doesn't want to leave me alone with Daniel? How crazy. "Uh, okay then. I'll see you tomorrow, Alyssa," he says.

I nod and glance around me to find the entire office empty. It's not uncommon for me to be the last one to leave, but today time really did fly by. Daniel walks out of his office with a document in hand and pauses as he looks around. He's equally surprised to find everyone gone and glances at his watch. I chuckle, because his reaction is exactly the same as mine. We have so much work to catch up on after our little holiday that neither one of us realised how late it'd gotten.

"Hmm. Now that we're alone, I guess I can finally touch you," he snaps. "Or can't I sit too close to you while we're at the office? Can I smile at you? Is that okay, or is that also not allowed?"

I sigh as he walks to my desk with the biggest scowl on his face. I take the document he's handing me and stand up.

"It's not like that, Dan."

He glares at me and I've gotta admit it makes my heart ache a little to see him so mad. "Isn't it?" he asks.

He grabs my hand and pulls me close before he changes his mind and turns me around so my back is facing him. He pushes against my shoulders and I stumble, bracing myself on Linda's desk. Daniel parts my legs with his knee and pushes on my lower back to keep me down while he grabs my hair and yanks it back. It doesn't hurt at all, but it turns me on like crazy. He chuckles when a small moan escapes my lips.

Daniel traces his finger down the back of my thighs and yanks my skirt up, exposing my ass. "Hmm, what a fucking view," he whispers. I yelp when he suddenly slaps my ass, the sound reverberating through the office. I clench my thighs and close my eyes. I didn't think that would turn me on, but it does. Daniel slaps my ass again, on the other side this time, and I moan loudly. He chuckles and pushes down my underwear, leaving it hanging mid thigh. I barely recognise the sounds that escape my lips as he pushes a finger into me.

"So needy, Alyssa. So wet. You want me, baby?"

I groan. "Yes. Yes."

Daniel chuckles and pulls away from me to open his zipper. It only takes him a couple of seconds to slide into me, but to me that felt too long. I moan in delight when he fills me up, ramming into me all the way.

"You could have my hands on you all the time if you'd just agree to go public with our relationship," he snaps.

He thrusts into me so hard that some of Linda's things fall off her desk, but neither one of us pays attention. Daniel's fingers find my clit and I ride them eagerly.

"You want to come for me, Lyss? If you tell me we can go public, I'll make you come like this every day."

I moan and trash against his fingers. "You already do anyway," I whisper. He increases the pace and pulls out almost entirely before slamming into me so hard that the desk moves.

"Say it. Say you'll be mine. I want to shout to the world that you're my girl. Tell me you want the same."

His words only add to my arousal, and I feel my inner muscles contract. I'm so close. He spanks me again when I don't reply and I come, suddenly and wildly. Daniel doesn't take much longer. Two more thrusts and he comes too, my name on his lips.

He collapses on top of me, both of us a hot mess. He pushes my hair out of the way and kisses my neck softly.

"Please, baby," he whispers. "I want everyone to know that you're mine."

I giggle and smile contently. If I'd known it meant this much to him... If I'd known he was this upset about it, I never would've asked him to keep our relationship a secret. Besides, it's not like we could keep it a secret forever. Sooner or later, the press would notice that I'm the only one he's ever seen with.

"I'm yours, honey. Tell the whole world if you must, but that won't change the fact that I'm already yours. Heart and soul, Daniel."

Forty-Three

T he atmosphere is tense when we walk into the office the next morning. Linda, Luke and Jake are all staring at us looking either shocked or concerned. Daniel and I glance at each other, neither one of us sure what's going on.

Luke suddenly jumps into action and walks towards Daniel, his hand curled into a fist. He swings and Daniel evades the hit easily. Luke is thin and puny compared to Daniel, so how he thought he'd get a hit in at all is beyond me. He grabs Luke's wrist and twists it behind him. Luke yelps in pain and I jump away from the two of them.

Linda grabs my hand and pulls me behind her as she grabs her phone with trembling hands. "I — you better stay away from Alyssa. I'm going to call the police," she says, her voice shaking. Daniel and I stare at each other in confusion. He lets go of Luke and holds his hands up in surrender.

"Can someone please tell me what's going on here?" he asks, his brows furrowed. Jake walks up to him and pushes against his chest. He fails to move Daniel and he shoves harder. I rush to get between them, but Luke grabs me before I reach them. He wraps his arms around me protectively, as if to shield me from Daniel. I push him away and stare at my colleagues, completely baffled.

"Okay, what the fuck is going on here?" I snap.

Linda looks at me with tears in her eyes. "We know, Alyssa. We know what he did to you. I'm sorry we didn't realise sooner."

I stare at her, unsure of what she's talking about. She bursts out crying and I panic. "I didn't know," she sobs. "I should've been there for you."

I grab her shoulders gently and pat her hair. "Sweetie, you need to explain to me what exactly you're talking about," I tell her, my voice soft. She sniffs and nods her head.

"This morning all my things were rearranged. The cleaners usually leave everything in the same spot, so I thought maybe someone stole something. I called security and used my credentials as an executive office member to access the security feed for our floor. And that's when I saw... I saw what he did to you."

I glance behind her as things start to click. I don't know whether to laugh or cry. There's a small window on her screen with last night's security feed. It's paused on the exact moment that Daniel spanks me. My ass is on full display and my skirt is pooled around my waist. My cheeks redden to a deep crimson and I jump to close the window entirely. I close my eyes and bury my hands in my face, not realising that that just makes it look like I'm distraught.

"I'm sorry," Linda says again. She hugs me and I pull away, moving towards Daniel. The look in his eyes breaks my heart. He looks devastated and I can see him overthinking the situation. He's probably wondering if he was too rough on me or whether he might have hurt me. Judging by our team's reactions, it seems like he violated me in the worst way. His expression tells me he's starting to wonder if he might have.

"Are you okay?" I ask Daniel. He takes a step away from me as soon as I take a step towards him, and my heart breaks even further.

I sigh and run a hand through my hair before turning back to Linda. "Did you actually watch that video? Because I was enjoying the hell out of that..."

She looks startled, and a hint of unease enters her eyes. "I —
you don't have to stand up for him. We all have your back,
Alyssa."

I sigh and look up at the ceiling. "Linda... Daniel and I are
dating. What you saw on the security feed was entirely consensual.
Hell, if that video had sound you'd know I enjoyed the hell out
of it."

She looks startled as understanding slowly begins to dawn on
her. I roll my eyes and walk up to Daniel. Without hesitating, I
throw my arms around him and pull him in for a kiss. He stands
there, frozen, but I kiss him nonetheless. "Don't you think for a
second that I didn't want that as much as you did," I whisper.

He relaxes into me and gently brushes my hair out of my face.
"I forgot about the cameras, baby. I never should've exposed you
like that. I never should've let anyone see your body like that."

I chuckle and rise to my tiptoes to press a kiss to his cheek
before turning back to my colleagues.

"Get the hell back to work, you absolute morons."

Everyone stares at us with wide eyes before they finally get
back to work. As Linda walks towards her desk, Daniel calls her
into his office. He sends me a reassuring smile when I glance at
them. I'm worried he'll reprimand her when all she did was worry
about me.

The atmosphere in the office is tense as we all try to work
despite the embarrassment. Eventually Luke clears his throat and
looks at me. "That guy... the guy you said you were dating and
that you were giggling about... it was the boss?"

I can't hide the guilt I suddenly feel and look down as I nod at
him. Maybe I should've been honest with them from the start.

"Ah... I see. I guess that makes sense," he murmurs. Jake looks
at me with eyes filled with regret and disbelief. I've been ignoring
the way he's been looking at me, and I've made sure to never
spend time with him if I don't have to. He, in return, has
respected my wishes, but it's clear that he's distraught now. I guess

he does see me as his ex-girlfriend, and finding out I'm dating Daniel is probably uncomfortable.

The morning goes by painfully slow and the silence is pressing. Just as I'm about to escape under the guise of lunch, my messaging system pops up with thirty different chats. I frown as I try my best to figure out what could have possibly happened. Almost everyone I have a close enough working relationship with has messaged me.

I click on the link in the first message and gasp as the website opens on my screen. Photos of Daniel and I in Singapore are all over the tabloids. How did they even manage to take these? Some of them are close ups of us making out in the pool, while others show us holding hands as we walk through the streets.

Hold your heart, ladies. Daniel Devereaux might soon be off the market entirely! It seems that Alyssa Moriani has stolen the Casanova's heart. Not only is Alyssa the late Charles Moriani's only daughter, she is also DM Consultancy's largest shareholder and a bona fide heiress. It makes us wonder who wears the pants in that relationship... Our sources tell us that Alyssa and Daniel have known each other all their lives and have worked together for at least the last four years.

After some digging, we found out that the two have been living together in Daniel Devereaux's luxurious penthouse. It's no wonder that our favourite heartthrob hasn't been seen in public in months now. We can totally imagine what the two lovebirds have been getting up to in their home. To our knowledge, this is the first time Daniel Devereaux has lived with a woman. By our calculations, the two have been keeping their relationship under wraps for months now. It's unclear when they started dating, but our source confirmed the two visited a prestigious jewellery store whilst on their romantic getaway. Is that wedding bells we hear?

I stare at the countless articles about us in disbelief. Some of them contain in-depth background information about me, while others are mostly speculation. Either way, it's an invasion of privacy I've never had to deal with before. I'm not as much in the spotlight as Daniel and Dominic. I rarely attend high profile social gatherings like they do, so I've never had to deal with paparazzi before. I sit back, completely shellshocked.

Daniel walks out of his office and immediately throws his arms around me. "I'm sorry," he whispers. "We can sue, if you want."

I shake my head. "It'd be too complicated, and it'll only fuel their interest more. I'll deal with it."

Daniel kisses my cheek gently, neither one of us realising that we're shocking our team members more than the articles possibly could. Daniel leans over me and opens the countless messages I've received. Most of them are tinged with hurt and betrayal. Most of the people I've worked closely with are wondering why I never told them my real name more than they care about whether Daniel and I are truly dating. "They're just surprised, honey," Daniel murmurs. "Take a moment to decide how you'd like to reply, but keep in mind that you don't owe anyone an explanation. What your name is shouldn't matter, and for so long it hasn't."

I nod, and Daniel tucks a strand of my hair behind my ear. "There's one more thing, babe. The lobby is swarming with paparazzi. We can either face them now, or we can take the heli to our apartment. I think the latter might be best for today. It'll give us some time to decide how to respond to this."

I smile and kiss him. "I agree, but there's no real need to think about it. Just get your spokesperson to draft a statement confirming our relationship and asking for privacy. I don't think we need to do more than that."

Daniel looks at me in wonder and grins to himself, looking oddly smug. "You're fine with it then?"

I glance at Linda's empty desk and chuckle. "Hmm, shout it to the whole world, baby. I'm yours."

Forty-Four

I walk into the lobby staring at my phone and accidentally walk into someone. I look up to find one of the guys in PR looking at me, startled.

"Oh, I'm so sorry, Ms. Moriani," he murmurs, flustered.

I sigh and stare at him. "Thomas, right? Thomas from PR? Please just call me Alyssa like you always have."

He nods awkwardly, and I just about keep myself from rolling my eyes. Everyone has started to treat me differently ever since the press blasted my name and identity all over the tabloids a couple of weeks ago. It's easier in some aspects, but I do miss being another worker bee. I miss knowing I earned respect of my colleagues because I'm good at my job versus them treating me respectfully because of my last name.

I glance at the stack of contracts on my desk and smile. I managed to bring in five new clients in the last couple of weeks. Daniel has been letting me run DM pretty much entirely by myself, and it's paid off. I feel a lot more confident now, and I know he's doing it to prepare me for taking on my role as his co-CEO. These days he'll be at Devereaux Inc. most of the time while he leaves DM entirely to me.

It's been tough to get used to him not being there and not

being able to walk into his office to ask a quick question. It's also been weird not seeing him most of the day. Since we both work long hours, we barely get to spend any time together anymore. I miss him, but there isn't much we can do about it. Thankfully, he's due to spend some time at DM today.

I'm antsy as I get through the day. I'm impatient to see Daniel. I'm planning on dragging him into his office for a little while, just to kiss the shit out of him. I smile widely when he finally walks through the door. He looks tired, but his eyes light up when they land on me.

"Hey, Lyss," he says, pressing a quick kiss to my lips. I lean into him eagerly and he chuckles against my lips.

"Come into my office for a bit. I need to speak to you."

I nod and follow him, the butterflies in my stomach going wild. Every day my feelings for him get stronger, and I'm pretty sure I'm already irrevocably in love with him. I'm pretty certain he feels the same way, but I've been scared to say the words. I'm scared he might not say them back.

Daniel closes the door behind us and chuckles when I pull him towards me for another kiss. He kisses me back passionately and lifts me into his arms to place me on his desk.

"I actually needed to talk to you this time, you know," he murmurs, his lips already finding mine again. He pulls back reluctantly and I hook my legs around his hips to keep him close.

"I'm going to call a board meeting, Lyss. You've done so well over the last couple of months. You've proven you can take on the role of CEO and I've spoken to all the board members, and they agree. The board meeting is just a formality at this point. I'm so, so proud of how far you've come in so little time."

I stare up at him in disbelief. I knew it'd be coming sometime soon, but it's still somehow shocking to hear him say it.

"Wow," I whisper. "Are you sure? I don't know if I'm ready."

Daniel laughs and kisses me again, his lips lingering on mine. "Baby, you've already been doing the job for weeks now. How could you not be ready? You even landed more clients this year than I did."

I nod and bite down on my lip excitedly. My heart pounds at the idea of becoming Daniel's co-CEO. It's all my dad ever wanted for me. Daniel seems to follow my train of thought and his expression softens.

"He'd have been so proud of you, you know. He always told me you'd do it in no time at all. That you'd be a better CEO than either he or I ever could be. He never had a single doubt that you could do it. I wish he were here to see you fulfil the dream the two of you shared."

My eyes fill with tears, and I bury my face in his neck. Daniel hugs me tightly and rubs my back as I try my best to compose myself.

He buries his hand in my hair and tilts my face up. He gently kisses my forehead before capturing my lips. He kisses me so softly that my heart feels ready to burst.

He leans his forehead against mine and closes his eyes. "I've missed you," he whispers.

I sigh and press my lips back to his. "I missed you too."

We've both been coming home completely exhausted every night. It feels like ages since we've had a chance to spend a couple of hours in bed together. Daniel kisses me again, more urgently this time.

"Baby," he whispers, a pleading look in his eyes. I chuckle and nod, wanting him just as bad. Daniel grins and slowly unbuttons my blouse while I make quick work of his shirt. I'm not as patient as he seems to be, and he laughs when I push the shirt off his shoulders. We've been married well over a year now, and I still can't get enough of his body. I place my lips against his chest and suck harshly, leaving a kiss mark. Daniel groans and returns the favour, leaving a mark on my breast.

He pushes my skirt up as I undo his zipper, and he grins when he finds out that I'm already soaking wet. "Always so eager for my cock, baby," he whispers. I blush and guide him inside me, impatient. He sinks into me slowly, inch by delicious inch. I lean back on his desk and tighten my legs around his, wanting him in deeper and harder.

"More, Daniel. Please."

He laughs and grabs my hips, finally giving it to me the way I want it. "Fucking hell, baby. I won't last long if you want it like that."

I moan loudly, and he kisses me to shut me up. My fingers find their way between my legs and before long I'm contracting around him. He moans and increases the pace, erupting inside me.

He holds me tightly as the two of us try to catch our breath. Neither one of us has said anything about it, but me becoming Daniel's co-CEO means we've fulfilled the terms of my father's will. What will that mean for us? Things have been so perfect between us, but even though we've been married for over a year, neither one of us has ever said those three little words. The sex between us is amazing and we always enjoy spending time together. But just liking each other isn't enough to sustain a marriage.

Forty-Five

I walk into the office a couple of days later to find the whole floor dark. I fumble around with the buttons until I finally manage to turn on the lights.

"Surprise!"

Jake, Luke, Linda and Daniel are standing in the middle of the office and the entire ceiling is covered in balloons. I grin and try my best to hide the emotions I'm feeling. Daniel walks up to me and sweeps me into his arms, twirling me around in a tight hug. I giggle and kiss him as he puts me down.

"Congratulations, CEO dearest," he whispers. The rest joins us excitedly. Linda is clapping and jumping up and down with a wide smile on her face. The official announcement was made early this morning, but I'm still in disbelief.

"Thank you," I whisper. They all hug me one by one and Daniel hands me a large gift. I frown and unpack it slowly, grinning when I see what it is. I run my fingers over the new nameplate. It says Alyssa Moriani, CEO. I'm giddy as I stare at it and smile at him, my heart overflowing. He presses a kiss to my forehead and pulls me into his office.

He takes the nameplate from me and places it on my dad's old desk. I stare at it incredulously. When did he move this back in here?

"I'd like to take credit for the gift, but your dad actually had it made years ago. He knew you'd need it one day and he was as impatient as you were for you to get here."

I trace the letters with my fingers, my eyes filling with tears. "He had this made for me?"

Daniel nods and wraps his arms around me. I inhale deeply and try my best to smile. My dad wouldn't have wanted me to cry today of all days.

Linda walks in with a bottle of champagne while Luke carries the glasses. I smile at them and shake my head as I pull away from Daniel. "It's only 9 am guys," I say.

Daniel shrugs and pops the cork, a grin on his face. "It's five pm somewhere, baby." He hands me a glass of champagne and the five of us toast.

"To our new CEO," Daniel says. I giggle and clink my glass against the others. I'm pretty sure we won't get any work done today, but I'm not even remotely upset about it. I glance back at my dad's desk and sigh. I always thought he'd be here with me to celebrate when this finally happened. I hope he's looking down at me and feeling proud.

I glance at Daniel and smile. I might not have my dad here, but once again he's proven himself right. Daniel is indeed the best partner I could ever ask for, both in life and at work.

The morning passes by quickly, and Daniel had to get back to work at DM. I would've loved to have him with me all day, but both our schedules are far too hectic to allow it. I spend most of my day answering congratulatory calls from old friends and business partners. I smile when I see Vincent calling me.

"Hey, kiddo. I knew you'd do it, but even I'm impressed with how quickly you were appointed CEO. I'm so proud of you, and I know your dad would be as well."

I smile to myself. "I know he would be. I wish he could've been here to celebrate with me, though. I would really love to share a glass of champagne with him. We've both worked towards this most of my life. I can't believe it finally happened."

Vincent sighs and clears his throat. "I wish you could have as well, sweetie. Speaking of your dad, you and Daniel have now fulfilled the terms in the will. You've been appointed as CEO, so the shares are unconditionally yours. You two are free to get a divorce. I've had a copy of the papers prepared since the start, so I'll send those over to you."

I freeze, all the cheer draining away from me. I don't really know what to say to that. Daniel hasn't brought it up, and I haven't either. We'll need to talk about it, but I'm scared of how that conversation might go. Even if he doesn't want a divorce, will I always wonder if he's only with me because circumstances forced us together?

I'm absentminded for the rest of the day. All I can think about is whether Daniel will choose to divorce me.

Forty-Six

I 'm still distraught when I get home that evening. Both of our security guards smile at me as I walk in.

"Congratulations on your new job title, Mrs. Devereaux," they say.

I smile at them shyly. "Thank you. How did you know?"

They both laugh and glance at each other, exchanging an amused look. "Mr. Devereaux has told every single person in the building at least a couple of times."

I blush and smile to myself. I thank them again as I make my way upstairs. When I walk into the house, everything is quiet and I pause in the doorway. There seem to be a hundred candles throughout the apartment and even more roses. Daniel is standing by the dining table with a wide smile on his face. I walk up to him and kiss him. He laughs and kisses me back gently.

"Well, if it isn't the new CEO. I'm so proud of you, Alyssa. You have no idea."

I hug him, and he wraps his arms around me. Just looking around sets my heart at ease. He wouldn't have gone through all of this effort if he's planning on divorcing me.

"Everything looks beautiful, Daniel. I can't believe you did this for me."

He kisses my forehead and pulls a chair out for me before pouring a glass of wine. He serves and pampers me all night. He cooked us a three course meal that I'm beyond impressed with. I know he's worked much harder than I have today, so for him to have done all of this on top of his regular workload warms my heart. I can totally see us spending the rest of our lives together like this. I can only hope he feels the same way.

"And how does it feel?" he asks.

I grin and lower my eyes shyly. "It's the same as any other day. I don't know how hard it'll be going forward, but you were right to say I've already been doing the job for weeks. I might not have said it yet, but I'm grateful you've continued to train me. I'm grateful you trusted me with DM when many said I was still too young and too inexperienced. Thank you for standing by my side and for always being there to catch me when I fall. I could never have done this without you. It's not just the last year either. Even before that you've always had my back, and I want you to know I've always appreciated it. You've always been my role model, you know."

Daniel stares at me with wide eyes and lowers his eyes humbly. "I just did what I was meant to do. I've been your mentor for years, Lyss. I always knew this was the end goal, and I never once doubted you'd make it. If I wasn't going to have your back, then who would? I'm honoured I got to be the one at your side as you learned and grew as a person. You never cease to amaze me, you know. Every year you surpass my expectations, and every year you become more and more dazzling. Sometimes it's hard to believe that you're here with me at all."

I get up and walk around the table to sit in his lap. He hugs me tightly when I bury my face in his neck. I'm overflowing with love for this man. He's been there for me since I started at DM five years ago. He's always challenged me, and he's always taken me seriously despite my age. He's always trusted me and given me responsibility that even my father didn't want to give me. It's thanks to him I've managed to grow as quickly as I did. It's not just professionally that he's always been there for me. Subconsciously, he's always been the one I've trusted the most. He's the first one I called when the hospital told me about my dad. He's the one I called when I needed help with university applications and when I had doubts about interning at DM. He's also the one I'd call if I got too drunk on nights out with my friends and he's the one I'd plead with if my dad was being unreasonable about anything. I've come to rely on him a lot throughout the years. I just never realised it.

Daniel cups my cheek and kisses me gently before dropping his forehead against mine. "My amazing wife," he whispers. I smile and bite down on his lower lip before kissing him fully. Daniel buries his hands in my hair and deepens the kiss. It feels different tonight. There's a sense of desperation laced with emotions neither one of us dares to name.

He carries me to our bedroom and I hold on tightly. We're both quiet as we undress each other. We've mostly been rushed and passionate, but tonight everything feels sacred. The way he touches me makes me feel like he loves me as much as I love him.

My eyes fall closed when he slides into me. He tangles his tongue with mine and then pulls back. "Look at me, Alyssa," he whispers. I do. I look into his eyes as he slowly makes love to me. I'm overcome with emotions. Everything feels more sensitive than usual, and I can barely take it. I feel like I might fall apart.

Daniel bites down on his lips and I know he's close. "Alyssa, my love," he whispers. He thrusts into me slow and hard, driving me crazy. I'm done for. I'll never get enough of this man.

Forty-Seven

I stare at my phone, confused. I've texted Daniel a couple of times and I've called him too, but he hasn't replied. Even if he's in a meeting, he'll always message me to let me know, but today he's been awfully quiet. He hasn't been in the office today either. He's mostly been working at Devereaux Inc.

"Alyssa, Daniel just called to confirm the client meeting with Basel Tech. Will you be attending this with him? I'll put it in your schedule if so," Kate says. I frown at her.

"Daniel just called? When?"

She hesitates before she answers. "Uh, a few minutes ago."

I glance back at my phone and nod. "Yeah, plan it in," I murmur. Kate has taken on the role of my secretary in addition to being Daniel's, and so far she's doing an excellent job. It's just right now she annoys me, even though she hasn't done a single thing wrong. I'm annoyed Daniel managed to find the time to speak to her but can't find time to reply to my texts.

By the end of the day, I'm alarmed by the radio silence. I rush home as soon as I'm done with work and my heart sinks when I walk in to find the apartment dark and empty. I walk into the living room and jump in fright when I spot a dark shadow.

I rush to turn the lights on and find Daniel sitting on the

chair by the window. He doesn't look up when I approach him. Instead, he merely stares out the window as though I'm not there and takes a sip of what looks to be a glass of whiskey.

"Daniel?"

I place my hand on his shoulder, but he doesn't respond. My eyes fall to the stack of papers on the floor and I lean down to pick them up. My hands freeze mid-reach. I'm trembling when I finally grab hold of them.

"Divorce papers?" I whisper, my mind racing back to Vincent's call. He said he'd get them delivered, but I assumed he'd get them delivered to me at DM. There are several post-it notes on the papers and I flip through them out of habit, as I would with any contract. I stare at the pages in disbelief and flip through them again and again, but the result never changes. Daniel has signed everywhere he needed to.

I truly thought we'd talk about this and laugh it off. I thought we'd remain married and rip the papers up together. I knew there might be a chance that he'd want to get divorced, but I thought it'd be a small chance. I thought I could've changed his mind. I sink to the floor with the papers in my hand and look up at him. When he finally glances at me, his expression is cold.

"You signed them," I whisper.

Daniel smiles without a trace of emotion. "Hmm, I signed. Our time is up. You reached your goal of becoming CEO. Your father's shares are yours, and my stake in DM is secure now."

He sighs and looks away, as though he can't stand to look at me for a second longer. "It's been fun playing house with you, but enough is enough. I guess the sex wasn't bad and I'll definitely miss your sweet pussy, but there are plenty of fish in the sea. You're too young to be married. Hell, you were a fucking virgin. I definitely didn't think I'd be married now either."

I clench the papers in my hands, wrinkling them. "Playing house? That's what our marriage was to you? You're telling me the sex wasn't bad? I thought you didn't mind me being a virgin. I never once heard you complain about it."

He turns so I can't even see his face, and I long to cup his cheek and make him face me. But that feels wrong now. He feels out of reach.

"Alyssa, of course we were playing house. You and I were never together because we wanted to be. We were forced together. If your dad hadn't written that will, then you and I never would've gotten married. Hell, we never would've even gotten together. I'm ten years older than you. You've never even really dated."

I glance at him and try my best to keep it together. "So what were we doing last year if we weren't dating?"

He turns towards me, and the look in his eyes chills my bones. "We were making do."

I lower my face and hide behind my hair as a tear rolls down my face. I wipe it away furiously.

"So when you asked me to make our relationship official, you were just making do? If you knew you wanted to divorce me, then why did you insist on being with me? Why did you tell me we'd be faithful to each other and why did you publicise our relationship? If all you wanted was sex, then why didn't you just agree when I suggested that we both keep our separate lives? It makes no sense, Daniel. Please tell me you're joking. Please tell me this is all just a misunderstanding."

He stands up and walks away from me. I rush after him and grab his arm, but he shrugs out of my hold. When he turns to face me he looks cold, an unreadable, bored expression on his face. It's like he's an entirely different person from who he was yesterday. How can the man standing before me be the same man that filled our house with roses and candles?

"Fine. I did want to see what might happen between us. I did want to fuck you, and I didn't want anyone else to have what was mine. We got that out of our systems, and it's time to move on now, Alyssa. I guess we were dating, so let's break up. We're done."

I grab his shirt and shake him, as though that might make

him see reason. "Don't do this to us. What we have is something other people can only dream of. Aren't you happy with me?"

His expression falters and he buries his hands in my hair like he's done so many times and lowers his forehead to mine. I take the opportunity to pull him closer and kiss him. Daniel freezes and for a second panic grips me, but then he kisses me back hungrily. His hold on my hair tightens and before I know it I'm pushed against the nearest wall, Daniel's tongue tangling with mine. I unbutton his shirt while he pushes my skirt up, our lips never leaving each other. As my hands find his zipper, his hands find my breasts. He undoes the buttons with so much force that he sends a few of them flying. He groans when I grab hold of him, and he pulls back long enough to lift me up and push me back against the wall. I squirm in his hold and he smiles against my lips when I finally have his dick right where I want it. He looks at me as he sinks into me, his expression intense.

"Oh god, Daniel," I whisper. His lips find mine again and he thrusts roughly as he kisses me.

"This is the last time, Alyssa. This is the last time I'm fucking you."

I bite down on his lip harshly. "No."

Daniel pulls out all the way and then thrusts into me hard. "Yes," he snaps.

I pull hard on his hair and drag his lips to mine, kissing him with all I've got before I move my lips to his neck. "No," I say as bite down on his skin. I suck down on his neck as hard as I can to make sure I leave a mark. "You're mine."

Daniel moans and changes the angle so he's pushing up against my g-spot, and I'm panting as I try to hold on to my sanity.

"I'm not letting you go," I tell him, my voice husky.

Daniel kisses me and fucks me so hard that I know I'm going to be deliciously sore for days.

"I'm not giving you a choice."

I close my eyes and bite down on my lip, but nothing I do will keep me from coming. Not when he's fucking me this good.

"Baby, please," I whisper.

Daniel grins smugly and slows down the pace, keeping me at the edge. "No," I whimper. "Please."

Daniel chuckles and fucks me slowly. I scratch his back with my nails and he groans. "I need you. Now, baby."

He bites down on his lip and nods, thrusting into me hard, his eyes never leaving mine. My entire body seems to tingle as I come harder than I ever have before. My emotions turn me on even more and I struggle to think rationally. Daniel comes seconds after I do, and the two of us collapse on the floor, still connected. Daniel shifts so he's sitting back against the wall and I remain in his lap, my hands on his chest.

"How can you call this making do?" I whisper, my voice breaking. Daniel looks into my eyes and he looks as hurt as I do.

"Is it her? Is it the girl you said you'd propose to when we divorced? Is that why you're leaving me?"

Daniel looks devastated and he grits his teeth. He looks away and inhales deeply before nodding.

"Yes," he says. "I don't know when and I don't know how, but I'm irrevocably in love with her. She occupies my every thought and all I want to do is make her happy."

I tremble in his hold and stare at him in disbelief, my eyes filling with tears. I blink them away as best as I can and push away from him. I turn my back and cover my face with my hands. While I've been falling head over heels for him, he's been falling for someone else.

"Did you cheat on me, Daniel?" I ask, my voice shaking.

My heart breaks as he remains silent, but eventually he answers. "No, Alyssa."

I hear him stand up and straighten out his clothes. He might not have cheated on me physically, but for him to fall for her, he must've been cheating on me emotionally. Is she someone that works for Devereaux Inc.? Is that why he's been there every single day? I assumed he was giving me so much responsibility because he trusted me, but is it because he wanted to spend his time with someone else? I turn around and try my best to cover as much of my body as I can, but my broken shirt buttons don't make it easy.

"Who is she?"

Daniel hesitates, but then his expression hardens. "It doesn't matter, Alyssa. You and I are done. You have no right to pry into my private affairs going forward."

I inhale sharply and try my best to ignore the dull ache in my heart. No right? I chuckle darkly.

"I haven't signed the divorce papers, Daniel. I have every right. I won't let you do this to us. I'm not signing. You might think you're in love with someone else, but you're wrong. I'll prove it to you."

Daniel runs a hand through his hair and closes his eyes. "You will. You'll sign the papers, eventually. I'm leaving, Alyssa. I want you out of my house by the end of the day tomorrow. If you refuse, I'll just find somewhere else to live."

He walks towards the lift and grabs a bag that he seemed to have packed before I even got home. I'm tempted to run after him, but he knows as well as I do that I can't in the state I'm currently in.

He doesn't look back once as he walks out of the door and out of my life.

Forty-Eight

I stare at my work screen blankly. Four days. It's been four days since Daniel walked out on me. True to his word, he didn't come back home once. I know, because I waited for him every single night. It seems like he truly won't return for as long as I'm there. I thought he'd change his mind soon enough. I thought he'd regret what he said and that he'd come back asking for forgiveness. Instead, I'm staring at photos of him with Olivia.

It's been less than a week since our marriage fell apart and he's going out on dates with someone else. With Olivia, no less. I scan through the article and my stomach twists painfully.

Trouble in paradise?

It's been some time since Daniel Devereaux has been spotted with his girlfriend, Alyssa Moriani. Instead, he's been seen hanging out with his childhood friend, Olivia Diaz, on numerous occasions. This isn't the first time the two have been spotted together and over the years we have wondered whether something was going on between them, but they've always denied it. This time both parties declined to comment. That on its own is telling. Will we soon get a statement from Daniel Devereaux confirming his new relationship?

We've done some digging and found countless photos of Olivia and Daniel throughout the years. Though we feel bad for Alyssa Moriani, who has also declined to comment, we must admit that Olivia and Daniel look incredibly cute together.

I stare at the photos of Daniel and Olivia. There are photos of them as kids, as teens, and finally as adults. In most of them, they're smiling at each other or Daniel has his arm wrapped around her shoulder. Is it her? Was it her all along? Is that why he tried so hard to hide his kiss marks... Why he ignored me throughout the lunch we had I feel sick as I glance at the photo of them last night. He took her out for dinner to the same restaurant he took me to on our first date. The restaurant I've come to think of as ours. I guess to him it wasn't even a date. He was just rescuing his little brother's best friend from a night filled with awkwardness. He probably enjoyed the restaurant a lot more with Olivia there.

I'm startled out of my sombreness when Kate knocks on my office door and walks in. She looks stricken, and I wonder if it's because she saw the article. "Uh, Alyssa," she says carefully. I raise my brows at her and she fidgets before she slides a document towards me. I stare at it in disbelief.

"He already handed in his resignation to the board, and they accepted it. He's using his leftover holiday days to cover his notice period. The board allowed it, since you've proven that you can handle the company by yourself just fine."

I tremble as I pick up the document. He's destroying every tie I've got to him. Why did he marry me only to abandon the company as soon as he signed the divorce papers? Was it just his shares he was interested in, rather than the company? What is he thinking?

I grab my phone to call him, only to remember that he's blocked my number. I bite down on my lip and throw the document in my bag.

I nod at Kate as I walk past her. "I'm going to be out for the rest of the day. Reschedule my meetings where required."

I'm absentminded all the way to Devereaux Inc. Daniel won't let me in if I ask him for a meeting. I can't call him either, but one way or another I need to see him today.

I walk into Devereaux Inc. and straight to the exclusive executive lift that I've seen Daniel and Mary use before. A security guard walks towards me, but thankfully the doors of the lift open as I press my thumb to the scanner. Like I thought, Daniel has given Devereaux Security the order to give my biometrics all the same privileges as his.

I sigh in relief as the lift moves up. I don't know what I'll say to him when I see him, but just the thought of finally seeing him again sets my broken heart at ease.

I get numerous curious looks as people recognise me, but no one stops me as I walk towards Daniel's office. I've got my hand on the door handle when I hear giggling coming from inside. My hands tremble as I turn the handle and push the door open.

Daniel is sitting next to Olivia on his settee. He's leaning back, looking relaxed, while Olivia leans into him. Her lipstick is smudged, traces of it all around her lips. My heart shatters as I glance around his office. His desk is messy and bears a disturbing resemblance to what his desk at DM looked like after he fucked me on top of it.

I feel sick. My entire body is shaking as I walk in, and I wonder if my legs will actually hold me up. Daniel sits up in surprise when his eyes land on me, his smile dropping instantly. He looks wary, and I'm sure he's already wondering how I managed to get in at all. Olivia jumps up when she sees me and looks at Daniel worriedly.

"Can I have a word, please?" I say, my voice clear and even.

Daniel glances at me as though I'm a cagey and dangerous type of animal and eventually nods.

Olivia looks at him and smiles tightly. "I'll go," she says as I sit down opposite Daniel.

He shakes his head and grabs her hand to pull her back down. She stumbles back into her seat and he wraps his arm around her shoulder, the way he did in all the photos I've seen of them. "Stay," he says, his voice gentle and caring.

I bite down on my lip hard enough to draw blood, and even that isn't enough for me to remain in control of my emotions. I look down at my lap and grit my teeth, praying I won't burst into tears in front of them.

"I received your resignation today. I won't accept it."

Daniel chuckles. "The board already accepted it, so I don't care what you think of it. It's done."

He's never been so cold to me before. Not even once. He's always been there for me, and he's always treated me with kindness. I'd have thought that he'd treat me with politeness, even if it's just because of the relationship we had.

"I would like you to reconsider. I'm not ready to handle the company by myself. I can't do this without you," I plead.

Daniel looks away and glances at his watch, as though he's wondering how long it'll take to get rid of me.

"Then you'd better look into hiring another external CEO. I won't come back."

Olivia fidgets in her seat, clearly feeling awkward, and Daniel grabs her hand. As far as I recall, he never used to hold hands with any of the girls he's dated. I was the first, and I thought I'd be the only one.

I clench my teeth and grab another stack of documents from my bag. "Very well," I murmur. I hand him a copy of the numerous photos the press published of him and Olivia, and then place a copy of the fidelity contract we both signed and a share transfer agreement on top.

"This needs to stop. I won't sign the divorce agreement, Daniel. Unless you want to lose your 300 million shareholding, I suggest you keep it in your pants. I won't hesitate to sue you. You've done most of the work for me. All I need to do at this point is to show these photos to a judge. I'll let it go if you stop now."

Daniel stares at me and then at the photos before finally settling on the documents. He looks oddly impressed when he should be looking worried. Eventually he bursts out laughing, and my traitorous heart skips a beat.

Daniel reaches for the pocket inside his suit jacket and pulls out a pen. He then proceeds to sign the share transfer agreement without hesitation. He glances at it with a bittersweet smile before handing it to me.

I take it from him with shaking hands. He actually signed it. He'd rather sign away the shares he worked so hard to keep instead of staying faithful to me.

"What does this mean?" I ask, my voice breaking. "Did you…" I can't even get the words out. I can't even bring myself to ask him if he signed the papers because he has already breached the terms. It's been four days. How could he do this to me?

I must look devastated because Daniel suddenly looks panicked and pained, the way he used to when I'd burst into tears whenever I'd miss my dad in the first few months after the funeral.

"No!" he says, losing his composure for just a second. When I glance up, his stoic expression is back in place. "No, I haven't… but I want to. So I might as well just sign now and settle, rather than having to go through court proceedings."

I stare at him in disbelief. He'd rather give me 300 million worth of shares than remain faithful to me? My eyes automatically travel to Olivia. I guess that type of money is nothing to him when it comes to love. He's a Devereaux, after all. I wonder if losing such a large amount would affect him at all. I doubt it.

I nod absentmindedly as I put away the documents I came in

with. I was so sure. So sure I'd be able to tie him back to me this way. Never in a million years did I think he'd sign. I glance at him before I walk out, but his eyes are firmly pasted on Olivia.

Forty-Nine

"God, you're such a fucking mess," Dominic says as he swoops me into his arms. "You work your fucking ass off during the week and drink like you're at uni on the weekends. It's been weeks, Alyssa. This is no way to live."

He carries me home on his back. I finally gave in and moved back into my dad's house, not realising how many memories Daniel and I share here too. I thought all I'd have to deal with would be memories of my dad, but that isn't the case. I think of him when I have dinner and remember the way he'd chat with my dad and the way he'd compliment me on the food. I remember him in his wrinkled clothes in the morning, fast asleep on the sofa because he worked late with my dad.

I wonder if he's back in his apartment now. I wonder if he thinks of me when he goes to bed. Has he shared the bed I thought of as ours with someone else? I burst into tears all over again and Dominic puts me to bed carefully. He holds me as tears stream down my face.

"Oh man, Lyss. I have no idea what's going on. Daniel is putting up a good front, but he's just as miserable as you. What the fuck are you two playing at?"

Dominic has questioned me about Daniel repeatedly, but I've

been refusing to answer. It's almost like it'll become real if I admit that he's no longer mine.

"Lyss, please. You're breaking my damn heart here. I have no idea what's going on. You won't talk and neither will Daniel."

I sniff and pull away from him, gathering my courage. "He dumped me, Nic. He didn't just dump me, he signed the divorce papers. Remember the fidelity contract I told you about? He gave me his shares."

Dominic stares at me as though he's trying to make sense of what's going on, but just like I have, he fails. "That's impossible. There's no way he'd ever let you go."

I laugh hysterically. "Haven't you seen the photos? He's been seen with Olivia all over town."

Dominic shakes his head. "I have seen the photos, and they're not intimate in any of them. Looks like they're just hanging out, you know. I don't know what he's thinking, but I doubt he's actually getting with her."

I grimace and look away. I know he's only saying that to make me feel better. I know what everyone is saying. Daniel and I were rarely seen together in public, but he's going on date after date with her. I've been stubbornly holding on to him when he's moved on.

"He signed the papers, Nic. It's done. All that's left is for me to sign them too. I was stupid to think he'd change his mind. You're right. It's been weeks. Who am I fooling?"

Dominic wipes away my tears and cups my cheeks. "I'm sorry, Lyss. I don't know what to do or what to say. I'm so sorry."

Dominic gets into bed with me and spoons me, holding me as I try my very best not to sob my heart out.

"I — I love him, you know. I'm so in love with him, and he's going around dating someone else. He didn't even care about me enough to mourn our relationship for more than a week. I'm unable to eat or sleep, but he's going on dinner dates with someone else. I thought he was the one for me. I thought I'd spend the rest of my life with him. How could I have been so foolish? So blind?"

Dominic tightens his grip on me and pets my hair, the way Daniel used to. It sends a fresh wave of tears to my eyes.

"Enough is enough, Lyss. If what you're saying is true... if he's signed the papers and paid his way out of the fidelity contract... I don't know. Maybe you should listen to what his actions are telling you. Maybe you should move on."

I fall asleep with those words echoing through my mind. I know he's right, but I don't think I can take it.

Fifty

My heart feels heavy as I stare down at the documents in front of me. It's been five weeks since Daniel and I separated, and I kept fooling myself into believing he'd come back. He hasn't, and he won't. If anything, he has perfected the art of avoiding me. He won't attend any event that I'll be at, and he'll leave if we happen to find ourselves in the same location. Dominic is right. It's time for me to listen to what his actions are telling me.

I yearn for a mere glimpse of him, but he walks away as soon as his eyes land on me. How long will I keep both of us captive in an unwanted situation? Thinking back to it, he always did his best to resist my advances, but I persisted. He didn't stand to gain as much from our marriage as I did, and he told me he married me to honour my father's wishes. In the end, he wanted out so badly that he gave up the shares that got us into this mess in the first place. It's time to set him free.

My hands tremble as I sign the divorce agreement, a single tear rolling down my cheek. With this, it'll be done. Daniel and I had a robust prenup that ensures a clean break. I drop the pen on top of the documents and stare at it, a bittersweet smile on my face. If I could go back in time, I'd selfishly do it all over again. I'd never give up on the memories we made and the love I felt. I doubt I'll ever love someone the way I love Daniel, and I'm grateful I got to experience it.

I grab a piece of paper and clip it to the top of the first page before penning the last message I'll ever send him. Another tear falls down my cheek as the ink flows from my pen.

Dear Daniel,

I'm sorry for withholding my signature when you've made it so clear where you and I stand. You were right. We do have an agreement and our time is indeed up. I'm thankful that you chose to honour my father's last wish and I realise that that was the only reason you married me. I guess along the way the lines started to blur for me. It was selfish of me to hold on to you longer than your obligation required. Especially since you told me from the very start that there's someone else you've got your heart set on.

I'm beyond grateful that you were beside me during the toughest time I've ever had to face. All I wish for is your happiness, and I know these documents are the first step to achieving that. I hope that over time you and I can find a way to be in each other's lives again. Perhaps we can even be friends one day. Until then, I'll give you all the space you need.

All my love,
Alyssa

I wipe my tears away and promise myself that this is the last time I'll cry. I smile sadly as I seal the stack of papers into the envelope.

It's really over now. My voice wavers as I call Kate,and she looks worried as she glances at me. I hand her the envelope but struggle to let go of it.

"Please hand deliver this to Daniel. I assume he's at Devereaux Inc, but you may need to check with his new secretary. It's important that you hand this to him personally."

She looks at me with a complicated expression and then nods, resigned. "Understood," she whispers.

I sink back into my seat and stare out the window. He'll probably be relieved when he finally receives the divorce agreement. I pick up my phone and hesitate before making a call.

"Liam?"

"Alyssa? It's so good to hear from you. How have you been?"

I sigh and consider lying, but then I decide against it. "Honestly, I've been a train wreck. But I'm trying my best to be better."

"I guess the rumours about you and Daniel are true then? You broke up?"

I inhale deeply before replying. "Yes, we broke up."

Liam is silent for a couple of seconds. "I want to say that I'm sorry to hear that, but I'd be lying."

I chuckle, my sombre mood lifting a little. "Hmm, well, I actually called you because there's a charity auction ball I've attended every year. I was kind of wondering if you might want to come with me?"

"Yes! Fuck yes, I'll go with you."

I laugh and shake my head. "I'm not sure I can even call it a date. I'm not in a good place right now, Liam. I need you to know that."

He sighs. "I do know that, Lyss. Regardless, I'd be honoured to accompany you. Even if it is just as a friend."

I hesitate before I speak again. "There's one more thing... It's hosted by the Devereauxs. Daniel will definitely be there. Will you be okay with that?"

Liam chuckles. "Hell, I'm looking forward to it. Can't wait to see you, beautiful. I've waited years for a chance to take you out on a date. I can't believe it's finally happening."

I laugh. "It's not a date," I tell him.

"Well, we'll see about that."

Fifty-One

I glance down at my Oscar de la Renta evening gown nervously. It's stunning and figure hugging, but I'm worried I'll look overdressed. After all, I ordered it months ago. Back when I thought I'd be hosting this event alongside Daniel. I thought this would become our first official public appearance together.

I suppress the heartache I'm feeling and take Liam's hand. "You ready?" he whispers. I nod at him. He's been wonderful tonight. He hasn't pushed me once, and he hasn't crossed the boundary of propriety.

"Don't worry. You look stunning," he says. I smile at him and try my best to settle my nerves. I'm not ready to see Daniel. I promised myself I'd let him go when I signed the divorce papers last week, but my heart isn't ready.

Liam looks torn and eventually pulls on my hand as he leads me towards the Devereaux mansion. This place has always been like home to me, yet now I feel like an intruder. We both pause at the entrance of the makeshift ballroom and stare at it in awe. Every year I'm stunned by how the large backyard gets transformed into a ballroom, and this year is no exception. I look around with twinkling eyes as I take in the countless chandeliers and the stone floor underneath us. I know Mary reuses most of the same materials every single year, but she still manages to make things look different every time.

I tighten my grip on Liam's hand when I spot Daniel. He's standing next to Mary and Dominic. I hate that I'm relieved to find that Olivia isn't with him. For all I know, he might just have walked away from her for a second. There's every chance I'll have to sit through a night of watching him fawn over her.

"We'll have to greet the hosts," Liam murmurs. I look up at him with my heart in my eyes and he cups my cheeks gently. "It hurts that bad, huh?" he whispers. "Would you like to leave?"

I place my own hands against his chest and shake my head. Liam looks at me with eyes that are filled with understanding, and I'm so grateful to have him here with me tonight.

"Come on," he whispers. His hand slides down my arm until he's holding my hand and I tighten my grip on him, as though that'll give me the courage I'm lacking. He smiles at me and leads me towards Daniel, my heart beating louder with every step. I inhale deeply and put my best corporate poker face on. Mary smiles when she sees me, her expression wavering for a second when she realises I'm holding Liam's hand. She recovers quickly and wraps her arms around me. "I'm so glad you made it, honey," she whispers.

I hug her back tightly before moving on to Dominic. "You look good, Lyss. Beautiful," Dominic says, a wide grin on his face.

I freeze when I'm finally standing in front of Daniel. I look up into his gorgeous grey eyes and my heart skips a beat. He looks handsome. I love him in a tux and my hands are itching to yank off the bowtie he's wearing. He looks at me and then at Liam beside me before looking back at me with a raised brow. He clenches his jaw and stares me down. He looks jealous and hope soars within me, but I squash it down. I clear my throat and try my best to smile at him. "I — It's good to see you, Daniel. You look good," I murmur.

"Hmm, what is this?" he asks, glancing at Liam. He doesn't hug me. He doesn't even really say hi. "Is this a date?"

Liam wraps his hand around my waist and pulls me in closer, intimately. "Thanks for having us," Liam says. Daniel scoffs and shakes his head. He looks angry and betrayed when he's the one who signed the divorce papers and moved out. The way he looks at Liam sends a chill down my spine. If I didn't know better, I'd think he was furious and burning with jealousy.

I breathe a sigh of relief when Liam grabs my hand and pulls me towards the dance floor. He smiles at me reassuringly and wraps his hands around my waist while I automatically put my hands around his neck. He pulls me in closer and bends his head to whisper into my ear. "We can leave as soon as you say so," he murmurs.

I shake my head. "I can't. I agreed to auction one of my mother's necklaces. I need to stay to buy it back."

Liam sighs and twirls me around the dance floor, allowing me to forget about my heartache for a couple of minutes. "Thank you," I whisper. "I know this isn't what you might have hoped it would be, but I'm still really happy that you're here with me."

Liam smiles at me sweetly. "Lyss, I've always adored you. I'm happy to spend time with you, even if it isn't a date. You don't ever need to feel like you owe me anything. I'm here because I want to be."

I lean in closer and rest my head against his chest briefly, the two of us swaying around the room. I'm dismayed when the song comes to an end and Liam chuckles. "We can keep dancing, you know. There's no limit on the amount of times we can dance together."

I laugh, but my smiles fades as Daniel leads Olivia onto the dance floor. He's smiling at her and she's smiling back at him. They're looking at each other like no one else exists. Has he ever looked at me that way?

I didn't think it'd hurt this much, but my heart genuinely feels like it's physically aching. Liam angles me so I can't see them and looks at me with such pity that I start to feel sorry for myself. I promised myself I'd be better, so why am I such a mess?

"I'm sorry," I whisper, pulling away from Liam. "I need a couple of moments. I'll just go to the restroom for a bit and I'll be fine, okay?"

Liam nods at me with a sad smile. I feel his gaze on me as I escape from the room. I feel bad for leaving him by himself, but if I stayed I'd burst into tears right there on the dance floor.

Fifty-Two

I enter the mansion soundlessly, relieved to find my biometrics still in the system. I open the first door I come across and walk into the large library, but I only manage to take three steps before I sink down to the floor. I bury my hands into my hair to try and force myself to keep my composure. I don't want to cry. I don't want to be that girl that can't let go of her ex. I don't know how long I sit there trying to swallow down my tears, but it feels like hours.

Just as I've finally convinced myself to pull myself together, the door behind me opens and I jump up, unsteady in my high heels. My heart does an automatic somersault when Daniel comes into view. He closes the door behind him and walks straight past me. I turn to follow his movements with my eyes and watch him as he walks to the corner and turns on the fire with the gas switch. The flames come to life instantly and I stare at them to keep myself from following Daniel.

He sits down on the rug in front of the fireplace and shrugs off his jacket before patting the space next to him. "Come here," he says, his voice husky.

I move towards him without thinking. My body moves automatically. I don't even realise what I've done until my knees sink to the floor beside him. The heat from the fireplace feels amazing and I raise my hands to the fireplace to warm myself. It takes me a while to gather the courage to look at him. I glance up, only to find his eyes already on me. He looks angry and intense, but there's also a flicker of something more. Something I don't dare to name.

"What are you doing here?" he asks. "Your boyfriend couldn't keep you entertained?"

I look down at my knees and ignore his question. "I'm sorry for intruding," I say. "Would you like me to leave?"

Daniel chuckles darkly. He turns towards me and within seconds he's got me flat on my back, his body on top of mine. He pins me down with his weight, rage flashing through his eyes. He buries his hands in my hair and tilts my face up towards his.

"Liam fucking Evans, huh? I thought you were madly in love with Dominic, so where the fuck did this guy come from?"

I blink in confusion and try to turn my face away, but Daniel won't have it. My entire body trembles with need. Just having him close to me has me craving more of his touch. I almost moan when he tightens his grip on my hair. I glare at him viciously in an effort to hide my growing desire, but I doubt I'm fooling him. He knows me too well. He knows my body too well.

"I don't see how that's any of your business, Daniel," I say. I meant to sound angry and detached, but instead I sound husky and breathless.

He laughs and lowers his face until his lips are hovering above mine. It takes all of my willpower to keep from closing the remaining distance between us.

"Is he the reason you signed the divorce papers after refusing so adamantly?" Daniel looks tortured, as though the answer actually matters to him. "Answer me."

I smile at him and push against his shoulder. "You'd better let go of me. I'm sure Olivia is waiting for you."

Daniel's hand slips out of my hair to cup the back of my neck, and he lowers his lips to mine until he's almost touching me. My heart is beating wildly and wetness pools between my legs. I want him so badly. I'm dying to have his lips on mine, just one more time.

"So are you dating him?" he whispers. His lips brush against mine on the last word and my eyes shutter closed.

"Does it matter?" I ask.

Daniel bites down on my lower lip and I tilt my head in a silent bid for more. He smiles against my lips before we kiss fiercely. Daniel moans when my tongue finds his and he pulls away long enough to grab my dress and push it up. I lift my hips to make it easier for him and tug on his bowtie.

"I've been wanting to rip this damn thing off ever since I saw you wearing it," I whisper.

Daniel chuckles and kisses me as his fingers find their way between my legs. His eyes widen when he realises I'm not wearing any underwear, and for a second I see a hint of insecurity in his eyes.

"I can't wear anything underneath a dress this tight," I whisper. The relief in his eyes is instant, and the way he smiles at me has my heart beating in overdrive. He slips two fingers into me and I moan loudly. He shuts me up with a kiss while I fumble with his suit trousers, trying to get it off. My eyes shutter closed when I feel how hard he is.

"Look at me," he snaps. I blink, startled, and look into his eyes. He looks tortured, turned on and hot as hell. "So fucking wet for me, Alyssa. Such a wet fucking pussy."

I'm trembling with need and bite down on my lip when he aligns himself right where I want him. He pauses there when he knows full well that I need him inside me already. My hands fumble with the buttons on his shirt and I push the fabric away, exposing his delicious skin. Instead of waiting for him to give me what I want, I lift my hips and push against him so he falls onto his back. He looks startled and I immediately climb on top of him, straddling him. He grins and yanks on my zipper. His eyes widen when my dress finally pools around my waist, exposing my breasts.

"Such fucking amazing tits. No bra, huh?"

He fondles my breasts roughly and the way his thumb grazes my nipple makes my inner muscles contract. I position him underneath me and lower myself on top of him, taking him as deeply as I can. He moans loudly when I sit back on top of him, fully stretched and filled. I move my hips up and down frantically, desperate for him. He grabs my shoulders and pulls me towards him, so my upper body is on top of his. He kisses me as I continue to thrust my hips. I can't take him in as deeply at this angle, but he's hitting my g-spot with every move. I'm not sure I'll last long like this. I lower my lips to his neck and suck down on his skin, marking him as I increase the pace. He's moaning loudly and meeting my every movement, the two of us frantic and eager. I lean down and suck on his collarbone, and he groans. I sit back up and rotate my hips slightly every time I come down on him. Before long, I'm panting and barely holding on. He grins and continues to thrust into me, doing most of the work.

"I can't... I can't hold on," I moan, sounding breathless.

Daniel looks at me smugly and smiles. "Then don't, baby. Come for me, Lyss."

My inner muscles contract hard and my entire body trembles as wave after wave crashes through me. Just as I begin to regain my sanity, he turns us over so I'm on my back and continues to fuck me.

"One more, Lyss," he whispers. He angles his hips and thrusts into me slowly, teasing my g-spot with every move. Within minutes, I shatter around him again. "Hmm, what a good girl. What a good pussy. Always so wet for me."

He thrusts into me harder and within seconds he comes too, collapsing on top of me. I grin up at him lazily. "You were so hard for me, Daniel. Did you miss this wet pussy?" I murmur, throwing his earlier words back at him. He grins at my foul language and kisses me. It's a wet and sloppy kiss and I love everything about it.

"Where did you learn that language, huh?"

Irrational anger grips me as the lustful haze wears off and the painful memories come streaming back in. "Hmm, well... Let's just say I finally understand why you said the sex between us wasn't bad," I say, lying through my teeth. He freezes while still inside me. His entire face scrunches up in pure agony and I regret my words instantly.

"You fucked Liam?" he asks, the colour draining from his face. He looks so hurt and all I want to do is take my lie back, but he speaks before I have a chance to. "Well, fair enough," he says. "To answer your question... I did miss your pussy, but it was better in my memories. I've had better since you," he murmurs. Daniel grabs my hands and pushes them above my head, trapping me with his weight.

"Since me?" I repeat numbly. "You slept with her?" I ask, my voice breaking. My eyes fill with tears and I try to get my wrists loose with all my strength, but he won't budge. I should've known better. Of course he's slept with her already. All those dates they've been on... It's just me Daniel wasn't eager to bed. "How long did you wait after you bought your way out of the fidelity contract? Did you do her the same day? Did you even wait at all? Were you sleeping with her before you left me?"

I sniff and try to get my hands loose again. Endless tears are streaming down my face, my agony and heartbreak on display for Daniel to see.

"Get off me, you asshole. I fucking hate you," I yell.

He smiles at me with twinkling eyes and kisses away my tears. I sniff and push against him again as a sob escapes my lips. He pulls out of me and rolls onto his side, keeping me in his arms. I push him away and sit up.

I wipe at my tears furiously, hating that he's seen me cry over him. I try to inhale deeply but keep choking on my sobs, making me seem even more pathetic. I yank my dress up to cover myself and try to stand up, but Daniel pulls me back to him, his own eyes filling with tears. He pulls me down to the floor and rolls on top of me, caging me in.

"I lied. I lied, Alyssa. I never slept with her. I swear. Of course I didn't. Please, baby. I'm begging you... Please stop crying. You're tearing me apart, Lyss. Please."

He cups my cheeks and wipes away my tears, his forehead dropping to mine. "You didn't?" I whisper.

Daniel shakes his head and wipes away my tears with his sleeve. "No. I didn't. I just lashed out because for a second I believed your little lie."

I look up to find him smiling at me indulgently. I push against his chest weakly and get up. This time he lets me go. His eyes follow me as I escape from the room, leaving him sitting there with his clothes and his hair all messed up.

Fifty-Three

I t took me ten minutes to fix my hair and makeup. Thank god my room at the mansion has been left untouched. I would've been so embarrassed if I had to walk out of here looking like I did.

Liam is looking around the room anxiously as I walk back in. His eyes land on me and he exhales in relief. I'm instantly swamped with guilt.

"There you are. You've been gone for an hour, Lyss. I was so worried. Are you okay?"

I blush and nod at him. Liam touches my hair thoughtfully and then glances at me, a question in his eyes that he won't voice. Daniel messed my hair up so badly that I had to let down my fancy up do and settle for loose hair instead. I feel compelled to give him some sort of excuse.

"Ah, my head was hurting," I mumble. Liam smiles tightly and looks behind me. I turn to find Daniel walking in. His bowtie is undone and hanging around his neck. He hasn't bothered to fix his hair at all. All he's done is fix his clothes... mostly. Even from this distance I can see a hickey and a hint of my lipstick on his neck. At least he wiped it off his lips.

I glance back at Liam, who's staring at the floor with a hard expression on his face. He bites down on his lip and then looks at me, shaking his head. Eventually he sighs and pushes a strand of my hair behind my ear gently. He looks resigned, and I feel bad for putting such a sad expression on his face.

I see Daniel walk up to Olivia from my peripheral vision. It hurts that she's the first person he walks towards. Did what happened just now mean anything to him? Was it just lust or break-up sex? He hasn't so much as glanced at me since he walked in. Olivia takes a good look at him and then bursts out laughing, confusing the hell out of me. He runs a hand through his hair and smiles smugly. Daniel looks around the room until his eyes find mine and I look away instantly, embarrassed.

Liam grabs my hand and tugs me towards the seats by the podium. "So you just so happened to disappear when Daniel did, huh?" he remarks. He doesn't sound angry. Instead he sounds hurt, and that's so much worse. "Did you know he followed you as soon as you walked out the door?"

I glance up and find him glaring into the distance. "I'm sorry, Liam. I didn't — I didn't walk out expecting to meet up with him or anything like that. It wasn't like that at all."

Liam nods and looks down at his hands. "I know," he murmurs. "That's what makes it even worse. If he'd stayed away tonight, I might've actually had a chance with you, eventually."

I'm spared from having to reply when Mary walks onto the stage. She greets us all and the auction commences. Some of us are here to buy presents for others while contributing to charity, while others are here to bid for the same items they've put up as a way to contribute to the auction and donate at the same time, without losing a precious item. I've done the latter every year. This year I considered pulling out, but neither Mary nor Dominic was having it.

I'm surprised when Olivia bids on the ancient vase she donated. I'd have thought Daniel would've bought it back for her for sure, but instead she's doing it herself. I keep glancing at the two of them. They're seated all the way at the front in the row to my left, so I have a far clearer view of them than I would've liked.

Eventually my mother's necklace goes up for auction. I lift my hand immediately, but Liam grabs it and brings it to his lips. He kisses the back of my hand gently while he raises his own.

"One million," he calls. Daniel clenches his jaw and looks back at us, his eyes lingering on our joint hands that are still pressed against Liam's lips. His eyes darken and he turns back to the front, his own hand rising.

"One point five million," he says, his voice loud and clear. The room falls silent as most people glance between me and Daniel. Our names have been on everyone's lips tonight. I've ignored the whispering and the curious glances as best as I could, but Daniel is just outright fuelling the rumours now.

"Two million," Liam says.

I shake my head and grab both his hands. "Don't," I whisper. Liam looks at me and tugs his hand loose. He cups my cheek gently and looks into my eyes with a lost expression. His forehead drops to mine and he sighs.

"Three million," Daniel shouts, his anger obvious. I want to glance at him, but Liam is still cupping my cheek, keeping my eyes on his.

"Three point five million," Liam says.

I look at him pleadingly, and he smiles, a mischievous look in his eyes. He presses a gentle kiss to my forehead. "He won't let me buy it for you. That man... I don't know what's going on between you two, but he's head over heels for you, Lyss."

"Four million!" Daniel calls.

I look down and laugh mirthlessly. If only that were true. Liam puts his finger underneath my chin and lifts my face up. "Since he came between me and you, the least I can do is lighten his pockets a little."

I laugh and shake my head. "You drove up the price knowing he wouldn't let you have it?" I ask. Liam nods and I giggle, slapping my hand over my lips just as Mary proclaims the necklace sold.

"I'm sorry, Liam," I whisper.

He shakes his head and throws his arm around my shoulder. "You told me this wasn't a date and that you weren't in a good place. I knew what I was getting into when I agreed to come. Am I happy that you disappeared with your ex and showed up looking rosy and far happier than when you left? No, not particularly. But I don't blame you either."

I sigh and rest my head on his shoulder as Mary wraps up the auction. "You wanna go home or do you want to dance a bit longer?" I ask. Liam chuckles and grabs my hand as he pulls me back towards the dance floor.

"I know this is going to be the only night that I'm sort of your date, so I want to make the most of it. Of course I want to dance."

Fifty-Four

M y eyes are on Daniel as I walk into the courtroom. After what happened at the auction, I was certain that he'd get in touch with me, that maybe he might want to try getting back together or at least postpone the divorce. I should've known better.

I sit down and barely respond as the judge reviews our case. It feels like my heart is ripped right out of my chest when the judge signs the paperwork that finalises our divorce. Daniel doesn't look at me once, yet my eyes never leave him. Part of me wanted to plead with him. To beg him to give us another chance. Would it have made a difference?

I'm surprised when he offers me his hand. I take it absent-mindedly, my body still so used to giving in to him. His fingers close around mine and he pulls me up. He's smiling brightly, and his happiness breaks my heart. Is he that relieved our marriage has officially come to an end?

"How about we get a drink?" he says.

"What? You want to get champagne and toast to finally getting rid of me?" I snap, unable to keep my cool. I grit my teeth and push past him, but he wraps his arms around my waist from behind and then closes the distance between us until my body is flush against his. The way he's holding me reminds me of the way he hugged me once when we were cooking together. It reminds me of better times, and it hurts to remember how good things were between us.

"Come on, Lyss. Just one drink, okay?"

I subconsciously lean back against him and sigh. Who knows? It might be the last time he and I will spend time together. He's become a master at avoiding me recently. If I walk away now, there's a chance I'll never get to have alone-time with him again. I'll have to rely on catching glimpses of him when we both happen to be at Mary's.

"Yeah, okay," I murmur. There isn't much I wouldn't suffer through to spend a bit of time with him. He offers me his arm as we walk out of the courtroom. I glance at him as I thread my arm through his. I've gotten so used to holding his hand, our fingers entwined. I guess I'll never feel his fingers against mine again.

Daniel takes me to the same hotel we went to on our first date and uses his black card to grant us access. The rooftop bar is almost entirely empty, but we sit down in a secluded spot nonetheless. I grab my purse with shaking hands and take out my own Devereaux black card. The ties between us are being cut one by one, it seems.

I place the card on the table and slide it towards him. "This is yours. I'm no longer entitled to have it. I'm no longer a Devereaux, after all," I murmur.

Daniel stares at me with an expression I can't quite decipher. "Did you ever really consider yourself to be a Devereaux?" he asks.

I'm startled by the question and unsure of how to respond. Daniel laughs. "Hmm, I guess you did. I recall you once ordering me to call HR and explain to them that Mrs. Devereaux, my own wife, was harassing me."

I blush at the memory. What was I thinking, acting so bold with him? Even back then, he pulled away from me so often. That was the same day he told me he wanted to see other people. He kept declining my advances and kept his distance, yet I refused to see the signs. I failed to see that he wasn't falling for me the way I was for him.

Daniel shakes his head and slides the card back to me. "Keep it," he says. "You're still family."

I frown at his words. "Family? You see me as family?" I ask, my tone sharp. The mere idea of him changing the way he sees me is excruciating. I don't want to be seen as his little brother's best friend. And I definitely don't want him to see me the way he sees Dominic — as a sibling.

Daniel freezes and stares at me for a second before shaking his head. "I meant that you're a family friend. You should keep the card. Who knows when you might need it. It'll guarantee you access to anything that I have access to. It's a duplicate of my card. You should be able to enter any Devereaux building with it, including our summer houses and the office."

"Family friend, huh? Did you give Olivia one of these cards?" I ask, my heart twisting painfully. I genuinely thought this was something special. Something I only had because I was Daniel's wife.

Daniel smiles and shakes his head again. "No. You're the only person outside of the family to have one. You'll always be the only one, Alyssa."

I pick the card up and stare at it. I know I need to insist on giving it back. I know I need to burn the bridges between us if I ever want to have a chance at getting over him. But I can't get myself to do it.

I'm not even remotely surprised when the waiter walks up with a bottle of champagne, but I am hurt. I struggle to smile when Daniel raises a glass.

"I thought champagne was only for celebrations. What exactly is it you're celebrating?" I ask him, knowing full well what the answer to that is. Maybe I'm just a sucker for punishment. Daniel grins at me, his eyes twinkling.

"A new beginning. Here's to us," he says.

He waits patiently for me to clink my glass against his. For a second I consider being petty and refusing to toast, but then I think better of it. If our divorce makes him happy, then I shouldn't stand in the way of that happiness. I tap his glass and proceed to empty mine in one go. Daniel chuckles again as I put the empty glass down. How is it possible to both love and hate the sound of his laughter? Every time I hear him laugh, a bit of my heart falls apart.

"We were here when we just got married, do you remember?" he says.

I nod and look around the restaurant. It looks different in daylight, but it's every bit as romantic. "I remember. We'd only been married for a day then."

Daniel nods. "Hmm, you told me then that you'd always been in love with Dominic. He told you he feels the same not too long ago, right? Now that you're finally free, you can follow your heart."

I chuckle mirthlessly. "Did you know back then? Could you see what I couldn't? Did you know I was merely comfortable with him and perhaps a bit infatuated... Did you know it wasn't love?"

Daniel looks down and then takes a big sip of his champagne. "Are you sure you aren't in love with him? There's no marriage and no fidelity contract tying you to anyone else now. You and I haven't been together in months now, except for that one time at the auction... You should follow your heart, Alyssa."

I stare out the window. Following my heart would mean losing Daniel forever. If I hide my feelings for him, then perhaps I can remain in his life as a friend.

"Hmm, I'm sure it wasn't love. I doubt that he's in love with me as well. He'll realise that it was merely infatuation when he truly falls for someone. I doubt Dominic knows what love is."

He nods and looks vaguely pleased. "So what's happening with Liam Evans, then? You brought him to the auction and he's clearly very fond of you."

I glare up at him. "That might have led somewhere if I didn't disappear with my ex, only to come back looking thoroughly

THE TIE THAT BINDS

ravished. I actually felt quite bad. He's a great guy, but I'm not ready to be in a new relationship. Maybe in a few years. Who knows?"

I shake my head and try my best to smile at Daniel. "When we were last here, you told me there's a girl you couldn't get off your mind, but you weren't sure if it was love. But by the time you signed the divorce papers, you told me you were irrevocably in love with her."

My heart hurts just saying it and my stomach knots together painfully. I need to take a second to breathe in deeply before I can manage to ask my question. "It seems like you fell for her while we were married. Was it Olivia or was it someone else? Someone who works at Devereaux Inc, maybe? You did spend most of your time leading up to our divorce there."

Daniel bites down on his lip and looks away. I hate how cute he looks. He looks just like a guy talking about a girlfriend he adores, and it absolutely tears me to bits.

"It's not Olivia," he says carefully. "Liv and I are just friends. Nothing more. We've never been more and we never will be."

I nod. I kind of figured as much after I saw the way they interacted at the auction. They were close, but not all over each other. Dominic was right to say they weren't intimate in any of the photos published either. I was just too jealous to see it.

"Someone at Devereaux Inc then. Will you tell me who it is?"

Daniel shakes his head. "You'll find out soon enough," he murmurs, a sweet smile on his face. He looks in love and happy just thinking of her. I wrap my arms around myself subconsciously, trying my best to shield myself from the damage he's inflicting on me.

"So you're dating her, then?"

I can't help but wonder if he's been dating her for a while now. Was he already in a relationship with her at the auction? Did he get with her right after buying his way out of the fidelity contract?

"It's complicated," he says.

I nod and empty my refilled champagne glass. Will I be able to do it? Will I survive seeing him with someone else? Seeing him kissing another woman and holding her hand... Can I remain friends with him and genuinely wish him well? I don't think I can.

"I'm sorry I stood in the way of your happiness for so long, Daniel. I know firsthand how good of a partner and husband you will be. Whoever she is, she's a lucky girl. I genuinely wish you happiness and love, because you really do deserve it. But I don't think I can be part of your life going forward. I don't think we should be friends, and I don't think we should stay in touch either. Maybe in a few years... but not now. I hope things work out for you, Daniel. I hope she gives you what I couldn't. I hope she makes you happy... but I don't want to be around to see it. I can't."

I stand up and walk away, leaving what's left of my heart in Daniel's hands.

Fifty-Five

"Just come over for dinner. You've been avoiding us for weeks now. You're breaking my mum's heart, you know?"

I clutch my phone tighter and sigh. "I know... I don't mean to. It's just been difficult. Do you think Daniel will be there?"

Dominic hesitates. "Nah, doubt it. He rarely comes home these days. He's usually at his apartment or at work. Don't worry about it. Just come over and have dinner with me and mum. Stay the night if you want. We could watch movies? It's a Saturday, so don't tell me you have to work."

I'm tempted. I've missed Dominic and Mary so much. They're the only family I've got left, but I've been avoiding them out of fear of running into Daniel. And partially out of fear they'd tell me he's moved on. I don't really want to hear about him and his new girlfriend.

"I guess dinner wouldn't hurt," I murmur. Dominic cheers and makes me chuckle. I guess a night of fun and laughter is just what I need. All I've done the last couple of weeks is work until I'm exhausted enough to fall asleep. It's an endless destructive cycle.

I'm nervous when I walk into the mansion. My biometrics all

still work. I wonder if they'll change that soon. Perhaps I should bring it up. Maybe Mary isn't aware of it.

"Darling, you made it!" she says, a wide smile on her face. She hugs me tightly. I keep hold of her for a long time, and she pets my back lovingly.

"I missed you," I whisper.

She presses a kiss to my cheek and pets my hair. "I missed you too, my darling. This is your home, you know. Come back whenever you want."

Dominic walks up to me and throws his arm around my shoulder. "That's what I've been saying. Come on. Mum made your favourite things. There's lasagne and apple pie for dessert. It's obvious that you're the favourite. She never cooks me my favourite foods."

I roll my eyes at him and follow him to the dining table. I'm relieved to find Daniel isn't here. I don't think I can face him. I don't think I can look at him, knowing his heart lies with someone else.

Dinner is filled with giddiness and laughter. Thankfully, no one brings up Daniel. I was terrified they'd tell me that he's happy and dating someone else. I can't help but wonder if they've already met the girl he's so intent on marrying. Are they just sparing my feelings?

Dominic wraps his arm around my waist and pulls me towards the living room. The two of us settle down on the sofa in our usual seats, cuddled together. I'm surprised when Dominic hands me the remote. Usually I have to fight him for it.

"Since you've finally showed up, I won't complain even if you make me watch a chick flick."

I grin and mentally go through a list of the cheesiest ones I can think of. There's no way I'm passing up this chance. I eventually settle on Friends with Benefits, and Dominic groans. He hugs me tightly as we watch the movie and I snuggle into him. I've missed this. I've missed hanging out with him, but even more so, I miss doing exactly this with Daniel. How many times has he spooned me on the sofa as we watched a movie together?

I watch Mila and Justin fall in love with each other and glance at Dominic. "Do you think we'd fall in love with each other if we slept together?" I ask him.

He's so startled that he sits up and lets go of me. He blushes and looks at me with wide eyes. "I'm not sure. I think we already established that it would destroy our friendship. Besides, your heart belongs to someone else."

I nod and sink back down into the pillows. "I guess so. A rebound with someone I actually know and like isn't the worst idea though."

Dominic grins. "Can you actually see yourself sleeping with me?" he asks. I glance at him, truly taking in his body. He's handsome as hell, but I can't imagine seeing him naked. My face scrunches up in disgust and Dominic bursts out laughing. "I guess that's a no," he says, shaking his head.

"Yeah, no," I agree. Dominic shrugs. There's a hint of regret in his eyes, but I'm glad we've successfully moved past the stage of crushing on each other.

"Maybe you should just bang Liam. I know he wasn't too pleased with how things played out at the auction, but I'm sure he'd forgive you. Even if you told him clearly that it's just sex, he'd probably go for it."

I seriously consider it. It's not even the sex I miss per se. I just want to get over Daniel already. I'm also worried that I might actually suck in bed. If I sleep with someone else, I might finally know. It wouldn't hurt to gain some more experience either.

"Yeah, maybe. Daniel told me the sex between us wasn't bad. Ever since he said that to me, I've wondered if I'm really bad at it. I'm embarrassed and insecure. I wonder if it was ever okay for him at all, or if he just humoured me. I'm so inexperienced... I guess sleeping with Liam isn't a bad idea. If nothing else, it might improve my skills. Maybe I should call him."

"Hmm... Is that so?"

I sit up in shock when I hear Daniel's voice. He's leaning against the wall behind us, obscured in darkness. How long has he been there? He walks up to us and sits down on the sofa right beside me. He looks good in his tight black tee and jeans. There are bags underneath his eyes and he looks tired, but it doesn't take away from his handsomeness at all.

I glance at Dominic suspiciously. He told me Daniel probably wouldn't be here, so what is he doing here now? He shrugs as though he doesn't know either, but I see the tell-tale twinkle in his eyes.

"I uh... I should go, actually. I have plans tomorrow that I totally forgot about," I lie.

I get up, but Dominic pulls me back down. "You said you'd stay over. Leave early in the morning if you must, but you're staying. Don't even dream of breaking your promise."

I roll my eyes and snatch my hand out of his grip. "Fine. But I'm going to bed."

Dominic knew Daniel would be staying the night here. He knew and he lied to me. He might be denying it, but I'm certain of it.

Fifty-Six

Not even a long shower could calm me down. My heart is in disarray from seeing Daniel, and I'm annoyed that Dominic lied to me. By the time I get into bed, I'm so frustrated that I'm wide awake, unable to fall asleep.

I sit up in surprise when my bedroom door opens. Daniel walks in wearing his usual sleepwear — pyjama bottoms and nothing else. How does his body look even better than I remember? I hate how hot he is.

He closes the door behind him and walks up to my bed. "Y... you... what are you doing here?" I stammer. Daniel's eyes are flashing with anger and he's silent as he sits down on my bed.

I can't keep my eyes off his pecs and abs. I'm longing to touch him and knowing I can't do it freely anymore just makes me want it more. His eyes land on my pyjamas, which happen to be one of his t-shirts that I may or may not have stolen from him. He smiles but thankfully doesn't comment on it.

"Overheard your little chat with Dominic. Sounds like you're looking for a rebound? That's no reason to sleep with someone, Alyssa. You shouldn't fall in bed with someone if there's no mutual affection."

I laugh. "Is that what you had with all the women that came

before me? Mutual affection? If that's the case, then there's plenty of affection between Liam and me."

His eyes flash, and he turns towards me. "You know what I meant. You shouldn't sleep with someone unless you love them."

I roll my eyes. "Are you serious? Are you telling me you loved all the women you've fucked? You either fall in and out of love frequently, or you're confusing lust for love. Either way, you're being a hypocrite."

Daniel groans and pulls a hand through his hair. "Lust, huh? You want Liam?"

He looks tortured and I'm embarrassed to admit that I like this look on him. I'm hurt and I want him to feel a tiny bit of what I'm feeling.

"Well, he's handsome, that's for sure. I doubt he'd ever tell me the sex wasn't good if I slept with him. I have a feeling he'll never make me doubt my own sensuality. Besides, even if I do suck at sex, the only way I'll improve is by practising."

Daniel looks hurt and looks down. "I didn't mean it that way. When I said that, I had no idea it would impact you so much. Hell, it isn't even true. Every time I've slept with you has been the best sex I've ever had."

I look away in disbelief. "The only man I've ever slept with told me the sex wasn't bad. What did you think that would do to me? I mean, it's fine. I'm glad you were honest with me. You don't need to take it back now, and you don't need to try to make me feel better. It's fine."

Daniel sighs. "It's clearly not fine. Very well. If you want to improve your skills, I can teach you. There's no need to sleep with anyone else. You and I are already familiar with each other, so it stands to reason that I'm the most logical candidate to help you with this endeavour."

I stare at him, speechless. "God, don't sound too excited to sleep with me. Damn. Forget it. I doubt I'll struggle to find someone that actually wants me. I doubt Liam would tell me he'd be a logical candidate to help me with this endeavour."

Daniel grits his teeth and glares at me. Before I can react, he rips away my blankets and spreads my legs with his knees. He lies down on top of me and pushes his erection against me roughly.

"You think I don't want you? Alyssa, does this feel like I don't want you?"

My body automatically responds and I subconsciously grind my hips up against his. He moans and bites down on his lip. My hands find their way to his chest, my palms moving up and down his skin. God, I've missed how he feels against me. I struggle to hang onto reason and push against him weakly.

"Aren't you seeing that girl you're oh so in love with? How can you even think of sleeping with me when it's her you love? Didn't you just say that I shouldn't sleep with someone I don't love? So why are you doing it?"

Daniel groans, his frustration obvious. "She and I aren't together. It's complicated. You're the last person I slept with, Alyssa. There's been no one else."

He pushes aside my underwear and slips a finger into me, eliciting a moan from me. I stop thinking, my brain malfunctioning.

He chuckles. "Such a good girl," he whispers. It only takes him a couple of minutes to bring me to the brink of an orgasm, and it takes all of me to not give in.

"Didn't you say you'd teach me?" I snap. He pulls away and grins as he undresses himself. I gasp when his dick comes into view. He's ridiculously hard and throbbing. He pulls me up and helps me take off my clothes, his eyes lighting up when we're both finally naked.

"What do you want to learn, Lyss?"

I lick my lips and look down. "Teach me how to suck you off good."

Daniel's eyes darken, and he swallows hard before scooting towards the headboard. He sits up and then beckons me closer, instructing me to sit between his legs.

I grab his dick eagerly and bite down on my lips as I pump my hand up and down. Daniel grabs my hand and positions it so I'm holding him at the base.

"Now try to take it in. Don't go all the way. Just have some fun first. Use your tongue and move however you like. It's important that you're enjoying this."

I nod and follow his instructions, swirling my tongue around the tip as I move my head up and down.

"Good, baby. That's so fucking good."

I pull away from him and look at him with flushed cheeks. "I want to learn how to take you in deeper, Daniel. Can we try something?"

He nods, a curious and heated expression on his face. What would he say if I told him I've looked up how to do this? Would he think I'm crazy? I clear my throat and pull him up.

"Stand in front of the bed like this," I whisper, positioning him how I want him. His eyes widen when he realises what I'm up to. I lie down on the bed so my head is over the edge and tip my head back. Daniel guides his dick into my mouth eagerly, his eyes on me. He pushes in slowly, steadily, and I press my tongue down to prevent myself from gagging. He stops when he hits the back of my throat and I breathe in deeply. He doesn't move and instead grabs my breasts, playing with my nipples. Once I'm comfortable, I shift my head a little and he starts moving his hips, thrusting into my mouth.

"Fucking hell, baby. This is incredible," he moans. He doesn't last long at all and pulls out, coming all over my breasts. "Where the fuck did you learn to do that?" he asks.

He grabs his underwear and uses it to wipe away the mess he made on my skin before getting into bed with me. "Google," I whisper, giggling. "Remember when you googled how to make sex more comfortable for me after we slept with each other for the first time?"

Daniel blushes and cuddles into me, hiding his face in my hair. "Where did things go so wrong for us?" I ask, my voice breaking.

Daniel rolls on top of me and looks into my eyes. "You and I started off with an expiration date, Lyss. We always knew that our marriage was going to end. Besides, we were forced into our marriage. There's no way we could've survived that. We would've always wondered who we might have married had we been given the choice. We always would've wondered if there's something else out there for us. Something better, maybe."

My eyes fill with tears and I blink them away furiously. "I never once thought that, Daniel. You were it for me. I would've happily stayed married to you."

He drops his forehead to mine and sighs. "Maybe that's true. Maybe it isn't. You went on a date with Liam, didn't you? You never would've had that chance if we'd remained married."

I throw my arms around him and hug him tightly. "I understand," I whisper. "I don't wish to tie you to me when it's someone else you want to be with. I get it."

He chuckles and lowers his lips to mine. He kisses me so gently that my heart feels like it's ready to burst. I feel him harden against my inner thighs again and smile. He pulls away from me a little to look at me.

"It's not just an end, baby. It's also a new beginning. You now have the choice to do whatever you want... to be with whoever you want."

My heart breaks. I guess that sums it all up. He wanted a chance to be with the girl he said he can't get off his mind. A chance to find out whether she might make him happier than I did.

He kisses me again, this time passionately. He doesn't pull away until I'm breathless.

"Lyss, I want you," he murmurs, aligning himself with me. He looks at me through lust filled eyes and I nod, eager to have him inside me. I gasp when he pushes into me. It's been weeks since I've had him. Weeks since I've felt so deliciously stretched out.

"Baby, I need you rough and hard," he tells me. He rises to his knees and lifts me up by my hips. He thrusts into me hard and deep, just the way I like it. With every thrust he strokes my g-spot, keeping me on the edge.

"Daniel, I need you. Please. Stop teasing me, baby."

He grins at me and increases the pace, still pulling out almost entirely before thrusting back into me. "Yes," I moan. "Fuck yes, Dan. I fucking love the way you do me," I moan, urging him to go faster.

He gives it to me and I shatter around him, wave after wave of delicious tingles coursing through my body. "God yes... I love you, Daniel," I whisper, still high on lust. Daniel comes inside me, hard. He moans loudly and thrashes against me before collapsing on top of me. He takes a deep breath and then drops his forehead to mine. It seems like he didn't hear the confession that just slipped out of my lips and I breathe a sigh of relief. I don't want him pitying me or questioning me about my feelings. He kisses me with such intensity and such emotion that I'm almost fooled into believing he loves me back.

"So how are you going to repay me for these lessons?" he whispers against my lips.

I freeze, startled. "What?" I murmur.

Daniel chuckles. "Let's take the yacht out tomorrow. You can repay me by accompanying me. If you're lucky, I'll assist you with another lesson tomorrow."

Daniel doesn't wait for my reply. Instead, he gets comfortable in my bed and closes his eyes, his arms wrapped around me.

Fifty-Seven

T he wind blows through my hair as I glance at the horizon. I can barely see other boats around us. Daniel beckons me closer and pulls me in. He lets me take the wheel and stands behind me, caging me in. I lean back against his chest and he drops his chin to the top of my head.

"I love this," I murmur. Daniel leans in and presses a kiss to my cheek. "I may need to buy one of these for myself."

He laughs and shakes his head. "Why would you? We've already got one. We've got a bigger one too. We should take mum and Nic out on the big one next time."

My heart skips a beat at his words. Does he even realise what he's saying? I guess right now it feels like we never even divorced. It hurts to think he'll be doing all of those things with someone else someday.

Daniel kills the engine and leads me to the lounge deck. I laugh when he grabs a bottle of champagne and two glasses. He tilts his head towards the fridge and instructs me to grab a bowl of strawberries. Is there anything he hasn't thought of? It's no surprise I fell hook line and sinker for this guy.

I join him on the lounge bed and take a glass from him. Daniel's eyes roam over my body, lingering on the bits that are covered by my bikini. I glance at his swim shorts to find that he's already aroused. I blush and raise my glass to his.

"To us," he says, as he always does.

"To us," I murmur, my heart aching. This toast is one I've come to associate with our marriage. It seems ironic now.

Daniel grabs a strawberry and holds it over my lips. I take a bite, and a drop of juice runs down my chin. Daniel chuckles and leans in, licking it clean before brushing his tongue over my lips. I open up for him eagerly and clench my thighs as he kisses me. I'm disappointed when he pulls away instead of turning it into more.

Daniel takes another sip of his champagne and grabs another strawberry. This time he puts half of it in his mouth and I lean in to take the other half, startling him. I bite down on it and run my tongue over his lips before pulling back. I chew slowly and smile at him. "Delicious," I whisper. Daniel chuckles nervously and runs a hand through his hair.

I can't even remember the last time I was this turned on. My entire body is tense and I'm just waiting for him to make a move, but it looks like he won't. I'm not sure why, because his swim shorts resemble a tent and he isn't exactly trying to hide it.

He closes his eyes to soak up the sun and I take that moment to move closer to him. I straddle him so that he's pressing up against me delightfully and grab the bowl of strawberries. I grab one and hold it up to him. He's staring at me with heated eyes and opens his lips. I feed him half before popping the other half in my own mouth.

Daniel's hands move from my hips to my waist and back again. I doubt he even realises he's doing it. Eventually his hands settle on my ass and he grabs on tightly. He's throbbing underneath me and grinds his hips up. I tangle my hands into his hair and pull his lips against mine.

I don't know what we're doing here together. We're divorced and we should be going our separate ways, but all I want is to be here with him. I don't want this moment to end. If this afternoon is all I can have, then I'll take it. Daniel moans and kisses me desperately, his hands roaming over my body. He unties my bikini top from the back and is about to push it out of the way when his smart watch starts buzzing. He glances at it and freezes, retying my bikini top with a serious look on his face.

"There's a bit of trouble, baby. Looks like there are paparazzi near. Our security team just notified me of a potential media team trailing us. They're handling it now, but we'd better keep our clothes on until we get the all clear."

I look away, dismayed, and move to get off him. Daniel grins and pulls me back. "I said we should keep our clothes on, my love. I didn't say you should move."

He hugs me tightly and cups my head, angling me so his lips are on mine again. He takes his time kissing me, driving me wild. I'm soaking wet and ready for him. I breathe a sigh of relief when his watch buzzes again and he smiles.

"All clear," he whispers. His hands move to my neck and he undoes my bikini top with a tug, exposing my breasts. I glance around us cautiously. It looks like we're alone on the water, but who knows if a boat might come by soon. Daniel leans in and takes my nipple into his mouth, dismissing all my thoughts.

"Am I lucky?" I whisper.

Daniel grazes my nipple with his teeth and looks up at me. "I think the lucky one is me, baby."

My hands slip into his swim shorts and he moans when I grab him tightly. He tugs on the strings that keep my bikini bottoms together and I lift my hips so he can remove them. I sigh in delight when I feel him against me. I grab his hardness and align it with me, sinking down slowly. Daniel moans and drops his forehead to mine. "Fucking hell, baby. Didn't even give me a warning there. I was planning on playing with you first."

I shake my head and move my hips up and down frantically. "No. Can't wait. I need you now."

Daniel looks pained as I ride him, and he bites down on his lip hard. "Can't hold it like this, Lyss. You gotta go easy on me, baby."

He buries his hand in my hair and tugs on it while wrapping his other hand around my waist. I lean in and kiss him, slowing down the pace slightly. I watch him with satisfaction. Not bad sex, my ass. He's barely holding on and we've only got started. I move my hips around in circles and Daniel tightens his grip on me. "Fuck, Alyssa. My love, when you move like that..."

I come down on him harder and within seconds Daniel's body tenses. He jerks his hips up into me as his eyes shutter closed. He looks embarrassed and annoyed that he couldn't last longer, but I'm oddly pleased with myself. I stay where I am, the two of us connected, and pull his head towards me. I kiss him gently and he smiles against my lips.

He turns us over so I'm lying in his arms and he strokes my arm gently. I stare up at the cloudless sky and grin. He kisses my hair over and over again, making me feel intensely loved.

"Hey, since I helped you practise the whole sex thing, don't you owe me another date?"

I turn towards him so we're facing each other, our bodies pressed tight. "A date, huh? Is that what this is?"

Daniel chuckles and presses a quick kiss to my lips. "Of course it is. A boat trip, champagne, strawberries and mind blowing sex... for me at least. How is it not a date?"

I giggle and kiss him, my lips lingering on his. "I guess so. But then again, we divorced a couple of months ago. Does it even make sense for us to date? And what about that girl you're in love with... You're sleeping with me when you divorced me to be with her. How does that make any sense at all?"

Daniel groans and puts his arm over his face. "Fucking hell, baby. You have one hell of a memory, don't you? I only brought up this girl you keep reminding me of twice. Twice, babe. Once when I told you I couldn't get her off my mind when we'd just gotten married, and then again when I signed the divorce papers. Why is it you speak about her more than I do? I wish I'd never told you anything at all. Seriously, are you going to keep reminding me of this when we're grey and old?"

I glare at him and look away. "Grey and old?" I snap. "If you wanted to grow old with me, you never should've divorced me in the first place. Why the hell do you want to date me now when you dumped me a few months ago?"

Daniel rolls on top of me and pins me down. He grabs my wrists and pushes them above my head, locking me in. "You're right. We're divorced now. We can date whoever the hell we want. There's no stipulation that says we can't date each other. If that's what we want, then why can't we?"

I squirm underneath him and he lowers his body on top of mine, locking me in further with his weight. My nipples graze against his pecs and I hate that I'm immediately turned on again. This asshole.

"Forget about that girl, Alyssa. There's no one but you. You're all I can see. You'll always be my one and only."

He's looking at me so intensely that I can't help but look away. "If that were the case, you never would've divorced me, Daniel. Let me guess, you pursued her and she rejected you? So now you've come running back to me. I don't want to be second best, Daniel. I want to be with someone who puts me first. Someone who will always put me first."

He sighs and drops his forehead to mine. "Alyssa, baby. What am I going to do with you? I wonder if you'll forgive me when you finally figure it out..."

He kisses my forehead and then pulls away to look at me. "It's just a date, Lyss. It won't hurt to have some fun together, right?"

He lowers his lips to mine and kisses me thoroughly. I'm so tempted to say yes, but I know I need to be strong now. I pull away from him and shake my head.

"No," I whisper. "All we'll have is today. When the day ends, we're through."

Fifty-Eight

I walk out of the lift to find my entire team giddy with excitement. They're smirking at each other and avoiding my eyes. "Morning, boss," Luke calls, his eyes firmly pasted to his screen. I nod and frown at their odd behaviour as I walk to my office.

I freeze in front of my office door, my cheeks slowly turning crimson as I realise why they were acting so weird. I stare at the photo stuck on my door. The print quality is shitty, but it's obviously Daniel and me, wrapped up in each other on his yacht. I'm straddling him while his hands are buried in my hair, our lips on each other. I drop my forehead to the door in embarrassment. It looks like the tradition that used to apply to Daniel has now been extended to me. I grab the photo and rip it off before walking into my office with blazing cheeks.

I'm not even sure what that was. He and I are over. He's gone out of his way to avoid me over the last couple of months, and he's made it clear that he's done with me. So why couldn't he keep his hands off me? Why did he invite me out on his yacht? Why did he ask me out on another date after months of radio silence? I'm reminded of the way he looked at me when he told me that there's no one but me. Could it be true?

I try my best to focus on my work for the rest of the day. It's the only thing that keeps my mind off Daniel. It was so hard to get over him, and now I'm back at square one. All the feelings I thought I buried have resurfaced, stronger than ever before.

I'm startled when someone knocks on my door. My staff usually walk in, and I've never minded that. The door opens and my eyes widen when Daniel walks in. He glances around the room and smiles as though he likes the changes I've made.

He approaches my desk and sits down opposite me. I stare at him before snapping out of it. "What are you doing here?"

Daniel grins and slides a folder towards me. "I want to hire DM to implement the project I told you about a while back. I want to tighten Devereaux Inc's internal controls."

I shake my head instinctively. "No," I snap. I must've lost my senses in the last couple of days, but there's no way I'm going down this road again. I barely survived the damage he did when he walked out on me. I'd be stupid to let him back in so easily.

"It's a multi-million pound project, Lyss. Are you sure you can afford to say no? I know you have the resources and the knowledge to pull this off."

I grit my teeth in annoyance because he's right, but shake my head. The project would be great to have, but it's not like we aren't doing well enough without it.

Daniel crosses his arms over his chest and stares me down. "Saying no to this project would mean destroying shareholder value. Is that something you should be doing as the CEO? You're not one to let emotions cloud your judgement."

I sigh and cross my own arms, mirroring his stance. "I personally own 51 percent of the shares. I am the biggest shareholder. I'm fine with losing a bit of value."

Daniel looks down, his lips raised up in a tiny smile. "Hmm, I wonder if the board will feel the same way. I spoke to Christian the other day, and he seemed to think the project was a great idea and told me to run it by you."

I glare at him through narrowed eyes. He went behind my

back and presented this to the board? That means my hands are tied. If they already know about this project, I won't get away with declining. Not without getting into trouble. I can't have my leadership questioned only a few months after being appointed.

I grit my teeth and look at the documents he's presenting me with. It's a highly valuable project that we usually would've had to bid for. We're lucky Daniel is offering it to us without even having to submit a proposal. I bite down on my lip and nod tersely.

"Very well. It looks good. I'll have a team over it and get back to you."

Daniel grins and points out a specific clause. He looks smug and triumphant, and I'm already annoyed before I even look at it.

I frown and then glare at him. "Why would you need the CEO of a company to work with you directly?" I snap.

Daniel shrugs. "It's an expensive project. I need you to oversee it personally. Gotta make sure I'm getting my money's worth."

I close my eyes and try my best to remain calm. What the hell is he thinking? He's the one that walked out on our relationship. So why is he now the one that's asking me on dates? Why is he forcing me to spend time with him?

I grit my teeth as I read over the contract, beyond pissed off. He's got me backed into a corner. "Asshole," I mutter under my breath. Daniel grins but otherwise ignores the way I'm cursing him. I grab my pen, my limbs heavy with dread, and sign the contract.

Fifty-Nine

I'm filled with anticipation and nerves as I walk into Devereaux Inc with a team of five in tow. Daniel's stipulations mean that I have to check in personally at least once a week. I'd been so ready to move on with my life, and he's made it impossible now.

Daniel is standing next to his secretary, her hand on his arm. My eyes automatically zero in on where she's touching him, a feeling of unease overwhelming me. I shouldn't care anymore. I turned him down when he asked for another date, so I don't have the right to be upset now.

His eyes light up when he sees me, and he smiles fondly. "Hey, you're here," he says. He places his hand on the small of my back and leads me into his office while his secretary shows my team where they'll be stationed.

I'm so paranoid and my heart is so unsettled. Every time I see him with another woman, I wonder if she's the one he chose over me. There's no way he and I could date. I don't think there's anything he could do or say that would take away the insecurity I'm feeling. We're best off going our separate ways. Daniel looks at me with raised brows and I realise I've been lost in thought. I shake my head and nod at him politely.

"I apologise. My mind wandered," I say, smiling apologetically. I push a copy of our proposed timeline towards him. "This is our schedule. The five consultants I brought with me will be stationed here permanently. You should be familiar with all of them. You're welcome to reach out to me should you have any questions."

Daniel bites down on his lip and looks at me worriedly as I continue. "I'll go check up on the team and ensure everything is in place. I'll ensure that there are no delays and that the quality of the work will be as high as you're accustomed to."

I rise and Daniel jumps out of his seat, a grave expression on his face. I smile at him politely again and turn to walk out, but he grabs my wrist and stops me. I turn to face him, a stern expression on my face.

"Let me go," I whisper.

Daniel shakes his head and pulls me towards him, his free hand finding its way around my waist.

"No," he murmurs. He leans in and bends his head towards me, his lips hovering over mine.

I sigh and let my eyes fall closed. "We can't keep doing this, Daniel. You and I... we're done. We need to try to move on. You've got to let me go."

Daniel's lips come crashing down on mine and he kisses me as though I'm the very air he needs to breathe. I kiss him back just as desperately. My brain tells me not to do it, but my body can't help but give in. My heart pounds as his hands roam over my body. He deepens the kiss and lifts me into his arms. My legs automatically find their way around his hips and he carries me to his desk, setting me down on top of it.

"Never," he whispers against my lips. "I will never let you go again, Alyssa."

He kisses me as his hands roam over my body. I'm like putty in his hands, his touch searing hot. I moan when he strokes my inner thigh and he grins against my lips. He knows I can never deny him. He knows my body will betray me as soon as he touches me.

He slips a finger inside me and rubs his thumb over my clit and a small moan escapes my lips. I will never not want this man. Just one touch and I'm his. My hands fumble with his trousers, my movements eager and impatient. I smile in delight when I realise he's just as hard as I am wet. Daniel pushes my underwear aside and I guide him inside of me. He looks into my eyes as he enters me, slowly and steadily. He stretches me out deliciously and I'm panting by the time he's fully inside me.

He kisses me tenderly as he thrusts in and out, his hands on my hips. "We shouldn't be doing this," I whisper, clenching my muscles around him the way he likes it.

He moans loudly and leans in to bite down on my lip. "You vixen," he whispers. I grin as he thrusts into me harder. He kisses me viciously and fucks me so good... there's no way I'd ever get enough of this.

"Alyssa, baby... you better hear me when I say this," he groans, thrusting into me harder. "I won't ever let you go. I made that mistake once, and I'll never do it again. I'm going to pursue you until you give in and agree to be mine again."

Daniel pulls me closer and pulls my legs over his shoulders, fucking me even deeper. "You're mine, Alyssa. You hear me, baby?"

He thrusts into me hard, hitting all the right spots. I can barely think straight and look up at him pleadingly. I'm so close. So fucking close.

He grins at me. "You want it, baby? You wanna come for me?" I nod coyly, desperate for release. He's keeping me right on the edge and he knows it.

"Tell me you'll go on a date with me and I'll give you what you want."

He slows down the pace, and I groan in despair. "No!" I whisper. "I'll go, Dan. I'll go on a date with you," I say, falling for his trick. He smiles and gives me what I'm longing for. My muscles clench around him and he comes seconds after I do.

"Good girl," he whispers, pulling me in for another kiss. "I'll pick you up tonight."

Sixty

I'm nervous as I walk into Daniel's building. The security staff smile at me and nod politely as I walk into the lift. I haven't been here in a few months now. I press my thumb to the scanner and I'm half surprised when the doors actually close and the lift starts to move up.

I pause when I step out of the lift. Everything is just as I left it. A few months ago I lived here, and now I'm here as a visitor. Daniel and I have sort of been dating for a couple of months now. We haven't slapped any titles on our relationship, but as far as I'm aware, our relationship has been exclusive ever since he tricked me into agreeing to another date. After each date came a request for another, and before I knew it months passed by. Months filled with us dating like any other couple. Months filled with amazing sex, weekends away and countless dinner dates. We haven't spoken about a future together at all though, and I'm scared I want more than he is willing to give me.

"Hey, you're here. I thought I heard the lift. Why are you just standing there? Come in."

I snap out of it and enter the apartment. Daniel walks back to the kitchen, his black apron on. I follow him and hop onto the kitchen counter like I used to. He grins at me and spreads my legs to stand between them before pulling my face towards his. He kisses me before pulling away to get back to cooking.

We've gone on numerous dates and we've ended up sleeping with each other almost every time. A few times in his car, often in hotels owned by Devereaux Inc. and a couple of times at my place. For some reason, we never came back to Daniel's apartment. I guess we might've been avoiding it subconsciously, since it's where we spent our entire marriage.

It looks like he will be a little while longer so I grab the glass of wine he poured me and walk around the house. I gasp when I walk into the living room. Daniel comes running up and looks at me in panic. I point at his wall in horror and his eyes follow, a blush spreading along his cheeks. He scratches his neck in a cutesy manner and looks at me sheepishly.

"Dan, why do you have paparazzi photos of us on the wall?"

My eyes roam over the photos. In many of them, we're caught in compromising positions. There's one where we were making out on the yacht. I'm in his lap and we're all over each other. They're far from appropriate. There are other photos of us in Singapore or other trips away, and some on dates in restaurants. There are even a few of us walking hand in hand or smiling at each other.

Daniel shrugs. "Well, we rarely take photos together. And to be honest, these guys don't actually do a bad job. They're annoying as hell, but the pictures are kind of cute."

"Cute?" I repeat numbly. He nods and glances down at the floor, looking absolutely adorable. I shake my head and he grabs my hand to lead me back to the dining table. It doesn't take long for him to serve us dinner. Every time I offer to help, he declines and fills up my wine glass.

"I made you the stir-fry you used to love when we lived together," he says.

I smile and take a bite, a small moan escaping my lips. "It's still the best," I whisper.

Daniel smiles at me, his eyes twinkling. "I was thinking we could maybe watch a movie afterwards?"

I'm surprised and look down. Dinner and a movie at the apartment. It's exactly what we used to do while we were married. It feels nostalgic and it makes me miss living with him.

"Yeah, I'd love to."

Daniel grins and gives me two options. "Harry Potter and the Prisoner of Azkaban... or the Order of the Phoenix."

"Aw damn, trick question. I love both. Obviously, we must watch both."

He laughs and shakes his head. "Let's see if we get through half of one first," he mumbles, his eyes darkening. I blush and look away. We've been all over each other recently, and I truthfully don't think we could get through a whole movie without falling into bed together.

He spoons me on the sofa and I try my best to watch the movie, but the way he kisses my neck distracts me. I tilt my head to give him better access and he smiles, his lips moving down. We're only twenty minutes in when Daniel has his hand underneath my blouse.

"Baby," he whispers. "How about we watch the movie tomorrow?"

I giggle and nod at him. He lifts me into his arms and carries me to his bedroom. Everything still seems to be the way it used to be. Being here makes it feel like nothing ever changed between us, and we're still married.

He puts me down on the bed carefully and lies down next to me. He kisses me so softly and so gently that my heart skips a beat. I moan and deepen the kiss, eager to get his shirt off. I fumble with the buttons impatiently and Daniel laughs. He pulls it over his head and I ogle him shamelessly. Counting our marriage, we've been together for over a year and a half, and I still can't get enough of this man. He still steals my breath every time he undresses. He sees the appreciation in my eyes and smiles smugly. As he's about

303

to lean in and kiss me, I spot something red and lacy from my peripheral vision. I frown and reach out to grab it. Daniel tries to stop me, but I fish it out from underneath his pillow.

"Women's underwear?" I murmur. I'm so shocked I'm barely comprehending what I'm seeing. I sit up and stare at him in disbelief.

"You took someone home recently? To our apartment? In our bed?"

Daniel shakes his head and holds his hands up. "Babe," he whispers.

"I thought we were exclusive. I mean, we haven't specifically said it... but surely there was an implicit agreement that we were?"

"Babe..."

"How could you do this to me, Daniel? How could you break my heart over and over again? I'm done with this. I'm done with you. I'm done putting my heart on the line only for you to let me down time and time again."

"Babe," he whispers yet again, a hint of exasperation in his voice.

"Who the hell is it? Is it that girl again? The one you're in love with?"

"Alyssa!" he snaps. He grabs the underwear from where I threw it and holds it up to me. "Honey, these are yours. They're yours."

I blink at him and then glance at the underwear in his hands. My cheeks turn crimson as realisation dawns on me. He's right, those are mine.

"I — you — what the hell are they doing in your bed?" I shout, angry and embarrassed. Daniel chuckles and runs a hand through his hair. He looks shy and just as embarrassed as me.

"I... uh... well, you left them here," he stammers.

I frown. "Okay, but even so, why are they in your bed?"

He looks away and clears his throat uncomfortably. "I... uh... I just missed you. I forgot I put them there. I didn't really intend to get caught like this. I mean, I don't know... I don't really have an excuse."

He looks so uncomfortable and so awkward that I can't help but smile. I stare at my underwear again and burst out laughing. "Dan, what exactly were you doing with these?" I ask, holding them up. He blushes fiercely. Even his ears are red. I'm tempted to tease him further, just to see him looking so cute and flustered.

"Seriously, though. You gotta stop being like this, Lyss. There's no one but you. You keep bringing up another girl when the only one in my life is you. It breaks my heart that you don't trust me. We've been together for so long and you know what my schedule is like. Where the hell am I supposed to find time to cheat on you? I spend every free second I've got with you. I'm yours. There's no one else."

I look away, unsure of whether I should believe him. My heart feels unsettled. He's right. He has spent all his time with me, and I've never thought there might be someone else on his mind. But I'm still feeling insecure.

"I don't know, Dan. You divorced me. You left me. Things were going well between us and I genuinely thought we were happy, but then you just up and left. You signed the divorce papers and asked me to move out of the place I'd started to consider my own. You blocked my phone number and avoided me for weeks. You even went so far as to sign over your shares to me so you could be free of the contractual obligation of fidelity you had towards me."

I inhale deeply and try my best to remain calm. "I might be the only person in your life right now, but how long will that last? How long until you walk out again? How long until you go back to ignoring me? You ask me to trust you, but you keep breaking that trust. You might not have cheated on me, but you have taken away the security I used to have with you. You were all I had, Dan. And you left me. You left me saying you were in love with someone else. I spent our entire marriage falling deeply and irrevocably in love with you. But while I was falling for you, you were busy falling for someone else. How long will it be until you break my heart again?"

Daniel grabs my hands and rises to his knees to face me. He presses our joint hands to his heart and looks into my eyes. "Alyssa, I wasn't thinking clearly when I did what I did. It's no excuse, but I genuinely thought I was doing the right thing for both of us. I never should have ignored you the way I did, but baby, it's the only way I could stay away from you. I swear to you, Lyss... I will never ever leave you again. I'm only human, baby. I made a mistake. It was a grave mistake, but I'll spend the rest of my life making it up to you. Fucking hell, Alyssa, I'm so fucking in love with you. You're probably the only person around us that doesn't realise it. There's no one but you, Alyssa. I swear it."

I want to believe his words so badly. I've been longing to hear him say that he loves me for so long. But now that he has, it doesn't ring true. It feels hollow. You don't leave and divorce the person you love. I could never ignore Daniel, and I'd never hand him a resignation letter if I thought he needed me. I'd never ignore his pleas like he ignored mine.

"Daniel, if your version of love entails letting down your partner and abandoning them when they need you most, then I don't want it. I'm sorry, but I genuinely think we should break up. We should've just left things be when we got divorced. I don't know what I was thinking..."

Daniel tightens his grip on my hands and shakes his head. He looks panicked and stares at me pleadingly. "Lyss, no, don't do this to us," he says, throwing back the same words I uttered when he left me. "I know I made mistakes, Alyssa. Fuck, I know. But I love you. I love you so fucking much. I'd do anything to make it up to you. I'd do anything to regain your trust. I just need you to give me a chance. An honest chance. Just one, Lyss."

He drops his forehead to mine as a tear escapes my eye. I sniff and shake my head. "I can't, Daniel. I'll just destroy myself in the process if I do."

He throws his arms around me and hugs me tightly. He buries his face in my neck and inhales deeply, unsteadily.

"Baby, if you truly decide you don't want to be, with me I'll respect your wishes. But before you decide, give me a chance to tell you my side of the story. Meet me tomorrow evening at our restaurant. I'll explain to you why I did the things I did, and if despite all that you don't think you could ever trust me again... then I'll let you go, Lyss. Just give me that one last chance. Just hear me out tomorrow, that's all I ask."

Sixty-One

My heart feels heavy as I make my way up. Will I ever be able to walk into this restaurant without thinking of Daniel? I said I wanted to end things between us, but will I ever be able to?

The entire place is silent and I stand by the doors, my eyes on the candles on the floor. They make a pathway to the rooftop terrace and I follow it cautiously, my heart pounding wildly. This... this is extremely romantic. I thought Daniel and I would just talk today. That we'd air out our grievances and get some closure so we can decide whether our relationship is worth saving. This... I don't dare to continue my thoughts in the direction they're going. But when I see Daniel standing in the middle of the terrace, wearing a tux and thousands of candles and roses decorating the place, my heart can't help but hope.

He takes my hand when I reach him and looks at me nervously. His hand is trembling, and he tightens his grip on my hand in an attempt to hide it.

"I told you I'd tell you my side of the story today. Will you let me?" he asks, his voice soft and shaky. I bite down on my lip and nod. Daniel takes a step closer to me and brushes my hair out of my face.

"Where do I even start? I guess the story starts a couple of years ago. I came back to resume working for DM Consultancy after taking a break to do my MBA, in part because I owed your father so much, and in part because I wanted to fulfil my father's wish of succeeding him. Both our dads always wanted the company to fall into our hands, and I wanted to honour that wish. The day I got back to work was also your first day at the office. You started your internship and well... you'd changed so much in the two years I hadn't seen you. I was seriously awed. You were always beautiful, but seeing you then and there... Maybe it's because I hadn't seen you in so long, I saw you in a new light. But god, you were so beautiful. So beautiful, but so freaking young. So out of reach."

He looks away nervously, and I stare at him in disbelief. Is he saying what I think he's saying?

"You weren't just beautiful. You were so smart and so hard-working. You wowed me every single day, and I lost a bit more of my heart to you every single day. But you were too young. You hadn't even started university then. I knew there was so much of your life you still needed to live, and I didn't want to take away any of those experiences from you. Besides, you didn't see me that way at all. I tried so hard to forget about you. I tried to move on and deny my feelings, but it was all to no avail. You'd smile at me and I'd be lost all over again. I'd find excuses to see you all the time. When you were too busy to work from the office, I'd find a way to work late with your dad at his home office, just so I could have dinner with you."

He glances at me briefly and then looks down again, as though his admission is embarrassing for him. He seems really worried about how I might respond.

"I'm ten years older than you, so I knew I'd probably never stand a chance, and I was fine with that. I never intended to act on my feelings, and I kept telling myself that one day I'd get over it. But then something happened... The way you looked at Dominic started to change. You were falling for him right before my eyes.

You'd smile at him in a way you didn't used to, and it tore me apart. Do you remember the night you got drunk and confessed your feelings for him? I overheard it all. You two were so drunk and I was about to check up on you when I heard you. God, Alyssa, my heart fucking broke. The idea of you becoming my little brother's girlfriend, of you two being together. Fuck. I could barely cope with my jealousy every time you'd act chummy with him while you treated me with cold politeness. But seeing you in his arms? I don't think I could've survived that. When I heard your confession... I knew I'd truly never stand a chance. I knew I needed to give up, and for a while I managed it. For a while I convinced myself I wasn't in love with you. But then tragedy struck."

He inhales deeply and brings our joint hands to his chest. His eyes are filled with insecurity and all I want to do is take it away. I feel stupid... It's obvious to me now. The girl I've been so jealous of was me.

"You lost your dad and his will gave me a chance to be with you. I knew I could've contested it or I could've just bought you back your shares. He knew how I felt about you, and I guess this was his way of pushing us together. He'd told me to ask you out for dinner so many times, and I always refused. I was always scared of disturbing the status quo, and you'd never given me any indication that you even saw me as a man at all. I guess his will was his way of giving us his blessing. Even so, I never should've forcefully tied you to me the way I did. But I just wanted to be selfish. Just once, I wanted to call you mine. I knew it was a mistake when you walked down the aisle with Dominic. The way you two looked at each other... I felt fucking awful for breaking your heart. For taking away your chance at happiness. I knew right there and then that I couldn't keep you tied to me."

I grab our joint hands and press my lips against the back of his hand. I'm filled with intense regret. Would things have been different if I'd known then?

"The first couple of weeks of our marriage were rough on me.

It was so obvious that you were in love with Dominic. It hurt to know you were my wife, and it wasn't me you wanted. I knew I had to let you go someday. I was surprised when things slowly changed between us once we moved into the apartment. I could see the attraction in your eyes every time I walked around the house half-naked, and I guess I might've done it more often than I really should have. I just... I was just so excited to see you responding to me at all. But every time I thought we were getting somewhere, Dominic seemed to intervene. Every time I thought you might feel the same way, you'd show me it's still him you put first. Over time, we fell in love, but I just wasn't sure if any of it was real. I was certain you wouldn't have been with me if not for your father's will. It wouldn't have been me you'd choose, and I couldn't keep you tied to me when I knew I wasn't your first choice. It broke me to do it, but I had to let you go. I was so convinced that all you felt for me was lust. I mean... I was your first, Lyss. You hadn't had a chance to date and you didn't even get to be with the person we both thought you loved. I figured you'd get over me quickly and things would return to how they were meant to be."

Daniel hesitates and wipes away a tear from my cheek. I didn't even realise I'd started crying.

"But things didn't get better. You didn't get over me. I thought you would've gotten with Dominic soon after I ended things with you, but you didn't. I thought maybe you just needed some time... but then you showed up with fucking Liam Evans. I lost it. I couldn't stomach the idea of you being with him, so I ruined your chance at moving on. I felt horrible about it afterwards, but I just couldn't stand it."

He runs a hand through his hair and looks away, his face distorted by pure devastation.

"I don't understand," I whisper. "If you knew... If you knew I couldn't get over you, why did you still come to court to sign the papers?"

Daniel cups my cheek and looks at me sadly. "I didn't ever

want you to feel like you were forced into our marriage. I kind of figured that if you and I were meant to be, we'd come together naturally all over again. I wanted a chance to pursue you honestly, the right way. I wanted you to have a choice, and I wanted you to choose me."

Daniel drops down on one knee and pulls a ring box out of his pocket. My eyes go wide and I slap my hands over my lips.

"I've loved you for years, Alyssa. I know I've made mistakes and I know I'm a fool sometimes. I don't communicate my feelings very well and I've hurt you so many times needlessly, but I never meant to. I've always loved you and I've always wanted what's best for you. Please, Alyssa. Let me make my wrongs right. I'll spend each day of the rest of my life trying to make you happier than you were the day before. Please, will you make me the happiest man in the world and marry me?"

I burst into tears and nod. "Yes, Daniel. Yes. A thousand times yes."

He slides the ring onto my finger and rises to wrap his arms around me. I kiss him and giggle against his lips. The two of us are so wrapped up in each other that I haven't even had a chance to look at the ring. When I finally pull away to glance at it. I gasp.

"I — this... Daniel..."

He chuckles and kisses me again. "Hmm, it's the ring you picked out in Singapore a year ago. I bought it the same day. I always hoped I'd be proposing to you someday... and if I did, I wanted you to have the ring of your dreams."

Daniel drops his forehead against mine and smiles wickedly. "Hey babe, guess what? You owe me a new Aston Martin."

I burst out laughing and kiss the shit out of my soon-to-be husband.

Sixty-Two

I glance at myself in the mirror. Who would've thought I'd be in this same room in our local church all over again? It's been almost three years since Daniel and I initially said I do, and it's surreal how much has changed.

I glance at the stunning dress I'm wearing. It's exactly what I always imagined I'd wear if I ever got married, and I can't wait for Daniel to see me in it. I'm even more eager for him to take it off me...

I'm startled out of my thoughts when someone knocks on the door. Vincent enters and he smiles at me. "You look stunning, Alyssa. Your father would've been so proud."

I smile at the thought of my father. That old man was right all along. Vincent hands me a familiar-looking letter and I stare at it in shock.

"Your father instructed me to give this to you if Daniel and you chose to stay married. I thought now would be a good time to hand this to you. He rewrote his will and every single one of these letters every year, you know. He was so scared he'd one day have to leave you without being able to say his goodbyes. He always made sure you'd have a few handwritten letters as consolation. He loved you so much, Alyssa."

I nod and take the letter from him with shaking hands. Vincent smiles at me and leaves me to read the letter in private. I sink down on the sofa in the dressing room and open the letter carefully.

My dearest daughter,

If you're reading this letter, then my biggest wish has come true and you've finally realised how crazy Daniel is about you. It always used to make me smile whenever he'd gaze at you as though you'd hung the stars and the moon, when all you did was create a slideshow for a meeting. The man beamed whenever you'd offer him a cup of coffee.

I never would have admitted this if you'd chosen to divorce Daniel, because I fear you'd never forgive me. But there's something you should know, my child. The shares were always yours. I merely instructed Vincent to show you an earlier draft of my will that I created. He didn't want to, and he told me it's unlawful and unethical, but I'll be forever grateful that he chose to honour my wishes in the end. Had you said no to marrying Daniel, then I still would've left you my shares. There's no one in the world I trust more than you, my beloved Alyssa. Never, ever fear that I did what I did because I trust Daniel more than I trust you. I merely wanted to make sure you'd be happy, and I knew Daniel would ensure your happiness if you gave him a chance.

I'll admit that I'm glad I gambled and I'm glad it paid off. I doubt anyone will ever love you as much as I love you, but I'm certain Daniel is a close second. You deserve the world, Alyssa, and I know Daniel will try his best to give it to you. I hope the two of you will be happy together. I'm relieved you aren't by yourself now that I've had to leave you and I know you're in good hands. I wish I could be there to finally see you two together. I hope Daniel will always love you the way he did when I wrote this letter, and I hope you'll always love him the same.

Be happy, Alyssa.

All my love,
Daddy

I sniff and try my best not to cry a mere few minutes before I'm due to walk down the aisle. The last thing I want is for Daniel to think I might have second thoughts. Every day he'll stare at my ring in wonder, as though he can't believe I actually said yes. I can't wait to become his wife again and put all of his worries and insecurities to rest. I clutch the letter to my chest and inhale deeply.

"Thank you, daddy," I whisper. For a second I'm certain I can smell his cologne around me, and I wonder if he might actually be here with me today.

Dominic walks in and beams at me. He seems genuinely happy for me, and I'm just as happy to be getting married. It's such a contrast to the first time I walked down the aisle. He glances at the letter I'm clutching in understanding and wipes away the few tears that have rolled down my cheeks.

"You ready?" he asks. I nod and smile up at him. This time around he's Daniel's best man, and I'll be walking down the aisle by myself.

The church is packed this time. All of our friends and family are present. Daniel grins as I walk towards him, and I smile just as widely. He looks hot as hell in that tux. I can't wait to finally have a true wedding night. He grins at me mischievously and I know he's thinking the same thing.

He takes my hand when I reach him and beams at me. I'm

instantly reminded of my father's letter. How did I fail to notice that he's always smiled at me like this, when he'd barely even look at others? My eyes are glued on his as the priest starts the service. I'm giddy with excitement when it's finally time to say I do.

I look into his eyes as I recite my vows. He finally relaxes when I say I do, and I chuckle. Last time the priest skipped the part where Daniel is asked to kiss the bride. Thankfully, this time he doesn't.

Daniel kisses me and holds me by my waist, sweeping me off my feet. All our guests cheer, and I blush fiercely.

"Finally," he whispers. "Finally, you're truly mine. I love you to the moon and back, Alyssa Devereaux."

I giggle against his lips and rise to my tiptoes to kiss him again. "I love you too, husband dearest."

The End

Download for an exclusive sexy bonus scene, written from Daniel's POV from my website. It involves the red lace underwear he had under his pillow...

PS. If you're wondering what Daniel was thinking throughout the book, then check out the next page.

Serendipity

After writing The Tie That Binds, I received multiple requests for Daniel's side of the story — so I wrote it.

I never intended to write Serendipity, but I'm happy I ended up doing it nonetheless. It was my way of thanking readers that took a chance on my debut novel. Your encouragement means more to me than you'll ever know.

Serendipity starts a few years before The Tie That Binds, and it'll show you exactly what Daniel was thinking throughout the story.

So if you don't want Alyssa and Daniel's story to end, keep reading for Daniel's point of view in Serendipity. I've included the first three chapters for you. But if you just want the full book, you can get it here. It's in Kindle Unlimited too.

Serendipity: Chapter 1

I smile as I walk into DM Consultancy, the company my father and Charles Moriani built together. It's their legacy, and one day it'll be mine. Mine and Alyssa's. I rejected half a dozen offers from other consultancy firms to return to London, and I don't regret it for a second. I doubt I ever will. I'm excited as I walk into Charles's office. Too excited, clearly, because I walk right into someone.

"Ouch," she says, rubbing her nose.

I laugh and wrap my hands around her shoulders to keep her steady. "Still so clumsy, Alyssa," I murmur. She looks up at me in surprise and smiles from ear to ear before throwing herself in my arms for a quick hug. She's grown up a lot in the time I was gone. She was sixteen when I left for my MBA, so she must be eighteen now.

"You're back," she murmurs. I hug her back tightly and grin. Being back here feels like coming home.

Charles walks up to us and claps me on the shoulder. "You're back, son," he says. I nod and Alyssa takes a step back to stand next to her father. The two couldn't look more different. Charles looks perpetually grumpy while Alyssa looks perpetually cheerful.

She has her mother's looks and her father's eyes. It's the eyes that give away the relation.

"What are you even doing here?" I ask Alyssa. I expected to see her around the house now that I'm back, but I didn't expect to see her at the office.

Charles smiles proudly and throws his arm around her. "My baby is all grown up now, Dan. She's going to intern while studying at Imperial. Before I know it she'll be taking my job."

Alyssa blushes and my heart oddly enough skips a beat. Alyssa has always been beautiful, but I've never seen her as more than a kid — as my younger brother's best friend. She's ten years younger than me, so why do I suddenly find her so stunning?

"Interning, huh? I definitely wasn't doing that at eighteen," I murmur. I can barely even remember my first year at uni. I definitely can't remember Fresher's week. Alyssa has always been very responsible, but interning so young? I wonder if Charles might be pushing her a bit too hard. He's been pushing her to become CEO of DM consultancy since she was five. She should be having fun instead of interning here. Alyssa smiles back at her dad and my heart does it again. It skips a beat. I look away and stare down at my shoes, suddenly feeling awkward.

"That reminds me," Charles says, his face lighting up. He walks back to his desk and retrieves a rectangular gift wrapped package. Alyssa's eyes light up at the sight of it and I look at it suspiciously. Charles hands it to me and I shake it in an attempt to assess what might be in it. "Go on, open it," Charles urges. I frown and carefully unwrap the clumsily packaged gift. My heart races as I take out the new name plaque. It says Daniel Devereaux, CEO.

"I'm thinking that we can probably share this office, the way your dad and I did in the early days."

I look up at Charles in disbelief and he smiles at me proudly. "You didn't need the MBA, son. You were ready to become my co-CEO long before you decided you had to have one. Now that you're back, you can finally start easing my workload. I'm old, son. I want to go to less meetings and play more golf."

I laugh and shake my head. Charles Moriani is a devout workaholic. He enjoys what he does far more than he'd ever enjoy a round of golf. He's taught me everything I know. When my father died three years ago, Charles took me under his wing. He continued training me like my father used to and groomed me to take over my father's vacant seat as his co-CEO. He pushed me as hard as I'm sure he's going to push Alyssa. It's thanks to him that I can assume my new role with confidence.

"I think it might actually be good if you train Alyssa the way I trained you. I'll still supervise, but she's been complaining that I'm too harsh on her. I think it might benefit you both if you train her. After all, you'll be working together in the future anyway."

I nod and look at Alyssa. She's looking at me with such hope and excitement that I can't help but smile. It probably is better if I'm the one that trains her. If she's only just started she hasn't experienced the true horror that is her father's training regime. To say that he's a tough love kinda guy is an understatement. If I can keep Alyssa from going through that, I'll gladly do it.

"You'll need to hire an assistant," Charles says. I nod and stare at my new name plaque some more. I knew it was coming. I just didn't expect to be appointed on my very first day back.

"I've got someone in mind for that," I murmur. I immediately think of Kate, my friend Carter's sister. She's talented but she's had a rough couple of years. She did her MBA with me to try and make up for lost time, and a position as executive secretary might just give her the break she needs.

Charles frowns and looks worried for just a second before nodding. "Good. You sort that out then, lad."

I nod and tip my head towards Alyssa. "Wanna come with me to a department meeting?" I ask, checking my watch. Alyssa nods, her eyes brimming with excitement, and I can't help but chuckle.

To be this excited for a department meeting... oh the good old days.

I walk out of Charles's office and Alyssa follows me, her heels clicking against the stone floor. I glance down and frown.

"Since when did you start wearing those?" I ask.

Alyssa was a tomboy growing up, but it looks like she's outgrown that phase. She merely shrugs. "They're pretty," she tells me. I can't help but silently agree. She's wearing red bottomed heels that look surprisingly hot. I don't have a thing for shoes in the slightest, but these are different somehow.

"All you need to do for the next couple of days is shadow me and takes notes of absolutely everything, okay? I'll grill you on details every once in a while. I need you to understand everything that's going on to the best of your ability. Don't just repeat things verbatim, okay?"

Alyssa nods seriously, as though she already knows the drill. She probably does. I wouldn't put it past her to have interned here her entire summer. And I definitely wouldn't put it past Charles to let her.

Serendipity: Chapter 2

I walk into the office to find Charles shouting at someone. I sigh inwardly and shake my head. I pity the fool that managed to get in his way. Charles has endless patience when it comes to explaining concepts, but he has a zero tolerance policy for mistakes. Errors have gotten more than one person fired and I'm pretty sure I'll be signing a severance cheque later.

"How the hell could you miss such a monumental mistake? You put an extra fucking zero on that slide. At a *client meeting*. What kind of rookie error is that? Who the hell allowed you to work on client deliverables anyway?"

I sigh and check my meeting schedule for the day. It's only ten and I'm already tired. I'm pretty sure I'm going to have to do some damage control with the client now and I really can't be bothered with that.

"I'm sorry. I'm so sorry."

I freeze. I know that voice. I look up to find Alyssa standing in front of her father. She's trembling as he chews her out and my heart fucking drops. She looks fucking devastated. What the hell even happened? I didn't ask her to work on a client presentation, so why the fuck is she being blamed for this? She hasn't made a single mistake in the three months she's been working with me, so how could this have happened?

I glance around the room to find Christian hiding behind his screen. He's the one that was meant to make the presentation, and it's obvious he pawned off his work on Alyssa. I walk up to Alyssa and put my hand on her shoulder in a show of support.

"What exactly is going on?"

Charles looks at me and grits his teeth. "Is this how you train her?" he shouts. His face is red and he glares at me. Just a couple of years ago I'd have been shaking in my boots, much like Alyssa is now. I tighten my grip on her shoulder and she leans into me subconsciously.

"I didn't ask Alyssa to work on the client proposal. Either way, as an intern, she cannot be held accountable for this. If you want to blame anyone, blame me. You do not, however, get to speak to my trainee this way. Going forward I expect you to take it up with me directly if she makes a mistake. I am, after all, the person training her. Am I not?"

Charles looks at me through narrowed eyes and then looks at Alyssa. She takes another step closer to me and I wrap my arm around her shoulder fully.

"You're lucky Daniel is standing up for you, Alyssa. If it were up to me you'd be out the door by now."

I know he doesn't mean that. He's said similar words to me a thousand times, so I know he doesn't mean a word. Alyssa doesn't know that though. The way her body trembles makes my heart ache. Charles walks away and Alyssa stares at his closed office door, frozen. Eventually she snaps out of it and steps away from me. She rushes towards the bathrooms and I inhale deeply.

I follow her and lean against the wall while she disappears into the ladies room. I have no doubt that she's crying her heart out and indeed, she emerges ten minutes later with red eyes.

She looks startled to find me standing here and looks up at me with wide eyes. I sigh and hand her my bathroom card.

"This gives you access to the executive bathroom," I tell her.

She takes the card from me with trembling hands and stares at it. "I know this is probably hard to believe, but he's always acted the same way with me too. I know you probably can't see it now, but his craziness does work. Clients do actually behave in the same irrational angry way far more often than you might think. You'll get used to it soon enough, but it never gets easier. Feeling like you've let him down never gets easier, Alyssa."

She looks at me wordlessly and closes her hand around the card I gave her. She's clutching it so tightly than I'm worried she'll hurt her own hand.

"I may or may not have had to hide in the bathroom on numerous occasions after receiving a verbal lashing from your dad. At least the executive bathroom is private. No other stalls. No one witnessing your mini breakdown. And there will be many. Even I might sometimes upset you. I hope I won't, but I can't be sure. Things do get a little tense around here every once in a while."

Alyssa laughs and my unease settles just a little. "Did you really?" she asks. "Did you really hide out in the bathrooms too?"

I smile down at my shoes embarrassedly and nod. "Yeah. I respect the hell out of your dad, but he's a fucking psycho."

Alyssa bursts out laughing and puts the card away. "Thank you, Daniel," she whispers. I smile at her and fall into step with her as we walk back to the office. I can see Charles pacing nervously and he pauses when he catches sight of Alyssa smiling. His relief is palpable and I bite down on my lip to hide my smile. If he's going to feel this bad about it then why shout at her in the first place?

"Why don't you write up this morning's meeting minutes?" I ask Alyssa. She looks up at me and nods, her usual eagerness back on her face. I walk past her and pause at Christian's cubicle. He looks up at me with dread.

"Conference room. Now."

I walk away and he follows me reluctantly. He seems nervous and starts trembling as he sits down. I take the seat opposite him

THE TIE THAT BINDS

and cross my arms. I don't even have to ask him what happened. He starts rambling nervously almost immediately.

"I'm sorry, Mr. Devereaux. She was so eager to help, so I let her. I didn't know the quality of her work would be so poor. She seemed quite bright. Guess I was wrong."

Wrong fucking words, buddy. "So you asked an intern to do your job for you and then didn't even check for errors? *You* seemed quite bright. Guess I was wrong."

He looks up at me with wide eyes and shakes his head. "No, Mr. Devereaux. She said she double checked, so I assumed everything was fine. Like I said, she seemed so eager to help. I thought I was doing her a favour. It was bad judgement on my part."

I just about keep from rolling my eyes. "You thought you were doing her a favour by asking her to do a job I specifically assigned to you?"

He looks panicked and is no doubt coming up with yet more excuses. I sigh and check my watch. I have exactly seven more minutes before I need to be in my next meeting.

"You know the deal, right? You're fired, buddy. We have a zero tolerance policy for basic errors at DM. Especially in the executive office. Since the task was assigned to you, the end responsibility lies with you."

He jumps out of his seat and I rise too. I walk out before he can start begging to keep his job. If he'd just *done* his job, we wouldn't be in this situation. If he'd done his job, Alyssa wouldn't have cried her heart out the way she did.

Serendipity: Chapter 3

I press my hand to the biometric scanner at Charles's house and the front door swings open. The house smells amazing and my stomach grumbles immediately. When was the last time I ate? Did I even have lunch? I've been so busy all day that I genuinely can't recall.

"Hey, you're here," Alyssa says, sticking her head out into the hallway. She's got her long hair wrapped in a messy bun and she's in comfy house clothes. Looks like she's wearing nothing but a loose tee and some sleep shorts. My eyes automatically drop to her breasts. I can see a hint of her nipples through the fabric and my heart starts to race. I blink and look away. What the hell is wrong with me? I've known Alyssa all my life. Why am I suddenly attracted to her?

"Hungry?" she asks. My stomach grumbles again and she laughs. "That's a yes, then. Come in."

She disappears back into the kitchen and emerges minutes later with a large serving dish. I glance at the pasta she made longingly and she chuckles as I take a seat next to Charles.

"Alyssa and I started doing daddy-daughter dinner dates three times a week. We're both working so much these days, and working together isn't easy either. I kind of figured that having

THE TIE THAT BINDS

dinner a few times a week might help her not hate me. I'm not the easiest boss to have, and she has to live with me too. She's already threatened to move out twice."

I'm hit with an intense sense of longing but smile nonetheless. I'd give the world to work with my dad and to have dinner with him just one more time. Charles has done his best to treat me as his son, but it isn't the same. It doesn't make me miss my dad any less. If anything, it makes me miss him more.

Alyssa grabs a large serving spoon and proceeds to fill her father's plate with pasta and salad, before moving her attention to me. I'm so startled that I don't even have time to protest or to insist that I can do it myself.

I've gotten so used to the serving staff at home that Alyssa serving me instead makes me feel all flustered. How long has it been since I've had a meal that truly feels like a homemade one? One that isn't made by a chef and served by staff.

"Thank you," I whisper. She smiles at me and my stupid heart skips yet another beat.

"So you're buying an apartment, huh?" Charles says. I nod at him as I take a bite of my food and try my best to hide my expression. The food looks amazing but it doesn't taste quite right. Charles bites back a smile and shakes his head as I force myself to swallow down the pasta.

"Yeah," I say. "I found one I really like, overlooking Hyde park."

Charles nods thoughtfully. "Close to the office then. What area is it, Knightsbridge?"

I nod and he smiles approvingly. "Sounds great, son. I had a look at that Aston Martin you've been wanting to buy as well. Not sure about the options you picked."

Alyssa rolls her eyes and takes a bite of her food. Her eyes widen and she grimaces as she swallows the food down, and I can't help but smile. She grabs a large amount of parmesan and throws it all over her own food and ours, though I doubt that'll save the dish.

"God, stop it already. All this talk about buying apartments and cars. Next I know you two will make a cost-benefit analysis."

Charles and I look at each other and nod at the same time. "Excellent idea," I murmur, causing Alyssa to roll her eyes.

Dinner passes peacefully and I can't remember the last time I had such a homely meal. I love my mother to bits, but she's always worked so hard that we've never really done many family dinners. We've done even less of them since my father died.

I follow Charles to his office and the two of us finish up our paperwork while he advises me on client issues I've had. I've missed this. The MBA I did doesn't hold a candle to one-on-one mentoring sessions with Charles.

He seems fidgety and nervous as he reads through the proposal I crafted, and I lean back in amusement. I know there's nothing wrong with the proposal — it was a piece of cake. Instead he's gearing up to ask me something. Something about Alyssa, no doubt.

"So, how is my little girl doing?" he asks eventually. The edges of my lips tip up and I try my best not to smile. Charles Moriani is the most fearless and ruthless businessman I know, but he's a softie when it comes to his daughter.

"She's doing great, Charles. She's eighteen and she's already handling the workload of a graduate staffer. Even more than that, actually, considering that she's working in the Executive Office. I'm worried it's too much, though. I'm worried her school work and working at DM on top of that is too much."

Charles shakes his head. "No, not for Alyssa. This is a walk in the park for her. She's amazing."

I sigh and bite down on my lip. Nothing I say will convince him that the only reason she's working so hard is because of all the pressure he puts on her. Alyssa has always been scared of letting her father down.

"Don't you think you're a bit tough on her, though? That incident last month with the small error on the client proposal, that was a bit much."

Charles hesitates and looks away. "That's how I taught you, Daniel. Look how great you turned out. I want Alyssa to learn in the same way — in the way I know works."

I finish my cup of tea and nod respectfully. I don't agree with him but it's not my place to argue with him either. All I can do is shield Alyssa from his tough love training as best as I can.

I rise and grab my teacup. "Want a refill?" I ask. Charles nods and hands me his cup, seemingly lost in thought. I know he's worried about pushing Alyssa away, and he should be.

I'm surprised to find Alyssa at the kitchen table with her laptop and notepad. She's sipping a cup of tea of her own and looks up when I enter. I glance at my watch and frown.

"It's eleven, Alyssa. Shouldn't you be heading to bed some-time soon? You have classes tomorrow, don't you?"

She nods and yawns. "I know, but I have an essay due soon and I just don't have enough time to finish it."

I walk towards the kettle and refill it silently. "You know you don't have to come in every single day, right? If you're busy with classes then just reduce your working hours."

She sighs and shakes her head, her long brown hair falling over her chest. "No, I couldn't," she murmurs.

I walk towards her and sit down next to her. Alyssa pushes her laptop towards me and looks up at me with her stunning hazel eyes. "What do you think?" she asks, hopeful. She's totally giving me puppy eyes and I'm totally falling for it.

I read through her essay and highlight a few sections where she needs more references, and another few that aren't quite clear enough. "Work on this," I tell her, running her through my notes step by step.

She looks up at me with wide eyes, and I've never seen her look at me that way before. I've never seen her look so mesmerised. Or, well, I guess I've never seen her look that way *at me*. My cheeks heat up just slightly while my heart rate increases, and I push away from her.

"Thank you, Daniel," she murmurs.

I smile at her and shake my head. "It's nothing, Alyssa. I'm always here if you need help. I'm serious about work too. If you want to work less hours, let me know. I'll talk to your dad for you."

She considers it for a second and then shakes her head. I sigh and bite back a smile. I already know that I've got another workaholic on my hands.

Keep reading Serendipity here

Also by Catharina Maura

Forever After All: A Marriage Of Convenience Novel

Desperate and out of options, Elena Rousseau walks into a gentlemen's club, ready to sell her body in a last attempt to save her mother's life.

She didn't expect Alexander Kennedy to be there, and she certainly didn't expect him to propose a marriage of convenience instead.

Marrying Alexander means knowingly becoming a tool in his revenge plan. But what choice does she have?

Better the devil you know than the one you don't.

Until You: A Brother's Best Friend Romance

Left without a job and evicted from the house she so carefully turned into a home, Aria is offered two choices: move back in with her brother... or take the job her brother's best friend offers her.

Their lives weren't meant to collide — but everything changes when Grayson realizes that Aria is the mysterious woman behind a wildly popular vigilante platform.

She's the woman he's been falling for online, the one whose coding skills outdo his, the one he's been trying to track down.

It's her. And she's off-limits.

The Stolen Moments Trilogy: A Best Friend's Brother Romance

What if the one person you can't have is the one person you can't resist?

It was hate at first sight for Emilia and Carter. Neither can remember how their feud started, but that doesn't stop them from pulling some crazy pranks on each other.

Until one night. One kiss is all it takes.

The lines between love and hate blur, and things are forever changed.

They know they can never cross that line, though...

Carter is Emilia's best friend's brother, after all.

Made in the USA
Las Vegas, NV
08 June 2023

73142916R00199